TOMORROW'S
Treasure

TOMORROW'S
Treasure

A NOVEL

LINDA LEE
CHAIKIN

WATERBROOK
PRESS

TOMORROW'S TREASURE
PUBLISHED BY WATERBROOK PRESS
12265 Oracle Boulevard, Suite 200
Colorado Springs, Colorado 80921

All Scripture quotations are taken from the King James Version.

The characters and events in this book are fictional, and any resemblance to actual persons
or events is coincidental.

ISBN 978-0-307-45808-7

Published in the United States by WaterBrook Multnomah, an imprint of the Crown
Publishing Group, a division of Random House Inc., New York.

WATERBROOK and its deer colophon are registered trademarks of Random House Inc.

Library of Congress Cataloging-in-Publication Data
    Chaikin, L. L., 1943–
        Tomorrow's treasure / Linda Chaikin.
            p. cm.
        1. Mothers and daughters—Fiction. 2. Social classes—Fiction.
    3. Jewelry theft—Fiction. I. Title.
        PS3553.H2427 T66 2003
        813'.54—dc21

                                                                    2002013845

Printed in the United States of America
2009

10 9 8 7 6 5 4 3 2 1

PART ONE

The righteous man wisely considereth
the house of the wicked.

PROVERBS 21:12

CHAPTER ONE

Summer 1879, Capetown, South Africa

The four white gems of the Southern Cross had just risen from behind Table Top Mountain toward the deep expanse of sky over Capetown Bay. Though the scene usually set her heart humming, Katherine van Buren barely noticed the beauty tonight. Nor could she focus on remembered summer nights on the velvety lawn…for anxiety tightened its grip upon her.

At the baby's soft whimper Katie turned from the cloistered window of her upstairs bedroom in Cape House and went to the bassinet, gently lifting her three-week-old infant. She smiled down at her little girl, whom she had named Eve—now *Evy*—and sat holding her in the rocking chair.

"Poor baby, what shall become of us? But do not worry. Anthony will take us far from here. Yes, he will. Don't cry, my Evy darlin'."

Katie began to gently hum Brahms's "Lullaby." "Your eyes will be amber like mine. Your hair will be tawny gold. But your mouth will be like your father's…a beautiful, sensuous mouth." She hummed the lullaby again as she rocked.

The bedroom door opened. Katie looked up and gazed into the face of her guardian, Sir Julien Bley.

He stood tall and darkly forbidding. His complexion was scorched brown by years of trekking the land of South Africa. His one good light-blue eye burned. His jaw was strong, his sideburns tinged with white.

He came in boldly and shut the door too quietly. Apprehension darted up Katie's spine as she grew aware of the tension in the air—much as it was before a sizzling thunderstorm on the African veldt.

She licked her suddenly dry lips and counted the thuds of her heart in her eardrums.

"So, girl." Julien's voice was gruff, yet low-keyed, which only added to the devastation of his next words. "You insist on keeping the suckling infant though you are unwed."

Katie raised her chin, refusing to let him see she was intimidated. She made a small rocking motion with her infant.

"We must make plans, Katie. I have allowed you to keep her longer than is wise. You must be strong and give her up. It is best for her, for you. Your father, if he were alive, would agree with me. He trusted me to care for you, my girl."

She swallowed, and her arms tightened around her infant. She felt her cheeks turn scarlet at the memory of her godly father, Carl van Buren—memories she had continued to cherish since her arrival here twelve years ago to become Sir Julien's ward. What would her father think of her now, in her situation? Would he be ashamed of her? Embarrassed by her?

No matter what, he would love her. Though she'd been only six when he had died, she'd known his love for her was deep. And though most of her life before her father's death was but a hazy memory after so many years under her guardian's rule, she still remembered him and the religious ways of her Afrikaner people, the Dutch. How shattered she had been, as a small child, upon learning of her father's accidental death in the mine. The site at Kimberly was the first big diamond find he and Julien had made, and they had formed a partnership that went beyond business to a pact of friendship. After the explosion, her mortally injured father had pled with Julien to take his little Katie as his ward.

She stiffened now in her chair as Sir Julien walked up and spoke down at her. "Look at me, girl. Have you nothing to say for yourself? Must I force the infant's removal? Can you not see it is best?"

Her anger began to boil. There had never been so much as a word of condemnation for his sons and nephews who fathered the children he so lightly sent away to distant places, never to be seen again. *Not this time.* She thought and clenched her teeth. *Not with my sweet Evy.* She drew her infant against her heart.

"Well, girl?"

At his gruff demand, she nodded. "Yes, I have something to say, sir! But 'tis more important to me that you hear what Anthony has to say."

His tufted brow inched lower over his deep-set, pale eye. "You persist in laying the fatherhood of this child at his doorstep then?"

"He is the father, and no other, I vow 'tis true."

"You cannot keep the child, Katie."

Her chin lifted. "Anthony wishes to marry me, and I him. If he had not gone to London—"

"So you persist in deceiving yourself? You gaze too much in the mirror at your pert face and not enough at your books of learning." He took a turn up and down the floor. "The blame for your misbegotten baby lies in your willfulness."

She was not willful— She *loved* Anthony, had believed his promises—

"As for Anthony, I have spoken to him."

Her hopes brightened. She looked up at him, her knees too weak to stand and face him with any dignity. Evy was beginning to make little crying sounds, and Katie tried to soothe her.

"Did I not tell you this baby is your blood relation?" She did her best to force a merry note to her voice. Surely Anthony would own his own daughter to his uncle? "She will grow up to make you proud."

"Trying to wheedle me now, are you? It will do no good, my girl. I am doing this for your own fair future. As for my nephew… His marriage into aristocracy is important to the plans of South Africa, and to me. Such tales as laying this child upon my nephew would add to my burden and accomplish little good."

She moaned. Then the unthinkable could be true—that Anthony's marriage was already arranged to—what was her name? Her feverish brain would not let her think.

"Do you think it gives me happiness to see you mourning like this? Do you think I take fiendish pleasure in sending the child away? Nay! But it is your future too that is at stake. You are like my own daughter. Any marriage I make for you among the diamond families of Kimberly will not tolerate an illegitimate child by Anthony Brewster."

"Tales?" She took little note of the rest of what he had said. She gazed up at him, her sweet baby cradled close, and while his brows were tufted and cross, there gleamed a small flicker of pity in his return gaze.

"Anthony has denied everything. That does not surprise me. He is grieved you would try to lay this errant birth upon him, yet he has asked I deal with you gently."

"Of course he would deny it to your face. He fears you! But if you will accept Evy, Anthony will confess how much he loves me, how he wishes the three of us to be together always. Oh, Uncle Julien, can you not see how desperately I want to keep my daughter?"

"You have always been a willful girl bent upon trouble, my dear Katie, yet I have loved you. Part of this tragedy is my fault, I see that now. I should have arranged for you to be married sooner. You became a woman too quickly, and your will and good sense have not kept pace, I fear."

She managed to stand, despite the trembling that seemed to have taken over her limbs. "He is Evy's father, I tell you. Evy is a Brewster. Anthony told me he loved me, that he wished to marry me—"

Her voice cracked, and she sank back to the chair, bending her head toward her baby to avoid Julien's gaze. *He doesn't believe me… He has no feelings for Evy… She's just another baby—a girl at that—when he wants males to carry on his dynasty.*

A sob came from her tight throat.

"Do not be foolish, Katie girl." He spoke with gruff tenderness. "Even if I knew for a fact Anthony sired this infant, there can be no marriage between you and him. Nay, never." He walked to the window and looked out. "The Montieth family in London is important to South Africa, to forming a new state. Maybe Cecil Rhodes will call it Rhodesia."

Katie did not know what he meant, nor did she care at the moment. "South Africa? It is my *child* I care about."

Julien turned and looked at the tiny bundle in the pink cover. Then his square jaw set, the muscles twitching. "It's not a matter of kith 'n kin that's on my mind right now. It's that his Lordship Montieth and his daughter, Lady Camilla, will arrive from London, perhaps very soon. Anthony *must* marry Camilla. I cannot chance having this errant child waiting in the wings."

Katie looked up, brushing the tear streaks from her cheeks. Who were Lord Montieth and Lady Camilla? And what had they to do with her heartache?

Julien's face was wiped smooth of any emotion, and his brittle expression refused her any sympathy.

"Anthony will become engaged to Lady Camilla when she arrives here at Cape House. You are going to Europe for a year, and the baby will be adopted out to a loving family. I shall make sure of that much for you."

Katie's shoulders straightened, then sagged.

"In a fortnight"—Sir Julien's level voice brooked no resistance— "Anthony will place a diamond ring on Lady Camilla's finger."

This pronouncement had the effect of thunder clapping violently over the roof of Cape House. Katie's dry lips parted. She could merely stare at her guardian.

He frowned. "The marriage has been planned since Lady Camilla was twelve and Anthony thirteen. They knew one another while he took his schooling in London. Many a holiday he has spent at Montieth Hall. That he told you none of this does not surprise me." He paced. "But you should have known, Katie, that marriages must be arranged for the betterment of all—yours as well."

Unable to hold back her surging rage, she screamed, "*No!* No! Anthony loves *me!* I will not listen to these lies!"

The startled baby wailed, and Katie embraced her, tears rushing to her eyes. "Hush, hush, sweeting, you'll have your papa, you'll see."

"Stop that, Katie! I must do what is best for everyone concerned."

At her mutinous stare, Sir Julien continued gravely. "With your future at stake we cannot allow a child born out of wedlock to cast shadows on all our paths. You must give the child up. A journey to Europe will give you the maturity to see what is best. At the appropriate time, your marriage will be arranged. Your inheritance in diamonds will insure that some decent son of a government official will look the other way when gossip of a child makes its way into English social circles."

Katie wept into the baby's soft, pink cover. Her stomach ached and her pulse throbbed in her temples. She inhaled Evy's sweet fragrance. *I'll never give you up.*

Sir Julien turned away, shoulders oddly stooped, and walked toward the door and opened it. "I'm sorry, Katie girl, this pains me too. But I have no choice."

As the door opened, Katie saw Inga waiting in the hall. The sturdy Dutch woman held her hands hidden beneath her apron. Her faded gold-gray hair was braided and, as it had been since Katie was a child, coiled around her head like a wreath. Her once-round face and apple cheeks were now sagging and soft, and her small mouth drooped sadly.

"Inga, come in here. Do what you can to comfort Katie."

The old nanny entered the bedroom, bobbed a clearly uncertain curtsy in Sir Julien's direction, and then hurried toward Katie to take the baby from her arms. "There, there, Miss Katie, do not cry so, or you'll be upsetting the baby's milk. Shall I be seeing to her needs now, miss?"

The nurse's low voice—the same voice that had soothed so many of Katie's childhood fears—now filled her with fear. She held onto her baby tightly. What if Inga took Evy away? What if, once Katie relinquished her tiny daughter, Evy would be whisked away to some ship sailing for England or Scotland?

No, she would not let her go.

"I won't give up my baby!" She met Sir Julien's stony gaze. "Do you hear me? I won't! I won't! And no one can make me!"

An austere Sir Julien Bley left the room.

Katie jumped to her feet, still clutching Evy. "I want to see Anthony! Where is he? I want to talk to him! How dare he lie about Evy?"

Inga moved to lay a calming hand on Katie's arm. "Master Anthony is not here, miss. He left last night with them diamond buyers from London and he didn't return. Some say he's on his way to Angola. Something about emeralds."

The last of her hope ebbing away, Katie looked down at her baby girl. "Oh, my precious little one. What shall I do? Whatever shall I do?"

One Month Later

Katie's once-lovely cheeks were hollow and thin. Dark smudges beneath her eyes made them seem a lighter amber. She had made her decision the day after Evy was stolen from her bassinet and taken away from Cape House. *I loathe Sir Julien. And Anthony...*

She had thought she loved Anthony. Now she felt nothing but revulsion and shame. How could she have allowed herself to make such a mistake with her virtue? She had played the fool, and now what would happen to her baby?

"How dare he steal my daughter and lock me in my rooms?" She mumbled the question aloud. "Am I a prisoner? Yes! That is what I am!" For all her initial banging on her locked door, after two weeks she was still confined to her several rooms in Cape House. She ate little and hardly slept. She would have tried to escape when Inga came to care for her needs, but Sir Julien remained in the house as though he knew her thoughts. Inga worried about her, fussed and wiped sympathetic tears from her sagging cheeks, made her hot milk with honey, tried to cajole her into drinking it, but Katie did not respond.

Sir Julien, too, came to see her, frowning, worried creases around his grave eyes...but still he refused to relent.

"It is too late, Katie girl. She is safe with a loving couple. They are devotees of Christ and will treat your daughter as well as you yourself could have. Stop your grieving, and get on with a bright future."

An impotent rage swept her, making her fingers curl into a fist at her sides. "How *dare* you say that to me? What do you know about how a mother's heart aches for her infant? What right had you to steal this little soul from me? She was mine, I tell you, *mine!*" She burst into tears and threw herself in the big overstuffed chair, pressing her head against her arm.

"You leave for Europe in a week." Sir Julien's stiff words drifted through her sorrow. "Once aboard ship you will come to your senses. This was not the only child you will have. You will have others—and a husband and name to go with them."

He left her then, and as the door closed Katie heard the bolt slide into place with solid finality.

She ran to the door and pounded until her hands were sore. "Anthony, I loathe the very memory of your kisses, your wicked lies, the velvety grass that was our bed!"

As the days passed Katie soothed her torn heart with midnight plans and schemes of her own making. "I will escape," she argued to the four walls. "They won't stop me. I won't let them."

She had decided this morning—today was to be the day. She *would* gain her freedom. One way or another. She turned quickly as she heard the outer bolt on her door slide back. That would be Inga bringing afternoon tea.

The elderly Dutch woman entered cautiously, as though she did not know if a woman gone mad might attack her. She supported the tea tray on her hip as she closed the door. Katie noticed two flushed spots on the woman's cheeks. Her small eyes were as bright as polished coins. Sudden hope sparked in Katie's breast and she took steps toward her old nanny.

"What is it?"

Inga glanced back at the door as if it might suddenly develop ears.

"I shouldn't tell you this, miss, but if you knew the sweet baby was safe you'd rest much easier now, wouldn't you?" Her eyes searched Katie's as though looking to reinforce her decision. "Sure now, you would indeed."

Katie latched hold of the woman's arm. "Oh yes, Inga, I would," she whispered. "What do you know?"

Inga's eyes glittered and darted toward the closed door. Katie's old nurse did not like Sir Julien. He was involved in British policy to bring all of South Africa under the Union Jack. Inga had lost her husband years ago in the first skirmishes between the Dutch Afrikaners—the "people of Africa"—and the British. Since then, the Dutch-settled area of South Africa, the Transvaal, had been annexed to the growing realm of the British Empire.

But that did not put an end to the Dutch resistance to British rule.

Inga's low whisper pulled Katie back to the matters at hand. "Do you remember the missionaries who came here to see Sir Julien a year ago?"

"Vaguely." Katie frowned. "What about them?"

"Dr. Clyde Varley, his name is. An' the missus is a young mite. Junia Varley is her name. Junia's sister is married to the vicar of Grimston Way in England. Dr. Varley and Missus Junia have your little one at the mission station near Isandlwana."

Katie stood still, her fingers tightening. "Who told you this?"

"The Zulu woman. The one the missionaries turned into a Christian."

"Jendaya?" A hopeful excitement began to stir. Katie had seen Jendaya many times around the grounds of Cape House. The girl had been driven out of the Zulu *kraal* of beehive huts near Isandlwana, and she lived in danger of being put to death for her decision to be baptized in the Buffalo River near the mission.

Jendaya now spent her time between the Isandlwana mission and the African huts on Sir Julien's estate. Katie had seen the young woman in the stables with Dumaka and had at first mistaken them for lovers, but Jendaya had explained that he was her brother. Though Dumaka was not a Christian, he too had been driven from Zululand for not publicly disowning his sister. Jendaya was still trying to get Dumaka to visit the mission station and talk to the "wise daktari" about the God of gods, but Dumaka resisted. He was angry with his sister for causing him shame—and he was resentful of the "white skins" for interfering with his people. Though he lived and worked at Cape House, his gaze was not warm toward Sir Julien Bley or anyone in Capetown, be they British or Boer—especially the Boer, who were the Dutch.

Katie forced herself to release Inga's arm. "Send for Jendaya! Have her come below my window. I must talk to her."

Inga shook her braided head. "She is gone again, miss. She only came to the back kitchen door asking for me to say your little one was safe with the daktari's wife."

The sound of carriage wheels distracted Katie. She hurried to the window, drew the portieres aside, and looked down into the courtyard. The coach was a hired taxi, and a tall man in black hat and cape was paying the driver. The driver rushed to unload the gentleman's baggage, and the house butler was walking to meet the arriving stranger. Katie was startled when the man looked up toward the Great House.

"What's he doing here?" She turned to Inga. "Sir Julien all but tossed him out a year ago."

Inga joined her at the window. Her mouth pursed. Her glance at Katie seemed hesitant, cautious. "Why, that is Sir Julien's stepbrother, Henry Chantry. He had his eyes on you last time he was here."

How well Katie remembered. Henry was well known for his roving eyes, and she doubted he had changed since she had seen him last before he'd sailed home to Grimston Way, England.

"He's surely come back for diamonds." Katie watched him follow the butler up the walkway to the front veranda. From the looks of his luggage he expected to stay a time. What would Julien say?

Sir Julien and his aunt, Lady Brewster, the Capetown matriarch of the extended family, had long favored Henry, wild as he was. She had even arranged for Henry's blood brother, Lyle Chantry, to marry her niece, the lovely diamond heiress Honoria. But Lady Brewster was a strait-laced woman and so had no sympathy for Henry's lascivious lifestyle. She had stood firmly beside Sir Julien's decision to withhold an inheritance until Henry proved himself worthy of managing such a fortune.

So why had Henry Chantry sailed back here all the way from England after being rejected by the Bleys and Brewsters?

Katie turned her head and looked at Inga. "I wonder if Lady Brewster or Sir Julien expected him."

"Don't think so, Miss Katie. Leastwise there's been no hint of it in the doings about Cape House. And no word of getting his old room ready."

Katie wondered if Henry had known Lady Brewster was vacationing at her Dutch-gabled house at Pietermaritzburg some miles away in Natal, and that Sir Julien was planning a trek out to the Kimberly mines soon.

She turned back to the window. Her fingers ran along the smooth rich texture of the portieres as her eyes narrowed. Cousin Henry Chantry just might be the answer to her present dilemma. The sight of the knave of hearts, baggage in hand, brought Katie a new expectation. Schemes took shape in her mind. Perhaps he could help her escape to the mission station to find her baby, and even arrange passage on a ship to London, and America. Perhaps all was not doomed after all!

As she turned from the window she caught a glance of her image in the gilded mirror. She stopped short, surprised by her own expression. The little upturn of her lips looked sly. For a brief moment her conscience smote her—an uncommon experience since her father's death in the explosion. How disappointed Carl van Buren would be in his daughter if he knew how she had grown up!

Her tawny, wavy hair fell loosely across her shoulders, and her blue velvet empire gown showed a desirable woman. She clenched her teeth. *Too late…too late to undo the past. I am unwed with no prospects of marrying the father of my child. I need money for myself and Evy. No*—she met the amber gaze reflected in the glass—*there is no turning back for you, Katie van Buren. You have set your sails, and now the wild winds must bear you along.*

Ideas churned in her mind, like little weeds growing taller and stronger, and she paced.

How would she get money enough to escape, and a great deal more? It would do no good to flee if she ended up on the streets of New York with a babe in arms, no place to go, and nothing to make her new life respectable. That was no way to start if she was to realize her dream of one day establishing Evy in high society.

I am still young. There can be another love in New York with a respectable name who will marry me and adopt Evy as his daughter. Yes. That was how it would be. After all, she had a right—she was Carl van Buren's daughter. He had been partners with Julien Bley. Why shouldn't she have what had rightfully belonged to her father? What Julien was now keeping!

She must have the Black Diamond, the stone Sir Julien was always enticing buyers from London with by waving it under their noses. Once she had Evy and the Black Diamond, she would be free to do anything she wished.

Her mind made up, she felt nervous perspiration running down her ribs. The Black Diamond. How could she get it?

Henry Chantry was the man to approach about that. He insisted *his* father had found it, and that the diamond was by rights Chantry property, that Sir Julien had used deceit to secure it for himself.

Katie grimaced. She must be desperate indeed to turn to Cousin Henry.

A noise caught Katie's attention, and she spun to see that Inga was about to leave. "Leave the door unbolted. Don't you see? I *must* sneak downstairs and speak alone with Cousin Henry."

"If you get caught, Miss Katie, you know what Sir Julien will do to me for not bolting the door."

"I won't get caught. Please, Inga, I'm desperate."

Inga fiddled with her apron. "Just this once, miss, but do be heedful. Do, please."

"He won't catch me. I promise to be careful."

Katie waited until the woman's steps faded away down the hall, then inched the door open.

It was quiet. She crept to the stairway in time to see Cousin Henry entering the downstairs hall. He was looking toward Sir Julien's office with a dark countenance that matched his swarthy appearance.

Henry Chantry looked as dangerous as any blackguard pirate. He was tall, with black hair and mustache, and Katie suspected he carried a pistol somewhere beneath his white linen jacket. The last she had heard he had been in uncharted territory in Mashonaland on an expedition to locate a mysterious gold deposit that he avowed his grandfather had learned about from some tribal chieftain. No one believed Henry about the gold, although he claimed to have his grandfather's map. Henry's wife had died several years ago on an expedition, and the Brewster family held him responsible. Katie doubted Sir Julien would receive Henry at all kindly.

She stooped behind the banister, not wishing to be seen. She must approach Cousin Henry with caution—Sir Julien was downstairs in his office. What would he do when he heard of Henry's arrival? Perhaps she could learn something to aid her own quest if she could listen in on their conversation. Putting her scruples aside, she hid until Henry walked toward Julien's office, then prepared to sneak down the stairs to listen at the door.

Henry Chantry left the veranda with its bright sunlight and was now standing in the entrance hall looking toward the room he remembered to be Julien's office. His restless gaze flitted over the mansionlike amenities of Cape House, which was just as he remembered. He'd left for England two years ago, after his wife's death of African fever. They had been camped out on the Shangani River on their way back to Bulawayo to bring her to a doctor at the mission station when she had succumbed to the summons of death. Her aunt, Lady Brewster, had never forgiven him for bringing Caroline on the trek.

Henry forced his features into the semblance of a smile when he saw his stepbrother, Sir Julien Bley, standing in the hall beside the door to his office. Julien must have heard the carriage arrive out front.

Henry felt the icy stare of Julien's single eye; it seemed to bore through him with malevolent intent. So, matters had not changed.

"What are you doing here?" Sir Julien demanded, his voice low and chilled.

Henry felt the muscles in his jaw tense. The anger he had been living with ever since Julien had ordered him to leave Cape House blazed, feeling like hot coals in his chest.

"Did I not tell you two years ago"—Julien spoke as though through gritted teeth—"not to come back until you have turned your last allowance into a profitable business?"

Henry recalled that last meeting. He had relived the argument a thousand times over while in England. Each time he replayed the humiliating memory, he promised himself he would one day make Julien pay.

Henry felt his shoulders beginning to sag in the face of his stepbrother, who stood straight-backed, his head high, a diamond stickpin flashing loudly on his black lapel. The day of revenge had not yet arrived. Though Henry had worked hard in London, it seemed that money in his palm turned to straw, while in Julien's it multiplied into diamonds...heaps of them, all flashing brilliantly.

Yet was he not a son of the family as well? Didn't he have as much right to share in the family diamond mines as Julien?

"Well?" Sir Julien's tone was thick with disdain. "Have you come crawling back to me again? Cannot stand on your own two feet, eh? Well, you'll get nothing from me. Do you hear? Nothing. If you want anything to fill your empty pockets, my boy, you can go work in the mines along with the Africans!"

Sir Julien turned on his polished heel and strode into his office, shutting the door.

Henry stood there, tasting bitter gall. His heart slammed in his chest. Tiny beads of sweat formed on his upper lip. It was enough that he had to deal with his own constant string of failures, but when Julien's success was thrown in his face like this, it fed the resentment that ate at his heart like a canker.

I'll get my rightful share of the diamonds—or kill him in the trying. He walked with slow, steady steps toward the office door. His hand was sweaty as he grasped the doorknob and turned it. If it was locked—

It wasn't. He opened it and stepped in, shutting it quietly behind him.

Sir Julien sat behind his polished desk, a small, golden lamp glowing on the surface. The Black Diamond sat glittering under the light like midnight fire. The very sight of it—and the thought of its value on the world market—made Henry's breathing tense.

The corners of Sir Julien's mouth turned up, but his eye held no humor. "So you persist."

Curse the man, he sounded downright bored. Henry schooled his voice to be even, calm. "You will hear me out, Julien. I demand to be treated with respect."

Sir Julien's mouth widened into a smile that Henry loathed, then inclined his dark head with what was clearly mock gravity.

"Very well, I am listening."

Henry walked to the center of the room and stood. The diamond flashed. It was all he could do to keep from gazing at it.

"It was my father who found that." He nodded toward the diamond. "Both Lyle and I want what is rightfully ours—as his sons."

"Everyone suddenly claims to have found the Black Diamond, but I have an eyewitness who has sworn by the laws of England that it was I who discovered it, along with the Kimberly mine."

It seemed to Henry that the black patch on Julien's blind eye began to expand into a gaping pit into which Henry would soon be engulfed.

"A *Chantry* found the Black Diamond!"

"As you found a gold mine?" came Julien's impatient retort.

"I did find a gold mine." Henry braced himself with both hands on the wide desk as he leaned toward Julien. "One day I shall be rich. But I need that diamond to resume my expedition into Mashonaland."

"Don't be a fool, Henry. You've had these expeditions before. The last time it was emeralds. Until"—his voice grew even colder—"you filled your pockets with wind and had to bury your dreams beside Caroline's grave!"

He straightened as though he'd been slapped across the face. "Curse you, Julien. Leave my poor wife out of this!"

"It was you who dragged her into it, hauling her with you across wild, savage land—all while expecting your child! That they are both dead now lies at *your* doorstep—just as surely as though you had killed them."

Henry could bear it no longer. He would shut Julien up if it was the last thing he did! He made a lunge for Julien's throat, but stopped cold when Julien lifted a large caliber pistol from his lap. He aimed it at Henry's chest, his eye flickering in the lamplight—and Henry had the oddest impression that that one eye was a reflection of the Black Diamond.

"You will get nothing from me, Henry. And nothing from Lady Brewster. She blames you for Caroline's death. You robbed her of her only granddaughter—and her unborn great-grandchild lies buried in Mashonaland with her. Do you think either of us would give you a single shilling?" Julien stood. "Now get out of my office…and out of my life."

Dazed from bitter humiliation and weight of his guilt over his late wife, Henry just stood there. He felt as though he were in a trance, and the only thing that got through was the rage toward Julien.

His stepbrother walked around the desk and moved to open the door. He stepped back and gestured, still holding the pistol. "Get out."

Henry turned and walked with leaden steps toward the door, then paused to meet Julien's icy gaze. Neither spoke. Henry straightened his shoulders and walked out, his heels clicking on the polished marble hall.

The housekeeper loitered nearby, glancing from the office door to Henry before she hurried toward the front door and opened it. Her gray eyes darted here and there as she managed a curtsy. "A good day to you, Mister Chantry, sir."

Henry walked out of Cape House onto the veranda. He stood there for a moment, staring at nothing. Now what? What to do next?

He pressed his lips together. If it had not been for that pistol…

Katie had listened at the door of Julien's office through the entire exchange. When the housekeeper noticed her listening, Katie warned her to silence.

Katie hurried out of sight when footsteps approached the door. When Henry exited the office, the housekeeper showed him to the door, then looked only too glad to get away and be about her duties.

The house was still now, with a sense of impending doom. Katie remained hidden behind the bottom of the staircase facing her guardian's office. She was about to come around and go up to her room to think over what she had heard when the office door opened and Julien stood in the doorway. She dared not move…could not breathe. If he saw her, he would twist the truth from her, making her admit what she had overheard.

Julien's dark face was tense. He held something in his hand. At first she thought it was a gun, then she realized it was the Black Diamond.

Katie's heart pounded in her chest. Julien occasionally took the magnificent stone out of its hiding place and set it on his desk to admire it. Afterward he would put it away and go about his work as though he were fulfilled. No one knew where he kept it. He once taunted members of his family with his secret. "Do you think I would trust any of you to know where I keep it, eh? You, Anthony my boy? Or you, Katie?"

She held her breath, waiting for him to return to his office and close the door so she could go up to her room, but Sir Julien did not return to his office. He walked to the front door and stepped out onto the veranda. There was no time to risk going up the stairway. The library was just across the hall, and she sped through the doorway, slipping inside. A window faced the front veranda, and she hurried there to look out. Why had Julien stepped outside? Was he wary that Cousin Henry might come back to the house? Did he know Henry had a pistol, perhaps even under his coat, but had not risked reaching for it?

Katie felt weakened and sick. So much hatred and mistrust. Her hands were cold and tense as she quieted her skirts and peered out through the curtains.

Oddly, she could hear Sir Julien's low voice arguing with someone on the veranda, but she could not see who it was. It had to be Henry again. What if they killed each other? She was about to rush up the stairs to her bedroom when she heard the front door slam shut. Footsteps followed. She waited for them to disappear, but they drew closer. She caught her breath as she realized someone was coming. She did not want Julien to spot her now. He would see through her dismay and guess she had overheard the quarrel in his office. As the library door opened, Katie ducked behind the large leather chair and side table.

Muffled footsteps sounded across the burgundy carpet. She heard someone moving about the room doing something. She ventured a peek from behind the back of the chair and saw Julien's back to her. He stood facing the wall of leather-bound books. Katie realized he was not looking at the library books, but at a table in the corner near the fireplace. A carved teak lion, some elephant tusks, and a wooden box sat on top of the table.

She watched Julien turn his head and glance toward the closed library door. He approached a magnificently carved secretary and opened the two cabinet doors. Then came footsteps in the outer hall, and Julien hurried toward the library door. Katie saw lion etchings on the wooden secretary and two lionhead knobs. Julien bolted the library door and returned to the secretary, taking something from his jacket pocket and looking at it for a moment—

The Black Diamond! Katie's breath caught in her throat as Julien turned his attention to the two lionhead knobs. Once again he turned his back toward her, and she could not see what he was doing. She heard a click and then something like a spring releasing. She had the impression that he was placing something inside a compartment, then he pressed on something as the compartment clicked shut. He closed the secretary cabinet and walked to the library door, opened it and glanced out before he left the room. As his footsteps faded, Katie remained stooped behind the leather chair, too stunned to move.

The diamond was hidden in the secretary.

She moistened her dry lips and sought to calm her galloping heart. She could have sworn Julien had not used any key. Just a secret compartment in a hundred-year-old secretary, most likely used for maps and valuable papers. Why would Sir Julien hide the priceless diamond in a compartment in the desk instead of one of the safes in Cape House where the jewels and priceless items were kept? Perhaps he thought they were too far from his office.

Katie could scarcely take it in. She had actually learned where the Black Diamond was hidden! Her hands shook, but she did not move from her hiding place for an inestimable time. When all was silent, she crept out and went to the desk. She stood staring at it. It was enough to know the secret of the stone's hiding place…at least for now. She crept to the door, opened it a crack, and, seeing no one, slipped out and went to the stairway.

Safely back in her room, she collapsed in a tapestry chair, hugging herself until her nerves calmed and her shaking ceased.

She was still seated there, resting her head on the back of the chair, when Inga tapped on the door and opened it slightly. Seeing Katie, she opened it wide and came in with the afternoon tea tray.

"You're looking ill, Miss Katie. Are you needing a doctor?"

Katie shook her head and watched Inga pour her tea, add sugar and milk, and bring it to her on a gold-rimmed china saucer.

"Here, miss, drink it hotlike. It'll make your insides settle a bit."

Katie took it with a grateful sigh. "Inga?"

The old Dutch woman looked at her, a slight frown on her brow. "Yes, Miss Katie?"

"Did you hear anything in the kitchen about Cousin Henry?"

Inga's pug nose twitched. "Laddie says to his mum, the cookie, that when Master Chantry went to the stables he was mad enough to do Sir Julien harm."

Katie shuddered. "Did Laddie learn anything about where my cousin was going? Did he say he was leaving Capetown or anything of the sort?"

"Master Chantry didn't say a word, miss. Just swung himself onto the horse and galloped away like a hellion. But," she added in a low voice, "if you're wondering where the Master is staying, it's no hard thing to learn. There's all of a half dozen inns and hotels in town that's operating now. Would you be wanting me to send Laddie to find the Master's whereabouts?"

Katie leaned forward, setting her cup and saucer on the little table. "Can he go without Sir Julien knowing?"

"Oh, surely, miss." She grinned. "You know Laddie. He can do most anything and not get himself caught."

"Well, yes, I do not doubt that. Then I wish to write a letter to my cousin and have your nephew deliver it tonight."

Inga nodded gravely. "I'll see it taken care of, Miss Katie. I'll be bringing tea to the others, then I'll come back for your letter."

When Inga left, Katie drank her hot tea and poured a second cup, adding even more sugar and milk. She carried the cup and saucer to her desk, sat down, and drained the cup. When her nerves began to settle, she removed a piece of linen stationery and dipped the pen in the inkwell. She wrote hurriedly, folded the sheet, and sealed it in the envelope. On the outside she scrawled *Master Henry Chantry.* Then she went back to her chair and waited for Inga.

An hour later, the nanny came back into the room. Katie handed her the envelope. "Do not let Laddie tell anyone what he is about."

Inga nodded. "No one, Miss Katie. You rest easy. Laddie will find the Master."

CHAPTER TWO

Katie awoke with a start. She must have dozed off. She was still sitting in the chair, the empty teacup and saucer on her lap. She realized what had awakened her. Sir Julien's impatient voice rang through the open bedroom window.

Had Cousin Henry dared to return?

She set the cup on the tea tray and went to the window, looking down to the front lawn.

A tall young African in knee pants and a long yellow cotton shirt was leading a horse toward Sir Julien, who stood tapping his foot. Dressed for riding, he yelled something in Zulu to Dumaka, who was head groom. Dumaka trotted alongside the gelding, bringing the handsome golden horse to Sir Julien.

Julien mounted, took hold of the reins, and sent the horse galloping toward the gate.

Where was he going? It didn't matter. All that mattered was that with him gone, the task in the library would now be much easier to accomplish.

A soft tap sounded on Katie's door. She hurried to it. A moment later it opened, and Inga's light blue eyes shone.

"Laddie found Master Henry. He's in a room at the wharf. He sent a message to you, Miss Katie." After glancing both ways, she removed an envelope from behind her apron.

Katie read the brief wording from Cousin Henry: *I will meet you in the stables a few minutes after midnight. H. C.*

"Good news, miss? You're smiling pertlike."

Katie clutched the letter to her chest. "Yes! Leave the back kitchen door unlocked tonight. I will come down fifteen minutes before the stroke of twelve."

"Then the master will bring you to Isandlwana?"

"I shall do everything in my power to see that he does. This is my chance to get away, to have my daughter…and a new start in America."

Inga nodded. "With a guardian like Master Julien, it is best to leave if you can, miss. He's ridden to the harbor to meet someone from London. He didn't say who it was, but I don't suspect he'll be back soon. Luck, Miss Katie, is on your side, so it seems. Jendaya, too, has come back to her hut. She didn't leave as I had thought, but was selling vegetables at the open market."

Katie clasped her hands together. "Speak to her about having a four-horse carriage ready for me tonight. If Cousin Henry agrees, Jendaya can bring me as far as Natal. Afterward I can ride horseback with Henry toward Isandlwana." The ride would be rough and not without risk, but Katie would not turn back in fear, no matter how many rumors spread of the Zulus preparing for the first "washing of their spears."

Katie spent the rest of the afternoon on edge. She packed some of her clothing and personal items, then watched the clock on her table for the crucial hour to strike. After midnight the entire household would be asleep. Matters were turning out very well, what with Henry all but agreeing to help her and Sir Julien's being away from the house.

Perhaps almost too well.

Just whom might Julien be meeting on a ship from London? What if he had only pretended to leave for the harbor? He could return to the estate after nightfall, conceal his horse in the thicket, and enter without being seen—perhaps to wait in the darkened library for her and Henry.

"I'm being too suspicious," she murmured to the walls, "but it does appear that the Black Diamond, and escape to Isandlwana, is being handed to me on a silver platter."

Even so, this was the best opportunity to escape and to get Evy back. She narrowed her lashes, remembering the feel of Anthony's arms around her, but thinking of him now brought only a flood of bitterness. *I have borne all the shame, the suffering, the loss, while he tours about London in a fancy coach, sporting Lady Camilla at dinner balls and the theater. Oh, what a fool I was to give myself to him! To listen to his smooth sentimental talk, his declarations of love and protection.*

Well, danger from the Zulus or not, she was going through with her plans to journey toward the Varleys' mission station. There was also risk in Sir Julien's guardianship, considering his loathsome schemes to marry her off to a man of his own choosing. And if she stayed at Cape House, she would lose Evy forever.

I will not lose her! Not if I can prevent it.

As the clock struck eleven, she was dressed and waiting. She was not likely to hear Cousin Henry arrive. She doubted he knew that Julien was away, so he would avoid alerting him. Inga had told Katie earlier that evening that she had spoken to Jendaya, and the Zulu woman would have the carriage waiting behind the cluster of trees by the back road near the African huts. There was a narrow dirt road there that led from the farmland to the township. They could leave without going through the front grounds of Cape House.

Perhaps Cousin Henry was arriving by that road even now!

Once they reached the mission station near Isandlwana, Katie was sure Dr. Varley's wife would relinquish Evy. How could they with any Christian conscience refuse her if she insisted? She was sure they would not. Then, by the time they notified Sir Julien, she and Evy, and perhaps Cousin Henry, would be at Cape Elizabeth, boarding a ship bound for London.

She sat near the door in the darkness, her one bag waiting beside her.

America, yes—it will be a safe place to begin a new life.

She stood and began to pace the soft carpet. Her feet, encased in stylish flat-heeled morocco slippers, made no sound. She looked at the clock again. At last the hands reached eighteen minutes before midnight, and her heart began to leap. Though it was a warm night, she slipped into her dark, hooded cloak, caught up her bag, and slipped from her room. The upper hall was empty and silent.

Inga had left a small lantern burning near the table by the top of the stairway, and Katie crept down the steps, clutching the banister, her gaze riveted toward Sir Julien's office. No yellow glow came from beneath the oak door.

Below the stairs, hovering like a ghost, Inga waited, a small candle in her hand. Her fair face was taut and looked even more wan than usual.

"The kitchen door is unlocked, just as you said." Her whisper seemed to echo in the silence.

Katie nodded, then threw an arm around the older woman's shoulders. "Thank you, Inga, for everything. What would I have done without you these lonely years?"

Inga showed no particular emotion, but her mouth grew tight. "You be careful now. You watch that Master Henry. You might need him now, but he's a cagey one."

"Yes, yes, good-bye, Inga. You had best go to your room now and lock your door. Do not come out again, no matter what you hear."

Inga handed her the candleholder and slipped away. In another moment, the shadows had swallowed her from Katie's view. Katie glanced back up the stairs. All was well. She stood for a last moment listening. She heard nothing except the drumbeat of her own heart. She made her way along the hall, hesitated by the library, then went toward the kitchen. She would first explain about the Black Diamond to Cousin Henry. When it was taken, they must both be involved.

The kitchen was a huge room, usually warm and bright with a cheerful atmosphere, but in the sporadic moonlight it seemed more like a black cave. She edged her way along the counter and past the immense stove, past the sideboards, the tables, the pantry—

Her breath caught in her throat. What was that over there—that shadow that seemed to emerge from the darkness? Her trembling hand gripped the candleholder. A draft came from somewhere and drew the little flame aside, where it hovered, quavering.

Whoever was in the darkness must have already seen her candle. Too late to hide.

"Who is there?"

A shrill, feline hiss cut through the silence. Katie jumped, and the candle separated from the holder and thudded to the floor, bringing total darkness as the fleeing cat shot past Katie. Her heart fluttered, and she lunged for the back door. As she felt for the doorknob, pulled the door open, and bolted outside, she expected to feel someone's hands grabbing hold of her from behind. She darted to the porch, where damp mops, brooms, and trash barrels seemed determined to hinder her. She rushed down the porch steps and across the yard, toward the distant stables.

She looked back once, afraid she would see lights coming on in some of the lower rooms—but the windows remained dark. The tree branches around her sighed in the night wind. Above, the moon was like a silver disk darting between the clouds coming in from the bay. The beauty calmed her. She must have imagined that shadow, and her own prowling about had spooked poor Tabby, who slept on a padded footstool in the corner of the kitchen.

Katie released a tense breath, turned away from the house, and ran on to the stables to find Cousin Henry.

The stables appeared as low, rambling silhouettes against the backdrop of distant trees. The corral was visible in the moonlight, and a tall, shadowy figure moved away from a shade tree and came toward her. She paused and waited as a horrid thought struck her: What if it was Sir Julien, after all?

She gripped the handle of her bag until the leather strap began to press into her palm.

Cousin Henry came into view, a sardonic smile on his swarthy face, the wind ruffling his dark jacket. He could have passed for a riverboat gambler—not exactly the most trustworthy of folks. Yet she had little choice now except to turn to him.

"You called for me, my dear?"

Katie grabbed his sleeve and pulled him aside to the shadow of the stables. "We must not be seen in the moonlight."

His brows shot up when he saw her clothing bag. "Well, well."

Katie's cheeks heated at his smooth mockery. "So you've finally come to your senses and decided I am worth two of that insipid nephew of mine."

"Henry, you've got to help me. We must act quickly, and I haven't all night to explain. But I will ask that you keep your ill-bred remarks to yourself." She met his gaze. "It is not you I am interested in, but your assistance."

"Sounds typical of you, Katie love. If you were wise you would sound a trifle more...sweet and submissive? Well, go on, we are risking our necks out here if Julien finds us."

"He has gone to the harbor, but we must still be very careful."

"What did you mean by *assistance?*"

She read the hint of suspicion in his tone. Born and raised in England, Henry sounded more British than the rest of the family, who spoke with the Afrikaner accent. Henry's father, Squire George Chantry, owned the grand estate of Rookswood in the village of Grimston Way. Henry's older brother, Lyle, had married one of Lady Brewster's two daughters, Honoria—sister to Caroline, Henry's poor wife.

Katie clamped her jaw to keep her teeth from chattering and lifted her chin, hoping she looked brave when she felt otherwise.

"I have a bargain to present to you."

His dark brows arched at that. "What kind of bargain?"

She looked at him squarely; she needed to at least appear confident. "I overheard your discussion with your stepbrother. You need financial backing for your expedition. A gold discovery, isn't it?"

"You were eavesdropping?"

"Oh, Henry, there is no time for that. Do you want to hear my plan or not?"

"First things first. Why is it you are not turning to your beloved Anthony for help? When I left here two years ago you insisted you were madly in love with the innocuous fellow."

"And you, Cousin Henry, were about to be married."

"After you turned me down."

"That doesn't matter now. Are you interested in listening or not?"

"About my nephew Anthony—"

She tried to hide her consternation. "Never mind him. I don't know where he is, nor do I care! He lied to me. I loathe him." She clenched her hands to still the trembling that threatened to overcome her.

Henry's eyes narrowed as he studied her. Clearly, he was alert and not easily deterred. She should have known he would demand complicated explanations as to why her relationship with his wife's nephew had turned sour.

She stiffened when she felt his fingers on her face. He cupped her chin and turned her toward the moonlight, his gaze searching hers until he must have guessed what she was hiding, for the corner of his mouth tipped.

"So that's how it is, is it?"

She jerked her chin away and stepped back. "Please, don't. Sir Julien has humiliated me enough."

"So, you discovered too late that the cherished Anthony is a louse. I doubt he has given you a second thought since going to London. You should have listened to me. What has he done, abandoned you while he makes arrangements to marry Lord Montieth's charming heiress?"

"Oh, keep quiet!" She felt his words like a blow, and tears rushed to her eyes. She wished to throw his words back into his face, but common sense restrained her. She could not afford to anger him, not when she needed him so desperately.

"Your emotions tell me this is no ordinary jilt. What is it?"

She avoided his eyes and bit her lip, then turned her back. The words lodged in her throat like thorns. How humiliating to have to confess to a man like Henry Chantry that she had been a fool.

"I have a baby." How painful so few words could be!

He remained silent, and she thought he must be stunned.

She whirled to face him. "I *must* escape. I want to leave Capetown forever, to go to America with my baby—to get away from Sir Julien's power over me. He took my baby away." Her voice cracked as pain chipped at her heart. "I've found out she's at the mission station near Isandlwana—Jendaya told me."

"The Zulu woman?"

"Yes. I must go to Isandlwana, find my daughter, and board a ship at Port Elizabeth bound for England. From there, if my plan works, I'll sail for New York."

He looked at her. She began to fear he would utterly refuse her, but then he spoke at last, as brutally honest as she.

"And you want me to rescue Anthony's illegitimate child?"

"She is *my* daughter. I— I've no one else to turn to for help."

"You were a fool to trust him, Katie."

"Yes, I know that now. Will you help me?"

"It will take money to accomplish all this," he said flatly, "and I don't have it. Julien turned me down this afternoon, though I'm an heir to the diamond enterprise the same as he. He controls everything, thanks to old Ebenezer."

Ebenezer Bley. Katie knew he was the first in the extended family to come to Capetown. He'd been at Kimberly when the first diamond was found there, as well as on the river when the first gold was discovered. His wily ability to manipulate was well known. Hadn't he wheedled his way into the circle of just a few men who controlled these finds, thereby becoming wealthy and politically powerful both in Capetown and in London? Ebenezer died a very old man and left his son Julien the controlling interest over the family fortune. He must have felt that Julien would make the best financial patriarch.

Circumstances had proven Ebenezer right, Katie thought bitterly. Sir Julien even administered her portion of her father's fortune to control her future for the benefit of the diamond business as though she, a van Buren, were a relation.

"You understand what you're up against." Henry's question pulled her back to matters at hand. "How do you expect to pay for the ocean passage?"

"By taking some of what is being held back from me and from my daughter. What is partly yours as well. It— It would not be the same as stealing."

"Has Julien ever suggested giving you some diamonds from the inheritance your father left you?"

"He will give me little unless I marry according to his wishes. He took my baby and gave her to the mission and has plans to send me to Europe for a year. As if that would heal my heart! He intends to arrange a marriage for me that suits *his* plans for the Kimberly mines. That is all he devotes himself to—the diamond mines." Her voice quavered, and she cast another glance over her shoulder toward the house, where all was in shadow. The sound of the wind in the treetops and the creaking of the stables sent ripples of fear along her skin. What if Julien was watching, what if he knew? She remembered the pistol he kept. What if he was trying to trap her and Cousin Henry? He had used such a loud voice out on the front lawn—could it have been to draw her attention? To make her think he was leaving?

No, that couldn't be. Sir Julien would never expect her to take the Black Diamond.

"Then are you are thinking of taking some diamonds from Cape House?"

This time it was she who arched her brows. "As though you have not thought that very thing."

"I admit it. But if I help you, what do I get out of this?"

So like Cousin Henry to ask that, yet how could she blame him? She lifted her chin and confronted his hard gaze. She pretended brashness, using a masquerade of boldness to shield her precariousness. "You will get the same as what I intend to have—something of great value, Cousin Henry—the Black Diamond."

His breath stopped short. "The Black Diamond!" he repeated in a soft murmur. "Are you out of your mind? Julien keeps it well hidden—he worships that stone. It would be next to impossible to get your hands on it."

"You think so? It is because he worships it that he keeps his little idol where he can admire it anytime he desires without having to be seen going back and forth, to and from the safe. I know where he hides it."

"Ah!" He seemed taken aback, and she could well believe he wondered how she had managed to discover such a thing. "The Black Diamond. If I could just get my hands on it—"

"You say it belongs to the Chantrys?"

"It does," he stated firmly. "My father was there when it was found. Though Julien denies this, there is even some evidence that my father is the one who dislodged it from the strata."

"*My* father, Carl van Buren, helped to find that mine, yet Julien keeps the mine for himself."

"I can hardly believe you know where it is, Katie. You must be dreaming."

"Dreaming of escape and freedom, yes"—she took hold of his arm—"and desperate enough to take what is mine. I know where the diamond is. We can get it and be on our way to Isandlwana at once. I— I will share with you whatever price the diamond brings on the London market, fifty-fifty."

"It will need to be sold on the smuggling market. London, maybe. Russia, France—the Vatican..."

"But we need money now to get us to England!"

He regarded her, the flicker of condescension clear in his eyes. "If we are going to steal the Black Diamond, my dear, then we might as well help ourselves to anything else we need. In moderation, of course." He laughed and took hold of her arms, pulling her toward him. "We belong together, Katie love. What scoundrels we both are."

She wrenched free. "Speak for yourself, Cousin. I am not a thief."

"No? Dear Julien will come to quite a different conclusion, even though he's the real thief. Not that it matters to me. Evidently it doesn't to you, either."

It did matter. She could imagine her father frowning in sadness if he could see her now. She could remember him reading the Commandments to her when she was a little girl. "Thou shalt not steal... Thou shalt not—"

But all that was behind her now. She had grown up isolated from the religious instruction that had meant so much to her father and the van Buren family of Afrikaners. She would do whatever she must to be free. And to have her daughter restored to her. Surely her father would understand that?

She fixed her gaze on Henry. "Well? Do we have a bargain?"

In the moonlight she saw his mouth turn into a slender smile beneath his mustache. "We have a bargain, Katie. Now suppose you tell me where the Black Diamond is hidden."

For just a moment she could not escape the sensation that she was a fool to trust him—then, feeling his fingers enclose her arm and a tide of warm strength surge through her, she pushed the notion aside. She must take this chance.

"I will take you there. We must do this—together. It's in the library. Come."

"You are certain Julien's gone to Kimberly?"

She was as certain as she could be, and yet…there *was* that uneasy sensation that she was being watched. "I saw him ride away earlier this afternoon, but when it comes to your stepbrother, who can be sure of anything?"

"Here, leave your bag in that brush until we come back for the horses."

Henry was still holding Katie's arm as they came silently up the back porch steps. The door remained ajar from when she had fled. She reached for the knob.

The kitchen was in darkness as they entered, except for the stream of moonlight coming through the high window above the pantry cabinet. Katie stooped and picked up the candle she had dropped earlier. She went to the oven to relight the wick on coals banked in the oven for the morning cook.

Henry knew the house layout perhaps as well as she. He had come here from England several times with his father and Lyle. When his father had married Julien's widowed mother, there had been a time when Henry and Lyle had lived in Cape House. That, of course, was long before trouble developed between Henry and Julien. Lyle had been the silent one, the one who had made friends with Julien and married into the Brewsters.

When Katie turned around with the candle flaring, Cousin Henry was gone. She gasped, looking around. Had he abandoned her? No, she would have heard him if he'd opened the back door and gone out. She went into the hall. No sight of him. He must be in the library, waiting.

She trod the hall floor carefully, trying not to awaken anyone on the ground floor. The live-in Anglo servants all had their rooms near the kitchen and pantry, as did Anthony when he came to visit. Of course, Anthony had not dared show his face for some time. When she had written him about expecting the baby, he had not even replied.

When she came to the library, the heavy door stood open a few inches. She pushed it back and held the candle high. Henry was busy surveying the room of books, maps, and the hunting trophies Julien had collected from his trips into Angola.

She guessed he was checking his intuition as to where the Black Diamond might be hidden.

Katie pushed the door closed behind her. The candle flame reflected a bleak light in the mirror above the fireplace mantle, reminding her of a ghost.

She understood the danger with which she was flirting. Each step brought her closer to an action that she would never be able to reverse. *There is still time to turn back,* a small voice seemed to say.

No, not after getting cousin Henry involved. There is no other way out of my dilemma. I'm going through with it.

Henry came to take her arm. "Where?" His voice was barely audible.

Her hand shook as she led him to the old heirloom secretary. She hesitated—either she trusted Henry or she did not. There was no middle road. If he failed her as had Anthony, she would be twice a fool.

"Hurry!"

At his urgent whisper, she handed him the candle and turned to the secretary. Carefully she pulled aside the two cabinet doors, revealing the lion carvings and the two lion knobs.

"So that's it!" He sounded furious with himself. "A hidden compartment in this old heirloom."

Katie frowned. What had Sir Julien done when he'd had his back toward her? How had the secret door sprung open?

Outside the windows the wind rustled the leaves. The floors and walls creaked as the wood settled for the night. With her right hand she pushed against one lion, and used her left to maneuver the other, nothing happened. She tried again, her urgency increasing with the passing moments.

Her breath came rapidly. Standing beside her, she sensed Henry's impatience.

"Do you know what you're doing?"

"I'm trying!"

"Shh—quiet." His fingers clasped her shoulder as he glanced toward the door.

Katie tensed. Had she heard something? Maybe she had just imagined the sound that day of a spring giving way in a drawer? Now, in the candlelight, she could see there was no keyhole. Julien must have pushed on something.

"There must be a secret lever or something—somewhere." She looked helplessly at Henry.

"I'll try it." He pushed her aside, then set the candle on top of the secretary and began pushing on the lion knobs, then turning, shoving, twisting again.

From somewhere there came a heavier creak. Katie caught her breath and looked at Henry.

He was now so engrossed in trying to figure out the lion knobs and how they worked that he paid no mind. Her heart pounded with heavy beats that took her breath away. She continued to look toward the library door. If Julien had come home... But they would have heard his horse approaching the stables.

As Henry struggled to solve the puzzle, she inched her way toward the door. Was that creak from the wind, or a light footfall? Her mouth was dry. Her palms were slick with sweat, and her shaking fingers worked their way up the bodice of her dress to her throat. If Sir Julien found them here, he would use his pistol on Henry, she was sure of it.

Maybe on her too.

Oh, what have I done? What have I done? She hurried toward Henry, clawing at his arm. "I think I hear someone—"

"Ah!"

The exclamation caught her attention. She heard a faint click, and saw a section of the carved paneling open a crack. Henry pulled it farther out, then picked up the candle and held it close to a small, velvet-lined cavern.

Katie forgot all her fears as the Black Diamond winked at them.

They both reached for it, but Henry grasped first, turning it over in his hand before the candle.

Katie looked up at him. His eyes sparkled with an ugly humor that repelled her. "I've defeated Julien! It's mine!" Greed larded his rough whisper.

She snatched the diamond away from him. "It is *ours*."

"Look." He took some soft leather pouches out of the drawer, opened a drawstring, and poured some of the whites onto his palm. The diamonds glittered in the candlelight. He grinned, then put them back in the pouch and pulled the drawstring, stuffing three pouches in his trouser pockets.

"Give me that, we don't have time." He snatched the Black Diamond from her, rolled it in the velvet lining from the drawer, and shoved it in his inside jacket pocket. He pushed on the carved paneling and then closed the two cabinet doors.

"To the stables."

Henry surged ahead of her toward the library door. Katie rushed after him, her stomach clenching with fear and guilt. The candle went out, and she swallowed back her fear. Henry opened the library door a crack, looked out, then moved toward the back of the house.

The moon must have clouded over, for the room was in darkness—

just like Katie's aching soul. She was close at his heels when his steps halted at what must have been the kitchen. Her heart, too, nearly stopped.

She turned to look behind just as Henry lunged toward the kitchen door. A gust of wind sent Katie's skirts around her ankles. He reached back, latched hold of her arm, and pulled her toward the porch and down the steps. Crossing the backyard they started running.

When they reached the stables all seemed quiet. Laddie was nowhere to be seen, nor was Dumaka. Of course, they had not expected her to take anything from the house, so why would they be there? They would all certainly face Sir Julien tomorrow to be pounded by questions.

"Where is the Zulu?" Henry demanded impatiently. "She should have been here by now. It's after midnight."

"She's waiting farther down the road, behind the trees."

As he entered the stable for his golden gelding, Katie looked in the brush near the corral for her bag. Carrying it back, she paused, hearing the nervous neighing of the horses in their stalls for the night. Odd that they should be so nervous—probably not used to Henry's horse.

She waited. What was keeping him? She walked to the wide stable doorway and stared into the chasm of darkness, but could not see him. He must be farther toward the back.

She inched forward and whispered. "Henry? Where are you?"

The only sound meeting her was the nervous movements of the horses. She forced herself to enter, surrounded by deep shadows and the pungent odor of hay mingled with manure.

His horse, where was it? And where was the mare Inga had said would be saddled for her?

She turned full circle, glancing desperately about her. Then she heard a creaking sound—a door opening at the far end of the stable. The back door! She saw the wind moving it to and fro on its hinges. This discovery was followed by the one sound she feared: hooves, galloping away.

She ran through the stable and out the back door into the night.

"Henry!" she hissed. In the moonlight she glimpsed him, hunched low in the saddle, rounding a tree-lined bend, where he disappeared in the direction of the African huts.

Her heart sank like a stone. "No! *No!*" Her hands formed fists, and she doubled over. He had taken everything and left her here. *Betrayed!*

Bitter rage filled her mind. She pressed the back of her hand hard against her teeth until it bruised. Tears streamed unheeded down her cheeks. *Henry…Henry, come back! I hate you…hate you…*

She stumbled down the dirt road that led toward the African huts, running, sometimes staggering and stumbling, until she neared the trees. Here, she paused a moment to catch her breath.

A shrill bird's cry startled her. It was followed by a humming sound, loud, then louder still. Katie looked toward the trees. Jendaya had the four-horse carriage waiting in the myrtle trees and was drawing her attention, Zulu fashion, by the humming sound that made Katie shiver.

Jendaya held the reins with one sturdy hand and reached across the seat with the other to pull Katie aboard as she came hurrying up. She clamored onto the seat, gasping for breath.

"Hurry, Jendaya!"

The Zulu woman slapped the reins and the horses bounded forward onto the dirt road.

Katie clutched the sides of the seat as they weaved and bounced ahead. The horses galloped past the African huts. Katie feared the carriage might topple over on its side, but Jendaya handled the horses skillfully.

The warm wind swept Katie's face and sent strands of her tawny hair whipping. Soon, Cape House was left behind in the raw, dusty night.

Any hopes that Henry might be waiting for her along the road, or at the beginning of the township, proved vain. He, too, must be racing through the night astride his horse, the Black Diamond safely stashed in his jacket pocket. He must be throwing back his head and laughing with abandon at her folly for trusting him. She had delivered three pouches of cut diamonds, as well as the prized Kimberly Black Diamond, right into his hands, and he had simply ridden off.

Jendaya drove the carriage from the township and was on the road toward British-controlled Natal as the moon approached the hills that appeared like crouching lions on the horizon. They would reach the mission station near Rorke's Drift bordering Zululand by early morning.

Katie moaned. Her head throbbed, and desolation filled her mind.

Jendaya lifted a long, sleek dark arm with tight, beaded bracelets and made a sweeping motion inland toward the hills. "When the sun rises we will be near the Rock of the Crouching Lion. We will see the daktari and the mission station."

Above, the sky mellowed and cleared as the night wore on, revealing numberless brilliant stars. Thorn trees swept past, horse hooves pounded their drumbeat upon the path, and the South African yellow moon crouched over the hills of Isandlwana. Though exhausted, Katie could not rest. Her heart, sore and distraught, would not let her.

There was little hope of taking Evy away and escaping to America now, unless by some unforeseen chance the missionary Dr. Varley and his wife agreed to help her. Or unless Cousin Henry changed his mind about his treachery and came to Isandlwana? *Too good to be true,* she scolded her hopes. When Sir Julien returned and learned that his diamonds were missing, he would certainly search for Katie. If she failed to escape, how could she ever explain—or convince him that Henry had taken everything and fled?

No, she had no choice but to go on. If only she knew where she was going on to.

CHAPTER THREE

Henry Chantry groaned as he crawled from a layer of hay. He sat up slowly and peered around in the darkness. The stables, that's where he was.

He pushed himself to his feet and staggered a little, then caught his balance on a wooden post. How did he get here like this? He squinted, looking for his horse, for Katie.

Both were gone.

He touched the lump at the back of his head and his eyes narrowed with sudden, burning anger. The last thing he could remember was unhitching his horse, hearing a soft footstep—

So that was it! That treacherous, conniving female had struck him in the dark, then escaped on *his* horse!

Henry groaned as he felt inside his jacket pocket for the Black Diamond. His mouth turned. Gone… Of course it would be. What a fool to have trusted her pretty face.

"The Black Diamond—that rare Black Diamond." His hoarse whisper caught in his dry throat.

When his foot touched something among the scattered straw, he stooped down, wincing as the blood surged to his skull. He snatched up a heavy wooden mallet, glaring at it in the dimness. She might have cracked his skull open! He flung it aside, then started at an outside sound. He looked toward the stable doors. Someone was coming with a lantern—

He felt his trouser pockets for the three pouches of whites, amazed

they were still there. The snit must have been in a hurry. He took out
the pouches and stooped toward a corner, covering them over with hay.
He straightened up as Julien Bley's voice split the night.

"I suspected you would return to do your thieving business. You
thought you could get by with it, did you? Then you're a bigger fool
than I thought, Henry!"

Someone else was with him. Anthony Brewster held a sjambok, a
flexible, rounded whip a little over three feet long, usually made of rhino
hide, and first used by the Dutch settlers to drive their oxen.

*Was this why Katie involved me? She needed a handy culprit while she
escaped?* She was far more devious than he had thought.

"Where is the Black Diamond?"

Henry met Julien's angry glare. "I don't have it." He turned to
Anthony. "When did you arrive?"

"That's none of your concern!" Julien snapped the words out. "Take
that jacket off, then empty your pockets. Anthony, search him, and
check for his pistol."

"Don't be a fool, Julien." Henry leaned against the wall, crossing his
arms. "Someone clobbered me from behind. While we talk and delay,
the real thief is getting away."

Anthony, a broad-shouldered young man with a strong jaw and
platinum hair, came toward Henry, frowning. Henry made no resistance
as Anthony searched him. He knew there was naught to find but his pistol, which Anthony threw across the stable into the hay. Henry watched
Anthony, who seemed to have other concerns on his mind.

"Where is Katie?"

Henry met Anthony's clear suspicion. "Why ask me? You spent
enough time with her this past winter."

At least the knave had the grace to redden. "I've not seen Katie
for—for months. I've been at Lady Brewster's in Pietermaritzburg with
my fiancée until this evening. Julien had just discovered the theft of the
Black Diamond when Camilla and I arrived." He turned his troubled
gaze to Julien. "Isn't that so, Uncle?"

"Never mind that now, my boy. Search him again. He must have it. Inga says she saw him prowling about the library earlier."

"And knocked myself on the back of the head with that mallet too, I suppose?" Henry didn't even try to conceal his disdain. "Don't be ridiculous, Julien. I don't have the Black Diamond and don't know where it is. And don't forget, I'm an heir of Sir Ebenezer too. I'm just as concerned over its loss as you."

"You'll not convince me of that. And if this were not a family matter I'd contact the authorities at once."

"Would you? I wonder. You and I both know about the diamond smuggling going on recently."

"So what are you getting at?"

"I think you know a little too much about it."

The speculative gleam came cold and hard. "It's your word against mine. But I don't need the authorities to make you talk." Anger burned in Julien's eyes. "Hand me that whip, Anthony."

Henry straightened. "Try that approach, and I will live to kill you, Julien."

"Careful, Uncle Julien," Anthony said. "We must keep these squabbles to ourselves. We'll get to the truth." He turned to Henry. "You still have not told me where Katie is."

Henry smirked. "Dear little Katie has run away with the prize."

"The Black Diamond—? That's nonsense," Anthony snorted.

"Is it? She's determined to get her baby back—*your* baby, Anthony, and she needs the Black Diamond to do it."

A muscle twitched near the corner of Anthony's mouth. His cool gaze shifted away from Henry to Julien.

A footfall sounded behind them. They turned toward the stable entrance, where Henry saw a young woman standing. Her blond hair was elegantly attired and glittering, and there were large diamonds around her throat and at her ears. The tender gray eyes looked with surprise at Anthony, who still held the sjambok. Then she winced, her hand going to her throat. Her gaze swerved to meet Anthony's.

"Oh—"

Anthony looked evenly at Henry, and he got the message: *Say anything, and you will live to regret it.*

Henry smirked. A mere slip of his tongue and Anthony's prospects for marriage to Lord Montieth's daughter would be dust. He smiled and relaxed for the first time. "Maybe we need not be so quick about all this, Julien." He saw from Julien's start that he clearly understood the veiled threat: *Persist, and I just may open Pandora's box.* Lord Montieth was in the British Parliament under Queen Victoria, who, like Julien, wished to bring South Africa into the British Empire. He would certainly abhor any hint of scandal.

Julien's mouth tightened. "Anthony, take Camilla to the house." His words were as stiff as his carriage.

Camilla's questioning gaze swerved to Anthony. He went to take her arm, patting her hand. "There is nothing to be concerned about, my dear Camilla. Uncle Henry has had a minor accident, but he wasn't seriously hurt. His horse threw him and ran off. I'm sure one of the stable boys will find it roaming round the estate by morning."

Henry felt the woman's gaze. A hint of curiosity showed in her face.

"A golden gelding?"

"As a matter of fact, yes. You've seen it?"

She cast a glance toward Anthony. "I might have been mistaken about the color," she said in an apologetic tone. "I thought I saw a golden horse trotting loose when I walked up from the house just now. It seemed a little nervous." She twisted her lacy handkerchief. "It may still be there."

"I'll have a look—" Henry started for the doors.

"No need," Julien cut in. "Anthony can do it. Where did you see it, Miss Camilla?"

"By the outer rim of the corral, near the trees."

Henry looked at Anthony, then at the boy's wife-to-be. Was it his imagination, or did Camilla look strangely uneasy?

The woman's mood could be caused by her recent arrival in untamed South Africa. She did not look the sort to adjust well. Although pretty, she was thin and pale.

Then a thought stopped him. If his horse was wandering about, then Katie had not taken it. Had she walked all the way to the carriage waiting near the African huts? Had she intended to run his horse off to keep him from following after her?

"Go back to the house and wait for me, Camilla dear," Anthony was saying. "I will join you there in a few minutes."

Henry looked after them as they left the stables. Their footsteps faded into the windy night.

"What did you do with the Black Diamond?" Julien snapped.

"Don't be a fool. The longer you hold me here, the easier it will be for her to escape. She's already an hour or more ahead of me."

"You are still intent on blaming Katie for this theft?"

"Who else could have done it? You won't find her asleep in her room. Doesn't that tell you something? She told me she was determined to leave."

A moment later Anthony returned to the stable leading the nervous gelding by the reins.

"A bit shy, but otherwise unhurt."

Henry took the reins and led his horse to a stall.

"Then Katie might have been thrown," Sir Julien said. "We'd better get some of the Bantu together and search the area."

Anthony shook his head. "I looked in the trees around the corral."

"You won't find her." Henry looked from one to the other. "She sent a message to my hotel asking me to come here tonight. She had some kind of plan and mentioned taking a carriage. She wanted to escape to America."

"If you are lying—"

Henry cut Anthony off. "Why should I?"

"I can think of a few reasons."

Henry met the younger man's glare. "She had a most compelling reason to run away, thanks to *you*, my lad."

"Enough!" Julien fixed them both with an angry stare. "Henry, where is this message you say she sent you?"

"Naturally, I wouldn't keep it on me. I left it at my hotel."

"Naturally!" Anthony derided.

Henry ignored him, focusing on Julien. "When I arrived from my hotel, she said she was going to get the Black Diamond. She offered to sponsor my expedition to locate my father's gold mine if I would help her find her child and get ship passage. But when I was getting my horse ready, she struck me from behind with that mallet."

"You expect me to believe that?" Julien strode toward him and snatched the mallet up from the barn floor. "If she needed your help so much, then why would she strike you unconscious?" His black eye patch stared back at Henry like a bottomless pit.

Henry frowned. *Why indeed?* "I'm beginning to think the only reason she sent for me was so that I would be left here unconscious…to later waste time answering questions while she escaped in the carriage to the mission station with that Zulu woman."

"You let her leave for the mission station? At a time such as this, without even warning her? Have you gone mad?"

Henry had almost had his fill of this foolishness. "Warning her of what?"

"The Zulus, you fool!" Julien hissed the words. "If you had kept abreast of what London and Governor Frere have been up to these past months instead of chasing after bogus gold deposits, you might have stopped her."

Henry felt his muscles tense. "You'd better explain."

"The Zulus have been given a thirty day ultimatum to comply with British demands to leave the area or face Lord Chelmsford's troops in Zululand. Chelmsford rode toward Isandlwana a week ago."

"The general can expect to meet up with some twenty thousand Impi Zulus!"

Anthony's words struck Henry hard. "I had no idea!" He turned to Sir Julien. "The mission station is located near Rorke's Drift."

"If Cetshwayo's warriors are on the move, no one will be safe anywhere near Zulu territory, and Rorke's Landing sits on the Zulu borders." Julien's tone was dark.

"Uncle Julien"—Anthony looked pale—"we have got to find Katie tonight."

"Send for the Bantu servants, Anthony. I want every available man on the estate armed and on horseback."

"Yes, Uncle Julien."

"Send for Dumaka. He may be useful as a guide."

There wasn't a Zulu alive that Henry trusted, whether they claimed to be Christian or not. So far as he knew, Jendaya could be planning a trick, delivering a white woman as a hostage for the Zulu chieftain.

Julien started for the door. "I'd better send a rider to tell Sir Bartle at Government House. He may be able to send someone to Rorke's Drift."

"There's no reason for all of us to be idle while you gather up an armed force," Henry insisted. "I am well acquainted with the region. I'll ride ahead to Rorke's Drift—and I'll need to be adequately armed."

Julien's one eye glittered. For a moment Henry believed he would not permit him to leave.

"Stop by the house as you ride out." Julien gave a stiff nod. "Take a Martini-Henry rifle and whatever ammunition you need." He turned and stalked out of the stables.

Henry looked after him a moment, a little surprised by his cooperation. Julien must have serious concern for his ward after all.

Henry located his pistol, then retrieved the three pouches of diamonds and hid them deep inside his saddlebag. He mounted his horse and rode to the house for the rifle.

A short time later he was riding toward the Buffalo River at Rorke's Drift on the border between British-controlled Natal and the stony hills of Zululand. There, if he was successful in his quest, he would find not only Katie but also the Black Diamond.

Chapter Four

And he kneeled down, and cried with a loud
voice, Lord, lay not this sin to their charge.
Acts 7:60

*Rorke's Drift, Twelve Miles South of Isandlwana
House of Mercy Medical Mission*

The whitewashed walls of the House of Mercy mission station burned
in the dawn sunlight with the brilliance of bleached bone. The dwelling,
surrounded by wide, shaded verandas roofed with thatch, stood a little
apart from the church and its attendant buildings below the distant
rocky hills that marked the boundary of Zululand.

Dr. Clyde Varley was an early riser. He was fully aware that the
troops under Lord Chelmsford, some seven thousand strong, had already
ridden from Rorke's Drift and were well into Zulu territory. By now
Chelmsford would have divided his men into three groups, the smallest
camped at Isandlwana while the other two were out looking for the great
army of the Zulu chieftain, known to be up to thirty thousand strong.

Dr. Varley was worried. He was not pleased with this British mission into Zululand. The chieftain had ordered all missionaries out of his
land, and the House of Mercy at Rorke's Drift was on the very border
between Zululand and Natal. Varley did not think much of the British
general, for it was clear Chelmsford did not appreciate the strength of

the Zulu warriors. He trusted in his weapons and his experience in battle with other lesser tribes.

But the Zulus were fierce warriors. They had no friends among the other African tribes—too many of them had felt the deadly blade of the assegai, the broad, short, stabbing sword of the Zulu.

Dr. Varley was frowning to himself when a young man he liked, Captain Durbin, came walking toward him at the mission gate.

"Good morning, Doctor," the smiling young captain called.

"Good morning, Captain."

Captain Durbin walked beside a squarely built bear of a man, Hans Kruger, a Boer commander from the Dutch-controlled Transvaal. The Boer was wearing the customary Dutch leather jerkins and hat, in contrast to the British redcoated uniforms.

"Good mornin', Parson," the Boer called.

"You're leaving Rorke's Drift?" Dr. Varley knew they were; he had seen them readying the transport line during the night.

Captain Durbin nodded. "I received word last night from General Chelmsford. I and my men are to bolster the forces at Isandlwana. We wanted to alert you before we left. We know from scouts that the Zulus number about twenty thousand. We don't expect that great a thrust, but it might be wise to send Mrs. Varley and the baby into Natal with the other civilians under your charge."

"You think Cetshwayo will attack this far from Isandlwana?" Dr. Varley couldn't imagine it. Usually seven thousand troops were quite enough—especially when facing fighters with spears.

"I doubt if any of them will get past our troops, but with the woman here I felt I should mention the possibility."

The Boer made a throaty sound of disagreement and fingered his sjambok. "Yah, we have had battles with the Zulu afore now, Captain Durbin." He shook his golden head. "The Zulu must not be underestimated. They are fierce warriors. Cetshwayo's elite Impis are wanting a battle. They cannot marry until they initiate their assegais in enemy blood. Cetshwayo has kept them from war since he took over after his father, but they're wanting it, I can tell you so."

"Maybe. But you Boers tend to exaggerate when it comes to the Zulus." Captain Durbin's smile was indulgent. "If they do attack Chelmsford at Isandlwana, the general will defeat them without difficulty. What are spears against rifles and cannon? I fear it will all be over before I get there."

"You underestimate," the Boer said again. "Your general does not take wise precautions. Trenches should be built at Isandlwana, rocks gathered for defense lines, the wagons drawn in to form a wagon laager." He shook his big head again. "You do not worry enough, Captain."

Captain Durbin's impatient shrug was quick and abrupt. "We cannot waste the time, Hans. After this there will be no more skirmishes with Cetshwayo. He will go scurrying back to his kraal at Ulundi. At any rate, Dr. Varley, I'm under orders to leave soldiers here to man the guns and guard Rorke's Drift. But you might consider sending Mrs. Varley to Natal."

"Yes, Captain. The Scriptures say, "'With good advice make war.' And God be with you."

The three men shook hands, then Dr. Varley watched the soldiers mount their horses and ride toward the column. He continued to watch them until they had been ferried across Buffalo River into Zululand, then he sighed. *Dear Father in heaven, I am worried. War...and death! Souls will be entering eternity totally unprepared for Your holy presence. So few know the beloved Savior.*

Junia Varley cradled baby Evy in her arms and tried to hush her crying. *Father God, how You have blessed me! I feel like Sarah holding Isaac. With Sarah I can say, "Who would have said...that Sarah should have given children suck!" Yet you have given me this precious daughter to raise to know You.*

Perhaps, when Evy grew a little older, Junia would ask Clyde to let her go home to Grimston Way in England for a visit with her sister, Grace, who was married to Vicar Edmund Havering.

Junia secretly dreamed of the quiet rose gardens and village streets of England with its cool misty fog. The stony hills of Zululand, the thorn trees, and the wildlife were all a part of God's wonderful creation, but the heat, dust, and dangers from the different African tribes were a worrisome burden to live with, especially now with a baby.

She heard the sound of horses and carried Evy to the door in time to see the soldiers being ferried across the river to the hinterland. Thank God some soldiers were still left at Rorke's Drift. She walked out into the early morning to join her husband, who turned and smiled down at her and the baby, putting his arm around Junia's shoulders.

"There may be trouble ahead, Junia. The Boer might be right after all. Perhaps I should send you and the baby to Pietermaritzburg until this war with the Zulus is settled."

"They would never cross the river to the mission station, would they?" She did her best to sound calm and confident.

"I do not think so, my dear, but we'll take no chances. I'll arrange a wagon and ox today."

"I'm certain tomorrow will be soon enough, Clyde. Look, someone is coming in a carriage. Why, it's Jendaya…and an English woman. I wonder who that could be?"

"I don't know, but this is the wrong time for visitors to see the mission."

"Maybe they've come to warn us?"

Clyde shook his head. "Seems they would have sent a few men with rifles for that. Let's go greet them."

"She's a lovely young girl. Do you suppose she's one of the soldiers' wives?"

"If she is, I shall need to give her worrisome news. Captain Durbin's troops have ridden to Isandlwana to reinforce the base camp there."

They waited until the carriage drew to a halt, then Clyde lifted a hand in greeting. "Hello, Jendaya, you've brought us a guest?"

Jendaya did not get down immediately, but the young English woman did, as though she were exhausted from the ride. Junia watched her, taking in the dazed expression as the woman stood staring, first at the baby, then at Junia. She smiled again and patted the baby. After a moment of silence, Junia walked toward the woman.

"Welcome to Mercy House. I'm Junia Varley, and this is my husband Dr. Clyde Varley. We're the missionaries here, but I'm sure you've been told that already. Won't you come in and refresh yourself? I shall make tea. And you must be famished too."

The woman walked toward her with slow steps. She swayed a little on her feet, and Junia was relieved when Clyde stepped forward, taking hold of her. "My dear woman, are you ill?"

When she said nothing, he looked up at Jendaya for explanation.

"Bring her into the hut, Clyde," Junia said hurriedly. "She may have sunstroke. Jendaya can explain everything once we get the girl settled."

Odd, Junia thought, leading the way to the mission hut, *how she keeps staring at Evy.*

After they had gotten the young woman indoors on a cot, Junia sent Jendaya to start the water boiling on the outside earthen oven to make tea. Junia went for a jug of water so she could wash the woman's face and hands and feet. She looked so exhausted and frightened and she still had said nothing.

When Junia came back into the hut she stopped. The woman had gotten up from the cot and was kneeling beside Evy's little crib, rocking it gently and humming Brahms's "Lullaby."

Junia felt awash with pity. Was the woman—mentally ill? Had the heat gotten to her that badly on the trip from Natal? Maybe Clyde had learned what this visit was about from Jendaya. She glanced toward the carriage. What was taking Clyde so long? Junia saw Clyde talking with Jendaya some distance from the hut, near where the baking oven was located. She could see Jendaya stooping down while watching the water and talking to him. Clyde was standing, tall and lean and very British looking, a safari hat on his head, his arms folded, paying close attention to the woman. Junia knew her husband well enough after all these years to realize when something troubled him. He was not pleased with whatever Jendaya was telling him.

She turned back to the young woman and smiled at her, wondering what her name was. She must be a soldier's wife in fear for her husband who had decided to chance everything to come here. Some wives were like that when they knew their husbands were being sent into the hinterland during conflicts with the tribes, especially the Zulus. Yet she had not asked about her husband. Perhaps she had seen that most of the soldiers had already left Rorke's Drift and crossed the river. Junia went to kneel down beside the woman and the baby.

"Her name is Evy," Junia said gently, quietly, because the baby was asleep now. "Isn't she a precious one? She's only two months old. She's adopted—or soon will be. We must go to Capetown for that. Then she'll be our very own Evy Varley."

The woman had ceased her singing, but she was still rocking the cradle, staring down at the sleeping infant.

Junia tried again: "What is your name?"

The woman's hand stilled on the cradle. "Katie. Katie van Buren." She looked across the cradle at Junia, and Junia saw a look of tragedy in her eyes that brought a silence between them. The girl seemed to be watching her expectantly, as though she thought Junia would know who she was.

Junia smiled. "Van Buren? That is Dutch. Then you must be a Boer? Did you come from the Transvaal or the Orange Free State?" Although the Transvaal and Natal were no longer under Boer rule, the Transvaal had recently been annexed days after the new British governor and high commissioner, Sir Bartle Frere, had arrived from Bombay, India.

"Do you have family in the Transvaal?" Junia tried to restrain her curiosity.

At this Katie seemed frightened. "I… I don't know anymore." Katie's hand went to her forehead and she rested it there, closing her eyes. "I don't know about anything anymore. I'm so weary, everything is so hopeless…" Despair pinched her voice.

Junia frowned. Katie was indeed ill. "Come, my dear, you must rest for now. We can talk later, after you've eaten something and finished your tea. And a good sleep will do wonders to put worries into perspective."

"May I hold the baby while I rest?"

Junia saw the wistful look on the woman's soiled, sweat-stained face.

"Evy is fast asleep, but yes." Junia could feel the young woman's need to touch something fresh and beautiful. "You lie down, I'll wash you with cool water, and then I'll bring Evy to your arms."

Katie smiled, her lips quavering, and a tear ran down her cheek leaving a line through the dust. "Thank you." She spoke so meekly, so quietly that Junia could hardly hear her.

Worry nudged Junia as she removed the woman's shoes and socks and loosened her bodice. She washed her face and arms, then her feet.

"You're very kind," Katie murmured, watching her.

"It is the least I can do, Katie. A little tea, some food, and when you wish to talk I can listen to your worries. You are welcome at the House of Mercy."

"And you'll let me hold…hold the baby."

"Yes, you can hold Evy." Had Katie lost her own child? Was that the reason for her behavior? Junia felt growing sympathy for her.

Lord, please help this sad young woman. Meet her need, and heal the ache within her. And if I can help in any way, Lord, please show me.

Junia stood looking down at Katie van Buren holding the sleeping baby in her arms. The woman was smiling, her eyes closed. Junia started when Katie spoke in those quiet tones.

"Thank you, Junia. They were right. You are a worthy woman."

Junia frowned. What on earth? She shook her head, then left the hut and stepped outdoors. The afternoon sun was golden; a few fleecy clouds chased each other across the sky toward the distant hills. Jendaya had disappeared, and Clyde was standing alone some distance away by the river, hands in his pockets, staring off.

Something was wrong. She could sense it.

She came up quietly and tucked her arm through his. "So what is this mystery? You look worried, Husband."

He sighed deeply, then looked down at her, a frown between his brows. His deep-set eyes were kind and sympathetic.

"Junia, my dear, you mean Katie has not told you yet?"

"Told me what?" Tension rose within her as she searched his sober face.

"Then she has not." He rubbed his chin, watching her, his love—and his unhappiness—clear in his eyes. "I must say I am surprised by her actions and her silence. Jendaya says that Katie was very upset until she arrived here and saw you holding the baby. Then something came over her, and her emotions seemed to recede into a surprising calm."

"I don't understand." She searched his face for answers, growing more tense as she read his concern. "What's this all about?"

Clyde patted her hand between his, then clasped it tightly. "Katie van Buren is Sir Julien Bley's ward. She is Evy's mother. She's come to take Evy with her to America."

A sword might just as well have pierced her heart. Junia sucked in her breath and gripped his hand tightly, as though she would sink to the ground. He watched her, a worried crease between his brows.

"I see." She looked back toward the hut. "Yes, I see now. That explains her behavior." Her heart thumped, causing an ache in her chest. *Take Evy to America?*

"I do not see how we can turn her away. If she asks us for our help, we must try."

Junia's throat constricted. *Am I so soon to lose this brief time of fulfillment?* Her first cry to God was one of bitter disappointment. *Why? Oh, Father, why? It is unfair!*

"Junia?" he said in a ragged whisper, reaching a tender finger to brush against her cheek. "If she wants her baby…"

She tore her gaze from the hut and looked at her husband. His sympathy was so real, so visible, that his love for her warmed her heart and comforted her.

"Our faith is being tried." After an awkward moment he shook his head. "We can only trust His wisdom, His mercy in bringing Katie here to us. There must be a reason. If God gave us Evy for only a little while, then…though it hurts to release her—"

She had no answers, only questions that throbbed like festering wounds in her soul. Although she struggled for composure, all too soon the inevitable tears flooded her eyes. "Oh, *Clyde!*" She stepped toward him, and his arms wrapped about her and he buried his face against her hair.

"Darling Junia!"

She wept, trying to keep the sounds as quiet as possible, letting her sorrow flow, until her throat hurt. As all her happy dreams of having her own daughter ebbed away, she finally thought there were no more tears to flow. She looked up at her dear husband. "The LORD gave, and the LORD hath taken away; blessed be the name of the LORD."

"Now I know why God gave you to me, Junia." Clyde's voice was hoarse, and his eyes now filled with tears. "There are few as brave and trusting as you. Few with such a lovely spirit of submission to the Lord." He reached over and brushed the windblown dark hair from her face.

She tried to smile. "I love you for saying that, but I feel neither brave nor trusting." She only knew that she must choose to act upon what she knew of God's character. His good plans for them. Comforting words from Isaiah, chapter forty-three, breezed softly across her soul: "When thou passest through the waters, I will be with thee; and through the rivers, they shall not overflow thee: when thou walkest through the fire, thou shalt not be burned; neither shall the flame kindle upon thee. For I am the LORD thy God."

Her sigh seemed to come from the depths of her soul. "I suppose there are reasons… I *know* there are reasons, though I cannot understand them."

"The wounds are too raw, Junia, do not try to ignore the hurt. Wait. Time will prove our Savior can be trusted with pain. Perhaps there are reasons why God has brought us all here now. He knows the future, while we stumble along trying to understand."

She was quiet, just holding him. The wind came up and blew dust and brush along the rocky slope by the river. Though words failed them, their quiet embrace spoke volumes.

"Do you want me to talk to Katie?" he asked after a long while.

"Not yet, Clyde. She is asleep. But perhaps this afternoon, or even tomorrow morning. I wonder if Sir Julien will come here?"

"I'm sure he will. We need to pray about all this before he arrives. We need God's intervention."

Junia looked again toward the hut. Oh yes, they needed that. And His mercy. For without that, Junia feared she would not be able to endure what was coming.

Katie opened her eyes. Her mind and heart churned, and she looked around her. It must be early afternoon. Evy was still asleep in her arms. She held her little girl, running her palm along the baby's back. From outside she heard voices. Someone, most likely Dr. Varley, was reading from the Bible. She could hear his calm, kind voice carried on the wind.

"'The voice said, Cry. And he said, What shall I cry? All flesh is grass, and all the goodliness thereof is as the flower of the field:

'The grass withereth, the flower fadeth: because the spirit of the LORD bloweth upon it: surely the people is grass.

'The grass withereth, the flower fadeth: but the word of our God shall stand for ever.'

"This is a reading from Isaiah forty, verses six through eight."

Katie closed her eyes and felt her tears run down her cheeks and onto a pillow.

There followed a hymn. Katie had never heard it before; it was unlike any she remembered singing as a little girl. Whether because of the words Dr. Varley had read from Scripture, or because of the sweet voices of the missionary doctor and his wife as they sang, Katie felt a strange yearning and tugging at her heart. And for the first time in years, she found her soul crying out.

Help me, God! Help my baby, help these good people—help me do what's right. What do You want of me, Jesus?

The missionaries' voices filled the warm air and drifted in to Katie on the cot, the hymn like balm on chafing wounds.

"Savior, like a shepherd lead us, much we need Thy tender care; in Thy pleasant pastures feed us, for our use Thy folds prepare; we are Thine, do Thou befriend us, be the Guardian of our way; keep Thy flock, from sin defend us, seek us when we go astray."

From somewhere closer at hand another voice joined in, hesitant at first...a deeper voice struggling with the English language, yet resolutely humming the music. It was Jendaya, singing from where she sat on the hut floor: "Thou has promised to receive us, poor and sinful though we be; Thou hast mercy to relieve us, grace to cleanse, and power to free; early let us seek Thy favor; early let us do Thy will; blessed Lord and only Savior, with Thy love our bosoms fill;

"Blessed Jesus, blessed Jesus, Thou hast bought us, Thine we are; blessed Jesus, blessed Jesus, Thou hast loved us, love us still."

The baby stirred.

Katie looked at the sweet, innocent face. *Yes, early let us seek Thy favor; early let us do Thy will.*

She touched the perfectly formed little head, the intricately shaped ear. "May you grow up to do God's will, sweeting," she murmured, "may you learn early to do what is good and pure—"

She stopped abruptly, raising her head from the pillow to look at Jendaya. The Zulu woman had sprung to her strong legs like a lion and stood frozen, looking toward the hut door. She had heard something that brought her terror. Something in the far distance. Something far different than the music of the hymn.

This music did not bring peace.

Katie sat up, fear gnawing at her. She heard it now too. Humming. Humming from thousands of voices, like some great beehive on the move.

Katie struggled to get up, holding Evy to her breast. "Jendaya—? What—?"

"Night of the full moon. I forgot the full moon!"

"What?" Katie's teeth chattered.

Evy began to whimper as though hungry, and Katie tried to quiet her. "What do you mean, Jendaya?"

"Hide!"

"What?"

"Hide! *Hide!*"

"Jendaya!" From outside the distant hum grew still louder, and it seemed the ground shook from the pounding feet of a great and terrible army beating across the plain. Then there came a blood-chilling rattle, a sound Katie knew well. The Zulu Impi—the twenty-thousand strong army of bachelor warriors—were taking their short, wide-bladed spears and beating them against their shields.

Preparing for an attack.

The sounds grew deafening: the humming, the jogging feet, the rattle of blades—

"Oh, God in heaven!" Katie wailed. She ran to the hut door and stumbled out to where Dr. and Mrs. Varley stood shading their eyes with their hands, looking across the South African plain.

Katie looked too, and the sight nauseated her. A sea of black came rolling across the plain toward Rorke's Drift. The great Zulu Impi were trotting forward—thousands upon thousands of black and white cowhide shields. The warriors would charge forward like the buffalo to encircle their victims. They came with their assegais flashing in the sunlight, blinding her. The slow trot was more frightening than if they had been racing. They rattled their blades, humming steadily, coming in a human tidal wave.

The British soldiers were manning their guns, others were on horseback.

Katie screamed, and Junia came running toward her, her features pale but her expression unafraid. "The baby, Jendaya," she ordered quickly, "perhaps you can save her. If God makes a way, bring her to Pietermaritzburg to Lady Brewster. Tell her to send Evy to my sister and her husband in England. Understand? Vicar Edmund Havering! Go now! Take her!" Katie let the woman take Evy from her arms and hand her over to Jendaya.

The Zulu woman hesitated, looking from Junia to Katie, as though trying to think of a way to save them as well.

"If God wills, we will live." Junia pushed Jendaya toward the back of the hut. "Now hide the baby's white skin. Hurry, *hurry.*"

Jendaya took the baby and pushed her down between her breasts, then wrapped herself in the Zulu cloth. She looked at Junia. "Thank you for Jesus, Daktari." With that, she turned and was gone.

Junia threw her arms around Katie, then pulled her down to the hut floor where they knelt. "Pray. Pray to Jesus, our Savior."

Jendaya knew what to do. In the diabolical mayhem, she crawled beneath the black and white cowhide shield of a dead Impi and lay there, hidden, the tiny baby still concealed inside her bosom and covered by her wrap. As death stalked all around her, Jendaya spoke to the God of all gods in the name of His Son Jesus. She spoke for the poor white skins, who had brought knowledge of the Great One to Africa. She asked for safety for the babe and knew that amid the noise its crying was not heard.

The sound of humming stopped. Katie's heart pounded as a terror-filled silence encircled them, and then the clacking of assegais against Zulu shields started up, along with a death drum of pounding feet. Faster, faster came the crashing crescendo. Closer, closer…as many thousands of feet swarmed across Rorke's Drift.

Outdoors, the soldiers fired the guns. The Impi advanced.

Dr. Varley rushed into the hut and knelt beside his wife and Katie, encircling them both with his arms. His surprisingly calm prayer came in a steady voice and filled Katie's ears with amazing words of God's grace, power, and purpose. "God is our refuge and strength, a very present help in trouble. Therefore will not we fear, though the earth be removed, and—"

Katie squeezed her eyes shut and clung to Junia and Dr. Varley. She felt the firm, steady, comforting pressure of their fingers on her cold sweating palms.

"Jesus, forgive my sins," Katie kept repeating. "Forgive me, forgive me. Take care of Evy—"

"Into thy hands I commend my spirit." Junia's whispered prayer was calm, steady. "If you will, please save our baby—"

Katie could no longer hear Junia. The Zulu were all around now. She could smell smoke and hear the fire crackling…hear the dying shouts of the last brave soldiers making a stand outside the hut. The whinny of horses died away. And then…

The Zulus were in the hut.

Tall, chocolate brown Zulu Impi, with bright, fire-hot eyes. Their assegais were no longer silver, but crimson. The young warriors needed a battle before they were allowed to marry. At last, they had their first washing of the spears.

Katie heard Dr. Varley's last shout. Amazingly it was, "Jesus Lord, forgive them—!"

Katie slumped over at the first *whack!*

Strange that she felt such peace, like loving arms embracing her, strange that she was no longer afraid…no longer…

All was quiet in the darkness when Jendaya lifted the shield and crawled away over the bloodied ground toward the river. The mission station was a smoking ruin. Bodies were everywhere. The Impi had performed their ritual of cutting open the bellies of their defeated enemy, and as she crawled toward the riverbank she slipped on human remains. She crawled onward, down the embankment, down toward the Buffalo River, toward clean water. She moved through the water, swimming with floating debris, keeping the baby's head above water.

The stars glimmered in the sky now. Jendaya could see what the daktari had once told her was the Southern Cross. It looked down upon Rorke's Drift, upon Isandlwana, and she thought it looked down at her and the baby with a pure white glow that led the way through the deep, dark night to safety.

The sun rose over the distant hills of Zululand, its dawning rays turning the Rock of the Crouching Lion golden. Henry Chantry sat astride a brown horse looking off toward Rorke's Drift at the smoking ruins. He felt the grim line of his lips, and his fingers tightened on the trigger of his rifle. He was sure no one remained alive. He knew about the Impi rituals. Zulus would make sure everyone was dead before returning inland.

He had not arrived in time to save Katie. If only his gelding had not gone lame... If he had not had to stop at Ladysmith to get another horse...

His heart knew an unexpected pang as he thought of Katie van Buren. There were times in the past when he could have loved her as tenderly as any man could love a woman.

Never again, Katie love. May you rest in peace.

He rode the horse back along the Buffalo River toward Natal, where the stream was wide and low and tumbling over rocks. He saw something near the rocks on the other side of the bank and lifted his rifle.

"I see you, Master Henry. It is Jendaya! I have Miss Katie's child!"

Jendaya stood from behind the rock, holding the baby in front of her so that Henry could see she told the truth.

"I see you as well, Jendaya."

She carried the child close against her while wading across the water, coming toward his horse. She stopped and looked up at him, unsmiling, her great dark eyes shiny pools of sorrow. "They are all dead, Master Chantry. I could not save Miss Katie or Daktari and his wife. Impis surrounded Rorke's Drift, thousands of them."

Henry gave a slight nod. "You did well to save the child."

"I cannot keep child. I go to Ulundi."

Ulundi was the great beehive kraal of King Cetshwayo, where he ruled.

Again, Henry nodded. He accepted her decision, though he didn't fully understand it. To return might mean her death. "Why go there?"

"Because Dumaka will go there. I saw him. He was with the Impi."

Dumaka. Her brother. Then he had run away from Sir Julien's estate. Had he done so knowing of this attack on the British? "You know they may kill you."

"Yes." Her face was firm. "I go to turn him to the bright way."

She came up to the side of the saddle and handed him the infant. Henry took the baby as best he could and held it close to his thigh. The baby was crying, both fists and feet moving. *Your little girl is as spirited as you were, Katie. Let us hope she has the same strong will.*

Jendaya handed him a leather glove connected to a canteen.

"Cow's milk. That is how Daktari's wife feed the baby. I have words from Miss Junia. She says bring the baby to Natal. To Lady Brewster at Pietermaritzburg. Lady Brewster is to send the baby to England. To Vicar Edmund Havering."

Henry's brows lowered…and in that moment he decided. He would do it. He would do it for Katie. He would hire a nanny to make the voyage with him to care for the baby. Lady Brewster could help him locate one. Pietermaritzburg was not too far away. If he started out at once he could be there by noon.

Without a word more, Jendaya walked away, in the direction of Zululand, her head high, her shoulders straight. She was humming— but the sound was not like the humming of the Zulu Impi. Jendaya was humming a hymn that Henry had heard before in the vicarage of Grimston Way, as a boy: "Savior like a shepherd lead us, much we need Thy tender care…"

He frowned again, then looked down at the baby. With a final glance after Jendaya, he studied the track of land ahead of him—the track that led back toward Natal.

Katie was dead. The Black Diamond was missing. He still had no idea who had stolen it from him. Katie? Anthony? Julien himself? Maybe even Dumaka before he had run away to come here to join the Impi? If that was so, the Kimberly Black Diamond would be brought to King Cetshwayo!

Henry turned in the saddle and studied the smoking ruins of the mission station. But if Katie had taken the jewel from him in the stables, it was likely buried beneath all that smoking ruin, ashes, and body parts. His mouth thinned. Not even he would sort through gutted soldiers and women to find a diamond. Let it remain buried at the destroyed mission hut. Perhaps that was a fitting tribute.

He looked down at the baby. "I still have three pouches of whites and the map to the gold deposit in Mashonaland, little one. Maybe someday I'll leave it all to you. In memory of pretty Katie. But for now, you and I are going home to England."

PART TWO

He that troubleth his own house
shall inherit the wind.

PROVERBS 11:29

CHAPTER FIVE

Grimston Way, England
Fall 1890

The earthy blush of the autumn afternoon unexpectedly darkened under a sky heavy with the threat of impending rain. Evy Varley was out gathering lush red and gold leaves for Aunt Grace to use for the fall decorations in the rectory chapel when she realized she had been out too long. It was getting toward five o'clock. She had better find Derwent Brown, the curate's twelve-year-old son, and return to the vicarage before they both got a soaking.

Aunt Grace would be worried about her. Recently her aunt, who had raised her from infancy, seemed more anxious and protective than usual, insisting Evy come straight home from school. She knew Aunt Grace hadn't expected her to enter Grimston Wood today to gather leaves in her pinafore.

With a sigh, Evy started back in the direction of the dirt road. The air she breathed was moist and pungent with the odor of earth, roots, and leaves. Here and there, spicy evergreen scents reminded her of Christmas celebrations in the vicarage.

As she hurried through the woods, lightning suddenly struck above the tall fir trees, and Evy felt a shock of alarm jolt through her. Illuminated in the flash of light was a darkened figure, shrouded amid the trunks. Her skin prickled, for her sensibilities told her whoever it was might have been watching her since she had left the dirt road and entered Grimston Wood.

Thunder rumbled, echoing around Rookswood's gothic towers, with their hideous stone gargoyles. Was this cloaked stranger a visitor who had come to see the squire, Sir Lyle Chantry?

Apprehension tingling through her, Evy stood staring toward the trees. She did not run, as that would only bring her deeper into Grimston Wood. If only she had stayed closer to the road where Derwent was getting wood for the rectory stove! Derwent was the assistant to Evy's Uncle Edmund, the vicar. She had been friends with Derwent for as far back as she could remember, and she wished he would suddenly appear with his bag of wood on his back.

The wind picked up and sang in low, mournful tones through the tops of the fir trees. The first large drops of rain plopped against Evy's bare head, where her tawny hair was braided, pinned, and looped. Her dismay led her to release her pinafore, and the bright leaves she had been gathering fell into a pile at her feet. A mocking wind swept down, threatening to scatter them, seeming to laugh at her fears.

The figure stepped from behind the trees and moved toward her. Her heart leaped. She was sure he meant her harm.

"Don't be afraid, I only want to speak to you."

"Wh-who are you, sir?"

He did not answer, but came closer. She took a step backward, then spun to flee. She heard his footsteps behind, muffled on the thick bed of decaying leaves. She began to run, but a hand reached out and caught her, turning her around to face him. She nearly screamed until she noticed he was looking intently at her face, studying her.

Maybe he didn't mean to harm her after all. "I— I must go now. I'm late. My aunt will be worried."

"Your aunt? Is her name Grace Havering?"

Evy nodded, thinking he was not ugly like the gargoyles guarding the gates of Rookswood estate. He was handsome, with light blue eyes and golden hair. His skin was browned by the sun, and his voice sounded strangely different. Accented, somehow. His clothes spoke of wealth, there was something like a diamond pin in his lapel, and a ring on his tanned hand sparkled with white stones.

"Do you like living with the vicar and his wife?"

She nodded. He looked rather sad, she thought. She felt self-conscious at the way he studied her hair and face…the way he frowned at her scuffed shoes and mended school clothes.

"I must go, sir. It gets dark early in the autumn. I promised Mrs. Croft I'd help with the bread."

"Mrs. Croft?"

"She's the cook and housekeeper. She works at the vicarage."

He nodded, and a little smile lifted his lips. "Do you like helping bake bread?"

"Sometimes—if it's sweet bread. Then I can lick the bowl and spoon."

He laughed, and Evy smiled. There was something strong about him and he seemed to like her, even if he did not appear to like her clothes and shoes.

"I will let you go in a minute, then I will walk you back to the road. Tell me, Evy, do you ever visit Rookswood?"

"Rookswood? Oh no, sir." How did he know her name?

"Would you like to?"

She started. Why would he ask such a question?

"Right now—with you?"

"No, not with me. With the squire's children, Arcilla and Rogan."

Such a thing was impossible! And yet…something about this man convinced Evy he could manage the impossible. She shook her head. "Miss Arcilla does not approve of me, and Squire's two sons, Master Parnell and Master Rogan, think girls are a nuisance. They call me the rectory girl."

His mouth curved again. "I see."

She thought he did. "I'd rather visit there with you," she said impulsively, surprising even herself.

"Would you?" There was a look on his face that she took for sadness. "That might be nice. But you see, I am going away today."

"To London?"

"No, not to London." He looked up toward a riding trail, and Evy looked there too as she heard the beat of hooves.

"I must go."

Disappointment flooded her, though she could not imagine why. "Good-bye… Will I see you again?"

"Good-bye, Evy."

He walked away into the darkened trees as the hoofbeats drew nearer. Soon he had disappeared altogether, and Evy stood looking after him.

In the distance she saw a horse coming closer on the riding trail. Its rider was low in the saddle, and the sound of hooves reverberated among the thick trees. The rider must have noticed her from the corner of his eye as he swept past, for he slowed down a short distance later. The majestic black horse, rippling with muscle, reared up on its hind legs. The rider, seemingly unaffected by such a display, managed the reins and turned the animal around. He rode back to where Evy stood, then calmed the horse by patting its sweating neck and talking to it as though it understood everything he said.

Evy recognized the rider as the squire's younger son, Rogan Chantry. Though she had never spoken with him, she had often seen him riding around the village, his Austrian trainer at his side. She also saw him attending Sunday morning services at the vicarage church with the rest of the squire's family and with a new aunt who had recently come to Rookswood from South Africa.

Rogan looked to be around Derwent's age, but he seemed more mature than the curate's son. Evy thought this was due to Rogan's exposure to a wide range of experiences that Derwent, coming from a poor family, did not have. Rogan had the best tutors. His private tutor at Rookswood came with recommendations fit for royalty. Of course, Rogan had little interaction with the village boys, though he did have friends—the sons and daughters of lords and earls, who came from London to visit him.

Evy stood in the knee-high vines and grasses growing beside the riding trail, eying the splendid horse, remembering how Derwent said Rogan Chantry's first love was racing and jumping.

"Are you all right?"

She swallowed at his low question. "Y-yes."

He wore a dark blue riding jacket and breeches of expensive design. He was quite a handsome boy, with glossy black hair below a cocky cap, and his eyes were a rich chocolate brown with eyelashes as long as a girl's. Those eyes seemed as electric as the coming storm, full of boundless, challenging energy. He was conceited and arrogant too—or so Evy had been warned by Mrs. Croft.

"You might have caused me to crash into those bushes." he stated, his words and tone proving Mrs. Croft right. "I could have been thrown or worse—my horse injured. Never walk on a riding trail, little girl!"

What a lordly young buck! Stung, Evy momentarily ignored the manners so meticulously taught her by her aunt and uncle. "I was not even close to the trail, but *you* were riding too fast!"

He chose to ignore her jibe. "Are you with that silly red-haired boy you play with?" He glanced around, as though searching the wood.

"Derwent is not silly."

"Yes, he is. As silly as a Billy goat nibbling happy weed. You had better leave my woods. There is a thrashing storm overhead about to break."

"You do not own Grimston Wood. So I shall come here as often as I like."

Rogan gave her a rather surprised second glance. "The Chantrys own most everything around here…including the woods."

She should be afraid of him. Certainly she should think twice about challenging him. And yet…all Evy felt at the moment was exhilaration. She might not be a squire's daughter, but she had as much right to be in these woods as anyone of noble birth. "You do *not* own everything. You do not own the rectory, nor my cat, nor me."

"I'm sure I do not want your old cat."

"It is not old."

"I'm sure you are not worth much either."

She jutted her chin out at that. "Oh yes I am. My parents were very important."

He considered that boastful challenge for a moment. "Pray tell, then, who were they?"

"Dr. and Mrs. Clyde Varley from South Africa."

"Were they in diamonds?"

"No…"

A smile touched his mouth. "Then I daresay they were not important."

She stamped her foot. "Yes, they were! They were *martyrs*. Killed in the Zulu War of 1879."

He flicked the riding reins across his palm. "I shall find out about that. I have ways to discover things of importance. Where did they die?"

That stopped her for a moment. "I— I do not know."

"No matter. I'll learn all there is to know about your parents and see if you are only boasting."

"In the meantime I shall walk here anytime I please."

A smile suddenly altered the young man's expression, and Evy stared. So this was why Alice Tisdale, the daughter of the village doctor, tittered about *swooning* over Rogan Chantry.

"Walk here anytime you please, and be ready to meet a bear—a big black one."

"Bears? Here?" She scoffed but couldn't help a glance behind her. The action was not lost on Rogan.

"Why do you think I was riding so fast? It must have weighed five hundred pounds and had big white teeth. If I were you, I'd think twice before I came here alone."

Just then, a voice shouted plaintively from the trees closer to the road: "Miss Evy? Are you there?"

"I'm over here, Derwent."

He came through the trees and stopped when he saw Rogan astride the handsome black horse. Derwent's eyes widened, and he had the awestruck expression of one who had come in contact with royalty. He touched three fingers to his forelock.

"Afternoon, Master Rogan. Fancy meeting you here, sir."

Evy could have cuffed Derwent for fawning over the knave before them.

Derwent ambled toward them, a bag of kindling on his back. He was tall for his age, and looked gaunt in his patched breeches. His crop of russet hair was untidy from the wind, and in the nippy air, his rather long nose, salted with freckles, had taken on a rosy color. He was ogling Rogan's majestic horse and paying scant attention to where he stepped. His thick boot must have caught under a root, for he took a tumble, the bag of wood weighing him down in the moldy damp leaves.

Rogan laughed, and Evy shot him a glare before rushing to lift the bag from her friend. "Are you hurt, Derwent?"

"Ooh…I skinned my palms."

"Poor Derwent." She dragged the wood free, casting a glance at Rogan. The knave was simply sitting atop his beast, watching. Heaven knew it would tax him unduly to come help her!

Evy knelt beside Derwent. "You are always stumbling," she said sadly. "Mrs. Croft says you may need spectacles. Can you stand?"

"His feet are too big is all," Rogan observed with amusement. "Why do you baby him? I do not like girls who bleat like sheep."

Evy shot Rogan another glare. "I do not care *what* manner of girls you like, Master Rogan. If you were a gallant boy, you would have climbed down from your fine horse to help me get that heavy wood off him."

Derwent gaped at her as though she had sassed the king. Rogan, too, seemed at a loss. Then his lips thinned and he tapped his heels into the horse's side. It sprang forward and raced in the direction of the road.

"Ought you to have spoken like that to him, d'ye think, Miss Evy? The Chantrys are important folk in Grimston Way."

"A Chantry or not, he is arrogant and conceited. He's been nourished with exceptional manners, you can count on it, so he ought to use them on everyone, not just the sons and daughters of the aristocracy. I'm as good as any of them!"

At this passionate outburst, Derwent gawked at her. "Sure you are. But, well, Master Rogan's a son of the squire, whereas you and me—"

She jumped to her feet. "He treats us like *servants*. I'm not a servant's child. His father did not know the great missionary David Livingstone like my father did. You know how they were both great doctors. Missionaries," she repeated with emphasis.

Derwent ran his long, restless fingers through his russet hair. "I daresay you may be right, Miss Evy. Dr. Livingstone was a great explorer. I would like to go to Africa and explore the dark regions. I might likely find diamonds too."

"Are you able to walk?" She squinted upward, but the trees were thick, and the dark sky was blotted out. "It's soon to pour."

Derwent took a few steps and tested his ankles. "Good as can be. We best dash for it. Say—what happened to those leaves for Mrs. Havering?"

For some reason, Evy did not tell him about the stranger she had met. "The wind blew them all away."

She hurried through Grimston Wood, and Derwent struggled to keep up, loaded as he was with his bag of kindling.

Evy called over her shoulder: "As for being an explorer…Curate Brown will be unhappy if he thinks you're not going to follow his steps in life."

"Aye."

"You are to be a curate just like he. Sons always follow in their father's steps." She paused to let him rest a moment and catch his breath. "Your future waits here in Grimston Way."

"Aye, and yours, too, I'm thinking."

Evy thought of the gentleman who had spoken to her. Who could he have been? Had he been staying at Rookswood?

More lightning streaked across the darkening sky, prodding them onward.

Thick fir trees hugged the side of the road as they emerged from the woods. She could look up the road and glimpse the big stone gates leading onto Rookswood, so named because of the many black rooks that nested in the nearby wood and made such a fuss in the spring with their cawing.

Rookswood, prominent on the hill overlooking the village of Grimston Way, was even more mysterious and interesting to her now that the stranger had spoken to her and asked her if she wished to visit. Somehow the mere question gave her the exciting sensation of being connected to that huge gray-stone mansion and its forbidden halls. At least, she secretly liked to imagine such things, even though she was not likely ever to be invited there.

Cold splashes of rain from the roiling dark sky splashed on Evy's face, shaking her from her daydreaming. She turned away from the mansion and started down the road toward the rectory.

Derwent switched the heavy load to his other shoulder and followed behind. "Your folks were saints all right, Miss Evy, and important ones too, dying the way they did in Zululand years ago, but most folks in Grimston Way' agree that no one is as important as Squire and his family."

It was rather a blow for her to hear that it was not her martyred parents who filled the good villagers with admiration, but the local squire, Sir Lyle. Well, she knew far better. No matter how she might hold the squire in respect as master of the village, the ofttimes arrogant Chantrys could not compare with Dr. Clyde and Junia Varley.

"I do not believe you, Derwent Brown! Why, my parents' photograph hangs in the rectory hall. Aunt Grace says I look just like my mum." She threw him a glance. "I do not see Squire's photograph there."

"She said that? I don't see it, myself. If you don't mind my saying so, your hair is—er, prettier. Goldenlike. Your mum's is black, like your aunt's."

Evy stopped on the road and turned to face him.

"So? My hair will turn darker when I get older. What are you trying to say, Derwent Brown?"

His eyes widened. "Say? Why, nothing Miss Evy. Nothing at all. Just that I think you're prettier—but I wasn't suggesting—" He stopped, red filling his freckled cheeks.

The rain splashed cold and startling against her face. The gusts of wind whipped at her hooded cape as a nameless fear suddenly whipped at her heart. Evy turned and ran down the road toward the village green.

Fancy his saying she did not look like her mum's photograph. Her father had light hair didn't he? Of course he did. The photograph showed that he did. And she'd wager his eyes were like hers too, amber with flecks of jade green. Derwent could be so exasperating at times.

Perhaps Rogan Chantry was right after all. Derwent *was* silly.

At that, her conscience smote her. She must not be so hard on Derwent. He was a kind boy, and she knew he would never deliberately say anything about her or her parents to make her unhappy.

By the time she started across the green Evy was thoroughly soaked. Aunt Grace was going to be upset with her again. "You are so willful at times, Evy," she said time and again. "You must learn to be more like Junia."

Evy saw the old sexton persevering across the rectory yard toward the cemetery. The village gravedigger was carrying a large piece of canvas.

He must be on his way to cover the trench he was digging earlier this morning. If he could keep the rain out, he would be able to finish tomorrow. Uncle Edmund said the sexton was the most superstitious person in Grimston Way, even more so than Old Lady Armitage, who hung garlic on her kitchen door to keep the vampires away on Allhallows Eve. According to the good sexton, if the rain interfered with digging a grave, it meant the Grim Reaper on his horse had been delayed.

Evy waved at the old man, smiling. "No Grim Reaper is going to overtake me," she sang out and took off running toward the church and the rectory house.

The soggy lawn sank beneath her shoes as Evy dashed through the wicker gate and up the walkway, through Aunt Grace's heavily pruned rose bushes. Little remained of the summer flower garden except a few worn-out daisies. The seedpods that her aunt had out on a drying screen for the next spring's planting were getting a drenching. Evy put them under the porch before entering the front door, remembering to wipe her shoes on the mat.

Inside the rectory hall she removed her shoes, then stood quite still, looking up at the photographs that hung over the landing at the top of the first flight of stairs.

Evy went to stand and look as she had done unnumbered times in the past. There they were, Dr. Clyde Varley and his wife, Junia, servants of God to the savages in Zululand. A handsome couple. He had grave but kind eyes. "They are amber colored with flecks of jade green," she assured herself in a whisper. "The color just does not show up in the photograph."

And there was her beloved mother, Junia, with her bright, sweet smile and her dark hair pulled back in a knot.

Evy pulled her own wet hair back from her face and tried to wind it into a knot, but it was so thick, heavy, and wavy, that it ended up spilling from her grasp. She gave up and let it fall about her shoulders. "I look just like you, Mum. I know I do."

She reached a hand to touch her mother's portrait, closing her eyes, imagining as she so often did that she could feel her mother's loving embrace across time, across the miles. *Mother is a heroine.* After all, they died as Christian martyrs, in much the same way other Christian leaders laid down their lives throughout the centuries. Evy was learning about many of those heroes in her Sunday studies at the rectory. "But I wish I had your heart for God too. Your gentle spirit. Aunt Grace says I have a willful spirit. But where did I get it? Not from you. From father?"

Evy could hear Mrs. Croft's twanging voice singing in the kitchen. She turned from the photographs and ran down the stairs and to the back of the rectory, where the fragrant smells of hot bread wafted to entice her.

Aunt Grace was out calling on the parishioners with Uncle Edmund, and they must have been delayed by the rain. She would ask Mrs. Croft about it. Evy had learned early that if one wanted to know anything about what was going on in the village, the person to ask was the sexton's wife, Mrs. Croft. She had a full basket of relatives, so it seemed, and they all apparently worked in Rookswood as parlor maids, downstairs maids, grooms in the stables, cooks and washers in the kitchen, or gardeners. Whatever gossip was astir, be it upstairs or down, it was sure to drift down the hill from Rookswood to the big rectory kitchen to Mrs. Croft.

Aunt Grace would scold them for gossiping if she happened to walk
in and catch Mrs. Croft talking to one of her kin. Vicar Edmund, too,
would point out the inherent evils of the tongue when unyielded to the
lordship of Christ. Nevertheless, gossip flourished "like dandelions in
the lawn," Uncle Edmund often stated with a resigned sigh. "Proof the
devil walks to and fro seeking someone to devour."

Evy carried her wet shoes and stockings, along with her cloak,
placed them by the glowing hearth, then went straight to the oversized
kitchen. Her gaze traveled the huge stove, long sideboards, and floor-to-
ceiling cupboards stashed with dry foodstuffs, dishes, and great beat-up
pots and blackened kettles.

Mrs. Croft had been employed by the rectory to help with cleaning
and cooking for as long as Evy could remember, and she was as much a
member of Evy's family as her aunt and uncle. In some ways Evy felt
even closer to Mrs. Croft, since she could tell her almost anything that
troubled her, be it unsavory or fair, and Mrs. Croft would speak her
mind plainly. Whereas Evy loved and respected her aunt and uncle and
was on her best behavior around them, she could take off her shoes and
tuck her feet up under her when sitting in the big kitchen chair in the
company of Mrs. Croft.

Mrs. Croft was singing in her off-tune voice when Evy came rushing in, her wet hair loose and wild around her shoulders and back. She
breathed in the heady smells of hot, steaming cinnamon scones.
"Mmm…I'm starving."

"Humph. You keep eating scones before supper, child, and you'll
soon turn into one."

Evy took a mouthful. "Mrs. Croft? Derwent says the Chantrys are
more important than my parents."

"Does he now? Still trying to become friends with the squire's
young son, is he? Dreams of Kimberly diamond mines and gold fields
in the wilds of Africa, that's why. But the good curate won't be letting
him go on any such adventure, you'll see. 'Tis best. Derwent will make
you a good husband, child."

Evy wrinkled her nose. "That cannot be true about my parents. Not if my father knew David Livingstone! The stories about Mr. Livingstone were in all the newspapers. They don't write about Squire."

She chuckled. "You be right there. Leastwise in the society page."

"Then Derwent is wrong."

"Nay, he be right, I am afraid. Folks in Grimston Way don't be caring much about Master Livingstone, but they do be worrying their heads about the doings of Squire."

"But *why?*"

Mrs. Croft's beady eyes twinkled. "Because Squire be the biggest landowner in Grimston Way, that's why. Most folks in the village works for him. That makes Squire Chantry mighty important in the minds of hard working folk. Not *all*-important, mind you. God be all-important and all-powerful. But folks get their wages, you see, from Squire. Them Chantrys own just about everything, including diamond mines in South Africa."

"Then I wonder why the Chantrys come to Sunday service." Evy sniffed her indignation. "Surely they're too important."

Mrs. Croft laughed, clearly tickled, but when Aunt Grace suddenly came through the kitchen door Mrs. Croft coughed to clear her throat. Evy turned for the door.

"Evy, dear"—Aunt Grace Havering's tone was disapproving—"I am ashamed you would say such a flippant thing about anyone."

Evy winced and automatically pulled her shoulders back, hands tucked behind her. She became aware of her disheveled hair, her wet clothes and bare feet. She curled her toes inward and bit her lip.

Aunt Grace took in her condition and sighed. "Darling, you're soaked. And after you were ill all last week. You can be so careless in your behavior sometimes. You worry me."

Evy looked down at her toes. "Sorry, Aunt. The storm sort of crept up on me and Derwent, and before we knew it—it was pouring."

Just then Evy's cat meowed from under the hardbacked chair. She went to it and rubbed the sides of its golden face, then got up and poured it a saucer of milk.

Aunt Grace went to check on the scones, making sure there were enough to send over to Old Lady Armitage. "She has the grippe, poor old dear," she told Mrs. Croft. "Can you add some cold chicken, Mrs. Croft?"

"Surely, Missus Grace. There's plenty. I'll deliver it on the way home."

Evy watched her aunt as the cat drank its milk. Aunt Grace was a great lady. She was ten years younger than her husband, the vicar, and her hair was a shiny blue-black. Evy held fond memories of being rocked to sleep surrounded by the fragrance of the lavender lotion on her aunt's hair. She wore it in a sedate bun at the back of her neck, much as Evy's mother, Junia, wore hers in the photograph. Aunt Grace's eyes were also brown and often appeared to be sad—

"Were you in the woods with Derwent after school, Evy?"

Evy hesitated at her aunt's unexpected question. Should she tell her about the stranger in Grimston Wood? Her aunt was not the sort of person to approve of meeting and exchanging words with strangers, especially a man in the woods. Even if Evy said she had not wanted to speak to the man, she doubted if Aunt Grace would approve.

"Yes, Derwent was gathering wood for the stove, like Mrs. Croft asked. He should have brought it by now." She glanced toward the back porch, where the wood was stashed in a bin out of the weather. "I thought I'd surprise you with autumn leaves for the chapel," Evy went on. "I knew you would be going there tonight to decorate for Sunday worship."

"That was thoughtful, dear. I did want some leaves. You had better get out of those wet clothes right away. You have a propensity for chest colds, as I do."

"Yes, Aunt." Evy left the kitchen, smuggling the half-eaten scone under her pinafore.

The rectory hall was dim at this hour, and Aunt Grace was going about with a candle, lighting the lanterns. She always did this to make things cheery for when Uncle Edmund came home for supper.

Evy paused on the steep stairway and looked back down. She vacillated. Should she mention the exciting stranger and the interesting things he had said to her? Maybe Aunt knew who he was.

Her aunt became aware that she was standing there and looked at her, waiting. She smiled. "Yes, Evy?"

"I was wondering…do many visitors come to Grimston Way to visit Rookswood?"

Aunt Grace tilted her head. "Yes, why do you ask, dear? Did you see anyone arriving today?"

"No, I just wondered. I suppose they might go walking in Grimston Wood if they did, but hardly on a day when it was about to rain."

Aunt Grace was still. Then she came to the bottom stair. Her face above the glowing flame was unsmiling; her brown eyes shimmered like fathomless pools.

"Did you see a stranger in the woods today from Rookswood?"

Evy swallowed. "No—that is, I do not know where he was from. He did know something about Rookswood, though. He asked if I would like to go there and be with Miss Arcilla."

The candle slipped from Grace's hand and crashed to the floor at her feet. It burned brightly for a moment before going out. The wind lashed the front windows with heavy rain, and the leaded panes rattled.

Quickly, Aunt Grace stooped to the spilled wax and tried to scoop it onto the candleholder. "Oh dear, I've made a terrible mess."

Evy knelt beside her to help, but Aunt Grace had already gotten the candle back onto the holder. "I'll need to scrape the rest up later. Evy, who was this stranger, and what else did he tell you?"

Evy stared into her aunt's face. She looked frightened…but why? Her aunt's fear made Evy's own uncertainties leap out of bounds, so that her voice sounded tight and nervous even to her own ears.

"He hardly said anything. Just asked if I—if I was happy. And if I wished to be friends with the squire's children."

"And what did you tell him?"

"I said I was very happy. That Miss Arcilla did not approve of me."

Aunt Grace did not reply—she only looked down at the candle as though she had never seen it before. Suddenly she stood. "I'd better relight this in the kitchen," she said tonelessly and turned away.

"Aunt? I wonder who he was?"

"I do not know." She spoke quietly, her back toward Evy. "Just a stranger, I suppose. I would not give it a second thought if I were you, dear."

Evy watched her until she disappeared into the kitchen. She stood, taking it all in, then turned and went up the stairs to her room.

In the following days the incident seemed to have been forgotten, though Aunt Grace was more thoughtful than usual and kept a most watchful eye on her niece. Evy began to think she may have imagined the meeting in Grimston Wood. Hadn't Aunt Grace always told her when she was small how fanciful she was? Certainly the thunder and lightning and the darkened atmosphere of Grimston Wood could affect her imagination.

Just a few days later Evy had an opportunity to ask her uncle about her parents. It was a Saturday afternoon, and though the sky was clear and the wind chilly, she was happy to be seated beside the vicar in the horse-drawn jingle as he went calling on one of his parishioners for afternoon tea. Evy held the cloth-covered reed basket of pastries that would be given as a gift.

Evy liked Uncle Edmund's quiet, unassuming ways. She liked how his brown eyes were thoughtful, yet merry. He had a shiny scalp fringed with a mane of gray, and he was full at the waist, blaming it on his love of creamed gravies and flaky cobbler crust. He was the only father she had ever known, and she loved him dearly, despite her daydreams of her missionary parents facing down the Zulus.

"Uncle, Mrs. Croft says you went all the way to Capetown, South Africa, to bring me to Grimston Way after my parents were killed. Is that how I got here?"

He flicked the worn leather reins, and the dappled mare quickened her trot along the wooded road. Squirrels scampered up the tree trunks, chattering as they approached.

"You need to be cautious about listening too much to Mrs. Croft.

She's a splendid woman in many ways, and a great cook"—his eyes twinkled—"but she has a carnal propensity to say things best left unspoken."

"You mean about your trip to Capetown?"

"Oh, I would not say that, Evy." He looked down at her as she looped her arm through his. "Actually, I did not voyage to Capetown at all. You see, the mission board in London contacted your aunt and me about Dr. and Mrs. Varley's death. We had no child, so we were delighted to have you come live with us." He bestowed a kindly smile on her.

She beamed. "Then it was the mission board who brought me here to England?"

"Well, no, as a matter of fact, someone else brought you to Grimston Way. He was a friend of…your mother's…of sorts."

Evy looked at him.

"He brought you here to safety, but he is dead now. An unfortunate death at that."

There was something in his tone that she did not understand. "Who was he, Uncle Edmund?"

"I…er, never met him personally. He came from South Africa. I believe he was an explorer searching for gold. But never mind him. Your aunt and I chose you to be our own. You've made our lives very happy, little lamb."

The words warmed Evy inside. "Was I at the mission with my parents when the Zulus attacked?"

"Yes, you were there." Uncle Edmund sounded so sad, Evy was almost sorry she'd asked. "You would have been killed too, but someone rescued you and kept you safe until you were brought on a ship to London."

"I wonder who he was?"

He clucked at the mare. After a moment, he looked down at her. "Sometimes it is best not to ask too many questions, my dear Evy."

That alerted her. "Why, Uncle?"

"Oh, because some things in the past are best left forgotten. Your

life is here in Grimston Way now. This is as God intended. You have
nothing in South Africa. A fine marriage will be made for you here, and
here you will be happy, God willing. My fondest hope is that you and
Derwent will grow up to care for each other. You will make a fine vicar's
wife, Evy. You know everyone in the village, and you know all the ways
of the rectory. It is so sensible, so right." He reached over and put a protective arm around her.

So sensible, so right. But she couldn't quite still the inner question
that echoed within her: Wouldn't marrying Derwent, whom she'd
known forever, also be a bit…boring?

As the days passed, the story of her parents and how she had been
brought to live at the rectory would not relinquish its hold on her imagination—nor did the meeting with the stranger in Grimston Wood.
Both events developed into a rather heroic tale, which she began to
embellish until the players had become heroes and heroines of the high-
est order. As for herself, well, Evy imagined she was somehow most special. She would sit and dream of escaping tribal Zulus brandishing long
spears, of being chased through the trees toward a great lion with a flowing mane. She had come to Africa to do good and had been misunderstood, and was now fleeing for her life. All was hopeless, but as she fled
a stranger would suddenly appear and ask her if she needed refuge in his
mansion. Then the stranger turned into Rogan Chantry, who swept her
up on his sleek horse…just in time.

Neither Aunt Grace nor Uncle Edmund spoke to her of the matter
in the woods, and Evy believed they wanted her to forget that it had ever
occurred. She did not think, however, that they had forgotten. She even
heard that Uncle Edmund had called at Rookswood to see the squire
and ask if he had recently entertained a visitor from South Africa.

Evy frowned. Why would her uncle and aunt think anyone from
that wild, dark continent so far from Grimston Way would be watching
her picking autumn leaves in the woods?

Chapter Six

Mrs. Croft was nearly purring with excitement when Evy went into the kitchen on Sunday morning. Aunt Grace had departed earlier in order to choose the hymns, so Evy breakfasted in the kitchen without her before walking to the church.

This morning Mrs. Croft's niece Lizzie, an upstairs parlor maid at Rookswood, had come to see her aunt earlier than usual. Evy guessed this meant that the latest news from Rookswood was of an especially tangy flavor. Lizzie's cheeks had pinked with the rouge of excitement as she hovered near the big stove, chattering like a magpie, while Mrs. Croft whipped the bowl of eggs more energetically than usual into a foaming yellow froth.

"So I says, it's more'n her poor health that's the cause of her leaving South Africa without Master Anthony," Lizzie said in a hushed tone. "Lady Camilla Brewster's important, you know? So she wouldn't just up and leave her husband in Capetown, now would she? I mean, no matter how many giant spiders there is, an' heat, an' them naked heathen. So what if the weather be hard on her, I say. She put up with it all those years—since 1879, so it's said. Now, suddenlike, them savages makes her nervous so she can't sleep. It's all a bit too much for the poor woman's delicate constitution. So the Lady leaves Sir Julien Bley's big house and comes home to sweet England. Anyhow"—she reached across the stovetop for a cooling slice of bacon—"that's the tale." She bit into the bacon, her eyes shining like polished blue stones.

"Seems a bit long for the poor lady to learn the weather was draining her health," Mrs. Croft said thoughtfully, pouring beaten egg onto the sizzling fry pan. "If she went out to marry Master Anthony in '79, that was—" She stopped and pursed her lips, thinking.

"Twelve years ago." Evy offered this information cheerfully. She left the table where she'd been listening and came up to the stove beside Lizzie. Evy reached for a second helping of crispy bacon. She looked into Mrs. Croft's sharp, hazel eyes. "My age," Evy concluded and lifted her brows as she enjoyed the bacon.

"Ouch!" Mrs. Croft jerked her hand away from the splattering grease in the fry pan.

"Who are you talking about?" Evy looked from one woman to the other.

"The newcomer to Rookswood." Mrs. Croft frowned at the eggs, which were turning a lovely brown around the edges.

"A newcomer?" Evy became more alert. Her mind went back to the stranger in the woods.

"Lady Camilla Brewster. Lord Montieth wanted her to return to the Montieth estate in London, but she decided to live at Rookswood."

Evy had never heard of Lady Camilla. "Is she a relation to the Chantrys?"

Mrs. Croft poured Evy a cup of tea. "Anthony is a nephew to Squire."

"Not a blood nephew, though," Lizzie corrected as though teaching a pupil.

"Some of the Brewsters married some of the Bleys. And some of the Bleys married some of the Chantrys."

Lizzie grinned, satisfied whenever Mrs. Croft proved herself capable of explaining a muddled detail. "See?" She nodded to Evy. "It be simple, when you know it."

"Still seems a bit odd to me why Lady Camilla wants to come here instead of going to her family home in London," Mrs. Croft remarked.

"Seems so to me, too. It's whispered her marriage to Mister Anthony were never a happy one, and it's worse now." Lizzie lowered her voice. "Has something to do with a terrible scandal. Stolen family diamonds and a baby born on the wrong side of the blanket."

"So that's the way of it," Mrs. Croft said.

Evy drank her sweet tea. No wonder Lady Camilla was unhappy, if she was married to a scamp who fathered a wrong-side-of-the-blanket baby.

"Mister Anthony must have stolen the family diamond too." Mrs. Croft nodded, sure she was right. "He sounds like a scamp all right."

"That be the strange part." Lizzie joined Evy at the kitchen table. "Nobody knows what happened to the diamonds."

Evy spoke up. "Well, what happened to the baby?"

Lizzie stared at her. "Oh, it's got to be with the mum, what else? Mister Anthony probably paid the woman off and sent her away. That's what they usually do, I've heard. But it makes you wonder why Lady Camilla came here, don't it?"

"You mean she thinks the baby is in Grimston Way?" Evy stared at the older woman. How could such a thing happen?

"I'll wager we'll be learning something more before Lady Camilla leaves Rookswood," Lizzie said firmly. "Oh, I know the ways of these things. I seen it happen oh so many times when I worked them five years in London. Thought it'd be kinder here at home in Grimston Way, but them Bleys, Brewsters, and Chantrys—"

"'Tis the diamond that makes me curious." Mrs. Croft dried her worn hands on her faded apron. "If I'm remembering how it was years ago, it seems to me there was something sinister about that rogue, Henry Chantry."

"Aye, he came from South Africa, all right," Lizzie said thoughtfully.

"There was gossip about a Black Diamond," Mrs. Croft mused.

"That were before I worked at Rookswood. I was a girl here in the village back then. I remember him, faintly. A handsome man, he was. Young Rogan looks more like his Uncle Henry than he looks like his father, Squire Lyle."

Captivated, Evy looked from one woman to the other. A missing Black Diamond? Now *this* was exciting!

Lizzie stood and stretched. "Nobody talks about them days at Rookswood anymore. But I do see Master Rogan sneaking about Master Henry's old rooms sometimes."

"A real feisty boy, that one," Mrs. Croft warned, and Evy thought she glanced her way. Did Derwent tell Mrs. Croft how she'd met him in Grimston Woods?

Mrs. Croft just went on. "Curious, all of it. Curious and a bit scary, too, because Master Henry Chantry were a young man when he died the way he did."

Evy looked up from her plate quickly. "How did he die?"

Mrs. Croft and Lizzie exchanged glances.

Evy watched them. "Did he have an accident?"

"Nobody knows for sure." Mrs. Croft sounded grave indeed. "Some say suicide."

There was quite a scene when Lady Camilla Brewster and the three handsome Chantry offspring arrived that morning to attend the chapel service where Uncle Edmund, his small spectacles low on his short nose, would be reading his sermon. Evy wondered why neither the squire nor Lady Honoria was with them.

Lady Camilla must have been quite attractive when younger, for even now there was a certain prettiness about her, but it seemed any contentment with life had long ago been washed from her heart-shaped face. She entered, with Miss Arcilla, Rogan, and Parnell trailing behind. Many heads turned in their direction. The boys swaggered down the aisle to take their grand family pew at the front of the chapel, situated beneath a stained glass window of the Good Shepherd. Uncle Edmund once said the window was given to St. Graves by the squire's great-great grandfather, Earl Simon Chantry.

At fifteen, Parnell looked bored with Uncle Edmund's sermon as though he already knew more than the vicar.

Rogan, now thirteen, had managed to smuggle a book under his fancy jacket and sat reading it, his expression sober. Evy had once learned from Derwent, who had seen the book, that it contained maps of unexplored Mashonaland, South Africa, with tales about gold deposits. Evy cast Rogan a furtive glance. She always sat in the pew beside Aunt Grace, and he would know that, having seen her here often enough. She thought that the ice may have thawed between them by now, since two days had passed since their meeting at the horse trail. Yet, though she glanced his way several times, he seemed not to notice her. Was he ignoring her?

Evy saw Alice Tisdale, her strawberry-blond curls dancing about her face, and some of the other girls in the village glancing toward Rogan and Parnell. From the silly look on Alice's face, she might have swooned if either of the boys looked her way and smiled. The girls all dreamed of Cinderella romances.

Evy gave a soft snort. Silly twits. Fairy tales never came true.

She wished heartily that Rogan would cast her a glance just so he could see that she was one girl who was not watching him. She lifted her chin a little higher.

Arcilla fussed with her lace-trimmed frock. At twelve, she already had a propensity toward what Mrs. Croft called a "boy-happy" attitude. Not that any of the boys in the village would ever be suitable for Miss Arcilla Chantry. Like her brothers, Arcilla's marriage would be arranged for her. Most likely the three Chantry children would one day marry those from titled families in London—or else wealthy cousins from South Africa. After all, one had to keep the diamond dynasty in the clan.

Arcilla looked about, and Evy was sure she wanted to see what the other village girls were wearing. Just then her blue eyes fell on Evy.

She thinks she's a peacock, and I'm just a little brown wren. Naturally, girls from the families of farmers, merchants, gardeners, and servants, as well as the vicar's niece, would not be wearing frocks that could compare in the slightest with Arcilla's fine wardrobe. Oddly enough, Evy had the impression that this comforted Arcilla.

Poor Uncle Edmund! Was anyone listening to his sermon? Ashamed, she sat straighter in the hard-backed pew and concentrated on his message.

After the service Evy spoke with several of her friends from the village. "Did you see what Arcilla was wearing? Oh, to own a frock like it."

"She always dresses as if she's going to Whitehall instead of church. Mum says she only does it to be noticed."

"What do you think she'll wear next Sunday?"

"Silk." Emily, the blacksmith's daughter, sighed. "Pink. I always dream of owning a pink silk frock."

"Silk is impossible to wash." Evy crossed her arms. "I do not want silk." But even as she spoke, she felt a tiny nudge deep within. Was that completely true?

"Arcilla will wear velvet. Soft blue velvet." Meg, the daughter of the head groom at Rookswood stables, all but crooned the pronouncement. She ran her palm along her rough cotton pinafore as though she could feel the lush velvet on her callused fingers.

"You cannot wash velvet either." Evy said it in an effort to comfort her friend. "Cotton is…more sensible. We must be sensible, you know."

"Well, whatever it is she wears next week, it will make her look beautiful." Meg's sigh was deep.

"Every boy will stare at her as goggled-eyed as an old frog in Grimston's pond." Emily grimaced. "Like our silly brothers do."

"Milt has a terrible crush on her," Meg said with sadness.

"So does my brother Tom. As if Arcilla would *ever* look at him in his overalls. The Chantrys will have picked an earl for her to marry."

"I would not *have* an earl." Evy lifted her chin a fraction as she spoke.

"My brother insists she *did* look at him," Meg said.

"The boys' staring at Arcilla is no more silly than every girl in the village gaping at the squire's two sons." Evy shook her head. "Did you see Alice staring? I nearly laughed at her."

"As if Rogan would pay her any attention."

"Well, I could have told you Arcilla would come wearing the latest London fashion," Emily told them. "Mum says a new seamstress from

London arrived at Rookswood in the Chantry coach. Miss Hildegard, her name is. She is there to make Arcilla, Lady Honoria, and Lady Camilla new winter wardrobes. Mum was cleaning the sewing room when Miss Hildegard arrived. She had all manner of cloth—velvet, taffeta, and silk from India."

Meg and Evy moaned.

All this was fresh on Evy's mind when she returned to the rectory. The next day she was with Mrs. Croft in the kitchen learning how to cook and bake, and how to preserve jams and watermelon rinds in cinnamon. Cooking was part of Evy's schooling so that one day, when she became a vicar's wife, she would be able to bring food to the sick and infirm among the parishioners.

It was fully expected that Derwent would become curate after his father, and one day a vicar. In another few years he would be going away to divinity school in London. Marriage to Derwent would let Evy continue on at the rectory in a comfortable lifestyle. The idea was sensible and practical.

Evy grimaced. If only she felt some excitement when she thought about Derwent! He was like a comfortable shoe. Pushing the disloyal thought aside, she told Mrs. Croft how Rogan and Parnell ignored her and the other girls.

"As though we are a necessary evil to be tolerated."

"You wait a few years." A slight smile tipped Mrs. Croft's lips. "Sudden like, they'll be whistling a different tune. If they be anything like Squire or them before him, they'll be hanging about the girls of Grimston Way like ants around a honey pot. Every decent girl who wants herself a good husband had better watch her reputation. Squire thinks his boys can do no wrong. So if there's mischief to happen, who do you think will be blamed? It won't be Master Parnell or young Rogan—or that sister of his neither, for that matter," she said, showing Evy how to mash the berries for pound cake. "That young Master Rogan has wanderlust, he does, and he is too comely for his own good."

Evy licked the berry juice from her finger, and Mrs. Croft gently slapped at her hand. "Bad manners, missy."

"What does *comely* mean?"

"In the young master's case, pleasing to a girl's eye. Mark my words, little one. That means be cautious of him. He holds promise of becoming a rascally rogue, if you go wanting my opinion."

Evy smiled. Mrs. Croft would give her opinion whether anyone asked for it or not.

"He fits 'is name, I daresay."

Rogan...rogue. Yes, the words even sounded something alike, Evy decided.

Mrs. Croft nodded her gray head. "Aye, but he'll still rise above Parnell, I'm thinking. There's talk about, saying it'll be Rogan who inherits Squire's title, not Master Parnell. Lizzie's heard tales about young Parnell wanting more diamond shares in the Kimberly mines in place of the title and Rookswood lands. Don't know how this will affect Master Rogan, though."

Evy supposed she meant that Rogan, too, wanted to go to South Africa when he grew up, and would not look favorably on remaining in Grimston Way to rule Rookswood lands. However, since most of the villagers living in Grimston Way could trace their lineage back to the time of the Crusades, it seemed that if anyone even so much as wished to journey afar, they were accused of suffering from the reckless disease of wanderlust. Derwent also talked of adventure in faraway places, yet he was even more likely than Rogan to be denied his dreams.

Evy stared down at the bowl in her hands and sighed. Was there no one who could live life the way he—or she—wished?

October blew in on a chilly wind, bearing change in more than just the seasons. The village doctor, Dr. Tisdale, came through Rookswood's gate in his coach and called on Vicar Edmund. The vicar was needed up at Rookswood right away, he said. The long-ailing Lady Honoria, the squire's wife, had passed away in her sleep the night before.

A few days later the sky was roiling with clouds, and the fall wind shook away the few remaining leaves on the chestnut trees. Almost the entire village of Grimston Way lined the road from Rookswood to St. Graves chapel as the Chantry coaches made the slow procession down to the cemetery.

Because the vicar was Evy's uncle, she was permitted to attend. The Chantry family was all in black, including Miss Arcilla. She wore a veiled hat, as did Lady Camilla, who held the young girl's hand. Miss Hortense, the governess, was there too, wiping her eyes on a handkerchief and no doubt recalling being governess to Honoria when she was but a little girl in Capetown.

Parnell Chantry was very somber, as was Rogan, but neither shed tears the way Arcilla did. For the first time ever, Evy's heart went out to the girl. *So she's human after all.*

Evy watched Rogan put his arm around his sister's shoulder when she began to cry, and a warmth filled her. How splendid of him to care for his sister that way. He seemed protective of Arcilla, much more so than Parnell, though one would have expected the older brother to take the lead. Evy recalled what Mrs. Croft said about how the squire's title would be given to Rogan. That was odd, but then, so were many of the details about the Chantrys.

Evy was heartened when the service was all over and they could join the unhappy procession back to the rectory. When Aunt Grace went ahead to check on the tables of food waiting inside the rectory hall, Evy edged up alongside the vicar in his black robe.

"Uncle Edmund," she whispered, "did she go to heaven?"

"My dear child!"

"But Uncle, it's important where Lady Honoria went to."

He smiled and his eyes danced as he reached over to place his loving arm around her shoulders. "You make me a happy man, Evy. Yes, it is all-important where Lady Honoria went. And I feel confident, after having spoken with her many times on the subject of Christ our Savior, that Honoria Chantry is safe in the arms of Jesus."

Evy's relief escaped on a sigh. "Good. Now I can enjoy all the food everyone brought to the rectory."

The vicar threw back his head and enjoyed his laughter, then stopped quickly and cleared his throat when Miss Hortense, the retired governess, shot him a shocked glance over her pince-nez.

There was much food waiting in the hall provided by Rookswood servants, who had been sent down earlier that morning to get everything ready.

Evy marveled when she saw roast ducklings and partridges, a ham, and a big leg of lamb. There were breads, butter, pies, persimmons, and pears. But Sir Lyle, looking most unhappy, stayed only long enough to accept condolences from some of the villagers. Lady Camilla went back to Rookswood with Arcilla and the Chantry sons. Evy felt compassion for them. She had contemplated telling Rogan of her sympathy, but the opportunity had not come. Once again, he had not even glanced her way.

The death of a family member was such a lonely time, but Honoria was not lonely now. She was basking in the joyful presence of God.

Sir Lyle shook hands with the vicar and thanked him for his comforting words of sympathy, then he, too, departed.

The parishioners stayed, and after a while the mood cheered a little. Everyone ate so much that Mrs. Croft teased that no one should be able to eat again for another week, so she ought to take a week off from cooking and go home to clear out her old summer's garden and get it ready for the coming winter.

There was plenty of food left over. The wives all lined up to receive portions, commensurate to the size of their families, to take home. Meg's family got the most, while old Miss Armitage, who was all alone, received the least. She was quite dour about it and did not mince her words to Aunt Grace.

"Hark! An old lady who cannot be waiting on herself at every turn ought to receive a wee bit more. I'll be turning ninety in December."

Evy watched Aunt Grace add their own take-home portion to Miss Armitage's basket, assuring the old lady she was absolutely correct.

Evy sighed and nudged Derwent. "There goes my last hope for a piece of apple tart."

He carried Miss Armitage's basket outside, then drove her to her bungalow before the rains came.

That night Evy prayed especially long for Rogan, Arcilla, and Parnell, who now, like herself, had no mum. She wondered about Lady Camilla Brewster.

The fall rains lingered for several days, making everything chilly, damp, and morosely gray.

A week later Evy was sitting with her fellow students in the rectory hall, which was being used for a schoolroom. Along with her were Meg and her brother Milt, Emily and her brother Tom, Derwent Brown, and Alice Tisdale, the doctor's only child. As Evy sat before her open workbook, Curate Brown spoke.

"It seems Miss Evy is dreaming of faraway places. Do pay attention and begin your Bible lesson."

"Yes, Mr. Brown." Evy felt her face turn hot and she read the parable of the rich fool in the gospel of Luke.

"What happened to the rich fool?" Curate Brown studied the small class when Evy had finished reading.

Milt held up his hand. "He built himself bigger barns to hold it all. No sooner did he have himself a pile, then he up and croaked. He left it all in the barn and never saw it again."

"Just like Lady Chantry," Tom whispered, grinning at Evy. "You know where she went? Deep down below!" He used a deep, baritone voice to say this. He winked, and everyone chuckled except Evy.

"You should not talk so flippantly, Tom," Evy said. "You are gleeful about Lady Honoria's passing because she had so much and you have so little. But you should feel sorry for Arcilla, Parnell, and Rogan Chantry. How would you like to lose your mum?"

"Little Miss Vicar," Tom teased.

"She feels more sorry for Rogan, don't you, Evy?" Alice Tisdale's strawberry-blond hair was wrapped around her head in a braid. Her skin was sallow, and her small mouth puckered. Tom once said she looked as though she had been weaned on a sour pickle.

Evy blushed at Alice's taunt, and the other girl looked positively gleeful that she'd made Evy uncomfortable.

Derwent came to Evy's rescue. "Lady Honoria was a kind and Christian woman. She always came to Sunday services when she was feeling well. It seems her faith in Jesus was more than doing church rituals"—he fixed Alice with a hard stare—"which is more than I can say for others."

When Alice turned away, her cheeks a bright pink, Evy gave Derwent a grateful smile. Rogan wasn't the only one who could be protective. Perhaps life with Derwent would not be so boring, after all.

Three weeks after Honoria Chantry's funeral, Evy watched as Aunt Grace sat in the small rectory office, poring over a pile of papers. Were they debts? Evy wasn't sure, but she had noticed of late that Aunt Grace was mulling over many concerns, far more than the servants' gossip. Maybe Uncle Edmund's health had something to do with her aunt's worries. He had a heart condition that Dr. Tisdale was treating and, after the funeral, had taken to bed with angina. He was still in a weakened condition, so it had been left to the curate, Mr. Brown, to give the Sunday sermons in the chapel.

Toward the end of November, Sir Lyle left Grimston Way for Dover to board a ship for faraway Capetown. Rumor had it that he was to see his stepbrother, Sir Julien Bley. Would he also see Anthony Brewster? Maybe he was trying to bring him and Lady Camilla back together again.

Later Alice Tisdale claimed that Arcilla had needed a long bed rest. "Arcilla's even more unhappy now that her Papa has left. She doesn't improve."

"How do you know?" Evy asked as they walked to the classroom where Curate Brown waited.

A look of smug pride came to Alice's face. "Lady Camilla asked my father if he would send me up to Rookswood to be a companion to

Arcilla. Of course, since I'm the daughter of the village doctor, I'm considered quite suitable. I went last week to read to Arcilla. The house is so grand. Her room is pink and white, and she has dozens of slippers and frocks." Alice's mouth turned up at the corners. "I even saw Rogan and Parnell. They both spoke to me. 'Good morning, Miss Alice,' Parnell said."

"Indeed? Did you faint dead away?"

Alice's smile vanished. Her eyes turned hard. "You're jealous, Evy. And you the vicar's niece, too. You should be better than the rest of us. That's what my mama says."

Your mama says too much about everyone, Evy wanted to tell her, but of course she did not. Alice would run home and tell Mrs. Tisdale, who would then come calling on Aunt Grace.

Besides, Alice was right. Evy *should* be nicer than Alice because her parents had been missionaries and because her uncle was the vicar. She tried to control her tongue thereafter, but trying hard in her own strength did not always work.

When she got home that day, Evy found Aunt Grace in the vicar's office and told her about Arcilla Chantry growing worse.

Aunt Grace leaned back against the desk. "I daresay it has not been easy on her, poor child. Losing her mother, and now Sir Lyle has left for Cape."

"Mrs. Croft says it seems like a curse is on Rookswood. Another death in the family would convince her it was so."

"Nonsense."

"Aunt, who is Master Henry?"

Aunt Grace looked at her sharply. "Why do you ask?"

"Some people say he killed himself."

Aunt Grace yanked off her apron and threw it down on the chair. "I'm going to have a talk with Mrs. Croft."

"It— It really was not Mrs. Croft, but Lizzie."

"Ah, yes, the all-knowing eyes and ears at Rookswood." Aunt Grace sighed, seeming to forfeit any hope of stopping the gossip, and sank tiredly into the chair. "There is no big secret, Evy. Master Henry

Chantry was the squire's brother. He came to Rookswood from Capetown after the Zulu War. He fought in the battles. I think he was quite heroic, but I never met him. He was here in Grimston Way only about a year before he...he met with an accident. Now, enough chatter. I'm taking the jingle out to see Miss Armitage. Want to come with me? Better bring your hooded cloak, dear."

"Yes. Is... Was Master Henry Rogan's blood uncle?"

"Yes. He was somewhat of an explorer in South Africa. He was fairly wealthy, and he never did remarry after his wife Caroline died on one of his expeditions. He favored Rogan and left him everything he owned."

Evy thought of the diamonds, the Black Diamond. Was that how Master Henry made his money? She did not dare mention that to her aunt.

"That means Rogan is going to be a very wealthy man one day, doesn't it?"

Aunt Grace nodded. "Since he will receive a great inheritance from his father as well, yes." She looked over at her husband's desk, where she'd been going over some papers. The mention of money seemed to deepen the worry lines around her eyes. "Ah, well."

Toward the holidays an event took place that changed Evy's life. It was December, and some of the ladies were helping plan for the Christmas festivities at the rectory. Aunt Grace was teaching Evy to weave pine boughs for the garland that would decorate the chapel, and Mrs. Croft was telling the sexton in a low voice to put more pine boughs in the cemetery on the grave of Lady Honoria—"and some on the gate for the late great gentleman, Master Henry Chantry."

At the mention of Master Henry, Evy looked up, breathing in the pungent fragrance of pine. She had not forgotten what Mrs. Croft said about a curse on Rookswood, or that it somehow centered around Master Henry's death. The idea of a curse was just superstition; Evy knew it was foolish, but Mrs. Croft wanting her husband to add extra pine to the gate in memory of Henry Chantry's death convinced her that Mrs. Croft did not think so.

"Better to appease Master Henry," Evy heard Mrs. Croft whisper to her husband.

The tall, thin sexton nodded and ambled away from the rectory yard in the direction of the church cemetery.

Evy stood, about to follow him, intending to ask about Master Henry. But just then the Chantry coach rolled up, as sleek, black, and shiny as anything Evy had ever seen. Mr. Bixby, the footman, always shined it with a cloth, and the yard boy polished the wheels.

Everyone ceased what they were doing, as though royalty had just arrived from London. All eyes were on Mr. Bixby as he climbed down from the driver's seat, his shoulders straight and head high, then opened the coach door.

Though everyone knew Lady Camilla sat inside, they stared at the coach door, breath held, waiting.

Lady Camilla stepped down from the carriage, holding Mr. Bixby's arm. She was gowned in many yards of black satin, and her skin look like purest ivory.

She is prettier than I thought. Evy admired the woman's golden hair, which was so artfully arranged. Her large eyes were the color of slate, and Evy started when they looked directly at her.

Her heart jumped. *Why is she staring at me like that?*

"Good afternoon, Vicar. Mrs. Havering." Lady Camilla's smile was gentle. "I should like to speak with you in the rectory, if you have a few minutes to spare?"

Naturally everyone had minutes to spare for Lady Camilla Montieth Brewster, but Evy thought it rather gracious of her to ask rather than expect everyone to stop what they were doing.

"By all means, Lady Camilla, how good to see you." Uncle Edmund's smile was genuine.

"We were just about to have afternoon tea," Aunt Grace told her with an equally charming smile, and Evy had the clear impression that her aunt liked Lady Camilla.

"Mrs. Croft and Evy have baked fresh scones. I do believe they made your favorite, lemon curd."

Camilla looked over at Evy, and Evy smiled. When Lady Camilla looked quickly away, Evy felt her smile slip. *Is there something about my appearance that bothers her?*

She noticed there was no one else inside the carriage. Rogan must have stayed at Rookswood with Parnell. Parnell had been allowed to return to a prestigious school he attended in London after his mother's death, and was now home for the Christmas holidays. Rogan was to join him at school after the New Year. It would seem a little more deserted once they were gone to London. Evy often saw Rogan riding by on his horse. He would glance her way, pretending not to see her, but she knew he did. Once he had slowed down, but then had ridden on toward the woods, his dog close behind.

Something important must have brought Lady Camilla to see the vicar. Evy decided to help Mrs. Croft bring the tea tray and platter of warm scones into the rectory parlor. Afterward she lingered, hoping to hear what was said.

"I daresay, Vicar, I am at wits' end with worry," Lady Camilla was saying in her quiet voice. "I simply must try everything if Arcilla is to be cheered up. My husband's uncle, the squire, left me in charge of Rookswood and the children while he is away in Capetown. You did receive my message about Miss Evy?"

Evy's gaze swerved to Lady Camilla.

Uncle Edmund placed one hand at his heart. "I can assure you that my niece is a very sensible girl and will cause you no undue difficulty."

"Evy is at the top of the curate's class," Aunt Grace added. "Mrs. Tisdale, the good doctor's wife, also assures me Evy has a great love of and gift for music. It is our ambition to send her to Parkridge Music Academy when she is older."

What was this about? Evy's heart beat faster with anticipation.

"Yes, your niece seems a lovely girl," Lady Camilla was saying as though Evy were not standing right there. "She is quite sensible, indeed, Vicar, I'm well aware of that. I have noticed her in Sunday service. Very well behaved; she is not a little runabout. I have heard no ill talk of her in the village."

Had Lady Camilla been inquiring about her?

"Naturally, everything will depend on what Arcilla thinks. It was a great disappointment to me when she became displeased with Miss Alice. You do know how children fuss and quarrel so. Arcilla sent Alice home last week in tears. Alice has since apologized to Arcilla, but Arcilla has refused to let her visit." She looked at Evy for the first time, and it seemed Lady Camilla's eyes were bright and inquisitive. "Arcilla is willing to have Miss Evy come in Alice's place. Arcilla is very careful about her acquaintances, as you know."

"I daresay," Aunt Grace replied as expected of her.

"If they do get along as I am hoping, I, too, shall be very pleased."

Evy's heart quavered. Rookswood. She was going up to Rookswood, just as the stranger in Grimston Wood had said she might!

Aunt Grace did not look as pleased as Evy would have expected. Her hands were interlocked on her lap and her knuckles were white.

When Lady Camilla departed, Aunt Grace laid a hand on Evy's shoulder. "Dear, I need to discuss this with your uncle in private. Can you help Derwent with the Christmas boughs?"

"Yes, of course."

But as Evy left the parlor, she caught her aunt's quiet question to her husband.

"Oh, Edmund. Do you think this is wise?"

Evy hesitated.

"Perhaps it will be good for the child." Uncle Edmund sounded concerned as well.

"I wonder..."

Knowing she shouldn't dally any longer, Evy hurried out of the room. The next day the decision was announced at breakfast. Uncle Edmund looked at Evy over his lowered spectacles and told her she would become a companion to the ailing Miss Arcilla. Three afternoons a week, beginning on Saturday, she would walk up the hill to Rookswood to visit.

Evy was thrilled. At last, she would go inside Rookswood!

Later that night, Evy slipped from her bed and went to the window. She could just make out part of Rookswood mansion and saw lights glowing in the rooms like golden jewels. *Like diamonds...* She leaned her forehead against the cool glass. *I am going up to the house of diamonds.*

CHAPTER SEVEN

The old sexton, Hiram Croft, was digging a grave when Evy entered through the cemetery gate the next morning.

"Good morning, Mr. Croft."

He was older than Mrs. Croft, very tall, with hunched shoulders and a lined face. It was not polite to say, but Mr. Croft reminded her of one of the rooks that made such a racket in the trees. The birds were noisy now and jumping from branch to branch.

He leaned on his shovel at the bottom of the trench he was digging. "Mornin', Miss Evy. What brings you here?"

"The ghost of Master Henry Chantry," she said with a teasing smile. "I thought you could tell me all about it."

He grinned. "I remember Master Henry, I do. He used to ride by on a big gold gelding. Was the second golden horse he owned. Lost the first one in Zulu country, he said. He'd ride himself all over the village seeing how folks was. The women all swooned for him. Handsome rascal—some of his blood be in young Rogan Chantry, I'm thinking. More'n likely Henry had himself less concern for how folks was doing and more interest in dallying with the ladies than much else. Master Henry were a busy man when it come to that."

He began digging again. Evy stood on the edge of the trench looking down. "How did he die?"

"Now, missy, don't you go asking me that sort of thing. You ask the good vicar."

"I have. Uncle Edmund says gossip is a sin."

"Aye, so it is. A wise man, the vicar."

She held her hands behind her back. "It doesn't seem to me that my asking how Master Henry died is gossip."

"Well, that do seem a bit true, but when questions are whispered about how a man killed himself…well, then, things change quicklike."

"So it is true? The dark secret is that Master Henry did actually kill himself?"

He cocked one eye up at her. "Shot himself in the noggin, it's said." He tapped the side of right temple. "Right inside Rookswood. Third floor. And on Michaelmas, too. I daresay that will be a mark against him."

The morning seemed darker and somehow threatening. She realized she was holding her breath. Then—"But why would Master Henry shoot himself up there?"

"Why not? Better'n the first floor."

"I don't mean *that*. I mean, it seems a bit odd that a man as important and rich as Henry Chantry would kill himself. From what I've heard he was an adventurer, a bold man, unafraid of most things."

He leaned on his shovel again. "Aye, he was that. Odd, maybe so. I've seen me a whole lot odder things in my time."

"Like what?" She sat down on the edge of the trench, letting her high-button shoes dangle over the side. She wished she had a pair of pretty grown-up slippers like Arcilla wore.

"Well…one foggy Allhallows Eve, I come out here to hang the lighted lantern on the gate over there—so folks could come like they always do and leave things for the ghosts—and lo and behold, I saw the ghost of ol' Henry wandering around here just as plain as though he were alive and kicking. Makes me wonder if Henry killed himself, or if it was more violent than even that."

Evy swallowed, and a chilling breeze made her skin crawl. "You do not mean"—the word lodged in her throat—"he was…*murdered?*"

He looked up at the rooks with a faraway gleam in his eyes. "So some say."

"But who would *do* such a wicked thing?"

"That were long ago, missy. Who's to say? Only Henry's ghost can tell us."

"Oh, Mr. Croft, there aren't any ghosts. Uncle Edmund says ghosts are moldy suspicion from the Dark Ages. Miss Armitage is the oldest person in Grimston Way—nearly ninety—and Derwent vows he saw garlic hanging at her kitchen door. When he asked her why she hung it there, she said to keep vampires away. That's quite silly you know. When a man dies without believing in Jesus, he goes to a place to wait until God judges him. But those who believe go at once to heaven. So if all are accounted for, how can there be ghosts?"

"True enough." He removed his cap and scratched his gray locks, then shoved the cap back on. "I still think there be ghosts."

She smiled. "That is because you *want* to believe it."

He set his jaw. "Seen Master Henry plain as day. He be restless. So he wanders, seeking justice against the kin who killed him."

Evy stared at the man. "You don't think so! His own kin?"

"Aye. Who else coulda done him in?"

"Maybe a thief crawled in his window."

"Ha! You take another look at them tall windows. Why, you'd need to be a rook to fly to one of 'em."

"The bottom windows?"

"Locked, more'n likely."

"But who would that kin person be? And why?" Then it occurred to her. Of course! "The Black Diamond?"

Mr. Croft's eyes fairly sparkled. "Ah…so you know about it too, eh? Could be that diamond. Again, maybe not. Who's to say? Vicar be a good man, but even *he* don't know everything. Spirits wander."

"Human spirits can't wander after death, Mr. Croft. Maybe it was fog you saw instead. You merely thought you saw some unearthly thing wisping about."

"It were foggy that night, all right. So thick and white that swirls wrapped 'round me like snakes." He took a shovelful of dirt and tossed it, then looked up at her.

"There you have it, Mr. Croft. That's what you saw, plain old fog.

You know how thick it can become in autumn. So thick you can hardly see ahead of you."

At the amusement in his eyes, Evy wondered if all this was just one of his jokes.

"Think so, eh?" He shrugged. "Well, you go ahead and think that. Ye'll sleep better, Miss Evy. And Vicar won't be after me for filling your ears with nonsense. But I knows what I saw. And it were a ghost."

"I know a better ghost story, Hiram, but better not tell her more."

Evy nearly jumped out of her skin as the deep voice from behind her went on.

"The rectory girl is probably like Arcilla. My sister squeals and dives under the bed at such tales, and *she* probably does too, especially on foggy nights."

She turned her head to find Rogan Chantry standing by the oak tree, his dog on a leash beside him. Rogan wore a fancy black coat and trousers with gold buttons. His hair was dark and glossy below his cap, and one wave fell across his forehead. He walked up to Evy, and they looked at each other. He took in her scuffed, high-button leather shoes and the plain gray cotton skirt and pinafore she wore. As he studied her, she realized her pinafore was splashed with berry jam from the kitchen. She had not cared about that until this moment. She blushed. His eyes came to hers, and the corners of his mouth turned up as though she amused him.

Evy suspected he was as difficult to get on with as Arcilla. Not only did his father dote on him, but so did the old governess, Miss Hortense. Evy brushed her pinafore, but it did no good. She gave a furtive glance at his shoes. They were shiny—most likely bought in London. His trousers and jacket were of expensive wool, as was his cap. He probably received just about everything his heart could wish for. The leash on his red Irish setter was a shiny silver. The dog, too, seemed to dote on Rogan. It sat humbly at his feet, gazing up with adoring brown eyes.

Evy resisted feeling small and unimportant. Instead, she lifted her chin and folded her arms. "I do not squeal." She swung her high-button shoes. "Nor am I silly."

His smile held a sparkle of mischief. "You would squeal if I took you to my uncle Henry's crypt on Rookswood." Rogan's tone was full of challenge. "My sister is too afraid to go. *All* girls are afraid of everything, is that not so, Buster?" He patted the big dog's shiny head, and the beast whined as if to agree. Rogan's eyes danced as he looked down at Evy. "You see?"

Hiram Croft chuckled, and Evy's fingers itched to cuff that smug grin from Rogan's face. "I would *not* be afraid."

Clearly Rogan did not believe her, but he smiled. "Fine, then, I will take you there. When you come to Rookswood to see Arcilla. If you squeal, I win. Then you will have to do some task to please me."

"What if *I* win?"

The smug smile deepened. "You will not."

Her foot swung faster. "Maybe I will. Then you must do a task for *me*. I will think of one."

"No."

Evy stared at him. "That is not fair."

He shrugged, dismissing the subject, and turned to Mr. Croft.

Evy fumed.

"Now, Hiram, I do not see how you could see my uncle Henry's ghost here in the cemetery when he is not buried here."

"Eh, what? Er, you got me there, young Master Rogan." He chuckled again.

"Unless… Yes, that must be it—if he was riding his gold horse through the cemetery that night when you saw him. My father says his brother Henry was a wanderer."

"Aye, that must be it, all right. Master Henry were on that horse of his."

Evy folded her arms. "Now you are exaggerating, as Uncle Edmund says you do, Mr. Croft. I do not think you saw Master Henry at all, and I am *not* afraid of his crypt." She clambered to her feet, brushing the grass from her skirt.

Rogan shrugged, still smiling. "Never mind his showing up here. My uncle's ghost haunts the third floor of Rookswood Manor all year long. That is where he died. So he is not likely to be here in the cemetery anyway."

Mr. Croft grinned. "I won't be arguing with ye."

Rogan looked at Evy as if to make sure she did not challenge him either. She did not. Instead, to give vent to her miffed feelings, she said, "I will wager those are not real gold buttons." She was staring at his jacket.

"What makes you think they are not?"

"Because Lady Camilla is too wise to let you wear solid gold buttons when you are outdoors riding or walking Buster. You would lose one, and then what?"

Rogan smiled indulgently.

"I think Miss Evy has you there, Master Rogan. If ye did lose one and it were gold, then we'd all be out treasure hunting."

"Finders are keepers," Evy said with a grin. "Because I would find it before anyone."

"No, you would not."

He was positively insufferable! "Why wouldn't I?"

"Because it would be a small chance indeed for anyone to find it, even me."

And of course if *he* could not find it, no one could. How like a Chantry to think that of himself.

"Unless it caught the sun's rays." Rogan snapped his fingers, and Buster lay down. Rogan snapped them again, and the dog stood. "I have taught him a lot of tricks." He folded his arms across his chest and looked down at Mr. Croft. "I am going to find my own gold mine in South Africa. Just like my uncle Julien found a diamond mine in Kimberly. I could find a new diamond mine, but I want to do something different. So I will find gold. Lots. So much gold that I will have solid gold buttons on my jacket. And when I do, I will give you a small bagful, Croft."

"What about me?"

He pursed his lips and studied Evy. "We will see."

She had had enough. "I am not dumb. I would know what to do

with it. As for gold buttons— I daresay, it is a waste to have them. Do you not think so, Mr. Croft?"

Though Mr. Croft chuckled, he would not answer.

Well, she was not afraid to speak her mind. She met Rogan's gaze. "You would only be showing off wearing solid gold buttons."

"Evy!"

She turned to see Mrs. Croft, who was clearly dismayed to think Evy would speak with such flippancy to a Chantry. Mrs. Croft carried a basket over her arm, and Evy knew it contained gingerbread cakes because she had helped Mrs. Croft in the kitchen earlier that morning.

Evy looked down at the ground. "I was just watching Mr. Croft dig."

"You must be remembering your manners." Mrs. Croft smiled an apology at Rogan.

For as long as she remembered, Evy had been taught, whenever she might run into Sir Lyle, to drop a little curtsy and say, "Good morning, Squire Chantry. God bless you on this day and all your house." But this was not Sir Lyle. It was his insufferable son, Rogan, and he nettled her.

"Do not carry on so, Mrs. Croft. Do I look upset? It is nothing."

Evy looked at Rogan, surprised at how weary he sounded.

Mrs. Croft beamed at him. "So generous of you, Master Rogan. Don't you want to thank the squire's son, Evy?"

Evy did *not* want to thank the squire's son. She felt her face turning red. Just then Buster barked loudly and rolled over. Rogan picked up a stone and tossed it. "Go get it, Buster." He unleashed him, and the dog raced to retrieve the stone.

Evy stared at the boy in front of her. How convenient Buster's fetching trick was, coming as it did just in time to save her from embarrassment. Could Rogan actually have tried to help her out of an awkward moment?

Mrs. Croft was smiling at Rogan. "Would you like a cake?" She opened the basket and lowered it between him and Evy. Rogan inclined his head slightly, took the cake, then without another glance Evy's way, he walked off in the direction of the cemetery from whence he had first emerged so unexpectedly.

Evy felt a pang of regret as he left. Perhaps she should have been nicer to him. After all, he had recently lost his mother. He had not behaved sadly though, not like Arcilla, who had been confined to bed over the loss.

Mrs. Croft carried on about Mr. Croft eating his lunch. There was cheese and bread, she told him, and a jar of tea. He climbed up out of the trench and sat on a stump to eat, and Mrs. Croft steered Evy away toward the rectory. "You mustn't keep the vicar and his wife waiting for their lunch. Oh! Your skirt has grass stains, and your hands are smudged. Now Missus Grace will surely be upset. Run and decent yourself, Evy, while I get back to ladle the soup."

When Evy was seated at the polished round dining table, Uncle Edmund gave thanks for the food. Aunt Grace passed the bread plate while Mrs. Croft brought in the soup. Evy guessed from his contented face that Uncle Edmund was in a mellow mood, and even Aunt Grace seemed less worried than she had when Lady Camilla had first come calling. It seemed a safe time to ask questions.

"Where is Kimberly, Uncle Edmund? Isn't that where diamonds were first found in South Africa? It was not on the map I saw in your study."

"You and your curiosity, my girl. Yes, Kimberly is in South Africa, but that map is a very old one. It was not called Kimberly back then. The first diamond was not found there until 1867. At that time it was called the diamond diggings at Colesberg Kopje. It was renamed Kimberly after the colonial secretary who accepted the area into Her Majesty's dominions. After the big diamond was found on the river's bank, Kimberly grew by leaps and bounds. Miners came from all over the world to search for diamonds."

"Did my parents ever visit Kimberly?"

She noticed that her aunt watched her carefully. Did her continued interest disturb Aunt Grace…and if so, why?

"Junia never mentioned going there. Why do you ask, Evy?"

She laughed. "Would it not be a wonder if they had found a diamond of their own? I would be their heir, and we would never need to worry about paying bills again."

Aunt Grace spilled water from the glass she held, and Uncle Edmund reached quickly with his napkin and blotted his wife's sleeve.

"Oh dear," Aunt Grace breathed.

"No harm done, my dear," came Uncle Edmund's soothing tone.

Evy pressed on. "The squire's son isn't so interested in diamonds. He hopes to look for gold in South Africa when he grows up."

Uncle Edmund raised his brows. "You have been talking with Master Rogan, have you?"

"Only a little. It was quite by accident. He came to the cemetery with his dog and overheard Mr. Croft telling me about Master Henry Chantry. Mr. Croft thinks he may have been murdered."

Aunt Grace stiffened, a look of consternation on her face. Evy's uncle was more calm. His tufted white brows shot even higher. "Does he, now! And I suppose he told you Master Henry was murdered for diamonds?"

"He was not certain, just thought he was probably murdered. He did not say why, or who may have done it."

"Well, *that's* a blessing," he said wryly, exchanging looks with Grace. "There is absolutely no proof Henry was murdered."

"Then he killed himself?"

"Evy!" Aunt Grace's sharp tone startled her. "Spreading tales is an evil in which you must not indulge."

"But I did not spread them, Aunt."

"Listening can be just as bad. Words can hurt. Loose tongues can destroy people."

"Yes, and I would never mention this to Meg, Emily, or Alice. They would tell their brothers and it would soon be all over the village."

"I fear it already is." Uncle Edmund sighed. "That tale about Master Henry has been loitering in Grimston Way for many years now. I'm afraid there is not much we can do about it. The Chantrys are deemed mysterious at times by people, and all sorts of tales can spring up about them and grow like weeds."

"He said that Master Henry's ghost walks in the cemetery on Allhallows."

"Very unwise of him. Nonsense."

"That is what I told him, but then Rogan came along and said that his uncle wasn't even buried in the cemetery, so how could he haunt it? Then he told us his uncle Henry was buried in the family crypt at Rookswood." She considered telling them how Rogan offered the challenge to bring her there to see the crypt, but held back. Aunt Grace especially would tell her she could not go, and then she could not prove Rogan wrong about squealing like Arcilla.

"Master Rogan said that Henry's ghost haunts the third floor of Rookswood."

Grace tossed her napkin down on the table, frowning. "Edmund, you simply *must* do something about allowing this sort of chatter. It's unhealthy."

He reached over and laid his hand over hers. "I might as well try and bottle the north wind as end loose talk in the village. Do not fret so," came his soothing tone. "She will hear these tales regardless of our attempt to stop them." He looked across the table at Evy. "I trust you will be wise enough to sort the wheat from the chaff when it comes to truth and foolish chatter."

He trusted her, and Evy felt warm seep through her at the thought. But her aunt's reaction troubled her as much as her uncle's pleased her. Evy disliked worrying Aunt Grace. Lately, she fretted at the drop of a hat. What was worrying her so?

"I suppose you are right," Aunt Grace said uneasily, "but…"

"Aunt, I did not believe what they said about ghosts. How could I? It is silly. I merely thought it was strange about Master Henry. Do you remember him, Uncle?"

"Not well. He spent a good portion of his time in Capetown, as I recall. As to whether he shot himself, I cannot say. There was much confusion at the time." He glanced at Grace, as though to assure her all was well before he went on. "Henry had unwisely permitted himself to become entangled in some diamond scandal or other."

Evy saw her aunt's mouth tighten, and she hastened in another direction. "Master Rogan insists that when he grows up he is going to find a gold mine."

"He does, does he? Ambitious, like all the Chantrys." Uncle Edmund smiled. He took out his vest watch and glanced at the time. "I will be calling on Withers today, my dear," he said to Aunt Grace. "Would you care to come along?"

"I would, except the wind is so chilly. Looks like rain again too. I had better stay and work on Evy's dress. Saturday draws near, when she will visit Rookswood."

He pushed his chair back and stood. Aunt Grace went for his hat and gloves.

Evy came up, placing her arms around her uncle's pudgy middle. "Is it wrong to be ambitious the way Master Rogan is?"

He looked down at her with the kindly smile she loved and patted her back. "Not unless you allow your ambition to rule your heart. God must always have all your heart."

Evy wondered if Rogan would allow his ambition to rule him. "Is there lots of gold in South Africa?"

"I daresay there is a great deal. If you can find it."

"I suppose if you *could* find it, you would be very rich."

"Very rich indeed. And very prone toward trouble. Too much love for gold and diamonds usually brings out the worst in people. Some hoard diamonds and gold because it brings them power. Others put great trust in riches and never learn that possessions cannot give meaning to life. Only a relationship with Christ brings true security and satisfaction."

"Like the rich fool."

His smile deepened. "Like the rich fool, indeed. And we are wise to use Christ's parables to keep us from greed."

"I wonder if Master Henry was murdered for his diamonds and gold?"

"Evy!"

She turned to find Aunt Grace entering the room with Uncle

Edmund's hat and gloves. "You are becoming altogether too involved in this sort of chatter."

Quick remorse swept her. She did not want to distress her aunt. "Yes, I am sorry." With that, she hurried to gather the soup bowls into the kitchen.

When she entered the kitchen, she thought Mrs. Croft might have overheard, or rather had *listened*, for the woman stood by the door, her fingers clutching and unclutching her apron. Evy found her response curious. Why should Mrs. Croft be fidgety?

As Evy stacked the dishes, she began thinking of Saturday and her visit to Arcilla at Rookswood. Her excitement stirred to new life. She hoped it would be a clear and sunny afternoon. It would be such a shame to get her new dress rained on. Sure enough, before the dishes were even dried and put away, it begin to rain. Evy remembered the sexton and wondered if he had finished digging the trench before it became a slippery bed of mud. Mrs. Croft must have been worrying about her husband too, for she went to the window several times and scowled.

Thinking of a grave brought her mind right back to Master Henry. If he had not shot himself, then someone had to have murdered him. But why would anyone wish to murder Master Henry…if not for the Black Diamond?

Chapter Eight

The wind moaned throughout the rainy afternoon and evening. Though Aunt Grace had sent Evy up to her bedroom over two hours ago, she could not sleep, and so knelt to pray on the newly laundered rag rug beside her bed. She could hear her aunt downstairs in the rectory hall and knew how worried she was. When Uncle Edmund had not returned by supper time, Mrs. Croft told a few of the village men. They had ridden out toward Mr. Wither's farm to see if the vicar's jingle was caught in a bog. They had been gone longer than Aunt Grace thought necessary, and her concern had now turned to gravity.

Evy was still dressed, except for her stockinged feet. Her hands were cold, her stomach had butterflies, and her heart thumped with irregular little beats. She looked up from her prayer book toward the small window, shielded by eyelet curtains. The rain pelted against the leaded pane. A sweeping flash of lightning over Grimston Woods was followed by deep thunder.

"Like the death angel passing over Egypt," she murmured. Above the needling rain, there followed the sound of thudding horse hoofs in the rectory yard below. The jingle and Uncle Edmund!

She scrambled to her feet and rushed to the window, pushing aside the curtain. Even on sunny days the leaded panes kept the rooms dim, and now, with the darkness and rain, it was nearly impossible to see anything. She wiped the moisture from the pane and tried to peer into the darkness below, but she could not see who was hurrying across the muddy yard toward the door. Even up here in her small room she heard the loud rapping. Her heart sank like a stone. It could not be Uncle Edmund.

It was after eight o'clock, and Evy could not imagine a parishioner calling upon Aunt Grace now for any reason except unhappy news. With growing apprehension, Evy let the curtain fall into place and turned to look toward the open bedroom door.

She hurried into the narrow hall and leaned over the rail.

Aunt Grace stood below, Mrs. Croft beside her. Coming in through the front were the curate, Mr. Brown, and Derwent. Curate Brown had taken hold of Aunt Grace's shoulders, and his wet face was set with sadness. Evy saw Aunt Grace stiffen, then her head dropped and her body shook.

"Something has happened to Uncle?" Evy couldn't hold back the cry. She held tightly to the rail, and Derwent looked up at her. His wet face looked drawn and white, and his russet hair was plastered to his cheeks. He tugged at his father's arm and pointed toward Evy, and Mr. Brown looked up. The curate's expression confirmed her fears. He said something to Mrs. Croft, who left the others and moved up the stairs toward Evy.

Evy could not move. Her tearful eyes searched Mrs. Croft's pitying gaze.

"Oh, Evy, my poor lamb," she said gently. "I'm afraid the good vicar has met with a terrible accident. It was the rain and wind, no less. His horse must have bolted from the lightning. Dear Vicar has been taken to heaven."

Evy felt the room start to spin, and the last thing she heard was Mrs. Croft's alarmed cry as she plunged into darkness.

The rains continued on and off, and the perpetual dampness penetrated the old stone rectory. How strange that Lady Honoria would die in October and Uncle Edmund would die just a few weeks later.

Evy stared out the window at the rain. Maybe there really was some sort of curse connected with Master Henry and Rookswood. She could almost believe it if she did not know for sure that Christ was in control of life and death.

The names of the rectors for the past century were inscribed on a tarnished bronze plaque on the stone wall in the front hall, and now Uncle Edmund's name was to be there as well, freshly inscribed by the village engraver.

The Saturday appointment that Evy was to have had with Arcilla at Rookswood was postponed until after Christmas. Evy was confined to the rectory in the traditional state of mourning alongside Aunt Grace.

Though the kindly parishioners rallied to their needs and took turns bringing food, it was evident that in due time Aunt Grace would need to seek employment for the many years that loomed ahead. After all, she was still a relatively young woman.

"Times are changing, Evy," Aunt Grace told her two weeks later. "It's highly probable that you, too, will grow up with the need to seek employment. If that happens you will be aided by a good education. Even if you marry Derwent Brown, life is uncertain. We can depend upon the Lord to care for us, though He surely expects us to use our talents wisely. Consider how He gave the ant the instinct to prepare for winter. If we do nothing, and merely say we are depending upon our heavenly Father to provide, we are close to presumption."

Evy could see how grave and serious her aunt had become, and this affected her as well. After tasting pain and loss, Evy had made a terrible discovery: Life was dangerous.

The parishioners were helping with the many duties that were temporarily in the hands of the curate. No one had much doubt Mr. Brown would become the new vicar of St. Graves. He was well thought of by both the villagers and the bishop, and he was making quiet plans to move into the rectory house with Derwent, doing his best to do so without offense to the vicar's sorrowing widow.

Evy had no idea how this delicate situation would be worked out. It was obvious that once a new vicar was appointed, she and Aunt Grace would have to leave the rectory and find another place to live. The uncertainty was taking its toll on Aunt Grace, coming so soon after Uncle Edmund's death, and Evy felt great sympathy and concern. Life had suddenly become more difficult. The hard places had not been filed smooth. Tears were a portion of her cup. She wished she were older so that she could help bring in financial support. There was also some talk that Dr. Tisdale might arrange for Aunt Grace to live in a cottage on his farm for a monthly pittance, but Evy hoped that would not happen. Alice Tisdale was patronizing enough. She was going about whispering to the other girls that her father would be taking on the care of the vicar's widow and niece, even going so far as to imply that they would be receiving charity. Alice had sounded positively smug when she revealed she might need to go through her frocks to donate garments to Evy so she could continue to attend school. "Perfectly good frocks, too—ones that I want to keep. But Mum says I must be charitable to the poor and deprived."

It took all of Evy's control to not walk up and confront Alice with her silly lies. It wasn't so dreadful for her to say these things to Meg and Emily because they knew what poverty was and they knew better. But Alice was also spreading the tale among the boys. It was horribly embarrassing! Evy shuddered to think just how condescending Alice's manner would become if she and Aunt Grace *did* end up living in the old cottage on the Tisdale farm. *Oh, spare me! I will wear a potato sack before I ever wear a discarded frock from Alice Tisdale!*

Despite all this, as the days inched by, Evy was able to continue her piano lessons twice a week under Mrs. Tisdale, who had studied music when she was young, and whose contribution to the community was noted by the villagers.

"I'm in complete agreement with Mrs. Tisdale. Music is nourishing to the spirit," Aunt Grace said. "I see no reason why your uncle's death should deprive you of your piano lessons. Especially when you enjoy them so much."

There were four students: Evy, Meg, Emily, and of course, Alice. Although the other students paid, Evy was now allowed to attend at no charge since she had been the niece of the dear departed vicar.

Evy knew that Alice did not particularly like her. Alice blamed Evy for losing the chance to go up to Rookswood several afternoons each week to be companion to Arcilla. After all, Alice never ceased to remind Evy, *she* was the doctor's daughter. Though Evy thought her pallid and sullen, she considered herself quite pretty. Besides which, it was no secret that Alice dared to imagine herself romantically involved with Rogan Chantry. Emily and Meg would giggle about the girl's vanity.

"As if he'd ever look at her. He'll have someone special, like Lady Bancroft's daughter, Patricia. Have you seen Miss Patricia?" Meg asked Evy in a whisper.

Evy admitted she had not, nor did she wish to see another pretty girl romping about in fancy clothes and carrying on something awful in front of Rogan.

"She's very rich. She would be, of course; her parents are of the nobility, living in London. They even met Her Majesty at court. Patricia is thirteen now and wears gowns made in Paris. Her hair is auburn and she has what Tom calls forget-me-not blue eyes."

"Rogan is only a boy." Evy gave a sniff. "He is too young to marry."

"They make plans early for marriage among the nobility." Meg nodded, eyes wide and sober. "They even have someone chosen for Arcilla already."

"Oh, do not say so," Evy groaned.

"Indeed, so. Patricia's brother, Charles Bancroft."

"Pity the young man," Emily said.

"How do you know all this? About the Bancroft children I mean?" Evy had heard nothing of the sort from Mrs. Croft.

Meg shrugged. "Because Mum now works in the kitchen at Rookswood."

That appeared to explain everything from Meg's viewpoint.

Emily sighed. "If only I knew I was going to get a handsome husband, I'd be happy."

"Handsome! I should be happy if I get a husband at all," Meg said. "At least you're the blacksmith's daughter. Pa is a groom at the Rookswood stables."

"You'll marry Tom, Emily's brother." Evy patted her friend's hand.

"And you'll marry Derwent," Meg told Evy. "You're lucky. He's so handsome."

Evy's brows lifted. Derwent? Handsome?

Alice had finished her piano lesson and walked up. "You three are always whispering," she said crossly. "It's quite rude you know."

"So it is," Evy agreed, and stood, shaking out her skirts. It was time to start back to the rectory.

"We were talking about the squire's son." Meg's malicious tone made it clear she did not like Alice's superior ways of lecturing them. "Rogan's going to marry Miss Patricia Bancroft. *She's* rich and beautiful."

Alice's lips tightened. "Gossip…probably only from the kitchen of Rookswood. He'll marry whom he wishes to marry. He's very indepen- dent." She smoothed her strawberry blond hair with the palm of her hand. She looked at her fingernails with a secretive smile. "He talks to *me* all the time."

"Ta, *ta,*" Meg said, mimicking her lofty voice.

Alice fixed Evy with a cool stare. "It is quite unkind of you to have taken my place as Miss Arcilla's best friend."

"I have not been up to Rookswood yet. Really, Alice, you're being very unfair. Arcilla makes her own decisions as to whom she befriends. I had nothing at all to do with her choice."

Alice shrugged. "The doctor's daughter and the vicar's niece could be on the same social stratum, I suppose. But—"

"Always putting on airs." Emily shook her head. "You're really no better than the rest of us, Alice."

"That's not what my mum tells me. But never mind, both of you. Because now that the vicar has—well, now that he's not here any longer, Mum says Lady Camilla will ask me to return because I play the piano so well."

It was true that Alice was very good at the piano, and Evy longed to become as proficient. Alice was blessed to have Mrs. Tisdale for her mother, but Evy knew better about Alice being asked to return to Rookswood.

Emily looked at Evy and rolled her eyes, and Evy stifled a giggle. It vanished quickly enough, though, when Evy thought again about what she and Aunt Grace were to do.

Whatever was to be decided about the future, there was no question that they would need to find a new home soon.

Uncle Edmund had left Grace a small benefice, but Evy had learned the money would run out in the years ahead. The bishop in London had taken a sympathetic interest in their plight and written a letter to Grace, in which he told her that he would try to arrange something suitable for their sustenance. Grace wrote back that she preferred to find work in a household, perhaps in London.

Taking work in London loomed large in her aunt's thinking these days, when, on the wintry heels of change, the expected announcement arrived that the bishop had indeed awarded the St. Graves Parish to its curate, Mr. Brown. He had been faithful to Uncle Edmund, and, as Aunt Grace told her, it was fitting that he should become the new vicar.

"Your uncle would be pleased if he knew the position went to Mr. Brown. It will be good for Derwent, too, and ultimately for your future as well, Evy."

Evy understood what she meant. She was to marry Derwent.

Mr. Brown immediately offered to let them continue to live at the rectory for as long as they wished, but both he and Grace recognized the arrangement would not be wise. Her aunt declined. As she told Evy, Mr. Brown had lost his wife many years ago, after Derwent's birth, and it did not bode well for a widowed woman to be living in the same house with a widower.

"Besides, if we are to make a match between you and Derwent, we cannot have the two of you growing up in such close confines. You would soon begin looking upon one another as brother and sister."

Evy felt that way now. She had known Derwent all her life. The older she grew, the more difficult it became to imagine herself married to him. Her aunt assured her she would feel differently once she reached her teen years.

"Everything changes when you begin growing up. You will think Derwent handsome and wise."

Evy studied the quiet boy when they gathered for Sunday services the next day and wondered if such a miracle could happen. He was far from handsome, not that his appearance was of primary concern. A heart for God could supplant a handsome body. She thought this because her uncle had told her so. Evy hoped she would be wise enough one day to know this for herself.

Unfortunately, Derwent was not especially bright either, and that worried Evy. Although he was the son of the curate and so was expected to be interested in matters pertaining to the parish church, Derwent took more interest in hunting possum and rabbits and dreamed about searching for diamonds and gold in South Africa. He was quite good-natured, rather gullible about most things, and continued to look on Rogan Chantry with hero worship even though Rogan was a bit younger than he.

Perhaps Derwent would change?

Evy counted the years until she would turn fourteen, clearly expecting that she would wake up on that morning and find herself a new person, and Derwent—the fairy tale prince.

"I shall be taking the train into London to look for work."

Aunt Grace's words snatched Evy from her thoughts.

"Mrs. Croft has volunteered to look after you for the time I am away. I promise to return before Christmas."

Evy pondered this. "What kind of work will you seek?"

"Well, I was a governess before I married Edmund, so I can fall back on that. The difficulty will be in finding a family willing to take us both. We will make this a matter of prayer, Evy." Grace put her arms around her. "You are all I have left. It would not be good for either of us to be separated at this time."

Evy agreed and choked back her tears. What if she needed to live in an orphanage for the next five years? She asked the question that was uppermost in her mind, the one that was usually glossed over with indifference. "Aunt Grace, would not my father have had relatives? The Varleys, I mean? Someone we could turn to for help?"

Evy felt the familiar barrier slip between them. She guessed her aunt's response from the veiled look that came over her tired face.

"No, dear. I believe he had an older brother somewhere in the Cape, but we've never heard from him. He was quite a bit older than your father, so he may have departed this world by now. I believe he was a heavy drinker and a gambler."

Evy felt a rush of disappointment. "Oh…I see."

"Do not worry so. I shall find work. God is our Shepherd. He will provide. If not in London, then elsewhere. Your uncle had many friends and associates in the church. Perhaps the bishop will recommend me to some genteel family."

But Evy's troubled thoughts remained. "And my mother's family and yours?"

A cloud seemed to pass over her aunt's countenance, as though her memories were sad ones. "Our father died when Junia and I were children. I was thirteen and she was seven. There was no one else. Our mother—your grandmother, Victoria—died soon after Junia was born. Father never mentioned her family. When I was nineteen I worked as a nanny for the bishop's daughter in London while also caring for Junia. The bishop introduced me to Edmund, who was a young curate. Edmund and I married, and the bishop arranged for him to come to St. Graves. In due season he became its rector. That was many years ago." Her heavy sigh seemed to fill the room.

It was no use. Evy had heard most of this before. It was like knocking at the door of an empty house. Her aunt was never unkind about Evy's questions, but she was ever and always reluctant to talk freely. Perhaps Evy merely imagined that there was more to understand.

Before Aunt Grace left on the train for London, Evy overheard her talking with Vicar Brown. "We had such fine plans for her. Edmund wanted so much for her to attend music school in London. As you know, she loves the piano, and we both recognized her talent. To have become a music teacher would have suited her well. Now I wonder if I shall be able to manage it."

"These things can only be left to the Lord, Mrs. Havering. Surely God knew all this when He permitted the beloved vicar to meet with his tragic accident. In God's wisdom, what we now view as dark tragedies may be necessary for the final glorious design."

Evy eased the kitchen door shut, and behind her she heard Mrs. Croft sniff. Evy turned around to see the woman wiping her eyes with the edge of her apron. Her heart warmed toward Mrs. Croft. *She does actually care about us.* Rather awed at the thought, Evy walked up and put her arms around the woman's waist, and Mrs. Croft awkwardly patted her back. "There, there," she murmured, "there, there, Evy dear. It's all going to be all right. I daresay the future be brighter than any of us think now."

Evy and Mrs. Croft saw Aunt Grace off at the train depot.

Her aunt kissed Evy's cheek. "Good-bye, dear. Take good care of her, Mrs. Croft."

"Oh, I will indeed, Missus Grace," she said, holding the reins to the jingle tightly.

"And remember, Evy, study hard in Mr. Brown's classroom while I'm gone. It is even more urgent now to make good use of the three *R*s."

Evy blinked back tears. "I will, Aunt. Oh, good-bye, good-bye, and may God give you a wonderful post as governess."

She sat beside Mrs. Croft on the seat in the jingle watching her aunt wave as she boarded the train. A few minutes later the big steam engine pulled out of the way station, and the whistle pierced the cold morning air. Evy covered her ears. They watched the train leaving Grimston Way until it rounded the bend and was blocked from view by a stand of weathered oak trees.

The whistle continued to blow, growing fainter. Evy watched the boiler smoke on the horizon as stillness settled about her.

Finally Mrs. Croft flipped the reins, and the horse turned and started back toward the village rectory.

CHAPTER NINE

During the next few weeks life proceeded as normally as could be expected in such circumstances. Mr. Brown and some of the ladies in the village decorated the hall and church for the Christmas celebration, though the mood was anything but cheery. On the great table beside the host of inscribed names belonging to rectors of St. Graves Parish stood a Christmas bush in a pot. The decorated bush was an old tradition begun by the Cornish, and many in this area of England adopted the festive decoration instead of using Christmas trees. The bush had been sent down from the Chantry family with a hand-decorated card signed by the entire family, from Lady Camilla's elegant script to Arcilla's lop-sided handwriting. At the top of the card were the words *Merry Christmas.*

A few days before Aunt Grace's return Evy went with Derwent to the woods near the rectory to hunt for mistletoe and holly. She had spotted a large cluster of mistletoe in an oak tree, and Derwent shimmied up the trunk and onto a branch to reach it. When her basket was past half full he climbed down to rest, and they sat for a few minutes on a fallen log beside the dirt road. They agreed that after resting they would search for holly branches with red berries, then return to the rectory.

Derwent ran his fingers through his russet hair and looked at her. Red suddenly tinged his cheeks.

"Seems to me, if you go away to London to live, Miss Evy, I won't be seeing you anymore. Does it seem so to you, too?"

It did, but Evy tried not to think about it. Still, she couldn't keep her mind from traveling that path. What if she had to move to London? She would be taken away from her friends and from all she was comfortable with! Uncertainty was a constant companion as she wondered what would happen if she *did* move away. Would she and Derwent continue as friends, perhaps through letters? What a poor substitute for being with her lifelong friend!

She pushed aside these gloomy thoughts. "Oh, surely we will see one another. After all, you will be coming to London to attend divinity school in a few short years. And Aunt and I have so many friends in Grimston Way we could never simply turn our backs and disappear into the London throngs."

"Then you will come back and visit the rectory sometimes?"

Evy smoothed a tendril of her hair back into place, wondering why his question brought her a feeling of uneasiness. Perhaps because she noticed the hope in his eyes—a hope that appeared to question her more deeply than she was ready to answer.

"Quite often, I daresay. Aunt will see to that."

He cleared his throat. "I find myself hoping—"

A sudden thundering of hooves drew Evy's attention to the road, where she saw Rogan riding his horse. As usual he looked the squire's son, dressed handsomely in shiny polished boots, a neat hat sitting to one side of his head in a rather cocky manner. He looked surprised to see them sitting together on the log, and he rode up and took in the scene, noting the mistletoe in the basket at her feet. He studied Derwent, then looked at her, as though he had come to some conclusion.

"Is not that mistletoe?"

Evy stood quickly at Rogan's question and picked up her basket. "Yes. For the rectory hall."

"Mistletoe for the rectory hall?" He looked amused and then laughed. "I never thought of the rectory as a place for kissing."

"It's— It's not." Curse his mocking tone and the heat in her face! "It is simply—a decoration."

He held out his hand toward her. "I should like a piece of it, thank you."

Fighting the urge to throw the basket at him, Evy broke off a small twig with three leaves and handed it to him, eyes averted.

"Are you not going to ask me what I shall do with it?" Rogan's dark eyes were dancing.

"It's naught of my business."

Rogan looked at Derwent. "What do *you* do with this?" He waved the twig about, deliberately holding it over Evy's head.

Derwent turned pink, frowned, and shrugged. "Nothing."

"Nothing! I am disappointed in you."

Derwent looked at Evy. "What were you going to do with it, Evy?"

"Evy?" Rogan's tone showed his surprise. "Not *Miss* Evy, but just— Evy. Looks like I have interrupted a little rendezvous by the roadside, after all."

Derwent did not seem to know what to say. He stood and shoved his hands into his pockets, his gaze fixed on Rogan's purebred. Rogan leaned forward and patted the horse's muscled neck. Upon spying their picnic basket, he grinned.

"A little picnic. How charming. Shall I join you for lunch?" He swung down and appeared not to notice Evy's silence.

"Aye, help yourself, Master Rogan." Derwent went for the basket, all too willing to share. When Rogan smiled at Evy, she had the distinct impression he knew she did not want him to stay.

He sat down on the log beside Derwent, who opened the basket.

"Are you not you going to sit between us—Evy?" Rogan moved aside, providing a space.

Evy ignored him and pretended she had not noticed his using her first name. Why did he have to come along and spoil a perfectly lovely afternoon?

She walked over and stood across from them.

"Ah, my favorite!" Rogan seemed to be enjoying himself as he dug out a ham sandwich.

"Do you not get ham sandwiches up at Rookswood?" Evy crossed her arms and slanted him a glare. "I should think you could have any-thing your heart wished for."

"Of course"—he waved his hand as he talked around the sand-wich—"but I do not get to eat my lunch in Grimston Woods." He smiled. "I like picnics. Perhaps I shall have my own one day. I know of a special place on a hill. It's perfect."

"In Grimston Woods?" Derwent glanced about them.

"No. On Rookswood land. There is a grand view from the hill."

Derwent held out a second sandwich and an apple for Evy to choose. She knew he was hungry, so since Rogan was eating *her* sand-wich, she took the apple and bit into it. She nodded to Derwent. "You eat the sandwich."

"What fun," Rogan said, leaning back. "Maybe I shall decide to have a picnic of my own. Let me see... Whom shall I invite?" He looked at Evy, studying her.

"All your friends?"

At Derwent's suggestion, Rogan nodded. "Of course. That defi-nitely means you... What was your name?"

"Derwent."

He sounded so anxious to please the great Rogan that Evy wanted to stamp her foot.

"So it was. How stupid of me to forget my friends' names. Derwent Brown." He looked at Evy, his zesty dark eyes amused. "And Evy Varley. Let us think—where shall we have this picnic?" He hung his velvet hat on a twig above him and leaned back, watching Evy steadily as he ate.

"The hill you mentioned?"

"Maybe the crypt." Rogan ignored Derwent's idea. "Did I not say I would bring you there?" The look he leveled at Evy was replete with challenge. "Perhaps I will take you there after we eat."

What was he up to? He had never showed interest in either her or Derwent before now. A dart of apprehension shot through her secret plea-sure over the way he was noticing her. "It looks like rain this afternoon." She spoke quickly, hoping to cover how unsure she was of Rogan—and herself. "We had better return to the rectory soon, Derwent."

"Your aunt went to London, did she not?"

She met Rogan's questioning gaze head-on. "Yes. She will be back before Christmas."

"The crypt?" Derwent looked like a puppy promised a treat.

Rogan read the other boy's interest, and the smile that crossed his features was definitely smug. Clearly, he was enjoying how Evy's own friend was foiling her attempts to leave.

"Yes. My uncle's crypt. Henry Chantry is entombed there. I know all about the village gossip. They say he was *murdered.*"

Derwent stopped eating his sandwich and swallowed hard. "Murdered? I never heard about that."

"You would not," Rogan said meaningfully, "but the rector's niece has, have you not— *Evy?*"

"There is always talk." Rogan was beginning to irritate her in earnest.

He stood suddenly, wiping his hand on a napkin, still looking at her and Derwent. He caught up his hat and put it on. "We will go there now. I always have my way. Up, Derwent. Do not linger." He looked up at the sky and smiled. "Though rain it may, I would say we have at least two hours. That is still enough time."

Derwent was rushing, stuffing the picnic remains into the basket, anxious for the adventure with the future *Sir* Rogan. Evy, on the other hand, was far from pleased at the glint of mischief in Rogan's steady gaze. "I do not think—"

But Rogan had commandeered the moment, and Derwent was all too willing to follow him in whatever he wanted to do.

"Derwent, you can walk." Rogan nodded at the boy. "It is not that far. Evy and I will wait for you at Rookswood by the gate."

"Walk?" Derwent blinked.

Rogan's smile was tolerant. "You would not want to put the load of three on my excellent horse! It will be better if only Evy rides with me." He looked at her, his smile deepening. "You are not afraid to ride with me, are you?"

"Absolutely not," she said, though too forcefully. "Should I be?"

"Absolutely not," he repeated with that upturned smile of his.

Funny how she got the opposite impression from his words. "I will walk with Derwent."

Rogan's gaze narrowed, but before he could argue, Evy snatched her basket of mistletoe from below the tree and started up the dirt road toward Rookswood.

Just what was Rogan up to? Perhaps she ought to turn right around now and go back to the rectory. Yes, that was a good idea. If Rogan let Derwent ride with him on the horse, she would turn back to the rectory as soon as they were over the hill and out of sight.

But Rogan did not ride ahead, nor did he ask Derwent to ride with him. He brought the horse behind them allowing Evy and Derwent to lead the way.

Evy leaned close to Derwent. "Now, why is he doing this?"

"He is nice and friendly."

"I am not so sure."

Derwent's eyes shone, so impressed was he. "This will be quite merry, Evy. I always wanted to see a crypt, especially the Chantrys'."

"Whatever *for*, Derwent? Rogan Chantry will never make friends with you the way you hope." She tried to make the whispered observation as kind as she could, but Derwent was unaffected.

"Oh, I know that, but I'd sure like to hear about how his uncle found gold and diamonds in South Africa. Hunted rhinos, too. Heard there's a big rhino head and a Boer whip in his uncle's rooms."

Evy grimaced. "What uncle was that?"

"Oh…I don't know which one…the one that died here when we were just babies. He came from South Africa."

"Rogan Chantry is so arrogant he will never tell you about the family gold and diamonds."

But Derwent would not be turned aside. "Come on, Miss Evy, he was polite enough to invite us. Besides, I want to see the gargoyles again."

"You know you are afraid of them." She glanced over her shoulder. Rogan was a little way behind them, his posture in the saddle erect but relaxed. He certainly looked at home astride his horse.

The huge gate leading to Rookswood stood open between two ancient stone arches, which allowed them to look through what appeared an exceedingly long avenue that bent around some dark, wet fir trees.

"Sometimes I climb that tree behind us and crane my neck just so," Derwent confided in a low voice. "Then I can just glimpse the mansion. It's all gray, with three stories to it."

Evy looked toward the chestnut tree he was pointing out. "Uncle Edmund always said the mansion has leaded windowpanes, thick walls, gables, and all sorts of interesting porticoes and pillars. And he said there's a great iron-studded door built in the days of the Norman knights. There is a splendid polished suit of armor near the staircase, too, and even Norman swords on one wall." Evy couldn't help a little surge of pride at her knowledge.

Derwent's pale eyes bulged. "Knight's armor? Oh, to see *that*."

Evy too wished to see it, though she'd never admit it to Derwent. Or to Rogan. Better to change the subject so she didn't stir Derwent's hopes. "Christmas is the time to be invited to the mansion. Those who went caroling there last Christmas with Uncle Edmund got to see grand decorations. There were lots of candles adorning the baronial hall, and the carolers got cups of mulberry punch and sweet cakes. Mrs. Croft's family all came home with bags of tasty tidbits to eat."

Derwent gulped. "I remember. We were sick. Worst luck. How come Mrs. Croft's relatives get to partake and we don't?"

"Because they clean the rooms—so many you can't count them, so Mrs. Croft says. Everyone who works there got a gift, too."

Derwent looked as though he might have traded his position as son of the vicar to be the son of the chief stableman. Evy tried to imagine how each of the squire's children had their own big room with servants looking after them. There was a governess, an intelligent woman indeed, but she was soon to retire. So Mrs. Croft said that Squire was looking for just the right woman to be the new governess to his lovely Miss Arcilla. The old governess had served the previous generation of Chantrys and was to be given a small cottage on the estate where she would live out her final days with a comfortable pension. As for Rogan and Parnell, they had a male tutor, a young man who had studied in Paris and could speak several languages. He was preparing the two boys to be sent away to an exclusive school in London.

Evy looked up at the familiar gargoyles guarding the gate with their stone pitchforks. The rainwater still dripped from their mouths, and they looked like slobbering fiends. Uncle Edmund had told her they were medieval. Evy shuddered as she stared up at their leering faces. They seemed to challenge her, as though they knew something about her that she did not. Remembering the stranger in the dark woods, she trembled as the chill wind blew against her frock.

"Reminds me of the walls of Jericho," she told Derwent.

"Them gargoyles…"

She grimaced. "If I owned Rookswood, I would have angels instead."

"But it would be a pity to destroy them. They are ancient."

"You just say that because anything bearing the Chantry name leaves you awestruck," she half scolded. "I don't think you really like gargoyles."

Derwent's sheepish smile told Evy she was right. She knew he was afraid of the dark and prone to believe in the foolish tales of ghosts.

"Are you not afraid of the gargoyles, too?" Derwent's wide-eyed gaze searched her face.

She looked at the statues again. "They are ugly and—evil looking."

Rogan came up to them, leading his horse by the reins. "Those beastly things are all over Rookswood."

Evy studied him out of the corner of her eye. "When will you be joining Parnell in school in London?"

"Soon. Except I will not go to Oxford. I want to attend a special geological school."

That piqued Derwent's interest. "So you can better find gold and diamonds in South Africa, I suppose."

"Yes. What of you?" Rogan eyed the other boy. "I suppose you will go to divinity school?"

Derwent shoved his hands in his pockets. "It's expected."

"Can you shoot straight?"

Evy frowned. Why was Rogan drilling Derwent like this?

Derwent shook his head. "No, but I'd sure like to—"

"Can you ride well?"

"No, never been on a horse."

"That is what I thought."

At Rogan's bored dismissal, Evy spoke up. "Some *ordinary* people do not have the opportunity to do such things."

Rogan's mouth curved. "Such things as the Chantrys do, you mean?" He gave his horse to a boy who ran up to lead it away, then turned toward them. Evy didn't quite trust his smile. After all, he'd never shown such interest in her before, and she did not know how to respond. Perhaps it would be wiser if she did not.

Apparently Rogan realized she was not going to answer. "Follow me."

Derwent was quick on Rogan's heels, but Evy held back. "How far is it?"

"Not far." Rogan paused and looked back at her, that same irritating, amused glint in his eyes. He stopped when she merely stood there. He folded his arms across his chest. "So all your brave talk at the cemetery with old Hiram was boast. You *are* just like Arcilla and all her girlfriends." He seemed bored by the thought.

Evy's eyes narrowed and she set her mouth and followed. With another infuriating smile, Rogan led the way into what looked to her like a huge garden.

"Aye"—Derwent let the word out on a breath of awe—"it's beastly big, I daresay."

"Big enough," Rogan said.

"Too big." Evy knew she was being contrary, but she didn't care. "There's little reason for anyone to have such a big garden."

"Unless you are a Chantry."

Evy could have boxed Derwent's ears for his defense of Rogan.

"Squire can have anything he wants—and so can his family."

"I usually get what I want," Rogan agreed cheerfully.

"Must be like getting Christmas pudding every day," Derwent said with a sigh in his voice.

"And roast goose, too."

"I would not want Christmas pudding every day." Evy set her jaw. "It would soon become tiring. Then Christmas would seem like any ordinary day."

"But on Christmas we get a lot of other special things," Rogan parried. "So Christmas is never boring." He smiled at her. "You will have to spend Christmas at Rookswood sometime."

Evy said nothing to that. She watched Derwent following Rogan as though he were a prince. Rogan seemed to accept the other boy's sudden devotion as merely proper. That only reinforced Evy's determination to resist Rogan's arrogance—although, if she was honest with herself, she had to admit she could easily have gone to the other extreme and thought him special, too. In fact, he was quite out of the ordinary. She liked his dark, shiny hair much better than Derwent's russet hair. And those unusual dark eyes seemed to sparkle with a challenge of warmth. His smile was charming, yet it was mischievous at times, making him mysterious and a little dangerous—all of which was most intriguing.

Evy always knew what to expect from Derwent, so someone a little unpredictable seemed...appealing. *But I'm not silly like Alice or the rest of them. I shall never swoon for Rogan Chantry!*

The huge lawn was bounded by tall hedges enclosing wide flower beds. Trees behind the hedges made it completely private. Rogan whistled.

They walked through the garden for perhaps five minutes until passing through an arbor between two sections of a neatly trimmed hedge. They entered a courtyard enclosed on three sides with a high stone wall and three small gates. All three appeared to be locked, and Evy's imagination could only wonder at what might lie beyond them. At the end of the courtyard she saw what reminded her of an elevated stage with a roof. There were low, wide flat steps that went up. Below were tables and chairs, but they were old and it looked as if they had not been used for years.

"What is that?" Derwent pointed.

"Oh, we do not use this court any longer. In my great-grandfather's day it was for summer fetes, which I think quite boring. There would be an orchestra, and the girls would sit and listen to the music. The boys were supposed to come and keep them company. The best part was the feasting. That is the only part I would enjoy. Unless the girls were very nice to look at, of course. There aren't pretty girls in Grimston Way." But he looked over at Evy with a little smile.

"There is Evy."

Evy blushed at Derwent's innocent assertion. She turned away, steeling herself for Rogan's disagreement.

Oddly enough, it never came.

"They would roast an entire pig and ox on spits in that pit beyond the gate." Rogan pointed to the western gate. "There were big barrels of ale and wine, too. It became a very noisy celebration after the young girls went home…where they belonged."

Evy cast him a glance and saw his calculated smile. *He is trying to goad me.*

"Revelry, that is what it was." Evy nodded. "And debauchery, no less. Like typical lords, barons—and squires ruling over the fiefdom."

She expected him to get angry, but he looked pleased. "Not lords, barons, and squires, but earls and dukes. Now, admit it. You would be as impressed as my sister if a duke took your hand and walked you among the trees—perhaps with a bit of mistletoe."

"I would not. And if the duke tried to kiss me, I would slap him."

He tilted his head and regarded her, but he looked doubtful—and that worried her.

Evy turned away and shaded her eyes, turning her attention on the stage while Rogan gave a small push to Derwent's shoulder and gestured to the northern gate near the stage.

"That way to the mausoleum."

They walked away, leaving Evy standing there. Evidently Rogan was showing her that he did not care whether she followed or not. As she set down her basket she understood his message: She could go just so far in assuming a manner of equality. Any further and she would meet with his disapproval. She pressed her lips together. If he had imposed such boundaries at his young age, what would he be like at eighteen?

Not that she would ever find out. Nor did she want to!

Well, it was now up to her to either fall in line with his game or turn around and go back to the rectory. She stood there a moment watching Rogan open the gate and pass through without a glance over his shoulder. Derwent was at his heels, following, the happy puppy.

Why do I want to see a musty old mausoleum, anyway? She would not be Rogan Chantry's adoring subject. She was well aware that Alice would have followed him, and so might all the other girls, but—

Evy set her chin, whirled about, and ran back toward Rookswood gate. She would show Rogan he could not control her as he did everyone else. She would show him that Evy Varley was not like all the other girls in Grimston Way.

It took her ten minutes to find the front gate, for she had made a wrong turn and then had to retrace her steps. Rookswood was like a village all its own, she thought, looking around through the line of tall trees shadowing the flagstone walkway that circled around to the front of the estate. And now that Rogan was not there, she could allow her awe to come forth. She had never even glimpsed the mansion yet. It must be a good distance from the front grounds.

She did not see the boy who had been at the gate, so he must have taken Rogan's horse to the stables.

At last she found the gate, and with a lift to her chin, she left Rookswood—telling herself she was not the least bit sorry she had walked away.

It didn't take long for regret to sidle up alongside Evy. Her steps on the dirt road slowed as she made her way toward the rectory. How could she have let herself miss out on such a great adventure? No doubt Rogan would never ask her to accompany him on another one. *You have too much pride, Evy Varley.*

It was not until she went through the vicarage gate into the church-yard that she realized she had left her basket of mistletoe sitting in the Rookswood courtyard outside the mausoleum. *I hope Derwent notices and brings it back with him.*

But Derwent did not return with the basket—in fact, when Evy and Mrs. Croft went to the rectory to fix supper for Vicar Brown, Derwent had not shown up at all.

"A bit odd, seeing as how it's his favorite meal of mutton pie and cider," Mrs. Croft said to her.

Now I'll need to confess about going to Rookswood. Evy bit her lip and glanced from Vicar Brown, who was scowling at the dining room table, to Mrs. Croft, who was clearly worried.

"Odd, I say, Vicar. Derwent is not one to be missing his meals. He asked me just this morning what was for supper tonight, and when I told him, he was very pleased. And you know how he loves his cider."

"Yes, yes, very unusual. I wonder where that boy of mine could be?" The vicar's eyes glossed over the empty seat at the table and alighted on Evy, who sat with her hands folded in her lap, wishing she could vanish into thin air. His eyes fixed on her, and he smiled indulgently.

"Now, now, little Evy, maybe you have seen Derwent today?"

"Of course you did, Evy." Mrs. Croft smiled. "They went together to the woods to pick mistletoe and holly, Vicar." She frowned and looked at Evy. "Can't say I've seen where you put it though. Did you and Derwent not get it?"

"Um…"

Vicar Brown waited, his brows rising a notch, and Mrs. Croft continued to hold her hands under her apron as though it were a warming muff. When Evy fell silent, Vicar Brown's white brows climbed even higher.

"Yes, Evy?"

Bother. There was no way out of it. *Drat Derwent anyway!* "Yes. We went to the woods. We gathered the greenery. I…left it behind and… and"—she bit her lip and her eyes went down to her empty plate— "Derwent went back to find it."

"Ah, well, then, that explains it." Vicar Brown's brow unfurrowed. "He will soon be here, Mrs. Croft. Go ahead and serve supper before it gets cold."

"Aye, and I'll warm him a plateful when he returns."

Each bit of food Evy took seemed to turn to sawdust in her throat. She'd lied—and to the vicar!

After Vicar Brown went to his study, Evy slid from her chair. She had to find Derwent!

"Not feeling well, Evy?" Mrs. Croft eyed her when she cleared the table and saw her food hardly touched.

"No, Mrs. Croft. I shall go to my room if it is all right with you."

"Yes, you run along now. No doubt it's from traipsing about the woods in all this damp weather. I'll be up later with warm milk."

Mrs. Croft turned to leave the dining room, and Evy was edging toward the hall to find her cloak when there was a loud rap on the front door. Evy's heart jumped to her throat. Mrs. Croft went to answer it.

Evy heard voices, and when she entered the hall she recognized some of the fancy dressed footmen in hats and cloaks from Rookswood. They held bright lanterns.

A tall, slim young man with fair hair and skin stepped forward to speak to Vicar Brown, who had come out to see who was at the door.

"Good evening, Vicar."

"Hello, Charles, what brings you here tonight? Come in, come in, have some cider."

Evy hung back. She recognized the young man from Rookswood as Mr. Charles Whipple, the tutor who had come from London especially to teach Rogan.

"I cannot stay, sir. It is about your son, Derwent. He is quite beside himself about seeing Henry Chantry's ghost. We, er, have him outside now… We've taken the liberty of giving him something to quiet him down a little."

"Good grief! Derwent thinks he saw a ghost? What perfect nonsense. I shall indeed deal with him about this, you can be certain."

Evy winced.

"It might be best if you went gently on the boy, Vicar Brown. He is most upset."

"Such poppycock. A ghost! I shall have none of that devilish nonsense in my son. Where is he?"

"In the coach with Master Rogan. The squire's son happened to hear him calling for help at Rookswood and rescued him."

"Rookswood? You mean"—the vicar paled—"Derwent was up at the estate?"

"Yes, he was exploring the cemetery and wound up in the family mausoleum. The wind blew the door shut. He panicked in the darkness and could not get it open again. Master Rogan found him an hour ago. He's been looking after the boy ever since. They are together now." The tutor stepped aside from the open doorway and looked down toward the Chantry coach, parked in front of the rectory. The flames in the lanterns beside the coach doors were flickering.

Evy's cheeks burned and her hands were cold and clammy. Why that scamp, Rogan Chantry! He locked Derwent in the mausoleum, with all those old family coffins. What a dreadful boy he was! She had half a mind to tell on him.

She watched the coachman open the door, and Rogan stepped out, decked in his fancy coat with gold buttons and matching blue hat with a feather in it. He helped Derwent down, and holding to his arm walked him with what had to be feigned gentleness and concern up the path to the front door.

Derwent looked sick, his wide eyes going from his father to Mrs. Croft. His red hair was damp and drooping. Rogan looked calm and grave. He released Derwent, who wobbled toward Mrs. Croft.

"My, word! Why—he *has* seen himself a ghost."

"Nonsense!" Mr. Brown's tone was as stiff as his back. "I shall speak with you later, Derwent. Go to your room at once."

"Yes, Father." He looked anxious to get away. Mrs. Croft went with him, and Evy was willing to bet the woman could hardly wait to hear what the boy would tell her. She could imagine the wild tale that would grow in Grimston Way through the years. In another generation the old ghost story of Master Henry Chantry would increase by leaps and bounds.

Rogan removed his hat and bowed to acknowledge Evy, but not before she saw the slight smile he wore. "Miss Evy."

"Master Rogan, how can I thank you for helping my son?" At the vicar's expression of warm gratitude, Rogan inclined his head. "It was all my pleasure, Vicar." He glanced toward Evy. "Fortunately, Derwent was not caught inside very long." Rogan stepped over the threshold into the hall—clearly he was not anxious to leave. Left with little choice, Mr. Whipple came inside and removed his hat.

"Please, come in." The vicar gestured toward the drawing room. "Would you care for cider or tea, gentlemen?"

"Thank you, Vicar."

Evy stared hard at Rogan. *He can be as fancy in his manners as one would like, but it is a sham.* And yet for all her irritation, she could not deny the spark of excitement at Rogan's presence there.

When the vicar led the way, and Tutor Whipple followed, Rogan held back and turned to Evy. He started to speak but saw that the door was open and that the two serving men were standing with Mr. Bixby, the footman, by the coach. Rogan reached up and closed the door. He leaned against it and grinned, arms folded.

"I think you are horrid!" Evy stamped a foot.

"Can I help it if your beau is a bit of a coward, besides a bore?"

"Derwent is *not* my beau."

"He was only in there ten minutes, and he nearly spooked himself into a tizzy."

It was true that Derwent could work himself up into an excited state, but—ten minutes? She eyed Rogan. "Have you no heart?"

"Depends." He smiled.

"You know very well how superstitious the villagers are."

"He should know better. Is he not the vicar's son?"

"He is gullible."

"Granted." He looked to the ceiling, as though it were infinitely more interesting than their current topic of conversation. "I should think you would have more sense than to fall for a youngster like him."

"I have not fallen for him. He is a friend. A very dear one. As for being but a youngster—as you put it—he is a year older than you."

"One would hardly realize that." He studied her for a moment. "So you ran away from me."

A strange spark of excitement danced across her arms at the warm challenge in his tone. She tried to sound as bored as he did when discussing Derwent.

"I have no interest in being locked inside your family mausoleum."

The corners of his mouth turned upward. "I was not going to lock *you* inside. I was angry when you ran away, so I locked Derwent in to show you what a clod he is."

"So you *did* lock him in."

He placed hand on heart and bowed. "I confess to my warped sense of humor, Miss Varley."

"I shall tell the vicar—and your tutor."

His gaze narrowed. "I would not do that if I were you. They will never believe you."

"They will."

"My word against yours? Never. In their eyes I can do no wrong." He smiled. "So you'd best be wary."

Evy wanted to throw something at him. "So you admit you can get by with anything just because you are Sir Lyle's son."

He leaned there, watching her, but she thought his amusement grew somewhat subdued. "I would be lying if I said no."

"You are forgetting"—she glanced again toward the drawing room—"that it is my word *and* Derwent's."

That smile again. "No. I have convinced Derwent that the wind blew the door shut and jammed it. It took me ten agonizing minutes to get it open."

Evy felt her mouth drop open. What a fib! "He believes that?"

"I told him so." He smiled.

"You are worse than I thought. He believes you only because he is overawed by you. He thinks that giving him a few minutes of your time is a courtesy."

"There. You see? He does not think I am so beastly as you say."

"Because he trusted you."

"And you do not."

"I would never trust you now."

"Never is a long time."

"Not long enough."

"Oh very well, so I admit I took advantage of him a bit." He shoved away from the door, brushing the lapel of his coat as though to erase the incident. "He is rather dumb, you know."

"And to think he *likes* you."

For the first time her words appeared to have stung his conscience, if only briefly. "Very well. I shall be a good boy just for you and apologize."

Her brows lifted. "To me?"

"You are offended, are you not?"

"Yes, for Derwent's sake."

"What a waste!"

Evy stiffened. "You need not apologize to me, but to Derwent. And then confess the truth to the vicar and those at Rookswood you got all riled up over this, including your tutor."

Rogan touched hand to his forehead and groaned. "Heaven forbid. Anything but confession to the vicar."

"He is a nice man. He will likely accept your conduct as a mistaken jest and let it all pass with a subdued smile. That is the only thing we poor villagers can do to the Chantrys."

He tipped his head to one side, and his smile turned wry. "I cannot oblige you. You demand too much. I will not don sackcloth and ashes for anyone." With that, he straightened. "And if I were you, miss, I'd not be foolish enough to accuse me. As I said, I will deny it with great vigor. My word will always prevail over yours or Derwent's."

She felt even more frustration with herself than she did with Rogan. How could she have allowed herself to think for even a moment that he would comply with her wishes? "So you expect this to remain a little secret between us, is that it?"

"Yes, if you wish to put it that way."

For a moment he looked very young as he stood there, a flicker of uncertainty in those hooded eyes, his arms folded, a dark curl falling to his forehead.

"I make no promise to keep your secret." At her stiff words, he eyed her, saying nothing.

She knew she ought to turn and walk away, but she did not. They stood there, looking at each other.

Rogan broke the silence at last. "I think you will, actually. You could have told the vicar everything before now. Why didn't you?"

She had no answer. Footsteps sounded, rescuing her. Immediately Rogan became the perfectly mannered young gentleman. He pushed the lock of hair from his forehead and, hat in hand, put on a smooth expression. By the time his tutor appeared to see what was keeping him in the hall, he was definitely the future Sir Rogan.

He was deceptive and polished, and Derwent, in comparison, was an innocent child. Evy shuddered to think what this scoundrel was going to be like as an adult!

"Coming, Master Rogan?" Tutor Whipple asked.

"I have changed my mind about the cider. I think I shall go back to the coach. I sense that Derwent's ordeal has affected me more than I first realized."

Rogan opened the heavy door. He wore a slight smile as he looked at Evy, and then with a final bow of his head, he went out onto the porch.

"Good night." She forced the words through stiff lips.

"*Au revoir,*" came his low murmur.

Somehow Evy thought he had actually enjoyed the standoff between them. He found it entertaining that she refused to crumple at his feet.

And yet he had warned her too. It was her word against his. When it came to public opinion, she would never win against him. And when he decided he wanted something, he would persist until he got it.

Though she could not explain why, that thought sent a shiver down her spine.

CHAPTER TEN

When Aunt Grace returned to Grimston Way, she did not immediately discuss with Evy what had transpired in London. Several days passed by before she came to Evy's room and suggested they take a walk together into the village.

It was a chilly but otherwise pleasant afternoon, with the sun shining in a grayish-blue sky and the branches empty of the warm golds and reds of autumn. December holly smiled its wintry bloom with flame-colored berries amid waxy green leaves.

Donned in matching hooded capes, they might have been mother and daughter out on an afternoon stroll. Evy glanced at her aunt. She was still an attractive lady, and young enough to remarry. If only Vicar Brown were not so old and gray. But it seemed there were no acceptable widowers or bachelors in Grimston Way. Farmer Gilford had no wife, but his rheumatism was such that his knees were knobby, and he walked bowlegged.

"Will we be moving away to London?"

Her aunt shook her head. "Not yet. We will need more patience."

Then that was the reason she had not discussed the matter sooner. "You did not get the post you wished?"

"I went to several interviews, one arranged by the bishop, which appeared at first to be quite hopeful. Alas," she smiled, spreading her palms, "it did not turn out as hoped. Ah, well. We will trust and wait."

Evy watched her, concerned, and noticed her aunt hesitate.

"I was not what they were looking for in a governess," her aunt explained. "Lady Mildren wanted someone older."

"Was it also because you asked that I stay in the house with you?"

"Oh, that," Aunt Grace said too quickly and placed her hand on Evy's arm. "Perhaps it had a small effect on the outcome. Things will work out in due time. We will rest our need with God. He knows our situation. He has good plans. Bishop will also continue to do what he can to find me a post. In the meantime, I shall try my hand at sewing. Lady Camilla has been talking to Miss Hildegard, the seamstress at Rookswood. Miss Hildegard has kindly suggested she could use a little help now and then." She smiled. "So you see, we will not starve in the streets."

Aunt Grace spoke lightly enough, yet Evy could see she was burdened. How like her to try to put a good face on her disappointment. Evy admired her so, and her own conscience was smitten over her deceptive behavior where the vicar and Derwent were concerned.

"Aunt, I feel ashamed about…withholding the truth from Vicar Brown." She paused on the road, and they faced each other. The breeze tossed their capes. A few clouds blew in and scuttled across the wintry sky.

"It concerns Derwent and the episode at Rookswood mausoleum." Evy forced the truth out. "I suppose by now the vicar told you what happened?" Of course, Evy knew that he had—as far as he knew the truth. She had heard them talking.

"Yes. It is all over the village."

Evy saw an odd look on Aunt Grace's features. Had her aunt already suspected her dishonesty?

"Would you like to tell me about it?"

Evy would not, but knew she must if ever she would be free of the burden. She told Aunt Grace what happened when she and Derwent went in search of mistletoe, fully expecting to see her growing look of disapproval. She was heartened when her aunt revealed no shock. If Evy were telling her tale to Alice Tisdale, she would have behaved as though it were a scandal in need of a town meeting.

"Thank you for telling me."

"I should loathe it if my silence about this caused any excessive difficulties for the vicar."

"I will see to the matter. Derwent has already told his father everything, including how you were with him when the squire's son took both of you to Rookswood."

"But Vicar never spoke to me about it."

She smiled briefly and they walked on. "No. He was waiting for you to tell the truth. He was assured you would once I returned home."

"Oh dear… I suppose I shall need to go to him, too."

"Yes. And he will surely accept your apology."

Evy nodded. This was so humiliating. *And it is all Rogan's fault.* No… She could not blame him for her own response. It would have been much easier to have simply told the truth to begin with.

"Derwent believes the door to the mausoleum was jammed. The squire's son convinced him the wind must have blown it shut."

Her aunt kept walking. "And you do not think it was the wind?"

Evy drew in a breath. "No."

"You were not there, Evy. It is your word against Master Rogan's. We must understand that the Chantrys have special privileges accorded to their position."

"Yes. I understand that." And one of those privileges was that their word was considered law. *More's the pity.*

"I am not suggesting such privileges are right, but it has been that way for centuries, and I suspect it will remain so for centuries more."

Evy had no doubt.

"I think," her aunt said, "that we may need to dismiss this behavior as a boyish prank and let the matter die down of its own accord. Master Rogan did return to let Derwent out. If he were a really cruel boy, he might have left him trapped there all night."

Evy shuddered. "I suppose. He did say it was only around ten minutes, but he also said he did it deliberately."

"Did he? Curious… I wonder why. He did not need to tell you."

"No. I think he had not intended to. I have tried to tell Derwent that Rogan locked him inside, but he's not willing to accept that the squire's son would do such a thing."

Evy knew why, too. Rogan had been friendly to Derwent after the crypt incident. That was unusual because she knew that he thought Derwent *unstimulating*. Rogan normally would not choose him as a companion. Both Rogan and Parnell had many friends their own age in the nobility, who shared the same mind-set, abilities, and background. They were accustomed to involving themselves in all manner of exciting activities with well-educated people. Yet Derwent just a few days ago told her with a ringing voice that Master Rogan had brought him to the Rookswood stables and allowed him to choose a horse. And Rogan had brought him to his father's armory closet and had shown him how to handle a rifle so they could go on a rabbit hunt.

"I even saw the suit of armor!"

Evy could still see the way Derwent's eyes had shone.

"I think it wise that you not try to convince Derwent otherwise, Evy. He will need to make up his own mind about Master Rogan. And if you speak against him, Derwent may think you are merely envious that you were not asked to go riding with them. They seem to be getting on as well as anyone in Rogan's position can with peasantry, and that is what we villagers are considered. Not merely by the Chantrys, mind you. These distinctions reign throughout English nobility, as they do also in France and many European countries."

"In France the peasants overthrew the nobility."

"Ah, the Reign of Terror. Thankfully the peasant class of England holds no such vicious vendetta against the royal family. We are not as hotly volatile as the French peasants were."

Evy agreed. "*We* are cool and calm."

Aunt Grace laughed. "We hope. Then again, we are not treated as badly as were the peasant class in France at that time."

Evy felt a great respect and affection in her heart for the beloved Queen Victoria. She imagined herself, sword in hand, defending Her Majesty from a horde of angry British peasants storming St. James Palace.

That image was replaced by another, but this one was real. How surprised she had been when Rogan came riding up to the rectory to see Derwent two days after the mausoleum incident. Evy had been picking Michaelmas daisies with Mrs. Croft and pretended not to see him. Rogan had climbed down from his horse and talked with Derwent, who was weeding the garden. Then Rogan gave something to Derwent. Derwent brought it over to her.

"Fancy you forgot this," Derwent said with a grin.

It was the basket of mistletoe. Evy glanced from the now wilted greens across the yard to Rogan, but he behaved as though she were not there. He was either too friendly or not friendly at all. Of course, she *had* criticized him the night he had brought Derwent back to the rectory. Now he most likely was reminding her of her rightful place.

"Wager you don't know what Master Rogan just offered me." Derwent looked positively giddy.

"Another look inside the mausoleum?"

"Evy!" scolded Mrs. Croft.

Derwent grinned. "No, goose. A horse from Squire's stables."

"A...horse?"

"For riding. And hunting! Wager you'd never thought to see Derwent Brown going hunting with the future squire."

"No, I never did."

"You'd best cease using the word *wager*, Derwent. Your father is set against gambling," Mrs. Croft warned. "And you be careful how you handle them rifles, young man, lest you go shootin' your foot—or Master Rogan's."

Apparently the adventure turned out well. They had returned safely, and Rogan had made certain Derwent was home in time for supper. Certainly he was on his best behavior. Had her rebuke stung his conscience after all?

Derwent brought home a dead rabbit for the sexton to make a favorite stew, which he remembered from childhood (and which Mrs. Croft loathed and would not cook). Derwent confessed he was not sure whether he had shot the rabbit or Master Rogan had. At any rate the sexton, grinning, had been very pleased.

Recently Derwent was walking around with his head higher and his shoulders straighter than ever before, proud that he should have made friends with Rogan Chantry, who, he said, "rides better and shoots straighter than anyone else in Grimston Way."

"Derwent's unexpected friendship with the squire's son seems to be doing him much good," Aunt Grace agreed as they continued their walk. "He is gaining more confidence."

"Maybe, but Rogan orders Derwent about mercilessly."

Her aunt angled her a glance. "Derwent does not appear to mind. He has been a lonely boy most of his life. Not even the other village boys liked him."

"That is true." Now, of course, the other boys were treating Derwent differently. They gathered around to ask about his latest adventure with the squire's son, and could he use his *influence* with Master Rogan to allow them also to accompany Derwent on the next hunting adventure? Since the friendship had begun, it was as though Rogan had raised his scepter and knighted Derwent Brown.

Of course, Rogan's friendliness would not last. Rogan was to be sent away to school in London in February, and that would be the end of it. She hoped Derwent would not be too disappointed when the princely horse turned into a pumpkin at precisely the hour Rogan left Grimston Way.

So the incident at the Chantry mausoleum was to be dismissed as a boyish prank. She believed her aunt said this because she understood that Evy's persistence would hurt her more than it would teach Rogan a lesson. It was just as Rogan had warned her that evening in the front hall: No one in the village in his right mind would win anything by butting heads with the Chantry family.

Her aunt was right. Better to leave things as they were. Evy could just imagine Alice whispering, "Fancy that Evy just trying to get the squire's son into trouble. She's tattling about him because he won't pay her the slightest bit of attention is what I say. My *mum* says…"

Yes, she could imagine what her *mum* would say. Mrs. Tisdale, too, had influence in the village. Recently she had been trying to win Lady

Camilla Brewster with flattery. So that was that. Evy would not go up against Rogan Chantry.

He has won, but I will be even more cautious of him now. She remembered what Mrs. Croft had once warned her. Evy could not forget the words: "Every decent girl in Grimston Way had better watch out. Squire's two sons can do no wrong, so says Sir Lyle. So if there's any mischief to happen, who do you think will be blamed, eh?"

Yes, she would beware indeed.

CHAPTER ELEVEN

Christmas Day arrived chilly and damp, but the sky was clear of mist. The eve before, villagers from all over Grimston Way had continued their tradition of visiting the parish to enjoy platters filled with ginger cookies, mince pies, and a special cider that Mrs. Croft made each year. This time they also came to call on the new vicar and his son and to pay their respects to dear Edmund's widow and niece.

Evy found it a little odd to hear Christmas wishes and condolences in the same breath, but then, nothing seemed normal these past months. Her heart ached for Uncle Edmund, and she knew Aunt Grace grieved as well. Despite the loss, though, her aunt was determined not to spoil the holy day with her own sorrows.

"At Christmas we should not think only of ourselves, but we should also remember our Savior's birth and how it means good news of great joy for all people."

On Christmas Day, Aunt Grace gave Evy a light blue, barred muslin dress trimmed with eyelet lace, assuredly her prettiest and most adult frock ever—although her aunt admitted that the style was a bit behind the present fashion. There was even a pair of heeled slippers, and Evy admitted she looked quite grown-up. She threw her arms around her aunt. "Why, this is not the same dress you have been working on in the evenings!"

"So I fooled you. Well, good, that was my intention. And here is the one I was working on. Now you have two."

Evy, with the help of Mrs. Croft, had made her aunt a lace bookmark and a small reading pillow with tassels. The pillow had a small pocket in which to tuck away her book and reading spectacles.

There was a mince pie sent over from Mrs. Matheson and Tom, who had tried to be nice to Evy. Emily had wrapped up one of her favorite books of poems and gave it to Evy. Everyone was thoughtful and kind. But perhaps the biggest surprise of all came when the Chantry carriage pulled up in front of the rectory and Mr. Bixby got out, sporting a new shiny hat and looking quite proud of it. He came to their door, arms laden with gifts.

Evy and Aunt Grace each received a new hooded cloak and mittens from Lady Camilla. There was a box of bonbons from Switzerland, fruit-shaped marzipan from London, and tins of various cakes and puddings. And Derwent, to his delighted shock and everyone's surprise, had been sent hunting apparatus from Rogan Chantry.

It would be Evy's last Christmas dinner in the rectory, and they had bought a fat hen from Farmer Gilford so that there could be a feast, with Vicar Brown and Derwent as their guests.

"He shall come down like rain upon mown grass," Aunt Grace read from the Psalms before their meal.

The day became a very special Christmas, one Evy knew she would always look back on with fondness and sorrow mingled. They had known the sharpness of God's pruning, but God's kindness could also be depended upon to send soft, healing showers in this new season of their lives. Tomorrow they would set out once more on a different road, but Evy knew wherever that journey might lead, God would be faithful. Amid their loss had come blessing too.

A few days after the New Year of 1891 began, Evy came home one afternoon from her music lesson at Mrs. Tisdale's and noticed something different about Aunt Grace. Her aunt stood before the window, her small pince-nez clipped to the bridge of her nose, contemplating a letter with some uncertainty—yet also with obvious excitement. A fire glowed in the fireplace where water sizzled on the hob. Evy set her bag and cape down on the wooden bench and went to prepare some tea.

Finally she could stand it no longer. "Aunt Grace, what has happened?"

Her aunt looked up, startled. "Hmm? Oh yes. Yes, everything is going quite well, dear. How was your lesson?"

"It was wonderful. Mrs. Tisdale says I'm nearly as good as her Alice. Meg and Emily are all thumbs, she says. She becomes quite irritated with them because they have calluses on their hands and their finger-nails are soiled."

"I hope she did not say such things to their faces."

"No." Evy looked at her own fingernails and was pleased they were clean and filed neatly. But Meg and Emily could not help it. They worked so hard helping their poor families…

"Is that a letter from the London bishop, Aunt Grace?"

"No. It is from Rookswood."

Rookswood!

"Something unexpected has happened." Her aunt's eyes glowed. "Lady Camilla writes me that Arcilla needs a governess. Miss Hortense has retired to the servant's cottage, which is no surprise. Her retirement has been expected for some time."

Evy swallowed. Could that possibly mean…?

Aunt Grace's eyes twinkled. "Lady Camilla wishes to procure me for that position."

Evy caught her breath and stared at her aunt. "Are you going to accept?"

"I will be meeting with Lady Camilla on Wednesday afternoon." Aunt Grace touched her hair. "I will need to wash and arrange it nicely," she murmured to herself. "And I shall wear my gray organdy dress. If all goes as expected, Evy, we shall be moving up to Rookswood. We shall have two adjoining rooms on the third floor, vacated by Miss Hortense. I know that will please you."

Evy clapped her palms together, laughing. "Oh, how exciting! Living inside that splendid house. What would Uncle think if he knew?"

Aunt Grace's face lost some of its glow, and her eyes became grave. "I wonder."

Evy could have bitten back her words. Even so, what choice did Aunt Grace have but to go? Evy clasped her hands together. Her aunt, the new governess at Rookswood! It appeared to be the perfect solution to their present need and would even allow them to remain in the village of Grimston Way, among friends. Their prayers were answered.

And yet… Evy watched her aunt's face and was nearly certain that despite her own enthusiasm for the coveted position, Aunt Grace seemed troubled. It could not be over becoming a governess, since she already desired to do so in London. Nor could it be the wage, since it was known that Sir Lyle paid well. So what was it about going to Rookswood that caused Aunt Grace anxiety?

Evy soothed herself by believing that perhaps it was just the difficulty of being governess to spoiled Arcilla. It was well known that Miss Hortense had struggled for years, first with Parnell and Rogan, and then with Arcilla who was far worse than her brothers.

Aunt Grace handed Evy Lady Camilla's letter to read for herself. The silver lettering on the rich stationery bore the insignia of the Chantry family, and Evy fingered the linen texture of the paper with a degree of awe.

It was known among the village, wrote Lady Camilla, that Mrs. Havering was properly educated for the task of becoming Miss Arcilla's new governess. Grace was a woman of upstanding character and devotional discipline, having produced such a well-behaved young girl as Evy Varley. Therefore she appeared to be the "godsend" Lady Camilla had been praying for to teach Arcilla, who was not handling the loss of her mother well. Added to that grief was the absence of her father, Sir Lyle, still away in South Africa. Then there was the retirement of Miss Hortense, who had been like a grandmother to Arcilla. Lady Camilla remained in charge, and she was confident that offering Mrs. Havering the post, which would include room and board for herself and Evy, plus a decent wage, would please Sir Lyle.

The letter continued: *As we discussed before the vicar's untimely death, it comes to my attention that the calming influence of your niece as a companion for Arcilla will also benefit Evy herself, as she can attend the schoolroom here at Rookswood. The piano lessons would continue under the doctor's wife, Mrs. Tisdale, who has already agreed to hold the music lessons here, bringing her own daughter, Alice. And Evy would further benefit by joining Arcilla in riding lessons and other nurturing events, all of which would stand Evy in good stead in society.*

Arcilla would have another loss to face too. Rogan would be leaving soon to attend a private boys' academy in London for the next few years, and then he would go on to graduate university. Arcilla was especially close to Rogan, and so her brother's departure would certainly sadden her. Since he would be leaving in late February, it was imperative to have Mrs. Havering and Evy at Rookswood beginning the first week in February. That would leave the month of January for Mrs. Havering to conclude her affairs at the rectory.

Lady Camilla went on to write that she was quite sure that Vicar Brown would do all he could to aid them in moving to Rookswood. Camilla would also send two of her servants to help bring their belongings to the suite of rooms they would share on the third floor.

Lastly, Mrs. Havering's influence was deemed to be beneficial as she would be bringing with her the experience of having been a beloved and respected vicar's wife. The teachings of the church were to be used generously during the school day, for Miss Arcilla "is such a willful girl."

Evy frowned. Maybe her new life at Rookswood would not be as thrilling as she thought. She would need to get along with Arcilla regularly! To be her companion for a few hours a week was one thing, but living at Rookswood was likely to be another matter entirely. And while moving to the estate house would certainly provide adventure, Evy couldn't help but feel anxious about interacting with the other Chantrys either. Parnell remained a mystery. Perhaps she need not worry about him, who, being the eldest, would look on anyone younger with disdain—especially a girl from the rectory. Rogan, on the other hand…

Evy grimaced, then comforted herself with the thought that even he would soon be gone. And who was to say that she would even see him before he departed for London? He had, after all, been ignoring her ever since the incident over Derwent at the family mausoleum.

Perhaps that was best, since their previous two meetings had convinced her to tread with great caution where he was concerned. She was a little afraid of his dominant disposition, not knowing what to expect from him or how far his intentions would take him. Although locking Derwent in the mausoleum had been a prank, what else could he get by with if he chose to? She was sure Rogan's arrogance convinced him that he deserved to be obeyed just because he was a Chantry, and that she and everyone else should treat him with complete deference.

And that was one thing Evy knew she simply would not do.

Evy would always remember the day when Mr. Bixby arrived at the rectory in the shiny Chantry coach to bring her and Aunt Grace to Rookswood. As they departed that February for the last time, even the weather mirrored her emotions: temperamental, as though it could not decide whether to turn sunny or cloudy.

She and Aunt Grace had packed the last of their belongings the evening before. Their trunks and a few special pieces of furniture, going back to the youthful beginnings of her aunt's marriage to Uncle Edmund, had already been sent over to Rookswood two days before in a wagonette. So today she and Aunt Grace carried only a small portmanteau.

Vicar Brown, Derwent, and Mrs. Croft stood out in front of the rectory garden gate to see them off. Mrs. Croft tearfully reminded Evy that it wasn't as if they'd never see each other again, "The walk down from Rookswood to the rectory, and coming to my cottage for tea, isn't far at all." Evy agreed, trying to dispel the nagging sadness that all goodbyes tend to bring when what was shall never be again.

The coach wound its way up the road bordering Grimston Woods, and the estate gate came into view. Evy heard the eerie squabbling of the rooks seeking a perch in the gray branches.

Evy sat across from her aunt, who wore her best gray linen dress with matching hat and gloves. Evy, too, was appropriately clothed in her new dress with its frills. It made her feel quite adult and special. All her other dresses were so plain, or, as her aunt said, *sensible*. How Evy had grown to dislike *sensible*. Such dresses lasted too long—until Evy outgrew them—and most were out of fashion, too. Then the frock was taken apart, and the best cloth was recut into a blouse or petticoat. The dresses were all in the darker shades: blues, browns, and even one black dress, which she did not like.

Arcilla's dresses were always bright colors with lots of ruffles, bows, gold and silver threading, some with pearl buttons and trimmed in velvet. They weren't sensible at all. But then, Arcilla was not the one who had to worry about washing them. Some people could afford not to be sensible.

The Chantry horses trotted through the tall, arched gateway beneath overhanging oak branches. Harley, the old gatekeeper, stood near the small rose-covered cottage he occupied and lifted his cap before shutting the gate after them. He was Mrs. Croft's cousin and had been gatekeeper for as long as Evy could remember.

Once inside, the road changed from dirt to small cobbles. Evy looked upon mounds of green turf that gently rolled toward a horizon of trees on the perimeter of more private woods. Was that where Rogan had taken Derwent to hunt? The land went even farther back beyond the woods to farmland cultivated by workers employed by the squire.

The shrubbery along the lawns was meticulously manicured, the handiwork of Mr. Tibbs, Rookswood's main gardener. Not far from the entry gate was a narrower lane that she remembered well. It was the route along which Rogan had taken her and Derwent to the huge garden near the Chantry family mausoleum.

They drove the long S-shaped carriageway to the mansion, rimmed on one side with white birch and on the other with elm. When the horses at last came to the end of the S, Mr. Bixby stopped. Evy stared at the biggest house she had ever seen. And the most forbidding.

Why, it's more like a castle than a house!

A Chantry footman came to open the coach door, and Aunt Grace stepped down to the carriage block. Evy followed, unable to pull her gaze from the crenelated towers and turrets. She had learned from Uncle Edmund during her history lessons that they were from the twelfth century, as was the thick, high wall surrounding the main grounds.

What excitement she'd brought with her mingled with dread as gargoyles with bulging eyes and evil scowls glared at her. Evy imagined soldiers dumping boiling pitch down the castle's machicolations while fiery arrows flew from the tower heights to invading enemies scaling makeshift ladders against the walls. In one lesson at the rectory the curate had told of an early Chantry family fleeing into the woods and hiding for weeks while the enemy took over the castle. Someone in the family had been beheaded, but she could not remember who. Evy shuddered.

There was more than one door to Rookswood, and they were all studded with massive iron nails. Many windows included leaded panes, and Aunt Grace pointed out the intricate Gothic tracery on the stone mullions and arched transoms, looking so delicate in contrast to the grotesque faces of the stained gargoyle rainspouts.

No wonder Rogan behaved as he did. It was quite a change to leave Rookswood with its renowned family history and ride down to the humble village with its farm bungalows.

"What a...wondrous castle," murmured Evy as she followed Aunt Grace from the coach up stone steps that rose to a walled courtyard.

"Yes, indeed. Did you know that the first Lord Chantry went with King Richard to the Holy Land to fight the Saracen?"

"Yes, Vicar Brown taught us last year that Lord Chantry was killed in Jerusalem."

"I believe the present squire keeps the sword in the armory room. Perhaps one day when we study history we shall have a tour of the weaponry."

Mrs. Wetherly, the Chantrys' housekeeper, wearing a black bombazine dress and stiff white apron and cap, greeted them in the upper courtyard. Evy recalled that she was a nice, no-nonsense woman who attended Sunday services. Evy wondered what *she* thought of the nosy Lizzie, as well as the host of Mrs. Croft's relatives.

"Welcome to Rookswood, Mrs. Havering," she said. "Lady Camilla will be meeting with you after luncheon in the library. She didn't sleep well last night and hasn't risen yet. I daresay her health troubles her… Do come this way, and I'll show you and Evy right up to your rooms."

"Thank you," said Aunt Grace. "Evy?"

But a fluttering caught her eye, and she looked up to see Arcilla peering down at her from one of the windows. With gold hair plaited and wearing a maroon satin dress, she might have passed for a medieval princess trapped in a castle. Then the girl stuck out her tongue and wrinkled her nose.

Princess, indeed. More like the toad!

Evy finally followed her aunt and Mrs. Wetherly inside, where she came to a stunned halt in the huge baronial hall, adorned with a magnificent chandelier in its vaulted ceiling. She figured the hall to run at least fifty feet with windows on either side. Sunlight did not penetrate the leaded panes well, though, which made for lurking shadows in the far corners and increased Evy's sense of doom.

Drawing a steadying breath, Evy gazed about her. Crusader weapons lined the wall, and she tried not to see the empty eye sockets of the giant suit of armor at the base of the staircase.

Mrs. Wetherly chattered about balls and other musical entertainments that were held here in the great hall and remarked on how beautiful it was when decorated with Christmas candles and holly berries. "Not that there's likely to be any entertainment soon," she said, "not with Lady Honoria's death. And too, the master's been away, and his niece by marriage, Lady Camilla, isn't well enough at present. When Miss Arcilla grows a little older I'm certain we'll have many balls."

Evy lingered, trying to calm her palpitating heart. She ran her palm along the polished wood banister, feeling the hideous bulging eyes of the same style gargoyles carved so intricately there. Uncle Edmund had told her the carvings were done by superstitious people living in other generations who feared devils and thought to frighten them away by surrounding themselves with monsters equally as frightening. The more religious, he said, filled their abodes with carved relics and religious symbols.

She continued up the stairs, feeling the soles of her shoes sink into the thick garnet carpet. The color reminded her of the diamond-encircled ring she had seen on Lady Camilla's hand. She looked up to the gallery where the housekeeper and Aunt Grace now paused. Flickering candlelight glimmered and tossed shadows all around her. Evy took a deep breath and stopped. Foreboding drifted downward in the silent atmosphere and seemed to rest upon her shoulders.

"Evy?" came Aunt Grace's voice, seemingly from far away.

Evy shook her head, hoping to dispel her alarm, and quickened her steps to join them in the gallery. At least a half-dozen family portraits lined the wall. Evy tried to pick out which austere face would most likely be the *murdered* Henry Chantry. It was difficult. They all wore a faintly disdainful expression, even the women, but she finally settled on a piratical looking man with dark hair, mustache, arched brows, and a smirk loitering about his lips—*a rather cruel mouth,* she thought. *Rogan has some of his blood all right, except he's more charming and handsomer.* That had to be Master Henry.

She shivered, now with a strange excitement. Then motion in the opposite end of the long gallery caught her eye. She turned her head. No one was there. But she *had* seen something… She was sure of it. She stared. It was probably Rogan, trying to frighten her—

Just then, a man stepped through the archway and regarded her evenly. At first she thought it was the man she had met in Grimston Woods, but this was a stranger. He remained in the shadows, yet she could see that he had a black eye patch and wore a short-clipped beard. Certainly he was not a servant. His bearing was too proud for that, and his wardrobe was of the same expensive quality as Rogan's.

Aunt Grace and Mrs. Wetherly had left the gallery, and Evy could hear their fading voices. But she felt transfixed. His face was lean and hard and very brown…just like the stranger's in the woods. The man walked forward and stopped a short distance away. His good eye remained fixed upon her. A strange expression flickered across his face as he took in Evy's eyes and hair.

She could stand it no longer. Evy fled up the next flight of stairs after Aunt Grace and Mrs. Wetherly.

The man must be a guest, some important person in the nobility from London. Why had he stared at her like that? Almost as if he knew her!

Evy tried to concentrate on the housekeeper's words. Mrs. Wetherly explained that the nursery wing and big schoolroom were located on the third floor. Here, also, would be their rooms, not two rooms as first thought, but *three*. They had belonged to the retiring governess, Miss Hortense, who had first come to Rookswood with Lady Honoria after she married Sir Lyle in Cape Town. Miss Hortense had stayed with Honoria to nurse their children, Parnell, Rogan, and Arcilla. Honoria's death, Mrs. Wetherly said, had nearly undone the poor governess. "She loved Lady Honoria like her own daughter."

Mrs. Wetherly left them at their rooms, saying that she would have tea sent up at a half past the hour.

Their quarters proved quite pleasant and dispelled some of Evy's discomfort. A small parlor with a hearth and two adjoining bedrooms welcomed them. Behind a blue curtain was a private powder closet, holding a hipbath, a vanity cupboard, and a white dressing table with a large mirror. In the parlor were two chairs and a settee upholstered in cream brocade with pink roses, several good quality mahogany tables, shaded lanterns, and the secretary desk with matching chair that was sent over from the rectory.

Evy's own room was quite small but cozy. She liked the floor-to-midwall window that looked down on a courtyard. She was up high enough to have quite a nice view, though the woods on the other side of the wall looked ominous.

The four-poster bed was smaller than the one in her aunt's room, and though it did not have filmy curtains that could be drawn closed, she approved of the blue quilted coverlet and thick frilled pillows. There was a white dressing table with a fringed ottoman, also in blue, a hard-backed chair, and a small desk with an oil lamp and writing materials. The floor was not carpeted, but there were several area rugs to warm bare feet.

Only one painting adorned the walls: a young girl in a long blue dress, her golden hair undone, running through a meadow. Evy thought it enchanting at first glance, but the longer she looked the more uncertain she became. A dark forest waited on the other side of the meadow, and Evy could not be sure if the girl ran to escape something or to meet someone she cared about. Perhaps if Evy studied the woods more closely she would see someone standing in the shadows waiting for her.

Evy turned quickly away, trying to smile at her fancies.

Some minutes later, when her things were put away, she joined her aunt in the sitting room again. Aunt Grace smiled at her. "Well here we are, Evy. Our new home. In everything give thanks, and so we shall."

Aunt Grace took Evy's hands in her own. "Father God, we thank You for our new home. Encourage us to learn and accept Your purposes for us while we live here. Help us not to be too shy in showing others how much we trust You with the sudden changes in our lives. And remind us to be content with such things as we have, knowing You have promised in Your Word to never leave us or forsake us. We ask in our Savior's dear name, amen."

A few minutes later there was a tap on the door, and the maid, Lizzie, Mrs. Croft's niece, brought in the tea tray. There were cakes and frosted ginger biscuits sent up from the kitchen as a welcome gift by the cook, Beatrice.

"Welcome to Rookswood, Mrs. Havering, Miss Evy."

"Thank you, Lizzie. Do give our thanks to Beatrice in the kitchen."

"Yes, Mrs. Havering." The girl hesitated, as though she wanted to talk.

Aunt Grace remained noncommittal and expressionless, and Evy knew that she was showing the young woman she would not be engaging in servant gossip. Lizzie seemed to understand and quickly departed.

Later that afternoon Aunt Grace would meet with her charge, Miss Arcilla Chantry. Right at the moment, their unknown future seemed to Evy less than comforting indeed.

CHAPTER TWELVE

Evy's meeting with Arcilla was not going well.

The girl was sitting on the window seat that looked out over the tops of the tall beech trees. She stood, as social graces required, when Mrs. Wetherly introduced her to Aunt Grace, though of course Arcilla was well aware of who she was. Arcilla had been attending the church for years. Evy thought the girl looked pale and docile—though she knew Arcilla was certainly not the latter.

Most likely Arcilla's momentary good behavior could be attributed to ill health over her mother's death or perhaps to her brothers' orders that she mind her manners. There was little doubt that Arcilla set great store by Parnell and Rogan, that she cared for their opinions as much as she did Lady Camilla's.

"Hello, Mrs. Havering." The stilted words were spoken as though she had been forced to practice their simplicity. "I am glad you have come to Rookswood." After a pause her eyes flickered, and it seemed her thoughts fought their way to the forefront to master her demeanor. "Not that *anyone* can ever fill the shoes of Miss Hortense. She was our nurse and governess all our lives—me, Rogan, and Parnell."

Her challenge was clear. If Aunt Grace expected to take Miss Hortense's place easily, there would be resistance.

Mrs. Wetherly made a throaty sound of disapproval, but Aunt Grace remained poised and confident. "I am sure you are right, Arcilla, and I certainly have no intention of taking her place in your heart. I am here to teach you on certain subjects until your father sends you to a private school in London."

"I shall *not* go to London. I shall go to *France,* Mrs. Havering."

"Miss Arcilla, you forget your manners!" Mrs. Wetherly's tone was firm. "Your father has not decided where you should be sent to school, and since that is at least three years away—"

"It is Aunt Camilla who will decide, and she has already promised that I can go to France!"

"Mrs. Havering, I must apologize for—"

Aunt Grace gestured airily with her hand. "No harm is done, Mrs. Wetherly." She turned and smiled at the girl, whose cheeks now showed two bright spots of temperamental pink. "I am sure Miss Arcilla and I shall come to peaceable terms."

The housekeeper was clearly flustered. Evy pressed her lips together. Arcilla was apparently quite used to getting the best of the poor woman. Mrs. Wetherly said, "Are you going to show Mrs. Havering and her niece, Evy, around the nursery wing?"

"No. I wish to be excused. I am not feeling well again." Without waiting for permission from either Mrs. Wetherly or Aunt Grace, Arcilla rose and started to leave. On her way to the door her gaze momentarily fixed on Evy, and she stopped in her tracks. A little smirk touched her rosebud mouth as she brushed past and went out, not even troubling to close the door. Her voice was heard in the hall: "Aunt Camilla! Aunt Camilla!"

Most likely she was running to Lady Camilla with an outburst of dislike for her new governess and the demand that Miss Hortense come back.

Mrs. Wetherly plucked at her crisp white apron. "That girl can be positively horrid at times. She's grown worse since her mother passed away. And Sir Lyle leaving for Capetown so soon afterward worsened matters. She needs a strong hand, and I'm afraid she's not getting it. Lady Camilla means well, but Arcilla is such a strong-willed girl that she dances circles around her aunt."

"I understand, Mrs. Wetherly. These matters cannot be rushed. I have hopes that in time she and I shall cooperate."

"Well, I certainly do hope so," the housekeeper said doubtfully. "The only one she tends to listen to is her brother. The world rises and sets upon him by her estimation."

"Master Parnell?"

"Oh no. Master Rogan."

Aunt Grace's brows arched.

Mrs. Wetherly shook her head. "Now that he's leaving next week, there won't be any of us who can calm her down." She wrung her hands.

It was telling that Rogan could calm his sister's emotions, or would even try. Evy would not have thought it in keeping with his self-indulgent behavior.

"Then I shall have a talk with Master Rogan later, Mrs. Wetherly," Aunt Grace said. "Perhaps he and I can work out something between us about Arcilla before he leaves for London."

"Oh, I am sure he would be cooperative."

Evy held back a snort at that. It wouldn't do well to offend Mrs. Wetherly, who clearly thought well of Rogan. The woman proceeded to show Aunt Grace about the large schoolroom. Evy glanced around, growing more dubious about their new home as the minutes passed. *It will not be easy here.* A sudden longing to be back at the rectory, far away from Arcilla, swept over her.

The room was bright and sunny with many windows and had the smell of books, paper, ink, and blackboard chalk. There were three desks with inkwells, two of which had been pushed aside. They must have once belonged to Parnell and Rogan.

Evy pondered which one she would use. Going to school each day with Arcilla sounded most unpleasant. She did not need to wonder which unused desk had belonged to whom. Both Parnell and Rogan had carved their bold initials into the wood, along with the date when they had left the charge of their tutor. Rogan's was just the month before, when Mr. Whipple had departed from Rookswood. Evidently carving dates was a family tradition, because there were other initials there too, from earlier generations of Chantry children. Evy found it curiously interesting to see the initials *H. C.,* etched by Henry Chantry, the man who had died violently here at Rookswood.

There were numbers of books stashed neatly in the walled bookcase, and a large world globe stood on a table. A world map was pinned to a wall, along with a smaller one of Africa. Someone had placed colored pins with tiny flags at Capetown and Kimberly. There was a blackboard behind the teacher's large desk, and Evy knew her aunt would make good use of it.

Some old toys were grouped on one side of the hardwood floor, apparently from when the Chantry children had been small. Evy looked at the red painted rocking horse and worn teddy bears that must have belonged to Arcilla, and checkers and a card game. The toy wooden soldiers and wooden swords must have belonged to the boys. She could imagine the many bouts and tussles that the two brothers must have gotten into when playing knights, while Arcilla played princess.

The door opened, and Lizzie came in apologizing for the interruption. "Lady Camilla wishes to see Mrs. Havering about the schedule she had in mind for Arcilla."

Mrs. Wetherly soon left to carry on her own work, and Aunt Grace asked Evy to go to their rooms. "Our trunks should be there by now. You can begin putting your things away."

Evy entered the sitting room and saw that the two trunks had been brought up by one of the footmen. There were no locks on the trunk lids, and one of them lay wide open. Lizzie Croft must have thought she was to help unpack. Evy saw that it was her own trunk that stood open, her things rifled through. Who would dare!

She closed the door and went to her trunk, looking down. She stooped to her knees to gather a dress and petticoat, when from the corner of her eye she saw someone standing. She turned her head quickly. Arcilla was framed in the doorway of Evy's bedroom, arms folded, a bored look on her pretty face.

"I do not like your dresses."

Hot words rushed to her lips, but she swallowed them back and managed a stiff reply. "Since you won't be wearing them, you needn't concern yourself."

"They are very dull. More suited for Meg."

Meg's mum worked in the Rookswood kitchen, and her pa worked in the stables. Evy struggled to hold her temper.

"Not everyone can have their own dressmaker." Evy directed a pointed look at Arcilla's satiny frock with its full sleeves, narrow cuffs, and popular braid hem. "But you are a bit young to dress so grown-up."

"I am *not!*" Arcilla fell onto the divan and drew her legs up beneath the knife-pleated underskirt. "I am quite grown-up for my age. I cannot wait to go to France to school. I shall have a dancing master and new gowns."

Evy gathered her frocks together. "It was very rude of you to go through my trunk. You had no right."

Arcilla shrugged. "You have nothing of interest to me."

"Then perhaps you ought to go to your own room."

Arcilla stared at her, mouth open, then laughed. "This whole *house* is mine."

"Not these three rooms. My aunt is awarded them for her work here, which will be quite hard, now that she is *your* governess."

Arcilla's eyes flashed, and for a moment Evy thought the girl would pounce on her like an angry cat, but though her hands formed fists and her mouth tightened, Arcilla controlled herself. Suddenly she grimaced what Evy could only surmise was meant as a smile or a truce. She scanned her curiously.

"You are not like Alice, are you?"

"I am Evy Varley."

"I shall overlook your bad manners." Arcilla sniffed. "I would have expected something much better from the niece of the vicar."

"And I would have expected much better from the daughter of the squire. Excuse me—I must hang my frocks in my wardrobe." Evy gathered them up and went into her room. She began hanging them up in the small wardrobe, fully expecting Arcilla to flounce away, but the irritating girl came into the bedroom and gathered herself onto the middle of the bed, watching Evy, amusement sparkling in her eyes. Evy would have liked to order her out of her room, but she could not do so without Arcilla making a fuss about it to Lady Camilla. And Evy did not want to make trouble for Aunt Grace.

Doing her best to ignore her intruder, Evy came to the bottom of her trunk, to a few games and some books that she loved to read. Arcilla looked at them and wrinkled her nose. "How can you waste time reading?"

"It's not a waste of time. Books teach and broaden your under-standing of the world and other people. This one is Jane Austen's *Pride and Prejudice;* it teaches so much about the life of the upper class and their snobbery."

"It looks thick and full of words."

Evy laughed. "It is."

"You should come to my room. I have so many things to occupy my time, and so many dresses that Aunt Camilla orders Mrs. Wetherly to give my old ones away to the poor each Christmas."

"Then you have lots of reasons to thank God."

Arcilla sighed, and her smile turned sour. "That's just what Rogan said you would be like."

So Rogan had told Arcilla about her? How…interesting. "What did he say?"

Arcilla shrugged and wrapped a curl around her finger. "Oh, that you were disapproving and bossy. Always looking down your religious nose at everyone else."

Evy stared, surprised that he would have said such a thing. What shocked her even more was how the words stung. Had he actually put it that way? "I do not think I am any of those things."

"Rogan's right. He is always right. I am disappointed you came." She leaned back against the pillows. "I hoped you might be fun. Flirt with the boys and things like that. We might have fun together if you were different. But you are boring. An old stick-in-the-mud. But maybe not as trying as Alice Tisdale. That old stuffy sock! She actually thinks she will end up marrying Rogan, imagine!" She giggled. "He cannot bear the sight of her. Says she practically throws herself at him."

"He seems to have little good to say about anyone except himself."

"Well, he did not have anything good to say about *you* or that foolish boy, Derwent Brown."

"Perhaps your brother has nothing good to say because he feels guilty for locking the vicar's son in the crypt."

Arcilla shrugged, smoothing her puffed sleeves. "If he got himself locked in, it was his own fault. I hear Derwent is quite gullible."

"It was *not* his fault. He was deliberately locked in."

"Rogan is always right."

"No, he is not."

"He *is!* I am going to tell my aunt what you said about Rogan." She climbed from the bed and marched from the room.

So much for not making trouble. Heavy of heart and spirit, Evy finished her unpacking.

The incident did not die there. Evy mentioned the unhappy encounter to Aunt Grace, who in turn spoke of it to Lady Camilla. Soon afterward Arcilla was called downstairs to the library to meet with her aunt, who apparently told her that she did not have rights to the three rooms belonging to the new governess and her niece, and that Arcilla must not forget her upbringing. She must knock before entering, and preferably she was not to go there at all without being invited. There was no reason that Arcilla should feel upset, since she had access by right to the entire mansion belonging to the family.

Evy saw Arcilla again around four o'clock, when Aunt Grace called her into the schoolroom to inform her when classes would begin. "Tomorrow morning at eight o'clock."

Aunt Grace went to get her teaching desk ready, and Arcilla said to Evy in a low voice, "You can *have* those old rooms. What do I care? The whole mansion still belongs to *me*."

"No, it does not."

"It does!"

"It belongs to your father. Your brothers will inherit before you do. I have heard that Rogan will most likely inherit Rookswood."

"*Master* Rogan to you."

"No doubt *you* will be married off to someone and sent far away."

Arcilla glared. "I will not go to that horrid South Africa. I shall stay in England and marry Charles."

Evy had no idea who Charles was, but she almost felt sorry for Arcilla. The idea that she might be sent to the Cape had brought her genuine consternation.

"Africa is a boring place full of naked savages," Arcilla said. "Rogan showed me pictures of them. They have nothing on but a loincloth and run around with spears."

"I am sure you will marry whoever your father decides is appropriate."

"Evy."

She jumped at Aunt Grace's stern voice.

"We will not discuss personal matters concerning Miss Arcilla and her father."

"Yes, Aunt."

Arcilla shot her a look of triumph.

Later, Aunt Grace went out of her way to warn her against contesting Arcilla. "You must not expect Miss Arcilla or her brothers, when they are home, to treat you as your village friends do in the rectory. I am employed by their father, Sir Lyle. We must not forget we are considered help."

"I know that, but she is so *proud.*"

"You must concentrate on your own manners and pride, dear. You are not responsible for Miss Arcilla's behavior, but your own."

"Am I considered hired help, too?"

Her aunt hesitated, and Evy detected a moment of silence that might have been construed as sadness. "No, not yet."

Not yet.

"You are my niece. Nevertheless, you must be respectful to everyone at Rookswood and do as you are told."

❧   ❧   ❧

The days passed, and Evy settled into her new routine, as did Arcilla. Arcilla's manner had changed a little for the better. Much to Evy's surprise, Aunt Grace said she had spoken to Rogan, who in turn had a talk with his sister.

Evy did not see Rogan until the day before he left for school in London. It was during teatime when Lizzie brought up a tray for Arcilla. The girl asked Evy to stay and join her after Aunt Grace was called to visit Lady Camilla about Arcilla's recreation in the afternoons.

The tray was set nicely with jam tarts and milky tea. "You pour," Arcilla told Evy.

She did so, noticing the lovely chinaware cups with their delicate pink blossoms. "They come from far away in China"—Arcilla lifted a cup to her lips—"and do not take that blueberry tart; its my favorite."

"You are the hostess. You are supposed to allow your guest to choose first."

Arcilla laughed and took the blueberry. "You should know me better by now." She bit into it and rolled her eyes. Evy couldn't hold back a smile at the girl's enjoyment of her prize.

The door opened, and Rogan walked in. He leaned back against the door and watched them for a moment. For some reason Evy believed he was amused to see her here at Rookswood. She assumed it was because he was thinking of her as an employee, which in his way of seeing things would make him feel superior.

"Oh, Rogan"—Arcilla's lip drooped—"I am so sad you are leaving tomorrow. It will be so boring around here."

He walked up and lifted the plate of tarts, deciding which one he wanted. "You will have Miss Evy to keep you company." He chose one, then sat down near the window seat, stretching his legs in front of him.

"Evy is too religious to be fun." Arcilla wrinkled her pert nose. "Now if it was only Patricia—"

"If it was Patricia, you both would get into trouble and send poor Aunt to bed with a headache. You can learn from Miss Evy."

Arcilla laughed. Evy thought that if *she* had said that to Arcilla, the girl would have puffed up with offense.

Evy ate her apple tart and sipped her sweet tea in silence, aware of Rogan's presence, while Arcilla chatted constantly with her brother. He listened, making comments now and then, and all but ignored Evy. He was dressed in rich clothes as usual, with an almost bluish-white shirt that buttoned in the back according to the newest style. His ebony hair was wavy, and though Evy pretended to ignore him also, she was as stimulated by his personality as his sister was. His dark eyes glittered as though he held some secret.

"What do you think of the old vicar's niece living here at Rookswood?" Mischief peeked from Arcilla's gaze as she glanced from Rogan to Evy. Evy remained silent, looking steadily at her own teacup.

"You are the one who requested she come visit you in the afternoons," Rogan told his sister. "What do you think of her?"

Evy bit her lip. Was she but a commodity at scrutiny for the buyer?

"I have not made up my mind, and now I have dear Evy every day in school," Arcilla said with a mock sigh.

"You wanted her to come, and you know it, so stop being silly."

Arcilla looked first at her brother and then at Evy. "I suppose having her for company is better than being alone until I'm sent to school in France."

"If you do not do your studies, no school will want you." He looked at Evy. "I will wager Miss Evy knows her lessons every morning. She will soon show you up, Arcilla."

Arcilla flounced in her chair. "I'm sure I don't care at all. I do not intend to do anything when I grow up except dance at balls and have fun in London."

"Sounds positively wasteful," Rogan said.

Arcilla laughed. "*You* danced with Patricia at Christmas."

"Because I had no choice."

"Parnell's sweet on her too. You had better make Patricia happy, or Parnell will marry her instead. Then you will not get Heathfriar.

You know you want Heathfriar very badly because of Lord William's thoroughbreds."

Evy tried not to let her avid curiosity show. She turned to Arcilla, determined to change the subject. "Once lessons are done in the mornings, your afternoons are free, at least. I have things I must do for the rest of the day too."

"Like helping out at the rectory," Rogan said with a smile. "I suppose you and Derwent have a good time together."

"Derwent." Arcilla made a wearied face. "He is such an uninteresting boy."

"He is a *fine* boy." Evy couldn't quite keep the heat from her tone— or her cheeks. "*He* honors his father."

"Why should he not? His father is the vicar. He has no choice." Arcilla yawned.

"He has a free will, the same as you and the others."

"Always protecting little Derwent." Rogan tossed the last bit of his tart into his mouth.

"When she marries him, she will have to do the same," Arcilla teased. "And all their children will have curly red hair and freckles and become vicars."

"At least Derwent reads the Bible." Evy glared at Rogan.

"There you have it!" He sat forward with a grin. "The vicar's niece cannot *wait* to marry Derwent Brown."

"Oh, spare me," Arcilla cried. "A fate worse than death, if you ask me."

"You need not worry." Evy set her cup down. She stood with as much dignity as she could summon. "I must go now. I need to clean my room."

Arcilla giggled as though she had said the funniest thing in the world. "Oh, Evy, you are so perfectly the studious little girl from the rectory! 'I need to clean my room.'" She laughed again.

Rogan stood. "You cannot leave yet."

"My afternoons are my own." Evy faced him.

"Not for long. I heard Aunt Camilla is going to ask Mrs. Havering to let you take riding lessons with Arcilla in the afternoons."

Evy could not restrain her surprise. Was he just taunting her? She knew that Lady Camilla had mentioned riding lessons, but there had been no promise. The thought of learning to ride filled her with excitement. Rogan seemed to watch her reaction.

"Oh, Evy, do sit *down*." Arcilla waved her hand at Evy's chair. "We promise not to tease you anymore. Will you ride at Milton's Academy, Rogan?"

"Not as often as I would like. On weekends Parnell and I will be going to Heathfriar. I can ride there."

Arcilla turned to Evy. "Heathfriar is Patricia's family estate. You will meet Patricia one day when she comes here to Rookswood. She will marry Rogan. I like Heathfriar better than Rookswood because it's close to London. So many exciting things to do. You are so lucky, Rogan," she sighed wistfully. "Patricia wrote that Lord William will let her attend the theater on her next birthday. I wish Father would let me attend the theater."

"Patricia is older than you. She's my age."

He sounded so grown-up, Evy thought.

"Will you be going to the theater with her and Charles?" Arcilla watched Rogan, eyes wide.

Charles… He must be Patricia's brother.

Rogan shrugged and stood. "That is ages away." He folded his arms and paced the room, looking very wise and handsome. He snapped his fingers. "I have an idea. I know what to do this afternoon. Hurry up with tea, Arcilla. Tomorrow I leave, and I promised Miss Evy I would show her old Henry's ghost. You will come with her." He looked down at Evy, that challenging smile tipping his lips again. "That is, if you have not changed your mind about being afraid. You are so much braver than Derwent, aren't you?"

Arcilla drew back. "No! I hate those rooms. It is damp in there. No one's been there for years and years. It is dark inside too."

"We will light the lamps, naturally. Use your head, Arcilla. I have done it before when I was searching. Don't be such a coward."

Evy frowned. *When he was searching? Searching for what?*

Arcilla pouted. "Do you think we should?"

But Rogan waved her hesitation aside. "Of course." He looked at Evy. "You ran away from the crypt. You were shaking in your shoes that day."

Evy stiffened. "I was *not*. Nor am I afraid of the silly notion of ghosts. It's just—well, I do not think Lady Camilla would approve of me exploring the mansion."

"Oh, that," he said as though it were a minor annoyance. "Do not let that worry you. No matter what Arcilla says, Rookswood will be mine someday, not Parnell's. I do as I wish around here. Everyone knows that. And it is now my wish to show you Henry's ghost. That is, if you really are brave enough."

"I do not like Uncle Henry's rooms." Arcilla emphasized the repetition with a stamp of her tiny foot.

Rogan barely looked at her. "We need to go there. We have a crime to solve."

"How do we do that?"

"We solve his murder, of course," Rogan told his sister impatiently.

"Everyone says he killed himself over diamonds."

Arcilla's whispered comment sparked Rogan's interest. "Who said so?"

"Father, for one."

"Did he?" He seemed thoughtful.

"And Aunt Camilla for another."

Rogan grew pensive, as though Camilla's notions interested him a great deal. Evy wondered why; was it because she had come from Sir Julien Bley's estate in Capetown?

"There is no ridding Grimston Way of the gossip about Uncle Henry," Rogan stated. "Even old Hiram Croft thinks he was murdered."

"Then I do not want to go to his musty old rooms."

Rogan shook his head at his sister's fear. "Here is what we will do. I am the detective, and you and Miss Evy are my helpers."

"*I* want to be the detective."

Evy cast a glance to the ceiling at Arcilla's quick assertion.

"I am the detective," Rogan commanded. "I am older, therefore wiser."

That seemed to satisfy Arcilla, so he turned to Evy. He looked from her to Arcilla. "Are you afraid too?"

Evy refused to be compared to Arcilla! She would show them both she was far braver than either of them. "Of course not."

Rogan grinned, casting a glance at his sister. "Are you as brave as the vicar's niece?"

That brought a frown to Arcilla's face; she obviously did not want Evy to outshine her. She pouted for a moment, then she stood. "I will go if Evy does."

Rogan gave a quick nod. "Hurry. Bring a cape. I have only an hour before my riding lesson."

Evy wanted to refuse. Why on earth was she allowing him to manipulate her? And yet…she found herself growing more and more curious.

She and Arcilla went out the door and followed him down the corridor. It was anyone's guess where he was bringing them! And what if they were caught? The mansion was huge and dark, and she hoped she did not end up losing her way. Aunt Grace would be disappointed and displeased if Evy ended up embarrassing her so soon after she had taken up her position as governess.

Evy pushed these thoughts away as she followed behind Arcilla, who stayed close to Rogan. They came to a dim stairway at the back of the house. It was quiet here, as though it was not often used, even by the servants. At the top of the stairway a rope was drawn from the banister to the wall, closing off the rooms that were uppermost in the house. Rogan went up as though he had come this way often. Evy frowned. What was he searching for in his uncle's suite of rooms?

Her heart thumping, she climbed the stairs after him, one hand on the banister. She tried not to look at the carved gargoyles staring back at them, teeth bared. Arcilla paused, and grabbed Evy's arm. For once, Evy didn't mind the girl's presence. They went up together.

Rogan waited at the top landing. He wore a faint smile, and Evy had the clear impression he was trying not to laugh.

"Come," he said. "You both look as if you swallowed green frogs."

Green frogs, indeed!

Evy stepped forward. She would show Rogan Chantry just how wrong he was.

Chapter Thirteen

Evy waited, her heart in her throat, as Rogan tried the knob to Master Henry's room. When he found it locked, she was surprised at her own disappointment.

If the door to Master Henry's rooms was locked, they must turn back—

But Rogan merely smiled at them and took a key from his pocket. He unlocked the door with a flair.

The door creaked open, and he entered first. Evy was determined to be brave, but it wasn't easy entering the dim room and feeling Arcilla's fingers digging into her arm. For all Arcilla's boasting and professed dislike, she was clearly grateful for Evy's company.

The silent house seemed to close in about Evy. As she entered the room it was as though an eerie coldness touched her. The warm schoolroom was now a whole world away. In a sudden panic, she froze in the middle of the stuffy room. Rogan closed the door and lit a candle. His brown eyes were bright as he held the candle and looked at them over the flickering flame.

"This was Henry's Diamond Room," he said in a low voice. "He used to keep diamonds here from Kimberly to sell in London and Paris. He was also involved in smuggling. There was one particular diamond that he would not sell for any price."

"The Black Diamond?" Evy said it quickly, to show him she knew more than he thought she did.

The surprise on his face brought a smile to her own.

"How do you know that?"

"From Lizzie," she whispered ruefully.

His mouth turned. "You are right, Evy. It was called the Black Diamond of Kimberly, very unusual and as big as an egg."

"Ooh, is it still here?" Arcilla looked around.

"Uncle Julien came here and searched once or twice after Henry's death. So did Anthony."

Evy came alert. "Anthony? Is he another of your uncles from South Africa?"

He shook his head. "No. He's a Brewster—a stepnephew of Julien's, but because Julien had no sons, he decided to adopt Anthony when he married Lady Camilla. The Black Diamond was worth many hundreds of thousands of pounds."

Evy pursed her lips. "What could have happened to it?"

"That question remains unanswered. It is either hidden here somewhere, or—"

"It was stolen?" Evy whispered.

Rogan's eyes glittered. "Most likely at the same time Uncle Henry was murdered."

"Ooh." Arcilla's whisper echoed in the still room.

"Henry's ghost creeps about this room in search of his murderer." Rogan's voice deepened, and when the candle flame nearly went out, Arcilla broke for the door, but Rogan grabbed her arm. "Shh!"

Evy's teeth threatened to chatter, and she gritted them into submission. She looked about the room at a big desk and chair, a library shelf with books from ceiling to floor, and a glass case lined with black velvet.

"That was where he used to keep some diamond jewelry from Kimberly."

It never dawned on Evy to question what Rogan said, or to wonder how he knew this. She supposed his information had come in much the same way that he had gotten hold of the key. He knew many of the secrets of Rookswood and was bent on discovering the rest of what might be hidden.

"Of course there's no evidence Uncle Henry was murdered," he admitted, "or that someone came to Rookswood and stole the Kimberly Black Diamond, but whoever did it would be smart enough to make sure of that."

Evy agreed. Murder and diamonds… It was exciting and terrifying all at once, and she was in the very midst of the scene of the crime!

"D-did you ever see Uncle Henry's ghost?" Arcilla whispered to her brother.

"I once saw what I thought was a ghost," he said calmly.

"You do not think so now?" Evy peered at him in the darkness.

His dark eyes squinted at her. "I'll tell you this much. See that closet over there? That's where I hid when his ghost came creeping out from that door across the room. That was Henry's private room where he would sleep sometimes when he worked up here late. That's the room where he was murdered, but the constable and the family say he killed himself with his own pistol."

Arcilla tugged at her brother's arm. "I don't like it in here, Rogan. Let us go back to the schoolroom and finish the tea and tarts."

"Not until I look in the other room."

"What is it you are searching for? The Black Diamond?" Evy took a step toward Rogan. "You do think it's still hidden here somewhere?"

"I am searching for more than the diamond, but that remains my secret. I won't tell anyone."

Evy knew she shouldn't be here, but she couldn't leave. She was determined to win Rogan's admiration, to make him see she wasn't afraid. So she lingered, even when Arcilla tugged at her sleeve to leave.

"How many people in your family could have taken the Kimberly Diamond?" Evy whispered. "You mentioned Sir Julien Bley and Anthony Brewster—was there anyone else?"

"A passel of them. There are the great-greats. All Chantrys."

"Not all, there's Mama's family, the Brewsters. Lady Brewster, our great-aunt."

"I forgot about her. I think she is still alive. She must be as old as Miss Armitage by now. Henry was married to one of Lady Brewster's nieces, I think."

"Caroline," Arcilla explained. "Mother told me about her. She was a sister." Arcilla looked at Evy, and her blue eyes gleamed. "Lady Brewster's family helped find the first diamond in Kimberly."

"They did not!" Rogan frowned at his sister, as though she were foolish. "Uncle Julien Bley did. And his partner—a Boer."

"What is a Boer?" Arcilla wrinkled her nose.

"Ancestors of the Dutch, who went to South Africa in the 1600s from Holland. Julien is here now visiting Rookswood. He came from Germany on business and will soon be on his way back to South Africa. He didn't know my father had already sailed for Port Elizabeth weeks ago, or that Mother—" He stopped and looked at Arcilla.

Evy knew he had been about to mention Lady Honoria's death.

"Anyway, forget the Boer. Now, Sir Julien is partners with De Beer of South Africa."

"De Beer?" Evy frowned. There were too many names to figure them all out.

"You don't know who De Beer is?" Clearly Rogan found the idea incredible.

Evy realized the man must be someone very important and that if she were to be wise, she must know about De Beer.

"He owns almost all the diamonds in South Africa," Rogan explained. "He has a near monopoly."

"But he doesn't own the Kimberly Black Diamond," Arcilla protested.

"No one owns it now—except the person who stole it from Uncle Henry."

"It's the biggest diamond they ever found," Arcilla said smugly to Evy. "They will find it again, and we will be very, very rich."

"We already are." Rogan shrugged. "I suppose we could have anything in the world that we took a fancy to having." He looked at Evy. "Even people."

Evy's chin came up at that. "You cannot buy and own people."

"Sir Julien Bley bought his wife. He wanted her, so he bought her."

"That's horrid."

Rogan smiled. "Not to Sir Julien. Aunt Catherine Bley was very beautiful. She died as a bride after less than a year of marriage, and he never remarried. That's why he adopted Anthony."

He moved to the second door leading into the bedroom where Henry Chantry had either killed himself or been murdered, keeping the candle flame from flickering out. Evy followed, with Arcilla clutching her arm, the carpet silencing their footsteps.

"How did Master Henry come to have the Black Diamond?" Evy asked.

"There's a big scandal that says he stole it from Cape House—that's Sir Julien's estate."

"I'm afraid," Arcilla whispered.

"Then go back to your room." Rogan sounded as though he was growing impatient.

Arcilla looked at Evy. "Come with me."

She stood her ground. She wanted to see that bedroom.

"I'm going back." With that, Arcilla hurried out of the room, silently closing the door behind her.

Rogan looked at Evy. "Follow me, and because you proved you were brave I will tell you what I'm looking for."

"I already know. Diamonds. Master Henry must have stolen more than the black one."

"There were three bags of whites, too, but that's not what I'm searching for. No. It's a map. Henry's map. He left it to me in his will."

Evy's heart thudded in her chest. A map? "The map is lost too?"

"Or hidden along with the diamonds—that's my thought, and I'm going to find it someday."

"A map to what? A gold mine?"

"Yes, a very old map—hand-drawn by Uncle Henry, who was shown the gold deposit by a Zulu warrior, called an Impi. It shows a gold mine in Mashonaland. But Sir Julien and the rest of the family insist that the notion of gold is a folly. They call it Henry's Folly. But I'm betting on Uncle Henry. He was quite an explorer. He left it to me because he suspected I'd follow his interests. He was right."

She agreed with that.

"When I locate the map, I'll go to South Africa and start my own gold mining business. That's why I've chosen a geological university instead of Oxford like Parnell."

Evy could scarcely catch her breath! Here she was, the niece of the governess, prowling the secret rooms of Master Henry Chantry with the son of the present squire. Somehow everything Rogan did was adventurous and exciting.

No wonder Derwent liked to be around him.

As they slipped into the bedroom, Evy felt as though Rookswood welcomed her into its mysteries. For a short time she had what she had secretly dreamed about: She was important to Rogan and Arcilla. Arcilla needed her. And the more time they spent together as companions, the more Arcilla would depend on her. Rogan seemed to encourage it, as though he thought Arcilla was safe when she was in Evy's company. But Evy knew that while Rogan might accept her at times, as he was now doing by taking her on a tour of forbidden places, he never lost the demeanor that told her she was of a lower station, and that their relationship was a temporary experience. She sensed that as he went away to school and grew older, the relationship would end.

The bedroom was also in shadows. The large bed was made up as though Master Henry were expected at any moment. The room was cold and musty smelling, and the floorboards creaked beneath the carpet as they walked slowly across it toward another desk, smaller than the one in the other room.

"I've looked everywhere." Rogan held the candle high, letting the light play on the walls. "He hid the map in a good place, all right. Otherwise someone would have found it before now. I've tried to think like Henry, but somehow it doesn't work."

"He was much older than you are now. Maybe he knew things about Rookswood you do not."

"A secret hiding place for his map? Yes, I've thought of that. When I go to school in London I'm going to visit the historical libraries to see what I can learn about Rookswood architecture. I do know that Uncle

Henry studied architecture as a young man before he gave it up and went to South Africa."

"I'm sure you will win in the end."

He looked at her, and there was an expression in his gaze that made her breath catch in her throat. Aware of an unsettling tension between them, she hurried to fill the silence. "Because you will not give up searching."

He gave a slow nod. "You are right about that. When I come home from school I will keep on searching until one day I find it. If it's here. I think it is."

Her heart began to beat faster. She gazed at the painting on the wall showing tall Africans in leopard skins, with feathers, bones, and jewels in their headpieces. They carried fierce spears, and their eyes stared back with a regal defiance. Behind them was a lion with yellow eyes, and in the background, a great flat-topped mountain.

Rogan noticed her glance. "That is Table Top Mountain, overlooking Capetown. Those short spears or knives the Zulu are carrying are called assegai."

She shuddered at the sight of the painting. The Africans looked fierce and vengeful. "The Zulus killed my parents at the mission station near Isandlwana."

"Yes. I was looking at your mother's photograph in the rectory last Sunday." He studied her, and Evy felt a quick heat fill her cheeks. She was recalling Derwent's comment that she did not look much like her mother. Did Rogan think the same?

The door to the front hall opened quietly, and there came the dreadful sound of footsteps too heavy to be Arcilla's. Horror washed over Evy. Was she to be found out? Oh, what would Aunt Grace say?

Rogan put a finger to his lips and gestured for her to hide. She dove under the desk.

The moments crept by. Where was Rogan hiding?

She saw a flickering light, but it could not be Rogan's candle, for he had doused it when they'd heard the door open. Slow footsteps moved across the main room, and the stealthy sound of desk drawers opening

and shutting followed. Ghosts did not open dresser drawers. Then whoever it was must have noticed the bedroom door ajar, for someone came
to the threshold.

Evy held her breath. A man stood in the doorway—the same man
she had encountered the morning of her arrival in the upper corridor.
He carried a lantern, holding it high, so that the light flickered on his
face: squared-jawed, a craggy complexion browned from the sun, thick
jaw-length hair the color of ebony, a black eye patch. His good eye was
a burning pale blue. He wore a gold satin smoking jacket, and a large
diamond ring on his hand flashed in the lantern light. She saw his head
lift slightly, like a hunting dog catching the scent of prey.

"All right. Who's in here? Come out at once!"

Evy's shaking hand went over her mouth. She was just about to
crawl out and surrender when Rogan came forward.

"Hello, Uncle Julien. You smelled the smoke from my candle?"

"So it's you, Rogan. What brought you here?"

"I leave in the morning for school in London. I like looking at
Uncle Henry's maps of South Africa, so I wanted a final look before I
went away."

Sir Julien Bley was silent a moment too long, and then he appeared
to accept the explanation. "Yes, Camilla tells me you are anxiously looking forward to coming to the Cape after schooling. Well, that pleases me,
boy. Especially with Parnell showing so much interest in the diamond
business. But I wish you would get this notion out of your head about
searching for Henry's Folly. You will do far better in the mines. Prove
your worth to me, boy, and I'll leave you a double share in my will."

"I will remember that, Uncle Julien."

He sounded so congenial, but Evy suspected he was pretending.

"Well, Rogan, show me the maps that so intrigue you. I can tell at
first glimpse if they're up to date and accurate."

Sir Julien looked around the bedroom, then back down at Rogan.
"Are they in here?" The tone of his question implied he knew they were
not, which left the obvious question of what Rogan was doing in the
bedroom if he were looking at maps. Evy tensed.

But here again, Rogan proved himself quite foxy. "Your stepbrother Henry had a whole drawer full of maps, sir. He kept them here in this ottoman." He went to a round footstool covered with tapestry and lifted the lid. He stooped down and took out a stack of maps, pencils, and several volumes of books.

Sir Julien came to join him. "Well, well. So you *did* find maps. Brilliant, my boy. Ah yes, indeed. I definitely want you in Capetown in a few years."

"I like this one best." Rogan spoke quietly, spreading it out for his uncle to see. "It's of Zululand. Like that painting on the wall over the bed."

Sir Julien followed his glance to the painting that had given Evy shivers.

"That was the Zulu king Cetshwayo," Sir Julien said, unpleasantness in his voice. "His twenty thousand Impi attacked and slaughtered our British troops in the Battle of Isandlwana in 1879. A loss we'll never forget." His jaw tightened. "Reinforcements came in later, and the Zulus were soundly thrashed. We've no trouble with them now—not much, anyway. Let me see that map, my boy."

Rogan stood and handed it to him.

"Ah." Sir Julien nodded, apparently satisfied. "It is Zululand all right. So, you were telling me the truth."

Rogan's eyes widened, making him the picture of innocence. "Why shouldn't I?"

"No reason. Well, good enough. Hand me those maps. I shall have a look through them myself tonight in my room. I, too, am leaving in the morning."

Whether reluctantly or not, Rogan gathered them up and turned them over to his father's stepbrother. He closed the ottoman lid and went toward the door. "I have a riding lesson in fifteen minutes. Do you want me to lock up?"

"Yes. Lock it up."

Evy watched them leave the bedroom and heard Sir Julien ask, "How did you get a key to this room?"

Rogan answered something in a muffled voice. Sir Julien laughed as if Rogan amused him with his antics. The door closed behind them and a grating sound was heard in the lock. Evy's hands were folded and tightly intertwined. She must not be discovered. It would mean trouble for Aunt Grace. Relief washed over her that Rogan had kept her presence a secret. But now...

Her eyes widened. She was locked inside! When, and how, would she get out?

Surely Rogan or even Arcilla would come back and open the door. But Arcilla did not have the key and would be afraid to venture here alone anyway. Evy hoped she would not say anything to Aunt Grace.

Oh, Rogan, now what?

He had to go riding, or the instructor would let it be known to Lady Camilla and Sir Julien that he had not shown up. Then Sir Julien would want to know why he had not kept the appointment. Evy crawled out from under the desk and went into the next room.

She would need to wait until Rogan could come back up here and unlock the door. She hoped he would come before the afternoon shadows began to darken the rooms even more.

She walked toward the door to the hall and tried the doorknob, but it was secure. She made her way to the window and looked out. Unless she had a rope she could never escape through the window. Nor could she imagine herself shimmying down a rope even if she had one. She grew dizzy just staring down into the empty courtyard. If someone had murdered Master Henry, that person would have entered through the hall door.

No, there was nothing she could do but wait. With a heavy sigh, she sat down near the door, her eyes on the big clock. The pendulum was not swinging. Perhaps it had not been wound since Master Henry's dreadful death.

It seemed hours before she heard quiet footsteps outside in the hall. She stood and faced the door. A key turned in the lock, and the door opened slowly. Rogan stood there, looking grave. He studied her face.

"I was afraid you would start screaming in panic."

"I told you. I do not scream."

"You were brave," he admitted, unsmiling.

His words did more to lighten her mood than anything else.

"Come along, hurry. I'll need to lock it again. And whatever you do, don't tell Sir Julien you were in here with me."

"I won't. But he took your maps."

"I didn't want those anyway." He smiled. "I kept them in the ottoman for just such an emergency. I'm more clever than anyone thinks."

She was not surprised. "You don't suspect Sir Julien?" she whispered as they went quietly down the corridor to the steps.

"Of what, murdering Henry?"

Evy clamped her fingers over her mouth. Even to say those dread words sent a shudder through her spine.

"No, Sir Julien doesn't need the Black Diamond, although he wanted it badly. He has diamond mines in Kimberly. He's richer than the Chantrys. He's as hard as a diamond, but some say he has a tender streak too. You would hardly know it by looking at him. Not that I completely trust him. He is greedy."

They came down the steps and across the hall to the schoolroom. He opened the door and looked inside. Arcilla jumped up from the window seat and looked at them, questioning.

"It is all right," Rogan said. "I've got to go back to the stables. Mr. Kline is waiting for me. I told him I had to do something important. Good-bye," he told Evy, smiling, amused again. "I will leave for London early. You have lived up to your boast." He ran down the hall and disappeared around the corner. She heard his footsteps clattering down the main stairway toward the front door.

At least he had admitted she was brave.

When she was alone that night in her bed, remembering, she felt uncertain, even fearful. There was something dark about those rooms… about the maps, the diamonds, and what she'd heard about Master Henry.

But none of it seemed quite so menacing as Sir Julien Bley.

CHAPTER FOURTEEN

The days seemed to rush by because so much was new and exciting. Then, one quiet Tuesday afternoon, Lizzie appeared in the corridor outside the schoolroom, waving wild hands to catch Evy's attention.

Evy glanced at her aunt, who was busy with Arcilla on a history lesson. She stepped from the room into the corridor and pulled the door almost closed.

"What is it, Lizzie?"

She'd never seen Mrs. Croft's niece quite so excited. "Lady Camilla is sending for you. She wants you to take tea with her in the parlor." Her bright eyes searched Evy's face as though she might find the meaning of this unexpected invitation written there.

Evy couldn't blame her. She was surprised as well. "Are you certain?"

"*Sure* of it. Something is up, Miss. Lady Camilla's been behaving strange these days. I seen her watching you, nervouslike. She wrote a letter too—to Australia, no less. Then she says to me, funnylike, 'But he ain't there yet.' Only she didn't say *ain't.*"

Evy glanced at the schoolroom door. Did Aunt Grace know about this invitation to tea? If she did, she had not told Evy earlier. She smoothed her cotton dress and looked down at her shoes. Maybe she should change into her new frock, the one she wore on their arrival to Rookswood.

It was quite a compliment to be invited to tea. Evy recalled the way Lady Camilla had looked at her when they first met at the rectory before

Uncle Edmund's death. "Are you certain you're not making a mistake? Maybe Lady Camilla meant both my aunt and me."

"No, she said it to Mrs. Wetherly. I heard 'em talking. 'Bring her now,' her ladyship says. A bit unusual, don't you think, Miss?"

Quite unusual indeed. Lizzie's eyes fairly snapped with curiosity. "And just you alone to tea, without Mrs. Havering nor Miss Arcilla. I said to myself, now what's *this* all about? Lady Camilla has herself something on her mind; wonder what it could be?"

Evy couldn't imagine, unless… Perhaps Lady Camilla Brewster had some interest in her parents? They were martyrs, after all. They had lived in South Africa. It was probably nothing more mysterious than that. Lady Camilla might even have met them at one time and could share some interesting experience.

"And that letter to Australia, I tried seeing who it was addressed to."

Evy tried to conjure up an expression of disapproval. "It isn't wise to be snooping, Lizzie. Whoever Lady Camilla writes to is none of our affair."

The stair creaked. Evy jumped and turned to find Mrs. Wetherly, the housekeeper, stopped on the stairway, brows arched and lips pursed when she saw Lizzie.

"You are supposed to be helping Beatrice in the kitchen, Lizzie."

"Aye, Mrs. Wetherly, I was just going there." The maid cast Evy a secretive glance and rushed down the stairs toward the kitchen.

Mrs. Wetherly sighed. "That girl is a trial to my patience. If it were not for my friendship with Mrs. Croft, I'd have sought permission from Sir Lyle to be rid of her long before now."

"Lizzie's curious about things." Evy did her best to give the woman a patient smile. "She's harmless, though."

"I certainly hope so. She talks so much about everything." Mrs. Wetherly studied Evy for a moment. "I expect Lizzie has already brought you Lady Camilla's request?"

"To have tea in the parlor, yes. Is it— Is it proper?"

"When Lady Brewster requests something, it is proper even if out of the ordinary. You come along with me. You look perfectly acceptable and quite pretty."

"I had better tell my aunt first."

"I will come back and explain."

Evy followed Mrs. Wetherly down the wide staircase into the great hall and then toward another intricately engraved door. She knocked quietly, then opened it.

"Miss Evy is here, Lady Camilla."

"Show her in please, Mrs. Wetherly."

Evy smoothed her hair into place and entered the parlor, taking in the heavy dark wood furnishings done in burgundy and gold. Lady Camilla stood before an upholstered velvet wing-backed chair; she looked utterly elegant and rather royal. Her long, flowing dress of wispy green material flattered her pale skin and golden hair, but seemed more appropriate for relaxing in the privacy of her room than for tea. Evy had heard Lady Camilla was still "rather ill" and wondered if her having asked Evy to tea might have surprised the household.

Oh, to be so lovely…

Lady Camilla smiled wanly. "Come in, Evy. Do sit down."

She moved across the thick carpet and took the chair across from Lady Camilla. A low rosewood tea table was set between them. Mrs. Wetherly brought in the silver tea service and went out, closing the heavy door behind her. Evy smiled to herself. So much for Lizzie coming with some vain excuse to loiter about the door. No one could hear through that heavy wood. It looked to be fourteenth century, when it would have protected a Chantry baron who might fear an ax attack from a warring knight!

"Why don't you pour for us, dear?"

Evy did so, suddenly grateful Aunt Grace had taught her the manners and style of fashion: Always remember to lift the little finger. Point up and not down. Never *grip* the handle as if it were a weapon.

Lady Camilla Brewster watched her, and Evy had the impression the woman was pleased. Evy handed her the tea plate, breathing in the sweet fragrance of the delicately arranged sweet jam cakes. Camilla chose the only one without gooey filling. Evy supposed that said something about her. Evy chose a raspberry, and then wondered how she would eat it without getting any on her chin, which would never do.

Camilla studied her, seeming to take in every aspect of Evy's features. Why had she asked her here? Evy offered a tentative smile.

"I am pleased you are not shy, Evy. Being raised in the vicarage as you were might have turned you into what we call a shrinking violet. Yet you seem confident and interested in adventure."

"Yes, I guess I am, Lady Brewster."

"Why don't you go ahead and enjoy that jam cake and not worry about the raspberry filling?" she said with a sudden smile. "If it splashes, we will keep it our little secret."

Evy laughed. "You knew just what I was worried about." She liked Lady Camilla after all. "I am pleased you would ask me to have tea."

"I have been wanting to speak with you for some time. Just the two of us, ever since I arrived at Rookswood from Capetown. The death of your uncle, the vicar, delayed matters. His death was unfortunate for you, wasn't it? I noticed at the vicarage that you appeared to love him a great deal, and your aunt, too."

An odd observation. Was it not normal to love the only family one had?

"They raised me. I consider them my parents."

"Yes. Assuredly. You would be so inclined. Yet they were not your parents by blood."

Now why was she saying this? "Aunt Grace is my blood aunt. She was the older sister of my mother, Junia Varley."

"Was she?"

Evy looked up from her tea. There was something a little strange in the way she said those words.

"Aunt Grace and my mother? Oh yes, they were sisters by blood."

The corners of Lady Camilla's mouth pinched together, making her look older than her actual years. She could not be over thirty-five, perhaps even younger.

"I wanted to talk to you before Sir Julien returns from London."

Evy watched her, speechless, trying to gain her footing. So that was why she had not seen Sir Julien at Rookswood for the last few days since Rogan left for school in London. Not that she knew much of what was happening in the house. She was mostly confined to the third floor and to their suite of rooms, though she could use the backstairs to go outdoors from the servants' entrance.

"Lady Camilla, I don't mean to be impolite, but why would you have a particular interest in talking to me?"

Camilla's eyes deepened to a violet hue. She leaned forward, her delicate hands clasping together so tightly that the fine hands turned white. "You really do not suspect, do you?"

Evy tipped her head at the woman's amazed tone. Suspect what?

"They really have managed to keep everything from you. I should have known. When Sir Julien makes up his mind about something, there are few inside the family who would dare oppose him."

The energy with which she spoke appeared to have drained her emotionally, for she leaned back again, or rather slumped. Her heart-shaped face was drawn and weary. "Then, for your sake, my dear, I shall be…delicate about this."

Evy's fingers were trembling now, and her cup rattled on the gold-rimmed saucer. "What do you mean, Lady Brewster? Did you know my parents?"

"Oh yes indeed—I knew them. I knew your father *very* well. Or perhaps I should say, I thought I knew him. As for your mother, I saw her several times. You look very much like her—very little like your father. You have her traits, too, her confidence, her spirit—"

Suddenly Camilla went rigid against the back of the chair, and her face drained of whatever color it had possessed. Her action so startled Evy that she too froze. A door clicked shut, and Evy spun to find Sir Julien Bley standing beside the door to a room she had not noticed.

Evy's fingers tightened on the cup. He appeared just as forbidding as he had in Henry Chantry's rooms. This time he looked angry and intimidating. Perhaps the black patch that covered his eye gave him such a sinister air. But as he stared coldly from that one pale eye at Lady Camilla, Evy decided that the dangerous air was more than mere impression. It was quite certainly reality when his will was thwarted.

And though Evy could not understand why, it was clear that Camilla Brewster was doing just that.

"Sir Julien." Lady Camilla's breathy, thin tone set Evy's nerves even more on edge. Was the woman afraid of Sir Julien? Lady Camilla leaned forward in the wide chair, both hands clutching the armrests tightly. "I thought—"

"I know what you thought, Camilla. I have not yet left for London, as you can see. However, I have decided to take you with me when I do. You can wait in the hotel while I have my meeting with the colonial office. You will be going back to Cape House on a ship departing on Thursday. With Anthony ill and anxiously awaiting your cherished presence, I fear we cannot disappoint him."

Camilla dampened her lips and looked ill.

Evy's heart was pounding so hard that she couldn't breathe. The moment was horrid. She wanted to run out of the room, but her need to understand outweighed her fear.

She set her teacup on the table and stood to her feet, her knees shaking. Sir Julien's good eye swerved and pinned her to the spot.

"So you are Evy."

She tilted her chin and met his hard gaze. *There is no cause to be so afraid. Why should I be?* "That is my name, sir. I was just having tea with Lady Brewster."

His mouth quirked. "So I notice."

"She was about to tell me what she knew about my parents in South Africa."

Any faint amusement vanished. "I assure you, my ailing daughter-in-law can tell you nothing about Dr. and Mrs. Varley. Nothing that in the least will help you get on with your growing up. However, your Aunt Grace tells me you wish to attend music school in London when you are older."

"Yes. With all my heart." Now why was he asking her this? It seemed rather odd.

"You think you are good with music, do you?"

"Yes!"

The quirk showed again. "You have spunk anyway."

"But Parkridge Music Academy is out of the question since my uncle died."

Sir Julien did not respond. Evy shifted under that intense gaze and stole a glance at Lady Camilla. She was still slumped in the chair, defeat on her delicate features. Evy's heart went out to her in sympathy. Sir Julien could be a bully if people let him.

"If you will excuse me… My English class is about to commence." Evy turned to Lady Camilla, who was gazing at Julien. "Lady Brewster, thank you for the tea. Perhaps we can resume our conversation later—"

"I am certain Lady Brewster will be much too occupied packing her trunk for the voyage."

Evy inclined her head to Sir Julien. What could she say? What *dare* she say to such an authoritative man? She turned away and moved toward the door, but he came up, surprising her.

"One moment."

She looked at him, her hand hovering over the doorknob. He was unsmiling, yet Evy thought his rugged, dark features had softened ever so slightly. He reached out and cupped her chin, and she didn't let herself flinch as he lifted her face toward the light coming in from the window. His sharp eye examined her features, and there was no apology in his gaze or in the firm grip of his lean hand. He looked at her eyes, her hair, the line of her jaw and her throat.

Evy could not move.

After a moment his hand fell away and she heard a slight sigh escape his lips. "Yes."

There was nothing in that simple word or his weary tone that she could understand. Evy stepped back. How could he humiliate her this way, studying her like some colt being considered for purchase? And how could he be so mean to Lady Camilla?

"Why did you do that, sir? What did you expect to see?"

"What did I expect to see?"

The sound of rushing footsteps echoed in the outer hall, and the door opened. Aunt Grace stood there, out of breath. Seeing Sir Julien, she stopped abruptly. They looked at one another in silence, then Aunt Grace looked over at Lady Camilla. Finally her gaze shifted to Evy.

"You should not have left the schoolroom without permission."

"It is my fault." Evy turned with a start to look at Lady Camilla. Her voice was soft and childlike. "I wanted her to have tea with me."

"You need concern yourself no further, Mrs. Havering," Sir Julien asserted. "Lady Brewster and I are leaving for London as soon as she is packed. We will be on our way home to Capetown."

Aunt Grace had regained her studious composure. She nodded and looked at Evy. "Miss Arcilla is waiting for you in the schoolroom."

Evy's hands were clenched at her sides. "But—"

"Evy?"

She knew that quiet, determined tone well. There was no use in arguing. "Yes, Aunt." She glanced toward Lady Camilla. For a moment Evy thought she saw an apology in the woman's eyes before she looked away.

"Good-bye, Lady Brewster." Evy turned and saw Sir Julien's heedful gaze. She walked past her aunt into the great hall. She had started for the stairway when she noticed Lizzie dusting a spotless polished table. Mrs. Wetherly was nowhere in sight. Evy ignored Lizzie and rushed up the stairs to the third floor schoolroom.

Arcilla, waiting at the window, rushed at her as she entered. She must have wondered at Aunt Grace's hasty departure from the classroom. She looked as curious as Lizzie had.

"What happened? When Mrs. Wetherly told your aunt you were having tea with Camilla, she dropped everything and rushed downstairs as though the house were on fire. What did Camilla tell you?"

"Sir Julien arrived and interrupted everything. Why is Lady Camilla so afraid of him?"

"Isn't everyone?" She shuddered. "And that eye patch is hideous! And the way he stares at you with that one pale eye—it makes me feel like a butterfly pinned to the wall."

"But why is Lady Camilla so intimidated? She is married to his nephew, the man he adopted as a son. I would think they should all get along quite well."

"You heard Rogan before he left for London. Uncle Julien manages the entire family dynasty. Almost like a king with his realm of subjects. Never mind him... What did Camilla want with *you*? And why was your aunt so upset that you were alone with her?"

That was exactly what Evy wanted to know, but to share her bewilderment with Arcilla now would likely add fire to the matter. No, she must talk to Aunt Grace alone first.

When Aunt Grace came into the schoolroom and went around to her desk, Evy nearly went limp with relief. Arcilla watched Evy's aunt closely as well, and Evy was sure the girl was stymied when Aunt Grace sat down with a calm repose in her hard-backed chair. She lifted the spectacles from the silver chain that hung about her neck and placed them on the bridge of her nose. And then, as though nothing unusual had occurred, she reopened her big textbook.

"Open your workbooks to page ten, please. We shall be a little late with closing our lessons today."

Arcilla groaned. Evy avoided her aunt's eyes. If only she could so easily avoid the questions filling her mind, as though they were burned there with a branding iron.

After school was over, Aunt Grace came to speak with Evy.

"Let's walk in the garden. Better bring our wraps, there's a chill wind blowing."

They went down by the backstairs and out into the garden. The wind rushed through the treetops and sent the clouds scuttling across the sky. Rain threatened them as they strolled through one of the narrow rocky paths deeper into the huge garden. The green willows spread their lacy branches and drooped toward the clipped grassland, reaching out like the long arms of an octopus.

"You must have wondered why I was worried when you were having tea with Lady Camilla."

"What am I to think? It was all so strange and mysterious. And Sir

Julien—the way he looked at me. I felt like a specimen on display. Why is he insisting Lady Camilla leave with him this afternoon? I thought she was going to stay and live at Rookswood."

"So did I. She must have changed her mind. Her husband, I hear, is ill and needs her to return to Capetown. That must be another reason Sir Julien is concerned."

"He treats her like a prisoner."

Aunt Grace walked along, a small frown pinching her brow, her meditative gaze on the rocky path at her feet. Unlike Lady Camilla, Aunt Grace wore sturdy booted shoes.

"You might as well know the unpleasant truth, Evy."

Her heart pounded. Was she at last to understand all the mysteries plaguing her?

"Camilla Brewster is not well. I've learned that she is mentally ill. In the beginning she seemed quite normal, but after suffering through a stillbirth, she has not been able to recover emotionally. Afterward she desperately wanted a child, but the attending physician spoke privately to Anthony and Sir Julien about not taking the risk—a risk even to herself. Since then she has run away from Cape House several times since her marriage to Anthony Brewster."

Evy did not speak for a moment. Lady Camilla unstable? But she had appeared quite sane. She finally managed a question. "A risk to herself?"

"Yes. And there was the possibility of mental deficiencies in the children, as well. Anthony thought it best not to attempt having children again, which brought tension between them because Camilla would not accept such a thing. She was eventually placed under medical supervision at Cape House. And to make matters worse, while Sir Julien was away in Germany, she arrived here in England, looking forward to being with Honoria, only to receive the sorry news of her death. So it's really no wonder Julien thinks it best to take her back when he returns home to South Africa."

Evy paused by the holly bushes, still thick with red berries. She frowned as she pulled some off and tossed them. "I feel sorry for her.

And why was she especially interested in me, Aunt? I could see that she was. I'm sure she was about to reveal something personal when Sir Julien came in and stopped her. His very presence intimidated her."

Grace sighed. "I suppose it has to do with a story I've heard—about a scandal in the family at Cape House. After you hear it you will also understand why it would not have been wise for me to discuss it with you sooner. It must be kept in strictest confidence, as such stories, regardless of their lack of veracity, can ruin reputations as well as important relationships.

"The tale has to do with Camilla's husband, Anthony Brewster. There was talk of a baby. Sir Julien fears she has worked herself into a stressful emotional state after convincing herself that Anthony is the father and—that you could be the child."

Evy stopped cold, staring at her aunt. She tried to speak twice, but nothing came out. Then, "Me!"

Aunt Grace's features softened. "I know how you must feel. It is all wicked gossip and not worthy to be repeated. But you were so upset about Camilla's actions that I needed to explain what I felt was driving her."

"I had already heard about a baby, but—"

"From whom?"

At her aunt's sharp gaze, Evy turned back to the holly bush. "Oh, just Lizzie. She picked up bits of gossip here and there. When she told Mrs. Croft about it, I happened to be there. But why would Lady Camilla think *I* am the child? My parents were missionaries; she must know that."

"Who can explain the irrational notions in the mind and heart of a woman who lost her only child and desperately wants a substitute? Especially when she is convinced that her husband fathered another woman's child, and she cannot risk having one of her own. I believe the scandal includes a tale of diamonds that were stolen from Cape House years ago. She also believes Anthony had something to do with that. As you can see, it is enough to disturb any woman who fears such things about her own husband."

Evy plucked at the holly bush, not caring that she was being rough. "Poor Lady Camilla. I feel so sorry for her. I wonder if that's why Sir Julien looked at me like that?"

Aunt Grace started. "What do you mean?"

"The way he stared at me, searching my face, my eyes. I thought it very rude of him. He thinks he can do most anything." A little like Rogan.

"Yes, Julien can be rude, and yet there are characteristics about him that are also gentlemanly and generous. I am sure he meant you no harm."

"But why stare at me like that? What was he looking for?"

Grace walked on then, forcing Evy to leave the holly bushes and follow.

"Probably because he knew Clyde Varley and my sister, Junia. They occasionally went to Capetown to get supplies for the mission station at Rorke's Drift and would stop by and see Sir Julien at Cape House."

More surprising information. Was there no end to the things she did not know about her own family? "Sir Julien does not seem a Christian gentleman to me."

"I do not know about that. His interest in Clyde centered on a new British colony. Julien came here hoping to get a charter from the Queen to proceed. Originally, he felt that allowing missionaries to journey with the farmers would give the enterprise more respectability and acceptance."

"He intended to ask my parents to join the colony, is that it?"

"Yes. Junia once wrote to me about it."

"I wish you had kept her letters. It would make me feel closer to her and Father if I had them."

When Aunt Grace hesitated to respond, Evy glanced up at her. Was she hiding something? Quick denial and criticism swept Evy. How could she doubt her dear aunt? She must not be suspicious of Aunt Grace now, not after all she had been through, all the while saving some of her meager earnings in the hope of putting Evy through school.

Evy fixed her gaze on the hard ground. "So he stared at me because

I reminded him of my parents?" Could that be the real reason, or was there something else?

"That could certainly explain it. But it would be better to forget him, and Lady Camilla, too. In a way, I'm glad she is leaving."

Evy glanced at her. "Now there will not be anyone to oversee Rookswood."

"On the contrary, Sir Julien told me that before Sir Lyle returns, his maiden sister, Elosia Chantry, will be coming from London. Sir Julien arranged it. She is very fond of Arcilla and Rogan. So let's forget the unpleasant past and walk into the future with confidence and peace. Shall we?" She smiled, but there was a tension around her mouth and eyes that worried Evy.

She tried to smile to ease her aunt's concerns. "I want that too, but I'd still like to know everything I can about my parents. And I still keep wondering about that stranger in Grimston Wood months ago. Who could he have been?"

"Before your Uncle Edmund died, he had a talk with Sir Lyle. It seems that Lady Camilla had arrived from Capetown in the company of her cousin John from Natal. He journeyed on to the Australian gold fields. It may have been John you met."

"Australia?" She remembered what Lizzie had told her about a letter Camilla had written to Australia. "Yes, that's possible. If she confided in him, he might have thought I was related." So that was why he had suggested she should visit Rookswood. And yet…

"But Evy, I must warn you again. There is no end to the pain that reckless gossip can inflict. It is wise not to mention any of this. Lady Camilla's delusions must be kept secret."

Evy envisioned Lizzie repeating the tale, with her own enhancements.

"It is likely you will one day marry Derwent and live in Grimston Way. For your sake, your children's, and their children's, let's not make more of this than absolutely necessary."

Aunt Grace was right. Evy did not care to have any dark mysteries shrouding her parents' past, or her own!

They walked back to the house together and up to their rooms.

Later that afternoon, through a small window in the hall, Evy watched Sir Julien Bley and Lady Camilla Brewster being assisted into the coach by Mr. Bixby.

Was Lady Camilla actually ill? Or was it just a way for Sir Julien to control her? What could be the real reason Sir Julien did not want Lady Camilla to remain at Rookswood? Could there be more truth to Lady Brewster's claims about a secret child than even Aunt Grace knew?

As though she were once again in the tearoom, Evy could almost feel Sir Julien's chill, searching stare…feel the firm grip of those lean, hard fingers grasping her chin, forcing her to look up at him.

Just what had he expected to see—or hoped he would not?

CHAPTER FIFTEEN

When Rogan came home from school that summer, he did not mention Master Henry's precious map to Evy again. She began to wonder if it really existed. Had it just been a tale to entertain her and Arcilla, while he hoped to make them afraid of a ghost?

She was relieved no one in the house had suspected them of snooping in Henry's rooms. But one good thing came from it: The incident had triggered the start of Evy's friendship with Arcilla. In the months following that day Arcilla regained her weight, and there was now color in her cheeks. On her fourteenth birthday she carried a gilded mirror with her, which she took out during teatime to study her reflection, quite pleased with what she saw.

"One more year and I shall go to school in France. I can hardly wait. And you?" She turned to Evy. "Will you attend the music school?"

Evy looked away. She knew she did not have adequate resources for such a thing, no matter how much she wanted it. Uncle Edmund's death seemed to have closed so many desirable opportunities. "We must trust the Lord with our disappointments."

Arcilla smiled. "Spoken like a true daughter of the vicarage."

In spite of disappointments and uncertainties, Evy enjoyed living at Rookswood. On Sundays she and Aunt Grace would visit with Vicar Brown and Derwent, usually joining them for Sunday dinner. In the evenings Evy played the piano for them in the rectory parlor, then she and Derwent would walk in the garden and talk about his future. Soon now, he would be attending divinity school in London.

Aunt Grace naturally believed Evy's music would be a help to her as a vicar's wife. It would work well in the church services, and she could always bring a little extra money into the family by becoming a music teacher like Mrs. Tisdale, but Evy prayed for more than that. She wanted to become proficient, to study with the masters.

But how to manage those expensive years of study?

Evy's favorite times of the year were summer and Christmas holidays, for that was when Rogan and Parnell came home. Not that they noticed her, of course. On his first visit home from school Rogan had ignored her. It had hurt, but she told herself it was to be expected. He was there only two weeks before leaving again. She found out later from Arcilla that he had taken his horse to Heathfriar estate, the Bancrofts' home. It seemed that Lord Bancroft's daughter, Miss Patricia, was an avid horsewoman.

No wonder she appealed to Rogan.

Even so, everyday events were pleasant enough, and as time rolled by, Evy all but forgot the strange tales of Henry Chantry's murder, the Kimberly Black Diamond, and the gossip surrounding Lady Camilla and her husband Anthony Brewster. Even Lizzie seemed to have forgotten and turned her attention on Arcilla's comings and goings, as the girl was growing up fast.

Lady Elosia Chantry, Sir Lyle's eldest sister, had arrived the year before to take over the household, and Sir Lyle, whose voyage home to London had been long delayed, finally returned to Rookswood nearly two years after his wife's death.

"Papa, you are home at last!" Arcilla ran to throw her arms around his slim waist. "Do not ever leave again without me."

A wan smile momentarily softened his lean, craggy face. "It is good to be home, Daughter. How beautiful you have become. Where is Rogan?"

Arcilla affected a pretty pout and stepped aside as Rogan met him. "Hello, Father."

"There you are. Ah, a happy birthday, son." The squire threw an arm around Rogan's shoulders, and a happy smile lit his face as he looked his younger son over.

Evy, watching from the gallery, her elbows resting on the rail, thought it was clear which of his children he doted on.

"You are quite the young man at sixteen. Even taller than Parnell."

Rogan laughed, but drew away and pushed Parnell forward to his father. Parnell grasped his father's arms, meeting him at eye level.

It was a curious thing, Evy thought. Rogan so darkly handsome, so bold and adventurous, looked more like his Uncle Henry than he did his lean, ruddy father. It was Parnell who reflected his father's physical image, with chestnut hair and a slighter frame.

"Did you bring me any diamonds, Father?" Parnell asked.

Rogan shook his head wryly. "You sound like Arcilla at five, asking for candy."

"Candy diamonds." Arcilla giggled. "Oh, how tickling."

"Lyle, is that you?"

Lady Elosia came from the other end of the great hall, and Evy watched her brisk walk as she moved toward her brother, her hand outstretched. It was as though he were a guest instead of the squire. Lady Elosia was taller than her brother and, with her large-boned frame and silvery-blue hair, looked little like him.

"It is past time you returned," she scolded. "Dear Arcilla has been *demented* since you left. More's the pity, indeed, coming so soon after Honoria's death. Really, Lyle, you should not have left Rookswood when you did."

The squire dismissed Parnell as though he had not heard his question about diamonds and brushed his wide mouth against his maiden sister's white, powdered cheek.

"Hello, Elosia. I am afraid the call of the Kimberly mines could not wait." His tired voice contained an injured edge to it. "Missing Julien's arrival here at Rookswood as I did, I had to remain at Cape House until he arrived with Camilla. Bixby tells me she wanted to stay here."

"Trust a coachman to see through things. Truly, Camilla had no choice. Julien practically escorted her from Rookswood with a gun at her back. I daresay, I have never liked that stepbrother of ours."

"Jesting about guns after what happened to Henry is not wise, Elosia."

"No, naturally not." For the first time she appeared a little put out. "Well, at least you are home."

"I am very grateful for your being here, Sister."

"You always were doe-eyed and helpless without Honoria," Lady Elosia said in an adoring, albeit scolding voice, and she smiled and kissed both his cheeks. "Come along, dear boy, you must be famished. I say, Lyle! You've lost weight. I must do something about that!"

Rogan looked up at Evy with a half-amused smile.

Sir Lyle glanced in the direction of the great library. "Did my books arrive from the publisher in New York?"

"You mean all those geology books?" Lady Elosia wrinkled her nose the way Arcilla often did. "Sorrowfully, yes. I had Bentley stack them in your office. But look here, Lyle, I simply won't allow you to close yourself up with your books and meditations and ignore your need to find a new life. You cannot mourn dear Honoria forever, you know. By the way, that reminds me—we are invited to Heathfriar next week. Miss Patricia is having her birthday ball."

"Oh how grand!" Arcilla clapped her hands, tagging behind her father. "I shall see Charles Bancroft."

Lyle scowled down at her. "Forget Charles, Daughter. When you reach sixteen your uncle Julien wishes you to meet Peter Bartley. A marvelous man. I went there to meet him."

"Peter Bartley? But Papa, I love *Charles*." Arcilla whirled toward Rogan, grabbing hold of him. "Tell him, Rogan, *tell* him. Tell Papa how you and I are such good friends with Charles and Patricia."

"You have already told him."

"Who is Peter Bartley?" Lady Elosia frowned at Lyle. "We must be careful about Arcilla's future marriage. I will not have her unhappy."

"Now, Elosia, the situation is still several years off. I simply do not want Arcilla getting too involved with Lord William's son."

"Yes, who is Peter Bartley?" Arcilla fussed with the frills on her stylish leg-of-mutton sleeves.

"I know who Bartley is," Parnell spoke up, lightly yanking Arcilla's golden tresses. "He is a very important fellow, isn't he, Father? You see? I have been studying my politics just the way you expected." He tossed a competitive look toward Rogan. "Peter Bartley may head up Uncle Julien's new colony deeper into South Africa."

Sir Lyle turned toward him, brows lifted. "You are right, Parnell. That is why Julien wishes Arcilla to meet him when she grows up a little more."

"I am already grown-up." Her head tilted to the side, and a pretty smile showed a dimple. "But I simply will not go to that savage place, will I, Aunt Elosia?" She went and put her arms around her, looking at her father with what Evy was certain was an unexpected challenge, softened with a teasing tone, as if trying to woo him.

Elosia was quick to agree. "Of course you will not. My land, Lyle! Would you send your own daughter to live among heathen just to please Julien?"

"Uncle Julien controls the diamonds." Rogan's wry observation drew a nod from his father.

"Unfortunately," Sir Lyle said with a sigh.

Rogan tilted his head, regarding his father. "Where is this colony to be?"

"Mashonaland."

Evy noticed the smile fade from Rogan's face.

"Isn't that where Uncle Henry had his last expeditions?" Parnell glanced toward Rogan.

"He insists his interest has nothing to do with the map Henry left Rogan in his will," Lyle said, a little too sharply, Evy thought.

Parnell turned a wicked grin on his younger brother. "Better watch out, Rogan, or Julien will be staking his claim ahead of you."

"That supposed map of Henry's was never located," Lyle countered.

"I agree with Father. It probably does not even exist, Rogan." Parnell sounded almost gleeful. "You're wasting your time searching for it."

Arcilla jumped into the fray. "You are just jealous because Uncle Henry left it to Rogan instead of you, Parnell. Pay no mind, Rogan." She went to loop her arm through his, then reached up and smoothed his dark hair. "When you find Henry's Folly, then it will be Parnell who will look foolish. And you won't get one single gold coin, Parnell."

Parnell chuckled. "*I* won't need it—I will have the diamonds. Remember, Father, Rogan and I have already had our meeting with you and settled our inheritance. I get extra shares in the diamond mines of Kimberly, and Rogan can have Rookswood as he wants."

"And the title." Evy marveled at Rogan's calm tone. He seemed utterly undisturbed by all that had just gone on. "In fact, you can begin calling me *Sir* Rogan now." His face broke into a grin.

"You can have the old title and land. It means little to me. All I want are diamonds! South Africa! And unlike you, Arcilla, I *do* want Uncle Julien to arrange my marriage—to Darinda Bley."

"Who carries a tidy inheritance of her own," Rogan said.

"Listen to you two carry on about titles and inheritance as though I were already gone," Lyle said wryly.

"What do I get for my inheritance?" Arcilla complained.

"Rogan and Parnell will always look after you, Daughter, and of course you will have your shares in the mines."

"And Peter Bartley," Rogan tossed in, glancing his sister's way.

Lady Elosia put her arms around Arcilla. "I'm leaving everything that is mine to you, Precious."

Apparently Rogan had had enough, for he parted company with them as Lady Elosia led the way into the dining room, Arcilla on her arm.

When Rogan came bounding up the stairs, Evy started to return to the third floor.

"Running away again!

She didn't even spare him a glance. "I have my studies to attend to."

"It did not seem to worry you during my father's homecoming."

"I was not eavesdropping—not really." She hated the way heat rose in her cheeks when he teased her. "Aunt Grace thought your aunt might call us to meet the squire. I was simply prepared to go down if beckoned."

"As though my father does not know who you and the vicar's widow are." He smiled. "What do you think of my family?" His eyes glittered, but Evy thought there was a tinge of hurt in the humor.

"At least you *have* a family." She had not meant to sound wistful, but the note, though restrained, was clearly in her voice.

"I've been wondering what you thought of Camilla Brewster?"

Aware that he watched her alertly, she wondered if perhaps he understood more of the scandal originating in Capetown than just the part about the stolen diamonds.

"I felt sorry for her." She met Rogan's steady gaze. "Your aunt was right about the way your uncle treated Lady Camilla. He commanded her as though she were a prisoner instead of his daughter-in-law."

"Maybe being married to his adopted son is one and the same thing."

"At least you do not approve of Sir Julien's control over the members of your family."

"I hear Camilla talked to you before Julien burst into the parlor with his sjambok," he said. "What did she tell you?"

"Very little." Evy almost smiled at his description of the scene. Sir Julien might as well have brandished a Boer whip. She wasn't sure what he knew, and for some reason was loath to reveal too much.

Rogan leaned against the gallery rail, but his gaze never left her, and she felt her cheeks growing warm again under that scrutiny.

"Did she mention the mystery baby?"

So Rogan also knew about that as well. The heat surged from her cheeks into her whole face. It was absurd how she could feel so vulnerable about her past when there could be no truth to Lady Camilla's irrational beliefs. Nor was there any reason to try to hide the tale.

"She did not mention the gossipy tale to me, but my aunt knew about it and explained Lady Brewster's...illness." She hesitated, then gave in to her curiosity. "When did you hear about the child?"

"Just recently. When I came from Heathfriar to welcome my father home. I must say I was surprised to learn about it."

Then he had heard about it yesterday. "It is quite foolish, of course." She spoke with more firmness than necessary. "I know who my parents are. Dr. Clyde and Junia Varley. I was born at Rorke's Drift at the mission station two months before the Zulu War."

His regard of her turned pensive. "Rather a murky issue, though, don't you think? The rectory girl becoming my cousin."

"I cannot see myself as your cousin—or being connected to anyone in this family, for that matter."

"Then again, Anthony Brewster is not related to the Chantrys by blood, only by marriage. But I wonder how things would change should the impossible happen and you discover you are part of this mixed-up, daft dynasty."

"I do not know what you mean." But she did. She merely refused to think about it.

"I *mean*," he belabored the point, "you would be a diamond heiress, much like Arcilla. Julien would be your grandfather by marriage, which would mean he would be meditating on whom to marry you to. After all, he'd have to be sure to enhance his fortune and power."

Evy felt her mouth gape open, and she stared at Rogan. Not for *anything* did she want to be connected to this family dynasty. If she were somehow related to Rogan…

She pushed away the emotions struggling to overwhelm her and tipped her chin. "Sounds a bit frightening to me."

"Frightening?" That caught his interest. "How so?"

"For one thing, I would not want Sir Julien arranging my future. But this discussion is silly because the tale of a mystery child is mere chatter."

"Maybe not. I can see I will have to look into all this."

"Please do not."

His smirk was back. "Why? Are you afraid to learn the truth?"

"Of course not." Really, he was insufferable! "I already *know* the truth. It is gossip I wish to shun. Soon Lizzie or one of the other servants will start spreading tales and turning me into an heiress." She turned away. "Now if you'll be so kind as to excuse me, I must go."

He laughed, and the sound was deep and rich. "Wait. Are you not going to wish me a happy birthday?"

She hesitated. He was sixteen now, more handsome than ever, with a devilish grin and devastating gaze…and every inch a scamp. She pressed her lips together. "Happy birthday."

He mocked a frown. "Is that all?" She started when he reached out to take her hand. His eyes glittered. "All the girls like to kiss me on my birthday."

She could understand that. "Alice Tisdale was no doubt first in line."

"I only like the prettiest ones to catch me."

From the fire blazing in her face, she was sure her cheeks must be scarlet.

"Well?" His brows arched, and his smile deepened.

Did he actually think she would kiss him? She assumed her sternest expression, but could not restrain a small, teasing smile. "There is no accounting for boys with unwise tastes, or for silly girls determined to make fools of themselves."

He laughed. "Leave it to the rectory girl to put me in my place. So you won't kiss me on my birthday?"

"Indeed, no. Aunt Grace says a girl must never permit liberties until she is engaged and the wedding date firmly established. And then only a kiss on the cheek."

His grip on her hand tightened. "It is like that, is it? But you are not actually *that* old-fashioned are you? Where is your adventurous spirit? Why not do something just for fun? It's rather early till death do us part."

Her heart thumped at the feel of his warm hand around hers, and she tried to wriggle her hand free. The action only amused him.

"Rogan?" It was Sir Lyle, calling from below the gallery. "We are waiting for you at the table."

He let a slow smile work its way across his features and tugged her hand. "At least come down for birthday cake."

"You forget yourself. What do you think Lady Elosia would do if the niece of the hired governess walked into the dining room and sat down at your birthday dinner?"

"She would do nothing because I have just invited you as my guest. I told you before, Rookswood will be mine someday. I will do as I wish here. Everyone knows that."

"I don't doubt it," she said with a rueful smile. "Thank you for the invitation, but I really must go." Easing her hand from his at last, she backed away.

Was that regret in his eyes? She could not be sure.

"If I cannot change your mind, then…au revoir."

He bounded down the stairs to join his father, and Evy watched them retire into the dining room. When they had vanished from view, she made her way upstairs to the third floor. But her wicked mind would not let her be. All she could think of was what would have happened if she had accepted Rogan's outrageous invitation.

She drew in a steadying breath as she sank into a chair. It was hard to know who was more dangerous—Sir Julien with his schemes, or Rogan with his utter determination to have his way with everyone and everything.

In the two years since Evy and Aunt Grace had come to Rookswood, Arcilla had accepted Evy. Still, the girl was not above being catty or demanding her way at times. She had her own set of friends from London's aristocracy who came to visit on holidays and in the summer, and Evy did not belong. When they came to stay, she would occupy herself with practicing her beloved music.

And yet, though Evy was excluded from the circle of Arcilla's friends, she was closer to Arcilla than she would have thought possible. The fact that Evy's temperament was so different from Arcilla's permitted their unusual but complementary friendship to proceed without threat of competition.

"We're nothing alike," Arcilla told her one day, "and maybe that's the reason I like your company, while I cannot endure that imperious snob, Alice Tisdale."

Evy did not tell Arcilla that she, too, was often an *imperious snob.*

Lady Elosia had been thoughtful enough to have a piano brought up to one of the empty rooms on the third floor, and Evy would go there and indulge herself. One such time when London friends were staying the weekend with Arcilla, she came to the door of the music room and stood, hands on hips.

"Will you *stop* that moldy music? You are disturbing my friends."

She nodded to Miss Patricia Bancroft, who eyed Evy with disdain. When they went out, Evy heard Patricia say to Arcilla, "Is *that* the girl Rogan was talking about to Charles?"

"I suppose it was. What did Rogan say?"

"He said…"

Evy grimaced when their voices faded. Down the corridor Arcilla closed her bedroom door, and Evy let her hands crash on the keys. The noisy bedlam filled the room.

So what did he say about me? Was it too much to contemplate that he might have complemented her? *Keep dreaming, Evy Varley.*

That same afternoon Evy noticed for the first time a handsome violin in the corner of the large room. Investigating she saw initials engraved on the leather carrying case: *R. J. C.*

It could not be Rogan's could it? There must be some mistake. Could there be another R. J. C.? Hardly. But the thought of the restless, arrogant Rogan playing violin made her laugh. What an impossible notion.

❦   ❦   ❦

Arcilla's fifteenth birthday finally arrived, but it did not find her going to France as she had anticipated. Instead, she was sent to a private school in London, which did not seem to cause the degree of disappointment it might have due to her interest in one of Patricia Bancroft's brothers.

Arcilla often talked about Charles, but then she talked about so many boys that Evy merely smiled at her.

"Honestly, Arcilla. You've been in love so often you'll never know when you really *are* in love."

"Oh, you're such a disapproving girl. Really, Evy, I'm serious. By now you should have at least *one* boy you're interested in. Instead all you do is practice your music and read your Bible."

"That is not true. I do lots of other things. But I don't see why I should follow in your steps. They'll most likely lead you into big trouble one of these days."

Arcilla laughed at her. "Well, you do have Derwent Brown."

Evy gave a haughty sniff. "I don't know what you intend to imply by that."

Arcilla's grin was utterly wicked. "I daresay you *do.* You are going to marry him one day. You'll go live at the rectory and grow roses and hold the spring and summer fete. Whereas I"—and she smiled to herself at this and opened her arms wide—"will be able to enjoy the whole wide world. Isn't it positively *grand?*"

"Oh, indeed. Positively." Evy gave her friend a small smile. "But I warn you, Arcilla, you may learn that the whole wide world is not such a lovely place after all. As for Derwent, you appear to know more than I do about our future. Nothing is certain in this life. Only God knows whom I will marry, and that is the best choice I could have."

"Oh, Evy, you are *so* naive, yet I can't help liking you for it. Well, never mind that, what do you think of my new ball gown? Isn't it a dream? I'll wear it at Heathfriar."

While Arcilla had been to several balls by now, Evy had not been to even one. She refused to let Arcilla know she was wistful, or that she secretly dreamed of waltzing with Rogan and not with Derwent. Arcilla would enjoy making fun of her, and if she discovered her daydream about Rogan she might even be mean enough to tell him.

"The ball at Heathfriar—where dear Charles shall sweep me off my feet." Arcilla held her ball gown against her with one hand and placed the other at her heart. She waltzed about the room, eyes closed in dreamy reverie until she bumped into the bed and fell. Evy laughed. Today Arcilla was in love with Charles, and tomorrow—well, who knew? Certainly not Arcilla.

The gown was indeed beautiful, a minty green with a golden under-lining so that it shimmered in the light. Arcilla would look lovely in it, and of course she knew she would. She was mature in body, and boys were starting to buzz around her like bees.

"What about Peter Bartley of South Africa?" Evy leaned back. "Your father and Sir Julien have plans."

Arcilla made a face. "I will *never* travel to South Africa to marry a government official. Aunt Elosia agrees with me."

A surprise, indeed, Evy thought, then chastised herself for the uncharitable thought. For all of Arcilla's posturing, it had to be a diffi-cult thing to have one's future decided without regard to what one truly wanted.

For the hundredth time, Evy thanked God that she belonged to a simple and loving family. At least she would never have to worry about being handed off in marriage as a financial or business asset!

A few months later, Evy had her fifteenth birthday, and Aunt Grace handed her an envelope.

"For your birthday."

Evy unsealed the flap, removed a gilt-edged letter, and read.

This is to inform you that Miss Evy Varley has been accepted into her first year of studies at the prestigious and hallowed halls of Parkridge Music Academy.

Shock and then delight shivered through Evy. She jumped up and threw her arms around Aunt Grace. "Aunt! Oh, *thank* you, thank you! But how? How could you manage with our finances as they are?"

Aunt Grace smiled, looking as pleased and excited as Evy. "Oh, I have my little secrets. I wanted to surprise you."

"You have. And I'm thrilled. But your savings—"

"This did not come from my savings."

"Then where—?"

Her aunt merely patted her hand. "Now now, you must not meddle. A birthday gift is meant to be accepted, not questioned. The second year of your studies is another matter, however. We will proceed one year at a time, trusting the Lord."

Evy laughed and embraced her again. "I owe you so much, Aunt Grace."

"It is enough I have your affection." Her aunt's voice trembled, and Evy blinked back tears.

"You will always have that, dear Aunt." She kissed the older woman's cheek, then frowned when she noticed darkening circles beneath her aunt's eyes. She must be tired, Evy thought, but paid no more attention at the moment. Her happiness bubbled.

"I must go and tell Arcilla."

"Tell me what?" Arcilla came into the room, hands behind her.

Evy whirled, smiling. "That I trusted the Lord with my disappointment about going to Parkridge, and guess *what?*"

Arcilla laughed. "He answered your prayer after all!"

"Yes! I'm leaving for London in two weeks."

"I know. Mrs. Havering told me. And now…" She drew her hands from behind her and held out a gaily wrapped package. Arcilla's eyes sparkled as she looked over at Aunt Grace, who smiled.

"We've shared the secret of your going to London, and I bought you something."

Evy's heart overflowed. "Oh, Arcilla, did you really?"

"Of course I did, silly goose. Open it."

Evy tore open the paper and ribbons. "Ooooh…" She feasted her eyes on a stylish dress, one as elegant as anything Arcilla owned for evening wear.

"The jade color goes with my eyes." There was no doubting the pleasure in Arcilla's features, as she said this, then went on to exclaim over the lower half of the skirt, which was also embroidered. "It is wonderful."

The neckline was lower, as was appropriate for evening wear, with a delicately embroidered bodice. The sleeves were puffed to the elbow with silk ruching at the bust. The overskirt was pleated, which, Arcilla explained, was quite popular. The gold-fringed hemline on the ornate skirt came to the floor.

Again, Evy let a sigh of pure delight escape her as she touched the glimmering silk.

"And—this." Arcilla stepped back into the corridor, then returned with a hatbox and several smaller boxes. Her mischievous smile drew an answering grin from Evy. "These are from my dear, *dear* brother."

Rogan!

Evy felt her cheeks warming, and lowered her head to avoid Arcilla's sharp gaze. She took the packages and tore off the wrappings, then removed a positively darling green hat with bows, ribbons, and silk flowers that matched the dress.

"The hat is for day wear," Arcilla said.

"It's beautiful." Evy held the charming adornment in her hands as a riot of emotions surged through her. *Don't be absurd!* a sensible voice within her scolded. *He didn't buy this special for you. Good heavens, he probably sent a servant to purchase it. You can't possibly think Rogan would care enough to—*

She removed the fashionable silk flowers with tiny gemstones that were to be worn in an upswept hairdo for evening. Next followed gloves that reached to the elbow, and a lacy fan to complete her evening outfit.

Evy could not find her voice.

"He's busy in London, so he did not come home this weekend."

Evy met Arcilla's smiling look. So she was right. He hadn't bought it—

"But when he saw the dress I'd bought you, he went out and returned with the other accessories. 'For the rectory girl,' he told me, though I confess his tone was a bit goading. No matter. His taste is surprisingly exquisite." She nudged Evy. "Try them *on*. Let's see."

"Yes"—Aunt Grace came from behind her—"try them on, dear." She reached to unloose Evy's garments, then helped her slip into the new dress and set the jaunty hat on her head, brushing back her thick, tawny curls.

"You look lovely, dear." Aunt Grace's voice caught with tender pleasure.

Evy rushed to the mirror and could scarcely believe her eyes. Could that vision in the glass really be her?

"Such conceit." Arcilla *tsked*, an utterly shameless grin on her face.

"I—hardly recognize myself."

"You look quite grown-up," Arcilla agreed, as though she were a few years Evy's senior instead of a few months.

Evy turned back to the mirror, noting how the color of the gown made her amber eyes sparkle with jade flecks. Those eyes widened a fraction as she realized how the dress enhanced her figure.

She fondled the ribbons on her hat, more pleased than she dared admit to know Rogan had actually taken time to shop in London to buy her birthday gifts.

Her gaze slid from the hat to her aunt's reflection, and Evy stiffened. Aunt Grace's eyes shone with pride, but there was something more there.

Concern. Clearly, her aunt was worried.

And Evy had the uncomfortable feeling that it was because Aunt Grace had known what—and who—had been occupying her thoughts.

CHAPTER SIXTEEN

Evy and Alice Tisdale shared a room with two other girls at Parkridge Music Academy in London. Turning fifteen and going to music school had not changed Alice one whit. She was still as haughty as ever. She seemed to live in a dream world, and hinted time and again that she would marry Rogan. Evy discounted that idea, though she never said so to Alice. But it was well known that Rogan and Patricia were often placed together at social functions.

Thus it was a quite a surprise when Alice announced one Thursday afternoon that Rogan had arranged for her to spend a weekend at Heathfriar. Arcilla would be there, as would Rogan and Parnell, and there was to be some sort of lawn party.

"Naturally the Chantrys shall be taking me to Heathfriar with them tomorrow afternoon. We shall return here to the school on Sunday evening." Alice looked across the room at Evy, who was doing her homework. "It is such a shame *you* will be left here all alone, Evy."

Evy refused to rise to the bait. Alice had been insufferable ever since she learned about the pretty hat Rogan had bought Evy for her birthday.

Alice, however, wasn't to be put off. "Isn't it all a bit barmy? I mean, here you are, so much *closer* to Arcilla than I, but you have not even been invited. Then again, maybe not so strange, since it wasn't Arcilla who invited me, but Sir Rogan."

"Are you not rushing things, Alice? He is not Sir Rogan yet. Squire is still in good health, the last I heard."

Alice pursed her small mouth and remained silent, pretending to read.

Evy was not disappointed about not being invited to Heathfriar. She'd had no expectations of becoming part of the aristocratic circle of young friends surrounding Arcilla and her two brothers. Nor did Alice actually belong. It was Mrs. Tisdale who constantly pushed her daughter forward and manipulated events to have her included.

As for Evy, she was under no illusions. She was the governess's niece. The fact she was able to attend a school like Parkridge, where most of the students were wealthy, had been primarily due to her aunt's ability to save. That, however, in no way elevated her in society.

She *was* surprised, though, that Alice would be invited to such an event, knowing how Arcilla felt about the girl. It was even more puzzling to think of Rogan arranging for Alice to come to Heathfriar for any reason. From what Arcilla had told her about Rogan's activities in London, Evy could not imagine him the least bit interested in Alice. He attended riding clubs and was rumored to be seeing several girls besides Patricia. Did she know this? Probably not.

Evy shook her head. Perhaps she was just not familiar enough with Rogan to know for certain. After all, she had not actually spoken with him since his birthday nearly two years ago—and the incident in the gallery had been a singular event. When he did come home to Rookswood, it was only briefly, and then he and Parnell would leave to spend time with their like-minded friends. If it had not been for the sweet little birthday hat, Evy would have suspected he barely remembered her. And even the hat might have been an impulsive gesture because Arcilla showed him the dress she'd bought her.

Ah well…

Evy stole another glance at Alice, who had her smug nose glued to her reading assignment. *Could I be wrong about Rogan Chantry and Alice?* Alice was pretty, in her own anemic way, and Dr. Tisdale was esteemed in Grimston Way, though he was unknown in London's higher circles. That being the case, it did seem strange for Alice to get an invitation to Heathfriar. If Alice were to be believed, then Evy knew even less about Rogan than she had thought.

Stop it! Evy pinched herself. *Stop thinking about Rogan Chantry.* After all, Derwent was corresponding with her. He was well into his training and would come home this summer to become his father's assistant until September, when he would return for his final year.

Evy let a small sigh escape. If only she knew how she felt about Derwent. She had known him for so long that she was perfectly comfortable around him, and she believed he felt the same. Still, at times she thought of him more as a cousin than a beau.

Perhaps the most disturbing change in Evy's life came when Aunt Grace wrote her that her health was troubling her. Now that Arcilla no longer needed a governess, Lady Elosia had arranged with the bishop to have Grace help the new young curate teach school at the rectory. Grace wrote Evy that she was enjoying the work.

I teach three days a week. I am enjoying it and did not realize how much I had missed the vicarage. Walking up the path lined with the roses Edmund and I planted years ago when we first arrived is like coming home again. Next month is the spring fete, and Vicar Brown asked me to be in charge of assigning booths to our dear parishioners to sell their goods. Oh, did I tell you in my last letter? Lady Elosia is allowing me to stay in the governess cottage vacated since Miss Hortense passed away last month. The cottage perfectly meets my needs, and there is plenty of room for your arrival in the summer.

Evy frowned. Was her aunt's writing a little shaky? Aunt Grace was under Dr. Tisdale's care for "weak lungs," but she had insisted to Evy she would grow stronger by summer.

Evy was thankful that Lady Elosia, filling the role of squire for her preoccupied brother Lyle, had been such a help to dear Aunt Grace. Evy suspected most of the Chantrys' kindness toward her aunt was because of Uncle Edmund's position as vicar for so many years in Grimston Way, rather than the few years she had been Arcilla's governess.

Evy returned home to Grimston Way that summer, anxious to see for herself how Aunt Grace was progressing. Though thinner, she appeared well enough when she met Evy at the junction in the one-horse jingle. Or was her aunt merely adept at concealing her problems? Now that Evy was older, she could look back over those early years at the vicarage, and even at Rookswood when Aunt Grace had been Arcilla's governess, and recognize that her aunt had never been one to share her innermost feelings. No, not even when she lost her husband.

Life in the simple cottage on Rookswood estate was cozy and comfortable. Evy loved taking walks in the huge garden, and not entirely because she might *accidentally* meet Rogan. But he, as it turned out, came and went with little notice of her, spending most of his time in London or at Heathfriar.

Evy missed being privy to what was going on with Arcilla and her brothers. Arcilla had many exciting new friends and no longer needed her company as she had when they were younger. Even so, when things went wrong in her life or she had some tantalizing secret she felt she couldn't entrust to her rival girlfriends, she would have a horse saddled and ride down from the manor house to see Evy, bringing another mare with her so they could go riding together as they had done in the past.

"What kind of friends are they if they cannot keep your confidences?" Evy asked her as they rode along the simple wooded trail at a slow pace. It was a warm June day, and the cloudless sky and green trees made for a perfect outing.

"Some of them I would *never* trust with any of my secrets." Arcilla shifted in the saddle to look at Evy. "Whenever they get angry or jealous, they threaten to tell everyone."

"Then they are not friends."

Arcilla's laughter rang out. "That's why I like you. Dear, faithful Evy Varley. I know I can tell you *anything,* and you won't tell anyone, or think worse of me."

"Perhaps because I already know the worst." Evy winked at her.

Arcilla's response was a smirk with a definite secretive edge to it. "Oh no, you don't… And I'm not going to tell you, either."

"I'm quite sure I don't need to hear about it."

It was around this time that Parnell and Rogan both came home from London. Oddly enough, they were going to be at Rookswood the rest of the summer because Parnell, who had graduated Oxford, would be going to Capetown to take a position in the diamond business under Sir Julien.

"When will Parnell leave?"

"August, I think. So Papa and Aunt Elosia wanted them both home together this summer. I don't mind staying at Rookswood this year. We will all be together for a change. Then, too, the summer entertainments will be grand this year, thanks to Aunt Elosia. Papa takes no interest in such things. When my mum was alive, she would always have dinner balls. That is, until she became so ill…" She fell silent, but it was only a moment until she brightened. "And of course Charles will come, and Patricia." She cast an amused glance toward Evy at the mention of the Bancroft girl.

Evy looked off toward the trees. Arcilla was far too quick to discern emotions in other girls.

"Have you heard more about Peter Bartley from South Africa?"

Arcilla grimaced, making her lovely face quite unattractive. "He writes me. His letters are filled with political information. Dreadfully boring. Something about trouble with the Dutch. *Boers,* I think he called them."

"What does Charles Bancroft think of your family's wish to match you up with Mr. Bartley?"

Arcilla bit her lip. "I have not told him yet."

Evy arched a brow at that. "Is that fair to Charles?"

"Do you want me to lose him?"

"No. But you will if Sir Julien and your father agree about your marriage to Mr. Bartley."

"I'm counting on Aunt Elosia. She wants me to stay in England, and she is close to the Bancrofts."

Evy sometimes saw the guests arrive on Friday afternoon to stay the weekend—they were wealthy, well bred, and of high social rank. Usually their sons and daughters would come with them and have their own parties with Arcilla, Rogan, and Parnell. At changing seasons there were foxhunts and pheasant shoots. Sir Lyle had pheasants bred on the estate solely for that purpose. Then, in the evenings, the dancing and dining would begin. The sounds of music coming from the baronial hall would drift down to the cottage. Sometimes, when Evy was in a fanciful, romantic mood, she would feed her dreams by going out to Aunt Grace's small rose garden and sitting on the swing where she could listen to the waltzes. She'd pretend she was there, like Miss Patricia. Naturally her dreams would have her in the loveliest ball gown, and suddenly Rogan would notice her!

"Where have you been all these years?" he would say as he asked her to waltz with him. "Look at you—all grown-up and so very pretty."

Evy laughed at her own folly, yet she would dance in the shadows of the rose garden pretending Rogan was with her. In her dreams, even Derwent understood. "I see you are not the one for me, Evy. I let you go in peace."

"Silly goose," she reprimanded herself. "I am as bad as Alice Tisdale!"

A few times during the summer Evy did see Rogan, but always from a distance when he was out riding with his friends. Those few times they did ride near the cottage, she went on pruning the roses and acted as though she did not notice them. Rogan, typically, would be smiling and laughing at something Miss Patricia said. Evy admired the other girl's blue riding habit, no doubt especially made for her. It went so well with her auburn hair. She was an exceptionally pretty girl. No wonder Rogan was attracted to her. Patricia fairly outdid herself to keep his attention, and she appeared very good at it.

One weekend not long after one of Evy's rides with Arcilla, Lady Elosia and Sir Lyle were entertaining guests from London. Evy was with Derwent in the rectory garden, and Aunt Grace was helping Vicar Brown, as she did every year, to arrange for the late summer fete. As usual, the parishioners would sell everything from elderberry jam and sweet cinnamon pickles to dried herbs in little bouquets. The money from the sale would go to restore the rectory fruit orchard, where disease had damaged the apple and plum trees.

Aunt Grace, as she had done for so many years when Uncle Edmund was alive, was assigning locations for the ladies to put up their booths on the large rectory lawn. Vicar Brown, Derwent, Mr. Croft, and even Bixby the coachman from Rookswood were building a few covered cubicles for the older ladies.

Derwent was home from divinity school and helping run the rectory and aid his father, who was none too strong. Vicar Brown had suffered a mild stroke in the winter. Though Derwent was expected to become curate when he graduated, nothing was settled yet. Some in the village said that he did not have the true calling of a vicar, and these whispers had made their way to him and made him despondent.

"If my father must step down earlier than planned, it will change everything," he told Evy, nailing a piece of canvas onto a booth. Evy would be selling Aunt Grace's tarts. "I suppose I could become a private tutor and live in London, but it would not give the living that the rectory does." At this, he glanced at Evy meaningfully.

Evy understood what Derwent was hinting at. If ever they were to marry, he would need a post at the rectory. If they both taught, then they could afford a place to live in London. But Evy had no strong passions toward Derwent, and the thought of marriage to him seemed little more than duty. And yet, what could be more normal than for a vicar's son and a former vicar's niece to carry on the work at the rectory in Grimston Way for another generation?

"You both know the rectory so well," Aunt Grace often said when they were alone in the cottage.

"I would not worry about a position, Derwent." Evy winced as he struck his thumb with the hammer. He yowled and dropped the tool, which Evy picked up. "Come down. Let me see."

"I was never good at this." Derwent climbed down the stepladder.

"You will lose your thumbnail," Evy told him. "Here, I'll finish."

"No, Evy, you might fall. Besides, girls don't climb ladders and bang nails."

She grinned. "I do." To prove it, she climbed up and proceeded to nail the canvas closed.

"Anyway, Derwent," she said over her banging, "if your father's health forces him to retire earlier than planned, there will of necessity be a new vicar appointed from London."

"True enough."

"Eventually, though, you will get a post here, perhaps as curate. There are a great many duties that fall to the curate, and you will be able to prove your spirituality."

"I suppose." He ran his uninjured hand through his russet hair. "I sometimes wish… Well, I'd best not say."

"What do you wish?" She hammered another nail.

"You won't laugh at me if I tell you?"

She gave him a scolding glance. "I think you know me better than that."

"I sometimes find myself wishing I was going to Capetown, like Rogan and Parnell." His eyes shone with a longing Evy had not seen before. "I would like to work in the diamond business. I suppose you think I sound ungrateful. The church has been good to me, allowing me the grant to go to school as they did. I wouldn't be able to attend if they hadn't. I owe my best years to the church."

Evy listened, aware how much Derwent still admired Rogan. She could not deny that Rogan's plans in South Africa seemed much more adventurous than being vicar. The lure of diamonds and faraway places had set Derwent to dreaming.

"The work in the church is far more important eternally," she encouraged. "Nourishing God's flock is a great honor."

"Oh, I know that. That's what troubles me. I don't feel worthy. And let's face it, I'm not the spiritual teacher your uncle Edmund was, or even my father. Though his mind seems to be going on him. His memory is, anyway. I'm helping with his sermons. I mean in no way to make light of it, but perhaps some of the talk going on about me is more true than not. Not every son is called to follow in his father's steps. The Lord does not always gift father and son the same way. If He did, there would be something to say for godliness and spiritual gifts being passed on through heredity and environment rather than sovereign will and grace. I don't see the Scripture teaching that."

She turned her head and smiled down at him. "The fact that you say these things tells me you *know* the Scripture well enough to be vicar someday."

A crooked smile lifted his mouth. "That will need to be a long time from now, Evy. I mean it." He frowned at his sore thumb, then shook his head.

Evy turned back to her nails. "A long time... Well, that is not really surprising. It's hardly wise for the bishop to appoint a young man like yourself to fill the vicar's position so soon. You must be tested by time."

"Aye—I mean *yes*," he hastened. "A *seasoned* man is how they say it. A man who's walked with the Lord for many years." Again he shook his head. "But gaining a living will be hard."

"I doubt if sailing to the Cape to search for diamonds will give you anything more in your bank account. You may end up with a whole lot less."

"That is true, of course. They say Kimberly is a wild and woolly place."

"That's why my parents went there so many years ago to present a witness for God."

"And they died for it."

She hammered a nail, not responding to this somber reminder.

"Evy, I just hope— Oh, why hello, Rogan!"

Oh no! Evy froze, then looked down over her shoulder. Rogan sat astride his horse, an alert, surprised flicker in his gaze. He studied her with sufficient intensity to freeze the smile on her lips into self-consciousness.

At first she thought he was dismayed to find her atop a ladder—not exactly a ladylike activity. But something in that dark gaze told her that what had startled Rogan had little to do with ladders and nails...and a great deal more to do with Evy herself.

She shivered, though the day was still quite warm. Rogan looked quite grown-up. His wavy ebony hair still had a tendency to fall across his forehead. His slashing dark brows, bold eyes, and strong jawline gave him a handsome, roguish appearance. How different he was from Derwent.

Evy became aware she was staring, and scolded herself for that fact just as Rogan seemed to recover from whatever surprise she had given him.

"You have grown." The comment was deep and rich, and his gaze held hers.

She loathed herself for blushing.

"Miss Evy, Derwent"—Rogan looked at Derwent as though suddenly becoming aware of him—"this is Miss Patricia Bancroft." Though he nodded to the young woman at his side, his gaze came back to rest on Evy.

Her gaze swerved from Rogan to confront the girl sitting proudly on the horse beside Rogan's magnificent mount. She seemed expert at handling her horse, another reason for Rogan's interest. The cold appraisal Patricia gave Evy made her cling more tightly to the ladder. Clearly, it had not been Patricia's idea to turn aside from the road to say hello. She looked disapproving and even hostile. Did she resent that Rogan would show friendliness toward her and Derwent—or had she noticed the look he'd given her?

Evy glanced away. What was she supposed to say?

"Time goes by so quickly." The words sounded foolish, even to her own ears.

Rogan's smile deepened, and his gaze told her he was aware of her discomfiture. "So it does. We were out riding before lunch and saw you both from the road. Is Derwent teaching you carpentry, or does he prefer the shade?"

She ignored his amusement, but Derwent held up his injured thumb. "Alas, I'm a poor teacher indeed."

Rogan laughed.

Derwent, apparently unmindful of the undercurrent between Rogan and Evy, sighed. "I was telling Evy how I might enjoy choosing to go to Capetown and work in the diamond business. I admire you and your brother."

"And give up the opportunity for a quiet and peaceful life here at the rectory?" Rogan's measuring glance seemed to question whether Derwent might also be relinquishing his plans for Evy.

"Well, there is that, of course." Derwent glanced about the vicarage grounds, as though contemplating all of Grimston Way.

"It would surprise me if Miss Evy would approve of your giving up rectory life for the uncertainty and dangers of African diamonds."

Evy felt herself stiffen. Rogan talked as though she were not present.

"I'm sure," she said, hoping to sound casual, "that my wishes will not be the sole criterion for deciding Derwent's future."

Rogan's brows lifted. "I would expect your wishes to count a great deal in Derwent's thoughts about anything, but most especially the future."

She ignored his assertion, grateful that Derwent looked as if he hadn't understood Rogan's implication. She started down the unsteady ladder, clutching the hammer in one hand. Rogan gestured for Derwent to help her.

Derwent jumped up to hold the ladder, and Evy felt the heat in her cheeks. What was it about Rogan that flustered her so?

"Thank you," she said, not looking at any of them. She set the hammer down and wiped her hands on a cloth, choosing her next words carefully. "It shouldn't be all that surprising for me to have interests in South Africa as well. Most everyone knows how my parents worked there and were killed in the Zulu War." She looked up and met Rogan's challenging stare.

"You are not afraid to go to the Cape?"

"No, though I've no reason to think I shall ever do so."

"I suppose not. I was thinking of Arcilla. You have two more years at Parkridge Music Academy?"

"Three years."

"That's right…you are younger than she."

"Only by three months."

At her hasty correction, Rogan regarded her. "Then you are enjoying your schooling?"

His seeming interest warmed her, and she smiled. "Very much so." She had not yet thanked him for the pretty hat, but she dared not do so now. Patricia was already fuming. The girl was flipping her small horsewhip, chewing on her rosebud lips while Rogan spoke with Evy.

Patricia looked over her shoulder toward the road, as if expecting company. "It is getting late, Rogan." She sounded a bit cross, and Evy had to fight a smirk. "We are to meet Parnell and Christine for luncheon. Remember?"

He did not appear worried about luncheon, nor even the obvious tone of her voice, but obliged her by turning his horse.

Derwent's gaze rested on the horses. "Handsome animals. How is your riding proceeding, Rogan?"

"I shall know next month."

"Next month?"

He smiled. "I shall ride in the Dublin horse show."

Evy had heard much about the show and realized he must be very good indeed if he was in that competition.

Rogan gestured to the booth. "Yours?" he asked Evy, studying her features again.

"My aunt's." She shifted, longing for the cool of evening—and freedom from that dark gaze, "The annual summer fete you know. The proceeds will go to buy new fruit trees for the rectory," she managed, brushing her heavy hair away from her shoulder. Anything to cool her face a bit. If only he would stop staring at her so!

"Interesting and commendable. We will make sure to visit Mrs. Havering's booth, won't we, Patricia?"

"Oh, by *all* means." Patricia made no effort to hide her irritation.

"It is well that Vicar Brown gets some new fruit trees." Evy felt the situation deteriorating quickly and dragging her down with it.

Again, Rogan smiled. He watched her as though trying to figure her out, and Evy felt a tinge of trepidation dance across her skin. How could one look both alarm and please her so? It was the kind of look she had secretly dreamed Rogan would give her, yet it made her feel guilty and afraid.

Breaking his gaze from her, Rogan touched the tip of his smart-looking hat, nodding first to Derwent, then to her. "I will try to visit the fete. When is it?"

Evy tried to swallow, though her throat felt suddenly bone dry. "Saturday, but I doubt if it will interest you."

His look told her he knew she was trying to discourage him. "Oh, I am quite interested already. Au revoir." With that, he maneuvered his horse and rode after Miss Patricia, who had galloped ahead.

Evy sank to the footstool, her legs suddenly unwilling to support her.

"A talented young man." Derwent looked after Rogan.

Evy felt an unreasonable surge of irritation. Did Derwent understand nothing? Didn't it even bother him to have Rogan looking at her the way he had? It certainly had bothered *her*…far more than it should have.

But Derwent seemed oblivious to anything amiss. "Rogan is quite different from his brother. Some think he will gain notoriety in the Dublin horse show. It takes discipline to reach that level. He also graduates next year from the geological school, and is in the top of his class. Parnell was not so inclined and spent a good deal of time in London away from his studies, with friends. Parnell is leaving for the Cape in September, did you know?"

She did, and she knew Rogan was likely to sail there after his graduation. What she didn't know was whether she was glad about that…or utterly devastated.

CHAPTER SEVENTEEN

It rained on the day of the fete, which prompted a rush to reorganize inside the rectory hall. Of course it was impossible to move so many booths indoors, so there was a scramble to locate enough tables for the ladies to display their baked goods and preserves in the rectory hall.

"To think we spent all that time on them booths," Mrs. Croft complained to Evy. "It won't be nearly as attractive now. Let's hope the villagers turn out."

It was a tradition for the squire's family to support the fete, so about an hour into the event Lady Elosia arrived in the family coach with Arcilla and Parnell. Evy looked around for Rogan, but did not see him. Patricia Bancroft, she thought. If she could keep him away, she would.

Apparently, though, Patricia hadn't succeeded, for Rogan came a short time later. Patricia was not with him.

Evy admitted her surprise that Rogan had actually shown as he said he would. Maybe the Bancrofts had returned to London, and he had nothing to entertain him. Evy watched Rogan and Parnell from where she stood behind a long serving table covered with a white lace cloth embroidered with spring tulips.

Dr. Tisdale's wife was at the next table dipping a ladle into a huge bowl of punch, while Alice cavorted about as though she were a guest. Evy could not remember a time when Alice actually assisted her mother at any of the events. But then, Mrs. Tisdale thought her daughter too important for such menial work as the other rectory girls endured. Mrs. Tisdale looked none the worse for manning the table alone. She was doing a brisk business selling her punch, and she smiled as the coins continued to plunk into the container.

Alice stopped by to see what Evy was selling. "Our punch bowl is Viennese crystal." She flipped her hair back. "Mum bought it in Vienna when we went there on tour two years ago." The pitying glance she directed at her set Evy's nerves on edge. "You should have *seen* the music theater! *Too* awfully grand! I simply *must* go again."

Evy held her tongue, but her thoughts would not be silent. *Alice will be in for a bumpy landing once she comes down from her high horse. How can she possibly expect to marry Rogan when Patricia Bancroft has already been approved by the Chantry and Bancroft families?*

Evy turned her attention from Alice to Parnell Chantry. He looked a great deal older since having finished at the university. He divided his time now between Rookswood and the London branch office, where he was learning about the family's South African diamond business.

Both brothers looked dashing in their rich attire as they stood beside Lady Elosia and Arcilla. They were soon performing the social duties of the squire's family, bowing to the ladies and complimenting them on their goods.

A woman holding a tray approached Evy's table. Evy held the tongs to a fat apple tart, watching Rogan as Alice approached him.

Rogan clearly was the more friendly of the squire's sons, with an easy smile and an appealing way about him that made him more likable in the village. It also made him more dangerous. The village girls were already hopelessly beguiled by him, a fact that both amused and irritated Evy as she looked on. Alice was fanning herself with a new white Vienna lace fan though it was not a bit warm. In fact, Evy had contemplated putting on her wrap. Alice's giggle carried on the breeze, and Evy glanced at her just in time to see her toss her strawberry blond curls and mince about in her blue dress.

Evy huffed when Rogan smiled at the ridiculous girl and carried on a polite conversation. But just as Evy was about to look away, Rogan glanced in the direction of her table. He caught her gaze, and his smile broadened.

"Oh! I am so sorry, Miss Armitage!" Evy's cheeks blazed as she looked down at the dear old lady's tray. She had just released the apple tart over her cup instead of her napkin! The cup instantly overflowed, and punch ran across the tray.

"My *dear* girl," Miss Armitage said, alarmed.

Evy grabbed a cloth and hurried around the table to where the elderly woman stood, clearly offended.

"Oh, my dear Miss Armitage, I do hope the Holland lace is not stained." She tried to blot a spill that had run from the tray to the woman's bagging sleeve.

"*Tsk, tsk,* Evy. You simply *must* pay closer attention to what you are doing."

"Yes, Miss Armitage. I am so very sorry."

"You've said that already." The woman turned her silver head with its outdated 1860 hairdo and looked across the hall toward Rogan and Parnell. The two young men wore tolerant smiles as they talked with Meg and Emily, who had joined Alice. The three girls chattered like excited sparrows.

"So that's it." Miss Armitage's features pinched even more than usual. "I might have known it."

Evy pretended to not understand. "Beg pardon, Miss Armitage?"

"You know very well what I mean, I daresay. I would think a sensible young lady such as yourself, Evy Varley, would know better than to get absorbed in the likes of those two scamps. And you, with your upbringing in the rectory, should know better than to be daydreaming about them." She straightened her spectacles and looked around. "Where is that aunt of yours?"

"She's a bit ill, I'm afraid. We thought it best that she avoid the rain." Evy wished she could sink through the floor and hide from those shrewd gray eyes that fixed upon her. "Shall I— Shall I get you another tray of punch and a tart, Miss Armitage?"

"You do not expect me to eat *this* mess, do you?"

"No, of course not. Here, I'll take that tray away."

"I should hope so."

A short time later, Evy returned with a tray of fresh punch and another of Aunt Grace's apple tarts. But before she could escape, Miss Armitage grasped her sleeve.

"You watch those two scoundrels." The old woman's voice was low and full of dire meaning. "They will dance circles around a good girl like you every time. You are no match for them. They've been well trained in the house of Master Henry, and now that their father, the squire, is widowed—he could very well have his eye on your aunt."

Evy must have looked blank, because Miss Armitage made a sound of impatient dismissal. "Untrustworthy scamps, those boys. Word has it from my sister in London. She knows. Oh yes, indeed. Those two have already caused talk in London. Matilda read about it in the society page."

With that, Miss Armitage walked away toward Vicar Brown, no doubt to fill his ears with whatever she had read in the London papers. Evy watched her leave, then glanced at Rogan and Parnell. What on earth had the papers said about them?

She shook her head. Never mind. Whatever it was, it had to be just gossip.

She took a deep breath and sighed to herself. *Lord, do not let me become a gossipy hen when I grow old.*

At least Miss Armitage was gone. Evy moved back behind the table, glancing around her. Had anyone noticed the embarrassing incident? Fortunately, everyone seemed too occupied with conversations to pay attention to her disaster. She looked toward Arcilla, who was as lovely as ever, her hair plaited with silver threads and her summery frock of daffodil yellow satin flowing about her. She had matured into a beautiful young woman.

Evy's own dress was quite ordinary by comparison. Cotton, pale blue, with simple white cuffs and a high collar with a bit of lace. The long skirts were quite dignified and proper, and while the dress was no match for Arcilla's and Alice's, she would need to be blind to see herself every day in the mirror and not be aware that she, too, had blossomed into a beauty.

Arcilla was nearing seventeen now and was anxious to complete her last year at the finishing school in London. After that she would have her coming-out in London society when a marriage would be arranged, either to Charles Bancroft, if Arcilla and Lady Elosia had their way, or to Peter Bartley of South Africa, if Sir Julien Bley ruled his family realm. Evy, if she believed in wagering, would bet that Sir Julien would win.

Evy glanced about, seeking Derwent. She finally spotted him with Tom and Milt. All three were agog, watching Arcilla, who smiled and charmed them, making each one feel special. One thing about Arcilla: She never blushed. *If all the boys stared at me that way, I'd turn pink as a new rose!* Evy sighed at her lack of poise. Arcilla knew her effect on the young men and played it to full advantage.

Evy grimaced. Could Derwent and the others not see through the girl's insincerity? Even so, Evy could not help being fond of Arcilla. She was what she was, and it was simple as that.

"My Alice is having such a wonderful time." Mrs. Tisdale's voice drew Evy's attention. The woman was talking with the solicitor's wife. "I daresay she is very near the marrying age now. The doctor"—she always spoke of her husband in third person, as though he were nobility—"is seriously rethinking her future. Naturally, Alice wishes to graduate from music school in London, but we are thinking an engagement might be wiser. We have *just* the proper young man in mind."

Was it Evy's imagination, or did Mrs. Tisdale glance sideways at her?

"Derwent and Rogan are *quite* friendly with Alice," the woman went on. "They rode over yesterday to visit and stayed for tea and cakes."

So that was where Derwent spent yesterday afternoon. Evy had wondered when he did not show up to help with the final preparations on the booth. It should not surprise her that he had opted to take an afternoon ride with Rogan, who must have lent him a horse. But she'd never dreamed they had ridden over to the Tisdales'. Derwent said nothing of where he had been when he came by later, and she had not thought it her business to ask him.

So he'd had tea and cakes with Alice. Well, that was fine. It didn't bother her. Not nearly as much as the fact that Rogan had done so as well!

"Alice is a very nice girl," the solicitor's wife agreed.

"And very dutiful to her religious faith," Mrs. Tisdale said.

Evy knew differently. The entire time she'd roomed with Alice, the girl had never read from her small Bible and tried to avoid chapel.

A sudden frown pulled Evy's brows low. Why was Mrs. Tisdale suddenly talking about religion…and Derwent? Could she have Derwent in mind for Alice?

Evy looked across the hall at Alice, adorned in an extravagant apple green dress with matching slippers, her braided hair coiled about her head. That dress must have cost Dr. Tisdale a pretty pound. It was Mrs. Tisdale's idea, of course. Evy watched Alice carry a large basket of summer daisies, handing them out to the ladies and girls in celebration of the summer fete. She was doing so with a certain fanfare that drew attention to herself as she walked about the hall, making certain Rogan noticed her. Or was it Derwent she sought to attract?

She handed a double daisy tied with a pink ribbon to Arcilla, then stopped in front of Rogan and Derwent to talk. She was playing the coquette and looking quite silly, but what irritated Evy the most was that Rogan was smiling. Alice was looking up at him and turning from side to side while she held her basket behind her back, her apple green skirts rustling.

If Alice were outside in the garden, and if it were nighttime, she'd probably let Rogan kiss her! Then Evy caught herself and bit her lip. *How catty I'm being.*

She jumped when a voice beside her drawled lazily, "Hello, hello, hello."

Parnell Chantry had come up without her noticing and stood there, a small plate in hand. He dropped a goodly handful of coins in the offering container. "Did you make those tarts?"

Unlike Rogan's dark hair, Parnell's was chestnut and curly, and his eyes were hazel-brown. He was an inch shorter than Rogan, and was slim and agile. A small, dark mole on his chin gave him a rather a knavish appearance. Evy couldn't recall seeing Parnell smile, but, like all the Chantrys, he was comely.

Evy used the tongs to move the tarts around so they would show better. "My aunt baked them. I'm afraid all I did was dust them with sugar. Which one would you like?"

"The one with the most apples. Yes—that one. Delightful."

He held out his plate, and she placed it with careful precision, taking no chances of repeating her accident with Miss Armitage. Imagine the horror of doing such a thing to Parnell Chantry! She glanced at the lace on his velvet cuff. Clearly he enjoyed dressing with more French flair than Rogan. She watched him taste the tart with his fork.

"Absolutely smashing." He looked across the hall toward his brother and took another bite as Rogan looked past Alice and his gaze came to rest on them. Evy had the oddest impression that the two brothers were challenging one another.

Parnell turned back to her. "Your aunt is ill?"

"Yes, for some time now. We hoped the summer weather would benefit her, but it has not."

He nodded. "I'm glad we had her as Arcilla's governess for as long as we did. My sister is most fond of her."

Evy was not aware that this was so, but perhaps he was trying to be kind. "Thank you. My aunt is quite patient."

Again, he nodded.

There was a moment of awkward silence, as though he tried to think of something to say to her. She already knew she was not as easy to talk with as other girls, who giggled and said silly things. But Evy would eat a mouthful of dirt before she would dither and show off in such a coquettish way.

Parnell shifted, suddenly looking as though his shirt collar was too tight. Undoubtedly he was aware of the wide disparity between their social positions. Evy took pity on the poor man.

"You are through at the university now." She smiled at him. "I suppose you will be sailing to South Africa. Are you looking forward to it?"

He brushed the spotless cuff of his jacket. "Yes, it should prove deeply interesting."

"Will you be leaving soon?"

"It will be a few months more. There is so much to learn at the London office."

She nodded. "I can well understand that. What does your family do at the London office?"

"For one thing we hire master diamond cutters. It is painstaking work, but lucrative. Businesses the world over come to buy from us. I'm pleased to say I will not be involved in that part of the business. I haven't the steady nerves for it. Our father expects me to be involved in running the mines. I'll learn all that from my uncle, Sir Julien. My family is partners with another side of our extended family in South Africa as well. You may have heard of the them...the Bleys and Brewsters?"

"Yes, indeed. Sir Julien Bley is an important name in diamonds, or so I've been told."

"Very important. You have heard of De Beer Consolidated in South Africa?"

Evy considered this. "Well, yes, I suppose I have. He is the diamond mogul, isn't he?"

Parnell seemed pleased at her knowledge. "To be modest, yes. De Beer owns one of the four main diamond companies in Kimberly. Sir Julien is managing director of De Beer under the great Cecil Rhodes. Uncle Julien is one of the largest shareholders. And Mr. Rhodes and Sir Julien intend to make De Beer the owner of the other three companies one day."

She supposed that if one's values and worth were determined by their ownership of diamonds, then Sir Julien would be a very great man indeed. "Do the other three diamond companies agree that Mr. De Beer should own a monopoly on South African diamonds?"

Parnell's expression told her he was being tolerant of what he considered her ignorance. "One does not *ask* permission for such ventures. One prods and pushes until walls fall down."

Evy looked down at the tarts on the table. "Sounds very...cold-blooded."

"At times, yes." She noted he offered no apology. "So you see, Rogan and I have grave responsibilities ahead of us in South Africa."

Her heart constricted at Parnell's words. "Then the squire will send both you and your brother to the Cape?"

"Uncle Julien has requested him to do so. Father is in close correspondence with his stepbrother."

From what Evy had seen, Sir Lyle was apt to do whatever Julien told him. Which did not bode well for Arcilla and Charles.

"I believe Rogan is nearly finished with his geology studies at the university," she commented. "He once mentioned searching for gold in South Africa."

"My brother has ideas…some strange and wild ones. I think he will set them aside when he arrives at the Cape."

"Am I interrupting something important?"

Evy turned with a start, and her gaze collided with Rogan's. He had come up without their realizing it. How much had he overheard? She would have preferred not to be found discussing him with his brother.

"Hello, Miss Evy." He smiled, a sultry contrast to his light-haired brother. He offered the small bow expected of young gentlemen of aristocratic birth, but he seemed disingenuous. What was he up to?

Evy felt a shiver of caution and set her guard against him. Rogan appeared to notice the change in her demeanor, as his smile deepened and seemed to challenge her. Could it be that in distancing herself from him, she actually interested him all the more? The answer was clear: Rogan's conceit would make him determined to break down anyone's resistance.

Evy bit back her annoyance. Apparently, by just being herself, she presented a different challenge than the other young ladies around them. And, much to her dismay, this had sparked interest in both brothers.

So this was what a hart felt when encircled by two hunters.

Old Miss Armitage's dire warnings echoed in Evy's mind, and she glanced in the woman's direction. Sure enough, Miss Armitage was watching them, shrewd interest gleaming in those pale eyes.

Rogan took another look at his brother, and his jaw tensed. Thankfully, Parnell did not appear to notice his brother's displeasure. Evy did not want a scene right there in the rectory hall.

She almost clapped with relief when she saw Lady Elosia coming toward them.

"Ah, there you are, Parnell, Rogan. Have you made the rounds? We cannot stay long, you know. Sir Lyle has received correspondence from Sir Julien, and he wishes to meet with you both in the library at four o'clock. Ah, Evy, and how is Grace? Any better?"

"I'm afraid not, Lady Elosia, but thank you for your concern. Dr. Tisdale will see her before supper."

"Ah, yes, the dear woman. I'm glad she did not venture out in the rain. Such dreadful weather for June. Well, if there is anything we can do up at Rookswood, my dear, you send word up right away. Your aunt is such a hard worker. It is no wonder she's having difficulty recovering from last winter's chest cold. You tell her to drink herb tea."

Evy thanked her, and Parnell bowed and took his leave. Evy waited for Rogan to follow suit, but he lingered.

"Mrs. Havering is ill again?"

She explained that Aunt Grace had been fighting a lung ailment since last fall.

Rogan's frown seemed sincere. "Maybe she ought to visit a physician in London. There are specialists in bronchitis."

"I mentioned it to her, but I think you know something about my aunt. She would feel it a waste of time and expense to travel there and stay in a hotel."

She was surprised by his genuine sympathy, but strangely, instead of bolstering her spirits it undid her defenses against him. And that was far more disturbing than she liked. She changed the subject, not wanting to let her rioting emotions show. She did not want his sympathy, not when it made her feel so vulnerable toward him.

"I believe Lady Elosia mentioned you are expected at Rookswood." She sounded more disapproving than she felt.

His brows arched. "How like a teacher you sound." He gestured at the tarts. "I shall try one for this evening. You can wrap it up? Anyway, I rode my horse down, so I don't need to return in the coach. And my father's always late. She said four, so that means more like half past five."

She wrapped the tart while he put money into the container, and she noticed he put in more than Parnell. She handed the tart to him. "I must not keep you." She took special care to avoid that dark gaze.

"You make me feel so appreciated."

She would not be swayed by his teasing. "I am sure you are."

A faint, sardonic smile showed. "But not by you."

"I do not know why you say so."

"It is obvious. You disapprove of me."

She busied herself rearranging the remaining tarts. "That should not trouble you. My opinion is not important."

"Then you do still disapprove of me?"

"I did not say so."

"Your eyes say so quite clearly."

"Then you must not try to read them."

A quick heat filled her cheeks at her effrontery, but Rogan merely smiled. "They are interesting...and *very* readable."

"You are mistaken—"

"Unusual color, I think...like amber. Or is it tawny? Almost the color of a lion I saw in a painting from South Africa." He leaned toward her for a closer look, and Evy stepped back.

Oh, this cursed warmth in her cheeks! She searched for a way to distract him from his study of her eyes. "Truly, what does my opinion matter? You do not remind me of someone who worries about what people may think of you."

"Depends on the person, of course." His smile was almost her undoing. "Maybe I would appreciate your good opinion."

The idea was so absurd to her that she laughed, easing the moment and breaking his spell. Since there were no other customers, she sat down on the stool and glanced about the hall, as though uninterested in him. But she was almost painfully aware of him leaning there, amused, watching her.

"Still looking for Derwent?" The smooth question was replete with meaning.

Her gaze came to his, and his dark brow lifted. He glanced about the hall. "I think he is with the Tisdale girl. Interesting thought. Derwent and Alice." His eyes came back to her. "They make a charming couple, don't you agree?"

She knew what he was trying to do, and she would not rise to the bait. "I have not thought about it one way or the other."

"Maybe you should."

She paused at that, and his smile returned.

"I mean that Derwent is obviously such a very good friend of yours. You should be interested in his…affairs."

"I consider him a good friend, yes."

"Only a friend?"

She ignored the question, and he went on. "Ah, well, you need not explain. You have so much in common, you and Derwent. Everyone says so."

She tried not to let her irritation at this show. "Do they?"

"Don't you think so? You both were raised in the rectory. That should give you much to talk about."

"Yes, I suppose that is true."

He pursed his lips. "Derwent may one day wish to reconsider taking his father's position when the vicar retires. Especially if he had another offer, and of course, if the vicar approved the change in his career."

What was Rogan getting at? "Derwent wasn't serious when he mentioned South Africa, you know." She folded her hands in her lap, hoping to still their trembling. Rogan in such close proximity was far too disturbing for her peace of mind. "Derwent is almost obligated to enter the church. Vicar Brown would be heartbroken if his son became an adventurer instead of a parson."

Rogan inclined his dark head. "True enough, I am sure. And there is nothing like being plagued with guilt for disappointing the expectations of family. Yet Derwent freely admits he does not feel worthy of that position."

Evy's uneasiness grew, and she also wondered if Rogan might actually know something of the same burden…if he bore the weight of disappointing Sir Lyle. However, even his notion to mine for gold in South

Africa, which was a departure from the family interest in diamonds, had not been met with displeasure.

"Derwent will become curate." She nodded to emphasize her certainty. "I don't believe he would shirk his responsibility."

"You think he is really that dedicated, do you?" There flickered an inquisitiveness in his dark eyes. "How highly you've elevated him above the rest of us adventurous scoundrels."

She managed a smile. "I am impressed by the humble manner in which he deals with the difficult expectations placed upon him."

"You mean, compared to us Chantrys, who are arrogant and utterly lacking in humility. Well then, being a rectory girl, you should be qualified to teach me how to be humble."

Such a suggestion sent her heart skipping, but Evy managed to keep her voice light and steady. "I am sure there is little I could teach you, Master Rogan, that you would accept."

A warm smile lit his features. "Then we must find out."

Evy wished the ground would open up and swallow her. Either that, or swallow him! Rogan's veiled suggestion that he was interested in her was utterly ridiculous, she knew that. There could never be anything to his intent beyond a light and frivolous flirtation. So why did the idea set her poor head spinning so?

"And since you are so impressed by Derwent"—he inclined his head—"is it possible that I know him better than you do?"

Now that was absurd indeed! "I hardly think so."

"We shall see."

Evy felt her gaze narrow. "What do you mean?"

He lifted a hand, every inch the royal dismissing a lesser being. "Perhaps he has confided in me." His eyes glinted, and Evy was sure he was laughing at her. "After all, having taken advantage of our docile and trusting Derwent when we were boys, I may feel compelled to offer him advice and, shall we say...opportunity?"

Oh no! Poor Derwent! He had always looked on Rogan with such admiration. If Rogan should somehow convince him to give up the rectory life to follow him out to South Africa—

"If you should make the mistake of luring him to South Africa, you shall be doing him, and others, an injustice."

A veil seemed to fall over Rogan's expression. "I'm disappointed you would see it that way. May I assume that when you mention an injustice done to *others,* you speak of yourself?"

"I speak first of Vicar Brown."

"And yourself second?"

Evy had had enough. She slid from the stool and planted her hands on her hips. "There has been no promise made between myself and Derwent, if that is what you are hinting at. My concern has nothing to do with *my* unwillingness to pursue a future in South Africa. It has everything to do with what is best for *Derwent.*"

His mouth thinned, and she saw clear disdain in his dark eyes. "Is it necessary, then, to protect him as though he were a child, with no wisdom or determination of his own?"

Words failed her at the cold accusation. Was that what she was doing? She remained silent, considering.

After a moment, he changed the subject. "You are returning to the music school soon?"

She pulled herself from her pondering and nodded. "Yes…in a few weeks."

"Maybe I will see you in London."

"I do not see how or why you should bother."

A sardonic hint of smile touched his mouth at her candor. She hoped he did not believe she wanted to elicit some reason why he wanted to see her. She had not meant it that way, but he was quite capable, in his conceit, of thinking so.

"Ah well, I must be going or I'll be late for my father's meeting in the library. That would never do. Every letter from Sir Julien is a grand occasion. My uncle always has his way—even from across the Atlantic."

"Perhaps the letter has to do with your brother's voyage to South Africa," she said, trying not to sound too interested.

"Yes. And mine, no doubt. The family in Capetown have a sudden and particular interest in us, which is curious"—a slight frown settled on his brow—"and a little worrisome."

What could he mean by that? What *particular interest?* But Rogan did not elaborate, and she would not be so forward as to ask. Instead, she headed the conversation another direction. "Do you remember the time we were nearly caught by Sir Julien in Master Henry's rooms?"

She would have thought the memory would bring him a smile, but instead a certain thoughtful concern showed in his gaze, as though his mind traveled far away, perhaps to Sir Julien himself in Capetown.

"Yes, I remember. But he only caught *me* there. He has since made light of it, but somehow I do not think he really accepted my explanation."

"Did he ever learn that I was with you?"

Rogan shrugged. "I never told him. I would have expected him to question you if he knew. Then, again, Sir Julien is rather odd. Sometimes I think he did know. By the way, have you heard from Lady Camilla since she was here?"

"No. For her sake I hope she has come to know I am not her husband's mystery child."

Rogan didn't respond. He simply studied her features.

She met his gaze, wondering at the shift in his mood, and he smiled a little.

"Well, Miss Evy, it's been…interesting. We will talk again. Au revoir." He turned and walked away.

She watched him leave through the front hall door. Why had he brought up Lady Camilla? And why did she get the distinct impression that Rogan did not quite trust his Uncle Julien?

As she turned back to the table of tarts, she could not help but shiver. Rogan…Sir Julien…Master Henry… Try as she might, she couldn't escape thinking about them. Nor could she dislodge the uneasy feeling that their family secrets were more than a touch sinister.

She could only be grateful they had nothing to do with her.

CHAPTER EIGHTEEN

Evy's uncertainty over Aunt Grace took a swift upsurge during the next several weeks. It was late August, and Dr. Tisdale informed Evy that her aunt was suffering from a serious attack of bronchitis that might linger into the winter months ahead.

"She is quite frail and will need care."

She stood beside him in the doorway to her aunt's small room, watching Aunt Grace sleep. Her sallow cheeks were pronounced, as were the purplish shadows beneath her eyes.

"Keep the room warm and dry." The doctor nodded to Evy, and left—taking with him Evy's hopes of returning to London and music school.

She found solace in long walks in the woods, where she thought and prayed. She knew there were scant resources for her schooling, and her aunt's health required that she remain with her.

Evy wished she could go to the stables to borrow the horse she learned to ride when she first came to Rookswood, but with Arcilla away for a short stay at Heathfriar to visit Patricia and be near Charles, she was reluctant to impose upon the squire's kindness.

She went out in the late afternoons, when the sun dipped low and cast a shimmer on the yellow-red leaves of August. The starkness of color, combined with the moan of the wind through the treetops in the otherwise pervading silence, touched her spirit with a melancholy she could not understand. Walking seemed her only solace.

Once on the little-used trail that led into the woods, she could walk undisturbed until she came to a small hill. Here, she could see Rookswood, especially the west side of the great house.

How she had enjoyed her early years, both in the rectory and at Rookswood. Everything was changing now that they were nearly grown and out of school. What would the future hold? If Sir Julien arranged for Arcilla to marry Peter Bartley against her will, that would of necessity end Evy's friendship with her. Arcilla would be busy with her new life in Capetown, distance and change would leave no opportunity for a continued relationship with her old governess's niece. Their lives would be so different.

And what of Evy's plans? Everything was so uncertain. She only had three months of paid classes left. Once Evy returned for the Christmas holidays, they would have to pay for any further schooling. But even more important, her ailing aunt needed her here.

No, Evy had little choice. She would have to find work teaching piano to children in the parish. There would always be new Megs and Emilys who would come along. Already the two girls were engaged to marry next year, and they would soon be having babies. Evy smiled to herself, for she could almost hear Uncle Edmund's voice on the wind in the autumn leaves, quoting one of the Bible verses he had asked her to memorize: "For I have learned, in whatsoever state I am, therewith to be content."

As she stood on the windy hillock looking off at Rookswood, the dry colorful leaves on the trees rattled in the breeze, accompanied by another sound...hoofbeats?

She spun just in time to see Rogan maneuver his horse from among the trees onto an open area, holding the mount steady.

"I thought I'd find you here."

Although his presence disturbed the tranquility of her emotions, she felt a rush of exhilaration. Rogan always brought her a challenge.

He looked down at her. "I saw you walking up the trail. You come here often. You must enjoy the view."

She drew her shawl tighter as the wind swirled her cotton skirts at her ankles.

"Rather a bleak day for a comfortable walk." He lifted his face to the wind. "There wasn't much of a summer, was there?"

Somehow she read more into his words, hearing the truth that the carefree days of youth were fast coming to a close. There would be inevitable partings, some of them permanent.

"I like to walk in the cool brisk wind," she said just to be contrary and to avoid emotions that weakened her resolve not to respond to his almost magnetic appeal.

"Well, there's no accounting for people's tastes. I am surprised Derwent is not with you, though. An aptly secluded spot for a late afternoon rendezvous." He glanced toward the dim woods as he slid from the saddle. "Or did he see me and decide to hide?"

How could she be so attracted to one so very irritating? "Once again, you are wrong. And I think you know it. I did not come here to rendezvous with Derwent or anyone else. Besides, Derwent is no doubt busily attending to the vicar's needs, just as I must do shortly with my aunt."

"What is wrong with the vicar?" He walked up to stand near her on an edge overlooking the grassy meadow.

"Age, I fear… How do you know I come here often?"

His smile was quick and warm. "I cannot tell you all my secrets."

Had he seen her in the afternoons from a window in the west wing? Interesting that he had never troubled to join her until today.

"I remember you often enjoyed riding with my sister. Why do you avoid the stables now?"

"It would be rather bold of me, I daresay, since your sister remains at Heathfriar."

"Ah, you are timid about riding alone, then. That can be remedied. I don't leave for London until next week."

His nearness was entirely too distracting, and she forced herself to look away, struggling to appear indifferent. "I am so busy now."

"Why not go riding with me?"

"You misunderstood me about being timid. How I feel about my access to the Chantry stables has nothing to do with the fear of riding alone. I have always enjoyed being alone, to some degree. I meant that it would be bold of me to make use of the Chantry stables on my own. It was different when I was Arcilla's companion. The only reason I even learned to ride was because Lady Elosia wanted a companion for Arcilla during her lessons."

It was no secret that Arcilla actually felt reluctant about riding. She did so merely because it enabled her to be out and away from family eyes. Evy was the only one who knew that Arcilla had used those occasions to chatter with village boys.

"Granted, that is the reason you learned to ride"—Rogan inclined his dark head—"but now it is I who need a riding companion. So you can accompany me while I am here."

She gave a short laugh. "I hardly think you have difficulty finding a suitable companion."

"That is where you are wrong." His smile sent a shiver of awareness dancing up her spine. "I gather you think because I am a Chantry I can have everything I want?"

"Most everything."

"Ah, wrong again. It is not so. I am particular, you see. And I wish for your company. Who better could I have than the girl from the rectory, chosen by my aunt for our sweet Arcilla's betterment?" He reached out to pat his horse's neck. "I am sure my aunt would also agree that your company would benefit me."

Evy could find no suitable retort. What was he trying to do? Wrapping her shawl tightly around her, she warned her emotions to be still and moved away from him. "It is later than I thought. I must be going now."

He ignored her statement. "Arcilla never really enjoyed riding, but I noticed that you did. I doubt if she ever would have mastered it if not for your lead. Though she was nervous about it, she felt motivated not to be outdone."

Evy hesitated, turning back to him. "I'm surprised you recognized that."

"It goes along with her tendency to be in the spotlight." He laughed. "I know my dear sister very well indeed. Now it is balls and outings. Of course, Charles is ready to flatter and charm her. I think he has already fallen for her."

"Arcilla is a beautiful woman. Naturally men will notice."

"Yes. And she does many foolish things. I suspect she gets the tendency from not having a mother to teach her. Lady Elosia, bless her heart, is, well—Lady Elosia."

Evy smiled, rather surprised to hear him speak this way. He had never given any evidence that he thought Arcilla was unwise where men were concerned.

He met her smile with one of his own. "Feel free to use the stables whenever the fancy takes you."

The clearly sincere offer warmed her in ways she knew it should not. "Thank you, but presently walking suits me just fine. It offers me time to think."

"And you can't think while riding?" His smile told her he didn't believe her. "I thought you handled your mount in a very relaxed manner. You could learn to be an excellent rider. A shame I will not be here long enough to give you some advanced lessons."

At his meaningful smile, Evy looked away.

Run! her mind screamed. *Stay!* her heart pled.

She cleared her throat. "You are leaving for the university?"

"Next week." His tone turned cajoling. "Yet there is time for a few lessons."

He was nothing if not persistent. "The sun will set in an hour. I must get back."

"We have time. You needn't be concerned. I will see you back to the cottage."

"I— I really must get back. You see, I never stay here long. It is mostly the walk I enjoy."

"You rise early. Meet me at the stables at eight. You can ride with me just as you rode with Arcilla."

It was all she could do to meet that steady gaze. Her heart beat rapidly, and she scolded it, furious with both Rogan and herself.

This is nothing more to him than a mild flirtation, an amusing entertainment. A culmination of their childhood relationship before he went away. It would go nowhere, nor was it supposed to. But for all that she knew that was true, Evy felt as though a dangerous and life-changing trap was closing about her. She must not get involved with Rogan. Not even lightly.

"I have so much work to do tomorrow—"

"It cannot be all that urgent. I shall have you back before ten o'clock."

"It is urgent."

A dark brow shot up, and he offered the cryptic smile she was beginning to know so well. He did not believe her. He leaned his arm against the saddle, studying her. She could only guess what was in his mind.

She glanced away from him. "I told Derwent I would choose the hymns for Sunday. I usually go there by half past eight."

"How long can it possibly take to choose a few hymns? No more than twenty minutes, is my guess, not to make light of hymns, you understand. Actually, I am very fond of church music. I have even studied its history."

She turned and looked at him. He watched her evenly, as though measuring her response. Was he trying a different bait?

"You…studied church music?"

"There! You see?" He looked utterly wounded. "*Everything* I do is suspect!"

She couldn't help but laugh. "Not quite *everything*. But you do not remind me of someone interested in music or history."

"Suspicion, suspicion. My interest in church music should convince you not to avoid me."

Her brows arched this time. "Avoid you?"

"Like a frightened little bird, ready to peep and fly away the moment I come into view…especially when you are alone." His voice dropped to a soft murmur. "What could you be afraid of, I wonder?"

Her heart felt as though a hand had seized it, squeezing it with fierce determination. She spun away from him, striding down the path in the direction of the cottage and Aunt Grace, back to safety and security.

He was far too close to the heart of her true feelings. How had he known? It did not matter, but it was risky that he knew. What else could he guess from reading her eyes?

"Then I will see you at the rectory in the morning." His laughing voice chased her down the hill. "I will help you choose the hymns, and we will have our little ride afterward."

"You would not enjoy choosing the hymns," she called over her shoulder.

He caught up with her at that, leading his horse. A smile touched his mouth again. "You think I am really that crass?"

She jerked to a halt, facing him. "That's not what I meant."

He leaned close to her, and the warmth of his breath on her face nearly stopped her heart. "Then I shall surprise you, Miss Evy. Did you know I am quite adept at playing the violin?"

Her mouth fell open. The violin she'd seen in the piano room. So it had been his. She narrowed her gaze. Or had it?

"You?" She allowed a slight laugh. "I can't imagine such a thing."

Was there regret in his smile as he shook his head at her. "Oh, my dear Miss Evy, you've been quite wrong about me."

She crossed her arms. "You never played the violin before going to school in London."

"That is where you are wrong again. My mother hired a maestro to teach me for years until she died. After that I rebelled and wanted nothing to do with it. But when I went to London I realized I could not shake off a love for good music."

Could she believe him? He sounded so sincere…but then, he was a master at that.

"So I've been practicing again. Why should that shock you?"

She felt the telltale heat enter her cheeks, and turned to his horse to stroke its smooth nose. "Because I can hardly see you playing beautiful music."

"Then I must play for you sometime. How about Paganini's Violin Concerto no. 2 in B Minor?"

She stared at him. "You're not serious. It is a glorious piece! You're jesting, surely."

Clearly he found great satisfaction in her astonishment.

Piqued, Evy tossed her head. "Nothing you *say* you can do surprises me, but if you can *really* play Paganini—well, I shall certainly eat my words."

His eyes glinted at that, and Evy felt a sudden dread. "Then we will one day put an end to your misconceptions, Miss Varley, and I shall play for you. On one condition—that you also play for me. I should like to hear Beethoven's Piano Concerto no. 4."

She winced at that. "You ask a great deal of me."

She couldn't tell if the glint in his gaze was mockery or admiration. "I am sure you can prevail. Do we have an agreement?"

She hesitated. "Yes…but I would feel more confident if knew I was returning to school for more training."

"If?" He looked genuinely surprised. "I thought you loved piano."

"I— I do. But things are not well for us at this time. Not with my aunt the way she is."

At his thoughtful look she changed the subject. "If you give me enough time to practice, I will agree."

"Then it's done. This is wonderful. I have discovered something that proves you wrong about me."

She almost laughed at the delight in his voice. "I really must be going now."

"I will walk you back to the cottage."

"There is no need. I do this most every afternoon."

His smile opposed her. "I insist. I have detained you longer than usual, and the sun is setting. You need not be afraid of me."

"I am not!"

His sideways glance was skeptical. "Then why do you not wish me to walk you back to the cottage?"

It was clear he was going to have his way. It ought to have nettled her, but secretly, it did not. She could not fight him on this, so she would simply give in to the pleasure of his company. For the moment, anyway.

"I simply thought you were out for a ride and would wish to carry on with it." She knew the protest held little force.

He placed hand at heart, affecting a somber stance. "I shall be completely forthright, Miss Evy. I have been aware of your habits recently and suspected you would come here, so I followed. I fully expected to see our dear Derwent, but lo, such a happy turn of fortune—I discovered you alone. You see, I wanted to talk with you. After all, being such a close neighbor and knowing you for so many years, I think it is time we became more…personally involved. Do you not agree?"

That half lazy smile pulled at her, and she forced herself to look away toward the path. "We are not actually neighbors. It cannot be lost on you that I live with my aunt in one of the Chantry cottages on Chantry property."

"Now, now, there's no need for that kind of talk. Anyway, we've shared a few secrets in our time, which goes a bit of a way in making a bond between us. Don't you think so?"

"The secrets, I admit, were very intriguing. But I am not aware of the bond you hint of."

He smiled. "Then I need to cultivate it to bring your thinking around to mine. Let us see"—he pursed his lips—"perhaps in London, when you get there. In the past there was a time or two when I thought to contact you, but one thing or another came up. This year, I will simply make things happen. I am rather a prodder, you know. I want things to happen, and I usually help them along. And we now have an agreement."

Would he really arrange to see her in London when she returned to Parkridge Music Academy? She hoped not. She hoped so. Oh, she didn't know *what* she hoped. Their agreement to play for each other clearly made a way for them to meet, which otherwise might never come to fruition. But in London—away from the vicarage?

"One day," he continued, "I will show you Uncle Henry's map. If

I did not want to develop this…*friendship* with you, would I make such a promise?"

She had no sensible answer and was fairly certain that was just what he wanted.

"Then you actually found Master Henry's map?"

"I told you I would, remember? When I make up my mind to accomplish something, I do not give up until I have victory. Yes, I found it. And I have plans for when I arrive at the Cape. You see? I've even let you in on my secret. No one in the family realizes I have the map. Naturally, no one ever believed it was real, except perhaps Julien," he said thoughtfully. "I think that's his reason for backing a new colony in Mashonaland. He would love to get his hands on the gold deposit that Henry made such an issue about."

"You will tell Sir Lyle, of course. And your brother, when you arrive at the Cape?"

He lost his teasing grace at that. "Parnell? I doubt I will. First I need to locate the area where Henry claimed there was gold."

"The map does not show it?"

"Most of that area of Africa is unexplored by Europeans. Livingstone may have gone that way, but Henry had difficulty drawing the map as precisely as he must have wanted. Someday, of course, they will all need to know I found the map, but not until I own one of the greatest gold deposits in the area. What I'm hoping for is that Julien's colony is nearby. If it proves to be, then I will have a base to work from."

"The colony is deep in Mashonaland?"

"They are beginning to call the town Rhodesia—after Cecil Rhodes, who sponsored the colony—but it's known now as Salisbury. Julien is hoping the colonial office will send Peter Bartley there to represent the Crown."

She looked at him. "Arcilla would be most unhappy if she were forced to marry him and go to such a savage place."

"Yes," he frowned, "Aunt Elosia will have a fainting spell."

"Surely your father would not wish his daughter to go to such a place?"

"Sometimes I do not think he knows what is happening. Or cares."

Before she could think better of it, she put a hand on his arm. "Oh, please, you don't mean that."

Something flicked in his dark features as he looked down at her hand, and when he lifted his eyes to hers, she found her mouth going suddenly dry at the intensity of his gaze. She had the odd sensation of drowning…and pulled her hand away.

He hesitated, then fell into step beside her again. "I do, actually. Since my mother died, Father is not the man he once was. At first we thought it was Arcilla who would not recover. It turns out she is doing very well, but my father seems to have lost all real interests. He stays in the library most of the time and studies his books."

"I am sorry."

"Anyway, I will go to Salisbury."

What once seemed Rogan's boyish dreams Evy now saw were an ambitious man's determination to prevail. She knew he was quite capable, for Arcilla had boasted of her brother's grades in the university. A professor of geology had great hopes for his success, Arcilla had said.

Rogan could be quite serious when he wished to be, but she knew little of that side of his character. She was still learning just who Rogan Chantry really was. Indeed, he had surprised her today. She suspected there would be more surprises in the future. His declared interest in music both startled and pleased her greatly.

And yet, despite all this Evy still did not wholly trust him, not when it came to her heart. She must not become foolishly enamored with him, for she was sure that would lead to unhappy consequences.

Too late, too late, a voice within her chided. She ignored it. "I am sure you will succeed, or die reaching for your goal. Where did you find the map?"

"In Uncle Henry's rooms. Just as I had thought. The Black Diamond may be there too. I'd hoped it would be with the map, but it was not. But I did find a few very interesting letters."

He gave her a curious glance, and Evy sensed a cause for concern. "Letters?"

"Old letters, written in 1879. From Cape House."

"Oh? Are you going to tell me their secrets?"

His smile was as guarded as his words. "Not yet. I have my purposes first."

She waited, but he said no more, and silence reigned until the cottage came into view. Aunt Grace had already lit a lantern, and a golden glow was showing through the front windows, welcoming her inside.

Rogan opened the small wicket gate, where the bushy white roses grew in sprawling mounds. He bowed her past with exaggerated decorum, as though he knew she did not trust him to be a gentleman. She passed through, and he followed her. It was a short distance to the cottage door, and relief swept her when he did not attempt to see her there, or—even worse—force her to show hospitality to the squire's son and invite him in for tea.

"Au revoir, my dear Miss Varley."

She smiled at his typical parting. Never good-bye, but always "until later." He was letting it be known that he intended to see her again.

When she reached the porch, she glanced back. He was mounting his horse for the ride across the estate grounds to Rookswood. He caught her glance and touched his cap in a little salute, turned the horse, and rode away.

Her eyes half closed, and she tried to discern the emotions rioting within her. Pleasure and excitement that he had contrived the meeting on the hillock, and that he'd arranged for a meeting in London. And something else.

Apprehension.

She was no fool. She was on dangerous ground, and she knew it.

Inside the cottage, she stopped to peer into the small mirror hanging before the table with its bowl of autumn mums. She took careful consideration of her appearance.

Her thick hair, amber eyes, and blossoming figure were surely the reasons Rogan's head had turned in her direction. All wrong reasons, of course, but there it was.

She turned from the glass. Yes, she would need to be cautious indeed. It would have been far safer for her to remain a little brown wren when the fox was near the coop. She lacked father, uncle, or brother to safeguard her from interested hunters.

Well, I have my Christian upbringing to give me wisdom. I shall tread slowly and wisely in temptation's garden.

Hadn't Evy seen how beauty had spoiled Arcilla? And how it made Rogan sometimes too confident and bold? At a snap of their fingers, they could have just about anyone they wanted.

Well, she was not so foolish as to think Rogan truly wanted her. No, she would not be caught in his trap. She would let him spend time with her, but nothing more.

Certainly there could be no harm in that.

CHAPTER NINETEEN

The next morning dawned with a cool, crisp early autumn breeze that tousled Evy's hair as she walked down the narrow dirt road past Grimston Wood to the rectory. Derwent was already up and waiting for her.

"How is the vicar this morning?" she asked as he walked with her into the chapel.

"I found him in his study when I got up. He was seated at his desk, his Bible open to the Psalms. I think he fell asleep there last night. I daresay he looked very unrested." He scowled, running his fingers through his red hair. "I should have gotten up to check on him last night. I saw him to bed, but I'm a sound sleeper; he must have gotten up and gone down to his desk to read."

Evy sympathized. Hadn't she spent days and nights worrying about Aunt Grace during her illness? "You must not feel guilty because he slept at his desk, Derwent. The vicar is not a child that you must make all his decisions and feel guilty when he chooses one with which you disagree. I remember how Uncle Edmund sometimes rose at four in the morning to read the Bible in his office alone with God before duties pressed upon him."

"Yes, but, my father is growing so forgetful. I worry he will hurt himself someday. The stairs to his loft are steep, as you very well know from having used them."

She nodded. Toward the end of her uncle's life, Aunt Grace had expressed similar worries about Uncle Edmund climbing and descending those very steps. Yet neither her uncle nor Derwent's father ever wanted to give up the loft as a cloister.

Her gaze rested on Derwent's strained features. "I can see your present concerns lie far away from divinity school in London."

He made no reply, but he didn't need to. He bowed to her at the front steps of the chapel and walked back to the rectory. She went into the small church office used by the vicar and turned her attention to choosing the hymns for Sunday's worship service. She had several hymnals open on the desk when she heard footsteps behind her. She looked over her shoulder toward the office door, then stood as Rogan entered. She had not believed he would come.

"Hard at work, I see." He came up to the desk, noting the hymnbooks spread before her. He was dressed for riding. "You look surprised. I told you I would come."

Evy held a hymnal against her. "I suppose I thought you would change your mind."

"Why so? When I commit to something meaningful, I pursue it." Apparently he saw the small flash of alarm in her eyes, for he gestured to the hymnbooks: "I confided in you yesterday and shared my interest in music, remember?"

She looked down at one of the open hymnbooks. "Yes, I daresay, I still find the idea rather startling."

He offered an easy smile as he picked up a hymnbook and leafed through it. "Yes, it would be...if you think me a scoundrel. Well, I suppose it was not so very long ago that my family's ancestors *were* scoundrels. Barbarians who would just as easily throw their enemies to the bears as bother with them. But to get back to the present, Evy—I may call you by your Christian name? Thank you," he said before she answered. "By the way, what is Evy the familiar form of? Eve, is it not?"

"Yes, so Aunt Grace tells me."

"I rather like that:...Eve." He walked to the shelf of theology books and glanced over them, still holding the hymnbook.

She drew a steadying breath. "Eve sounded a little stilted for a baby, so my mother began calling me Evy."

"A month at the mission station was not very long to have you."

"A month?" She frowned. "It was longer than that. More like a year. Why do you say a month?"

He rested his shoulder against the bookcase and studied her. "All right, a year. Let's not discuss that now—you keep looking at the door—are you expecting someone? Derwent perhaps?"

"No, he has work to do this morning. Is there anything I can help you with?" She made her tone quite businesslike.

"Yes, remember how you told me you were going to select the hymns? Well, there is quite a history behind church music. Were you aware that eighteenth-century hymnbooks were usually only collections of texts which did not include musical notes?"

That did interest her, which she fully believed he had expected. "No, I was not aware of that."

"Or that the first American hymnal to place music together with text didn't appear until 1831? In fact, there weren't many hymnbooks at all, even here in England. The usual way of singing was called lining out. The leader would say one line, and the congregation repeated it. Hymnbooks were rare and too expensive." He turned the book over in his hands, as though savoring the feel of it. "What's more, most parishioners could not read, so they did not sing one verse immediately after another as we do now."

She studied him as he put the book down and picked up another, noting the open page she had chosen.

"Charles Wesley… It might surprise you to know how many hymns he wrote in his lifetime."

She folded her arms. What a fount of information Rogan had become. If only she could believe it was out of true interest in the subject rather than out of a desire to entice her. "I suppose you know?"

"Of course. I told you of my renewed interest in music, did I not?"

Her bewilderment must have shown on her face, for he broke into a teasing grin.

"Really, Evy, you must learn to trust me. As for Wesley, he wrote

8,989 hymns! And even more poems than William Wordsworth. Charles completed a poem about every other day. Prolific, wasn't he?"

"I must say, I am quite surprised when I thought—"

"When you thought I'd no appreciation for the finer things of life, which in your opinion would be music and religion."

She walked to the desk and straightened the hymnbooks, dismayed to see how her fingers trembled.

"So hard-working and dedicated. I think a change of routine, a bit of relaxation, would not harm you. Why not dine with me tonight at Rookswood?"

Her brows lifted, and she struggled to keep her pleasure from showing. "I hardly think Sir Lyle and Lady Elosia would approve."

"By now it should be clear that I keep the company I choose."

"Still, it seems hardly suitable…"

"Let me be the judge of what is suitable. Tomorrow night?"

"I can hardly accept such an invitation."

He came up beside the desk, standing next to her, speaking in a low tone of what sounded for all the world like entreaty. "Come riding with me, at least."

She wanted to. Oh, how she wanted to. "Thank you, but I cannot. Not today."

"Why are you afraid of me?"

"I am not!" But as she spoke, she made the error of looking up, and her protest fell as his gaze held hers. She wasn't certain how long they stood thus, but when she grew aware of the warmth in her cheeks, she looked down at a book again. She picked up her pen and drew a piece of stationery toward her. "Whatever gave you the notion I was afraid of you?"

"It's obvious. No use denying it."

"That is quite absurd."

"It is quite accurate." There was laughter in his voice. "You look as though you're being stalked by the big bad wolf."

Which may not be far from the truth.

"You must not be afraid of me, you know. " His smooth voice did odd things to her heart. "There is no reason for it, really. In fact, I am fond of you."

She caught her breath, but refused to look at him. "Indeed?"

"Yes. And we have known each other for so long that I take a particular interest in you."

"I did not know I was of concern to anyone at Rookswood."

"Then I must try harder to convince you."

She straightened and met his eyes. "Why should I suddenly be convinced of something that has never been so?"

"Your question shows how little we understand one another. Surely a matter deserving of remedy. In fact, I admire you and your dedication to things Christian, such as your attendance at music school."

"I am pleased you approve, though I have my own reasons for doing so."

"Which is as it should be. You see, that is one of the things that interests me about you. Most young ladies seem so shallow in their attempts to impress me."

True…and a goodly number of young ladies at that.

"I was serious yesterday when I said that we should go riding together. There are areas where you could improve in riding, and I would enjoy helping you."

She picked up her pen and shuffled the books on the desk. "I am certain anyone who will be riding in the Dublin show, such as yourself, would be well qualified as a teacher, but as I have said—"

"There is so very much work to do for our dear and humble Derwent." His smile was close to being derisive. "Then I dare not keep you any longer. I must say our little confab has been informative, however. I think I understand you a little better now. I will see you again—soon."

When he had gone, she found it difficult to stop thinking about him. She recalled his interest in the violin—or so he had claimed—and his knowledge of Christian worship hymns. He had seemed genuine there. Was she being unfair with Rogan?

When she returned to the cottage she was surprised to find Aunt Grace sitting at the kitchen table waiting for her. She held a sheet of Rookswood stationery in her hand and looked up as Evy came in through the kitchen door. Pale and thin, nevertheless her aunt was cheerful.

"There you are, Evy. I've a message from Rookswood. From Lady Elosia. She wishes to see you for tea this afternoon."

"Lady Elosia invited me to tea?"

"Yes, a lovely invitation, I daresay. It will do you good. I fear I've demanded too much of your time. A young girl such as yourself needs some diversions."

Evy looked at the sheet of Rookswood stationery. Aunt Grace's words sounded vaguely familiar. Had Rogan suggested to Lady Elosia that she invite her? "Rather odd she would suddenly find time and desire to invite me to tea."

"Perhaps not so odd. I understand she has heard from Arcilla in London. Arcilla would surely have asked about you and perhaps even sent you a letter."

"I doubt if Arcilla has time in her thoughts or schedule to be wondering about me. But I shall enjoy tea at Rookswood."

As Evy entered Rookswood Manor that afternoon it was like old times. Gazing about the halls stirred to life memories of living upstairs, of days spent with Arcilla, of Rogan...

The leaded windows still lent their aura of shadow and secrets to the dim corners of the baronial hall, and the solid, ironwork grandeur carried her imagination to another century of Chantry dominance over the village serfs.

Her steps echoed in the stone chamber beneath the vaulted ceiling. Above the stairs in the upper gallery, paintings of ancestral Chantrys gazed down upon her with robust disfavor and amused superiority.

The housekeeper, Mrs. Wetherly, had since retired, so this was Evy's first meeting with the new butler, Mr. Ames. The man's thin, angular face remained unaltered as he led her across the hall to her audience with Lady Elosia.

"This way, miss," he stated in a lofty voice, and led her from the hall toward what Evy knew to be Sir Lyle's large library. The butler discreetly tapped on the solid oak door, opened it, and stepped in with a slight bow.

"Miss Varley is here, sir."

Sir? Evy started as Rogan's voice drifted to her: "Show her in, Ames."

Evy entered the library, rich with polished dark mahogany, wine-colored carpet, and walls of leather-bound books. The door clicked shut behind her.

Rogan stood near the fireplace, looking satisfied with himself. He stood with hands behind his back, feet apart, and wore a faint smile as he glanced over her Sunday afternoon dress.

"How good of you to come."

Could he mean it? Since when did Chantrys welcome someone of lesser social stature to Rookswood, as though that person's presence favored them? She glanced around the room for Lady Elosia. She was not there.

The log in the fire crackled invitingly and emanated a woodsy aroma. Rogan walked toward her, gesturing for her to take a comfortable chair near the marble fireplace, and he did the same.

"Where is Lady Elosia?" The warmth from the fire was pleasant after the chilling walk up from the cottage. She had brought no wrap and shivered slightly.

"She developed an unexpected headache and retired to her room for the afternoon." He wore a grave face, but his dark eyes danced. "Most unfortunate."

She resisted the exhilarating excitement that wanted to weave its tempting spell around her. She stood. "I am sorry to hear that. Then I shall go and come again when she calls for me." She started toward the door.

"Wait—Evy, please."

She paused in the center of the room, though it was against her better judgment.

He walked up behind her. "I have offended you. Why?"

She turned slowly to face him. "You must ask? Because you arranged this, not your aunt."

His mouth curved. "Is that so terrible?"

"Need I remind you of your social status, and of mine?"

"No. I told you I was fond of you, did I not?"

"Surely you are aware, a man of your background, that neither your aunt nor your father would approve of your being *fond* of me, as you like to put it. Nothing can come of this so-called fondness, and you know that better than anyone. Your attentions are—are quite unsuitable and—" She bit her lip, angry with herself more than with him.

"I am going away in a week. I wanted to see you alone."

"So you arranged a ruse."

"I arranged to see you, yes. But it is not a ruse. I asked you to ride with me this morning at the rectory, but you refused. I at least thought I could help you to select the worship hymns, but you refused that, too."

"I'll wager Lady Elosia knows nothing about this so-called afternoon tea."

"I wouldn't wager, if I were you. Your uncle, were he alive, would not approve such an activity." His smile was warm, teasing.

"Nor would he approve of your deceit."

"Oh, come. Your reaction is a bit overdone, is it not? You behave as though I have committed some great wickedness by inviting you here. Did I not invite you earlier to dine with me at Rookswood? Then why so shocked over a bit of tea?"

"You did not invite me to tea. Lady Elosia did. At least it was her name on the stationery."

He smiled wryly. "If I had signed *Rogan Chantry,* you would not have come. You made that clear at the rectory."

"You deceived my aunt. She believed the invitation was from Lady Elosia." She turned and walked to the door, but he was there ahead of her.

She had thought he would be frustrated by now, but he was still smiling. "You are a most maddening young woman. I know a dozen brats in London who would be flattered by my attention, yet you shield yourself like a prickly pear."

"Brats!"

"I can tell, however, that you are not as cool toward me as you like to pretend. Your eyes deny your indifference."

She was furious. He was right, and she felt unmasked. But he seemed to think she evaded him because she enjoyed being chased.

He leaned his shoulder against the door, looking down upon her, and did not step aside. "I think I shall keep you here."

She looked at him evenly, wavering in her resolve.

"My aunt did send that invitation to Mrs. Havering. I know that surprises you, but it is true. And she did come down with an attack and take to her bed. I merely took advantage of an opportunity. Fault me for that, if you wish. I confess, instead of sending word to cancel tea as she suggested, I decided it might be helpful to see you before I depart, as there is a matter that I wish to discuss with you." He reached inside his coat and pulled out an envelope, handing it to her. The envelope bore a London postmark, and she recognized Arcilla's handwriting.

He watched her for a moment, as though trying to discern whether she would cooperate. He must have decided she would, for he straightened from the door and walked toward the center of the room.

Evy turned and watched him. There had been a palpable shift in Rogan's mood. He seemed pensive, as though involved in some internal debate. A minute must have passed before she spoke. "What do you wish to discuss?"

He looked at her, and the gleam in his eyes was grave, even a little intimidating. For once, there was no suggestion of a smile on his face. "Your father."

"I do not understand."

"You will." She wondered if he was truly as calm as his tone implied. "As you suggested, Miss Varley, it is time to set aside any fondness." His gaze narrowed a little as he held an arm toward the door. "It is necessary for you to accompany me to the top floor, to Henry's old rooms. I cannot hint of a ghost as I did when a boy, but I can unlock the mystery of the Kimberly Black Diamond. And that of your parents."

Evy's breath caught, and her heart constricted. Her parents? There was no mystery surrounding her parents…was there?

"Shall we go?"

For once, Evy didn't argue. She simply nodded and followed Rogan from the room, nearly overcome with an odd sense of dread, as though her life was about to change. And she wasn't at all sure she was going to like the results.

CHAPTER TWENTY

The stairway to the third floor was dark as Rogan allowed Evy to lead the way. They passed the familiar rooms she and Aunt Grace had occupied, went by the schoolroom and across the narrow, dimly lit hall to another smaller stairwell that was uncarpeted and bleak. It looked even dimmer toward the top landing. Evy paused, hand on the rail, looking up.

"Childhood fears of ghosts?"

Evy ignored Rogan's question and pushed aside the cowardly impulse to run. With resolute steps, she moved upward.

The rooms once belonging to Henry Chantry were much as she remembered. Little if anything had been done to them in the years since Rogan had brought her and Arcilla here. A musty odor of old furniture and draperies hung in the air. Rogan went to the window and threw it open. A chill, damp wind stirred the curtains as he turned to face her, arms folded, gaze firm, and a trace of a smile on his lips.

He took a key, opened an old metal box with engravings of lions and elephants on it, and took out a lump of what looked to Evy like rough rock.

"That is not gold, is it?"

He took her wrist and placed the lump on her palm. She rubbed her thumb over the rough surface, thinking only that it was unimpressive.

"There is a crystalline structure running through the rock. See it?"

It looked dull and was marbled with flaws and fissures.

"That's quartz you're looking at. It's held together by a substance that fills every crack and fault line." His eyes met hers. "Gold."

Evy looked at the thin layers of bright metal that twinkled in the light from the window. "Master Henry found this?"

"He and the Hottentot must have taken it from the ridge. It is gold, all right. If this ore is typical of the vein, it is an unusually rich find."

Considering Rogan's geological studies, she would take his word for it.

"Henry learned about this deposit as a young man in the mining camps around Kimberly. An old Afrikaner of Dutch ancestry from the Transvaal had a Hottentot slave who led them to the ridge of gold somewhere in what is known as Mashonaland. The Afrikaner and Hottentot were attacked by tribesmen and killed. Henry writes that he barely escaped with his life thanks to a fast horse and his skill with a rifle and pistol. During the next year he tried to retrace his steps back into the area to relocate the gold deposit, but was unsuccessful. His efforts gave rise to the suggestion that he was a deluded adventurer. That's when the mocking notion of Henry's Folly began. Soon afterward the Zulu War broke out, and his return to the region was impossible. So he drew a map from memory, detailing the trek with the Hottentot. I found his map, which he left me in his will, here with the quartz."

Evy looked from the rock to Rogan. "But if this proves there was gold, why did Henry come back here to Rookswood after the Zulu War? Why not return to Mashonaland and search?"

"That"—he took the rock and put it back in the box—"is the mystery I have sought to understand for several years. It never made sense that he returned to England. How could he be content knowing, yet not acting? He wanted another expedition. I know that for a fact. He wrote about it. Well, I now have an answer."

He locked the box and looked at her, his gaze steady and even. "Evidently Henry had to leave Capetown and promise never to return. If he came back, Julien would turn the matter of the theft of the Black Diamond over to the law. Henry was in quite a dilemma. His individual shares in the diamond mines were all in South Africa, as was the gold deposit. And yet he dared not go on another expedition without Sir Julien's permission."

"The law? Then it was Henry who stole the diamond?"

"Not according to Lady Brewster, his older aunt by marriage. I found a letter she'd written to Henry. It was with the map. She apologized for accusing him of stealing the Black Diamond and for rashly joining with Sir Julien to send him away."

Rogan paused, as though hesitant to go on, to unveil what came next. But why should he be? Surely there was nothing in this story that mattered to her?

She moved to sit in a nearby chair, disregarding the dust. "Then, if Lady Brewster claimed that Master Henry did not steal the Black Diamond, did Sir Julien ever locate it?"

"No, not that I am aware. No one yet knows what happened to the diamond once it was stolen from Julien's library at Cape House. Heyden insists it was brought here to Rookswood, that Henry was the thief."

"Heyden?"

"Heyden van Buren. The van Burens are Boers, of Dutch ancestry. At one time Carl van Buren was Julien's partner. They were both young men then. They located their first diamonds together in the river diggings in West Griqualand, close to the river Vaal. Van Buren was killed in the same mine explosion that cost Julien his eye. Later, Julien bought out Carl's younger brother for a handsome sum, and the man reverted to farming in the Transvaal. Heyden van Buren is his son."

She noted an edge to Rogan's voice. "You sound as though you do not trust this Heyden."

"Perhaps I do not. He is here in England now, traveling with representatives from the Boer Republic under their leader, Paul Kruger. The Boers are protesting British incursion into the Transvaal. There are rumblings of war. Heyden van Buren, from what I have seen of him, is a Boer zealot."

"Surely none of this concerns my parents?" Yet even as she spoke, uncertainty nudged her. Evy searched Rogan's face for clues. "What can you possibly know of my father or mother?"

"I knew next to nothing about what Mrs. Junia Varley was like until I read Lady Brewster's letter. A very telling letter that mentions Junia.

I wrestled with whether to share the information with you, since it is unpleasant. I decided I must since it involves the theft of the Black Diamond, and, unfortunately—your mother's involvement."

She stared at him mutely. "Oh, but surely there is some mistake! It just cannot be."

"I am sorry. The letter to Henry mentions that your mother was in Cape House the night the Black Diamond was stolen."

She watched him, trying to take this information in. "How could that be? How could she have been at Sir Julien's estate when she was with my father at the compound at Rorke's Drift?"

"Your mother knew not only Henry, but Sir Julien. Lady Brewster's letter makes that clear."

"Impossible, I tell you."

"Lady Brewster had no reason to lie. She wrote years ago, after Uncle Henry returned here to Rookswood. The letter was private. Neither Lady Brewster nor Henry expected anyone other than themselves to know its contents."

Evy jumped to her feet. "Preposterous! What would my mother be doing at Sir Julien's house on that night or any other? There is some mistake, there has to be."

"There is no mistake. Sit down, Evy." He came around from behind his uncle's desk. "There was no romantic affair, if that thought is upsetting you. That would indeed be a tragedy, would it not? If we were blood cousins. No, this ugly matter involves not the fire of passion, but cold, hard greed."

She caught her breath. "Then of what do you accuse my mother?"

He shook his head, the shadow of his usual smile on his lips. "I do not accuse her of anything. Someone else has accused her. Lady Brewster's apology to Henry in her letter pointed out the fact that it was your mother who stole the Black Diamond and ran away from Cape House."

Evy gasped and stood so abruptly that she swayed a little. Rogan reached to catch her, but she wrenched away.

"You *dare* suggest that my mother stole your family diamond? She was dedicated to teaching Christianity. If she had been greedy for gain, she would not have become a missionary with small hope of having anything more in this world than a medical hut. She certainly would not have been risking her life in Zululand, where she gave her life in martyrdom."

"I understand the complications, even the contradictions, but Lady Brewster wrote Henry that the family nanny finally confessed that she had helped your mother escape by arranging with an African worker to have a buggy ready near the stables."

"There is no proof to any of this. There can't be."

"It's all in the letter. Your mother stole the Kimberly Diamond, then ran away from the Capetown estate, taking the diamond and the buggy."

"I want that letter." Her voice shook, but she didn't care.

He frowned. "No. Not yet."

She stamped her foot. "You are lying."

His dark eyes flickered, and she shivered at goading him so. But it had to be a lie. It had to be.

"For what reason would I lie, Evy?"

"Only you would know. You brought me here to flaunt this in my face. Why that should be, I do not know."

"I brought you here to show you…this." He took the letter from his pocket and held it in front of her. "No one else knows about it, just as they did not know of the map. Sir Julien has accepted what he believes is the inevitable loss of the diamond. Henry was the only other person who knew about your mother, and he's dead, as is Lady Brewster who wrote this incriminating letter. There is talk, of course. But without this letter dated many years ago, it is only a tale. As far as everyone else is concerned, the guilt lies with my uncle. I could destroy this letter and there would be nothing in writing to incriminate the memory and reputation of your mother."

She searched his face. Why had he said this to her? What was on his mind?

"I was going to show this letter to your Aunt Grace and draw the truth from her. Your mother was her sister. She could have written Grace, who may be keeping matters quiet."

This was too much! "So now you are insinuating that Aunt Grace knows where the diamond is hidden!"

His frown was quick, impatient. "I did not say that. However, she may know something, and I need any information she has."

Evy hesitated. "Yet you did not go to her. Why?"

"When I learned of her frail health, I decided against speaking to her. If she knows anything about the diamond, it is for you to find out—at the appropriate time, when you believe it is safe to question her. This"—he held the letter up—"will remain in my control. One day I may surrender it to you to do with as you wish. But not until I have all the information I can get on the Black Diamond."

Evy stared at him, and one simple fact filled her mind: She simply must get the letter.

Before he could guess what she was about, she snatched it from his hand and darted to the door, flinging it open and dashing into the hall. Rogan reached her before she hit the dark stairwell. His strong fingers closed about her wrist, and he retrieved the letter from her trapped fingers.

She spun to face him and was met by his smile. "Your determination is commendable, my dear Evy, but I'm afraid I must disappoint you."

She hissed her frustration and lunged to grab the letter back.

Her fingers tweaked it from his grip, surprising both Rogan and herself. A burst of energy shot through her as she sped down the steps. She traversed the corridor, running hard past the schoolroom, past the rooms she and Aunt Grace had once occupied, and toward the flight of stairs to the main house.

She heard him behind her, yet she kept her pace down the stairs, the hall, and then the second flight of stairs.

Evy glanced over her shoulder and saw him. She would never make it back to the cottage. It seemed as though he was letting her stay ahead, knowing he could overtake her when he pleased, perhaps outside—

unless she surprised him again. Was there time enough to take his horse? She had noticed it tied near the tree.

Did she dare? The feel of the letter in her hands brought her the answer: yes. She had no other choice.

She ran past the gallery of Chantry faces, down toward the final flight of stairs into the baronial hall. Rogan took a shortcut over the banister and ran ahead, reaching the front door, smug and smiling. Evy paused. He blocked her exit, and yet...off to one side was the library. *The library! With the fire still crackling in the fireplace! Yes! Yes, of course—*

She reached for the library door, looking up to see his smile vanish. Could he stop her? She must not let him.

Evy burst into the library. *Yes!* The fire still burned. Gasping to catch her breath, she held the letter in her hand...and time seemed to move in slow motion. She all but stumbled toward the fireplace, ready to hurl the horrid letter to the consuming flames, when there came a movement from a high-backed chair facing the hearth. A man stood and turned to face her.

He looked as surprised as she felt. She had not seen him before. His hair was fair, his eyes a wintry blue, his build rather slender.

Rogan burst into the room and also stopped in his tracks when he saw the man standing there. Evy was caught between the two of them, the letter clutched in her trembling hand.

"Heyden!" The surprise in Rogan's voice wore a thin veneer of...what? Dislike?

"Hello, Rogan. Am I—er—interrupting anything?"

A tense silence fell between Evy and Rogan. His dark gaze glittered, and she could almost believe he had enjoyed the pursuit down three flights of stairs, while she was gasping and holding a cramp in her side. Rogan smiled, casting a quick, calculating glance from her to the flames. Then he sprinted suddenly in her direction.

Evy made a dash for the fireplace.

Rogan intercepted her, catching her wrist and whirling her straight into his strong arms, holding her fast. He plucked the letter from her fingers and stashed it inside his jacket. He was smiling again, his dark eyes dancing.

"You are a tougher competitor than I would have thought, my dear. But alas—though I promised I may surrender to your whims one day, that day has yet to arrive." And then, as though they were the only two in the room, he drew her closer. Before she could protest, his warm lips covered hers in a kiss that sent her senses reeling and a shiver scurrying down her spine.

When he finally released her, there was a faint look of surprise on his face.

Evy didn't think. Couldn't think. She simply reacted. She drew back and slapped him. The resounding smack split the silence of the room. Rogan did not even flinch.

She dragged breath into her lungs, painfully aware that her breathing trouble had nothing whatsoever to do with the chase she'd just been in. No, it was the capture that had stolen the air from her lungs.

Heyden looked on in silence, and, choking back a sob, Evy ran from the library and out into the hall.

The butler was waiting by the front door, wearing the same dignified expression as before, quite as though he had neither seen nor heard anything amiss. But Evy knew he must have seen part of the chase with Rogan.

The butler opened the heavy door and bowed as she swept past and out onto the front steps of Rookswood.

"A good day to you, Miss," he said with the same lofty voice.

Down the steps she went into the cold afternoon, the sky a blue-gray with oncoming clouds as the promise of an early autumn sent leaves scuttling along the stone courtyard about her feet. Though exhausted, she hurried on, sniffing back angry tears, forcing her head high as she made her way home.

How dare he kiss her? How dare he make her feel…things she simply *shouldn't* be feeling!

"He's a cad," she hissed to the darkening sky. "A frustrating, impossible cad!"

CHAPTER TWENTY-ONE

Evy did not return to the cottage immediately lest Aunt Grace question her about the teatime she was to have taken with Lady Elosia. Instead, she hurried along one of the garden paths, hoping against hope to rid herself of emotional upset and calm her facial expression.

And to give herself time to forget the feel of Rogan's lips on hers…the way his arms had both imprisoned and sheltered her…

"Stop it!" She clenched her teeth. "Stop thinking about the cad!"

She had wanted the truth about her past, and yet it loomed as a dark, ugly cloud. How could either of her parents possibly be involved in stealing? Especially the theft of something as valuable as the Black Diamond?

No! It was utterly preposterous. She refused to accept any such notion.

She rushed on, the wind cooling her feverish skin. Wasn't the horrid innuendo about her mother terrible enough? How could Rogan have compounded this awful day by taking hold of her that way…by lowering his dark head until all she saw were his eyes and the light burning in their depths?

"Oh, stop it!" Evy pressed her hands to her burning cheeks. How could he have kissed her? And in front of Heyden van Buren! Yet it had not troubled Rogan at all. He had seemed to enjoy the spectacle! Well, of course. Why wouldn't he? The cad had probably planned all along to take advantage of her. What a fool she'd been to trust him, to follow him to Master Henry's rooms.

"Cad!" she hissed to the blowing wind. Yet…she could not stop thinking of him.

She kicked at a rock in the path. *I should be indignant and dislike him heartily.* Unable to deny the truth, she looked to the sky and wailed, "But I don't!"

Her shoes crunched the leaves on the path. She came to a bench on the green beneath an overspreading oak tree. She brushed the leaves from the bench and sank down, limp.

"Oh, Rogan…what have you done?"

She closed her eyes. Could there be any thread of truth in Lady Brewster's letter? Could Evy's mother have been involved in stealing the diamond?

For all her staunch denials, fear nibbled at her. Fear that what appeared impossible might somehow be true… Oh, the idea was humiliating! And made even more so because she'd heard it from Rogan.

She sat mulling over the dark disclosure, over the picture of her mother changing from Christian martyr to thief. The cracked image left her shaking. First Lady Camilla's wild claim, and now Lady Brewster's letter.

Evy straightened. She must talk this over with Aunt Grace.

But even as she was ready to stand, her traitorous mind recalled occasions when Aunt Grace had behaved oddly. Rogan's tale could certainly explain why Aunt Grace had always avoided discussing details about Evy's parents. And there was her strange reaction when Evy mentioned Master Henry's death to Uncle Edmund several years ago.

Could it be…? Was her aunt wary of some sort of scandal coming to light? When the old sexton, Mr. Croft, had mentioned the possibility that Henry did not commit suicide but was murdered, Aunt Grace had been particularly upset. Evy had thought it was just the topic that upset her, but now… Could there be more to it? She frowned. If Aunt Grace discussed the notion of murder openly, wouldn't that eventually introduce the topic of the stolen diamond and her sister Junia?

As though she could not help herself, Evy remembered the strange anxiety Aunt Grace had shown when asked to become governess and live at Rookswood. Perhaps she had known Sir Julien was visiting at Rookswood and feared he might tell Evy that he blamed her mother for the diamond theft.

Feeling as though the weight of a thousand wagons rested on her shoulders, Evy stood and trudged back to the cottage and up the front steps.

"Evy, you are back so soon?" Aunt Grace regarded her, wide-eyed.

"Yes. Lady Elosia developed a headache and took to bed." Evy struggled to keep her voice from betraying her emotional exhaustion. "I shall put the tea on for us."

She poured boiling water into the teapot, then covered it with the faded cozy. A counter divided the small kitchen and sitting room. Chairs encircled the small fireplace. Though far from luxurious, the cottage was comfortable and, until the last few weeks of her aunt's illness, cheerful. Now the chilly wind blew about the chimney and windows, and the once sunny summer atmosphere took on a lonely isolation.

Evy stole several sharp glances at her aunt. How to bring up the stark subject gnawing at Evy's soul without making her aunt ill?

I will ask about the Black Diamond without mentioning Lady Brewster's letter... I could bring up Lady Camilla again...

Evy brought the tea tray with sweet biscuits made by Mrs. Croft to the low wooden table and sat down opposite her aunt.

Aunt Grace was propped up with pillows on two overstuffed chairs pushed together, improvising a daybed. Outside the window the bare branches on the old apple tree moved in the wind.

"Looks as though rain is on the way again." Grace lifted her teacup to her lips.

One look at her aunt was all it took for Evy to swim in dismay. Aunt Grace was watching her, her large brown eyes troubled and wide with alarm. Evy's heart knew a pang of guilt when she noted the gray in the woman's once brown hair. Aunt Grace had lost so much weight that the skin on her face was taut, showing the fine sculpture of her bones. The bluish splotches under her eyes persisted despite the energy tonic Dr. Tisdale prescribed.

Evy swallowed hard. Aunt Grace had raised her, loved her, and with Uncle Edmund had provided for her earthly needs. Even this cottage was an entitlement granted her because of her aunt's faithful service to Grimston Way. To badger her now with questions of the past seemed…cruel.

How can I break her heart by letting her know that I've heard the very worst, what she desired to keep from me, about my mother?

Evy bit back sudden tears. What if burdening Aunt Grace with questions now about a stolen diamond and possible murder shortened her life? She had been so upset over Lady Camilla's suspicions, what would she do about Lady Brewster's letter to Henry Chantry?

No. I cannot do this to her. Not now… She swallowed her disappointment and desperation. *Dear God, help me to be wise, to wait upon You.*

"You worry too much, Evy."

At her aunt's unexpected comment, Evy started.

"You heard Dr. Tisdale. My chances for recovery are excellent. Mrs. Croft has offered to come and help me while you are away at school in London."

Evy sighed. It was well enough that her aunt took her subdued mood for worry about her health. "School? Dear Aunt, we both know that it is out of the question now. It seems selfish of me even to contemplate using the little you have saved for another year at Parkridge. I would much rather take you to London to see a specialist. Dr. Tisdale is a fine man, but I am sure there are better doctors. And Dr. Tisdale, too, expects to be paid. I've been thinking. I could take a leave of absence from my studies and return in, say, another year or so to graduate. Perhaps I can take your place teaching school with the curate. Derwent may be able to arrange for it. He could convince Vicar Brown to authorize my acceptance, I'm sure."

Aunt Grace set her cup down. "I'll not hear of it, Evy dear. Your learning is more important than ever. Should something happen to me, which is entirely in God's timing, then I want to depart with the peace of knowing your education will provide for your upkeep. If not, I shall feel a failure in spite of my service at the vicarage with Edmund."

Aunt Grace went on: If Evy graduated music school she would be qualified to teach in London. But once a student left the path of learning to start earning a living, it could become difficult to return to that narrow path.

"Once in a race, it is wise to keep going."

Aunt Grace would know better than anyone about that. And then Evy paused; for once Aunt Grace did not suggest that marriage to Derwent would bring the secure life that she had always planned for Evy to have.

"Not that I am suggesting marriage to Derwent is the wrong choice for your future," Grace said as though she had read Evy's mind. "I am certain he will be a good and kind husband for you. Even so, it is wise to have something to fall back upon when I am gone. Just in case."

Evy shuddered. She could not imagine the quiet, isolated cottage without Aunt Grace, or even living in the rectory. Peering into the future to plan her life was like trying to see through the fog on the London wharf. Only God could see ahead. She did know that peace always came to her when she thought of His wise and caring nature.

Evy's decision came swiftly. She went around the table and knelt beside the daybed. "Aunt, I— I do not mind staying here in Grimston Way. I've had one wonderful year at Parkridge, and I have learned so much. Even now I'm able to teach children and receive a wage for it. True, it will not be much, but I am sure I can get two, possibly even three students whose parents will pay for piano lessons. Madame Ardelle at the London school believes I have talent as a children's instructor. I think she would be willing to write me a letter of recommendation."

Grace squeezed her hand. "Yes, I am sure you are qualified now. I was talking to Mrs. Tisdale only yesterday. She tells me she will soon need to give up her piano lessons and mentioned the possibility of you taking over for her."

"There! You see?" Evy really did try to sound enthusiastic. "God will provide for His children."

"Yes, even so, it isn't necessary yet that you not go back to London."

"But—the money. How will we manage?"

"I have the money."

Evy stared at this calm pronouncement. "Where did it come from?"

"Now, dear, did I not tell you before that I must be allowed my little secrets? It is enough that the money is available. No, you will finish your schooling, and who knows? Derwent may receive a living at a vicarage in another section of England with better possibilities than Grimston Way. Should he end up in London, you could get a position teaching in a music school. So you see? There's not a thing to worry about, Evy."

Evy could have told her there was plenty to concern them, but not wishing to put further stress upon her aunt's thin shoulders, she said nothing and simply returned her bright smile. She would keep her fears about her mother and the future locked inside her heart.

"If you say so, Aunt. I have much to be thankful for, I know. My future, it seems, is in God's hand."

"Most certainly. Like the pillar of cloud leading the children of Israel, there is One directing our path through the wilderness."

Despite her aunt's assurances that all was well, Evy still struggled with uneasiness. Concern—unnamed, unknown—loitered in the background like some ominous phantom of darkness ready to spring upon her. She took solace in the words of the psalmist: "My times are in thy hand."

During the following days, before returning to London, Evy tended to Aunt Grace's vegetable garden and fruit trees. In early September Mrs. Croft came, and they enjoyed time together with Aunt Grace, preserving the bounty.

Evy prayed often that whatever their allotted time together might hold, the favorable hand of their heavenly Father would overshadow and protect her and her aunt. Much to her dismay, she did not see Rogan again before he left for his final year at the university. She suspected that Heyden van Buren had also left with him for London.

It is just as well, she told herself time and again. She still fumed when she thought of the way Rogan had taken such liberties with her. He would not have dared if he had not been a Chantry.

As the days slipped by and she prepared her winter wardrobe to return to London, she wondered if the divine promise of God's protective oversight might not be gracious preparation for what awaited. For disappointment came only a few days before Evy and Derwent were to board the train together for London and their respective schools.

It was around five o'clock in the afternoon, and Aunt Grace was taking a nap, something she needed far more frequently of late. Evy was alone in the kitchen, kneading dough for the following day's bread, when Derwent showed up on the bungalow porch. He always tapped and looked in through the window on the door. She saw him outside, his hands pushed into the big pockets of his faded coat. She raised floury hands and gestured he should come inside.

He opened the door, and a gust of wind followed him.

"Brrr, it's getting colder by the day. Autumn's coming sooner this year."

The sun was dipping low in the pearl-gray sky, and she motioned toward the lanterns. "Would you light those for me, Derwent, please?"

"Sure enough." He looked over at the counter by the big black stove. "What are you stirring up?"

"Bread dough for tomorrow. I'm all done." She went to wash her hands, then removed the apron that had been Aunt Grace's. "I will put the teakettle on."

"Um…I really cannot stay that long, Evy. Thanks, anyway."

She was rather surprised. He usually had tea, then cleaned out any sweet biscuits left from the morning. "Is anything wrong?" She looked at him in the lantern light.

He shifted. "I would not say it that way, but, well, I would rather just get on with the news that brought me here."

"Well, all right." She sat down on the kitchen stool. "What is it?"

He cleared his throat. "I will get right to it. I won't be returning for my final year at divinity school."

Evy stared at him, not sure she'd heard right. Her first thought was that Rogan must have had something to do with this. He had already planted a song of high adventure in Derwent's mind. *South Africa again,* she thought shortly. *Gold fields and diamond mines!*

"So you are going to Capetown."

"No… That's not how it is, Evy. It is my father. I've been noticing it all summer, and maybe you have too, but it is getting unmanageable. He is just growing old, I expect. He forgets things. That's all right, if it does not hurt anyone, but that's the pain of it, you see. Last night he decided to make himself a mug of tea before bed. Next thing I knew, I woke up smelling smoke."

"Oh no! Derwent!" She reached out to take his hands.

"That's what I told myself. 'Oh no!' I went rushing down to the kitchen not knowing what to expect and found the water in the kettle had boiled away. The kettle was black and smoking up the kitchen. I took care of things, then checked on him. Do you know he was fast asleep! If I hadn't been home and smelled smoke, the rectory could have caught fire. And that isn't the first time… Two weeks ago he left some candles burning off the holder. Mrs. Croft found them." He squeezed her hands. "He is getting worse, you see. You know what that means."

"Is there any damage to the kitchen?"

"Oh, some smoky darkened areas by the stove. Mrs. Croft says she won't attempt cleaning up unless I help, so naturally I will. Wouldn't think of leaving the mess all for her, especially the ceiling. We'll do it tonight."

She almost smiled when he released her hands to reach for the plate of sweet biscuits. He frowned as he chewed. "My father's losing his clarity, that's plain to see. It is getting worse by the week. Seems to be coming on awful fast. He can no longer prepare his sermons. No one knows that yet. I've been helping him all summer. He has merely been reading them from the pulpit. So you see"—his tone was heavy, resigned— "I wouldn't feel good about myself if I just up and left him for school. You understand, don't you, Evy? You feel that way about Miss Grace sometimes. But she's not half as bad off as my father." He searched her eyes, as though seeking some kind of confirmation from her. "If it were just his leg or a knee, I could handle that. I could just get the sexton to come and help him with personal matters while I was away at school. But his mind…well, it is different. Sometimes he gets frustrated and cross about it. And he says I imagine it all."

Her heart nearly broke for him. "Derwent, I am so sorry. Of course I understand your dilemma. I wish there were something I could do to help."

"There's nothing anyone can do. He is my father, and I will look after him. But it does throw a corker into matters, doesn't it? I will need to delay graduation, and if I must do that, then I'll need to delay— well, a lot of other things." He took her hands again. "You know what I mean, Evy?"

"Yes, of course I do." And she did. But what she didn't fully understand was the rush of relief the news brought her. "That is very understandable. You must not worry about any of that now. You have enough on your shoulders."

"It is not that I was worried, or that I'm thinking things are too burdensome. It is just that setting future things by the stovepipe is inevitable right now. I worry something dreadful could happen. If I went away now, the rectory could burn down, or he could take a fall and break a hip."

"That would be dreadful indeed."

"So, at least until the bishop appoints someone to take over the rectory, I cannot return to school."

As he spoke she had the oddest impression that he was just a trifle relieved over the postponement.

Derwent gave a deep sigh. "When a new rector comes, then I can carry on at divinity school."

Evy nodded, but Aunt Grace's warning drifted through her mind, about the difficulty of getting back on the path to learning once one stepped off the narrow way.

Derwent stood, then hesitated, as though he wanted to say something more and could not find the words. He shuffled his feet and put the collar up on his coat. "Well…you will be leaving soon for music school, I daresay."

"Yes, in three days now."

"I will write you about how things are going here."

"Yes. And I will write you."

He maneuvered his way to the door. "Try not to worry about Miss Grace. I will look in on her every day, and so will Mrs. Croft."

She nodded. "That will be a great blessing for me." He was such a kind man. Why couldn't her heart react to him as it did to Rogan? "Thank you, Derwent."

He hesitated once more, then opened the door and stepped out to the porch. "G'night, Evy. See you tomorrow."

"Yes, good night. And I will be praying for you and the vicar."

He smiled. "I knew you would. You are good at that sort of thing. Better than I. It was your upbringing."

He shut the door, and she heard his feet leaving the porch. From the kitchen window she saw the chilling purple twilight settling into darkness.

Soon it was time to pack her trunk, and then Mrs. Croft drove her and Aunt Grace to the train depot in the one-horse jingle. Evy boarded the train and waved good-bye as the train chugged out of the station on its two-hour journey to London.

Now she would play the piano every day. How she had missed it. Of course, she'd played at the rectory when she had time to walk there, but now music would fill her life, her soul. What joy! Oh, to fill her mind and heart with glorious music and forget everything unpleasant that had plagued her these summer months.

Everything…and everyone.

As Grimston Way and Rookswood estate faded into the distance, Evy wondered if even her love of music would be able to free her mind of the dark clouds of suspicion surrounding the Kimberly Black

Diamond and Henry's mysterious death. Or if it could keep her from dwelling on the unthinkable—that somehow her mother had been involved in theft and deception.

Would Rogan let the ugly past alone? Could she? She did not know. She could only pray for God's wisdom and guidance.

CHAPTER TWENTY-TWO

On the first day of the new school year Evy and the other students were assembled in the great hall, where Madame Ardelle, who reigned over Parkridge Music Academy as though she were its queen, addressed them. She was clad fully in black, except for a bit of white lace here and there. Though formidable and demanding, she was otherwise a pleasant woman, who commanded the respect of her students, most of whom were pleased to be in this serious learning environment.

Madame emphasized how fortunate the students were to be here and that they must now live up to the reputation of the school. This seemed to worry her a good deal of the time, for Master Eldridge would teach the final year at Parkridge. She seemed to have no greater chagrin than that her music students would not measure up to his expectations. She constantly reminded them that Master Eldridge had played piano throughout Europe and was considered one of the great musicians in England.

"I think Madame is in love with Master Eldridge," Victoria, one of the girls in Evy's room said.

Another of the girls, Frances, dismissed this notion. "She's too old."

"Who said old people do not fall in love?"

"It seems quite obvious that romance and marriage are for the young."

"What nonsense!" Victoria grimaced. "Who wrote the great romantic plays, pray tell? Men with gray hair."

Frances considered, then shrugged. "Maybe you are right. I never thought of that."

Alice Tisdale was not in Evy's room this year. In fact, Evy had looked for her at all the large gatherings but had not found her. That seemed a bit odd. Was all well with Alice? She had seemed rather wan and quiet all last summer, as though something had been troubling her. In Evy's next letter to Aunt Grace, she asked about the Tisdale family and whether Alice had been seen in church.

The weeks went by slowly because Evy was concerned about her aunt. Also, she could not quite stop thinking about Rogan—and the memory of that moment in his arms would return at some of the most inconvenient times, such as during practice, when her fingers would miss a key and she would instantly glance up to see Madame Ardelle's sharp black eyes.

In the second year there was a good deal more freedom for the students. Sometimes in the afternoons and often on Saturdays the students would hire carriages and go to Regents Park, or take boat rides on the Thames and afterward have tea in Piccadilly. Evy enjoyed choosing a bakery treat and taking it out to one of the sidewalk tables, joined by her two roommates, Frances and Victoria.

Life was molded around a pleasant routine. Besides her music, there were language classes, dancing, and twice-a-week classes on deportment and conversation. Evy took them all, as though she knew her days for such opportunities were short. But piano was a grueling five hours a day, overseen by the watchful madame. Sundays, of course, were worship days. A good many of the students did not attend, but Evy would find her way to St. Paul's each Sunday morning where she hung on words the minister gave from the pulpit of the great cathedral.

When Frances told her about Grand Tabernacle, she began attending and was awed and inspired by the preaching of the great Reverend Charles Spurgeon. After hearing him she began taking a greater interest in the Scriptures. Evy had been raised to believe in Jesus and His redemptive work, but through Spurgeon's eloquent exposition, Christ became more precious and personal to Evy's heart. She read the Bible before bedtime now, whereas before it was mostly a book for Sunday at the rectory. Her prayer life also became less dependent on the *Book of*

Common Prayer, and hymns took on new meaning. She read about Wesley, Isaac Watts, and Newton, and gained a new appreciation for Bach and Handel as she recognized that their inspiration came from their Christian faith.

The month of November rolled around, and letters arrived from Aunt Grace explaining that Alice would not be returning to music school.

She may take her final two years in France, with this year as a sabbatical. She has been such a help at the rectory, taking over many of the duties you performed so well. I must say I'm surprised. Alice never appeared committed to the Lord until this year. Derwent is depending on her help a little too much, I fear. At any rate, we are all so grateful Alice can help since neither I nor Mrs. Tisdale is quite able to do all that we once enjoyed.

Derwent and Alice?

Derwent also wrote telling Evy of his father's regression and of how difficult things were for him. *I do my best, but I have always said that I am not as gifted as my father. Miss Alice thinks I should speak of my concerns to Sir Lyle and Lady Elosia.*

Evy looked up from the letter. What was Alice doing advising Derwent like this? He seemed quite satisfied to allow it. What was going on back in Grimston Way?

She read on…

We all know what a great influence Sir Lyle and Lady Elosia have over the rectory and what goes on here. Did I write you about the good man and his wife who may take my father's place as vicar when the hour comes? I daresay, everyone likes him. He was here for a week last month to meet the villagers. The bishop is likely to appoint him. He and his wife will be coming in the spring, around Easter, to hold services and get to know the parishioners better. There is some assurance that I may become the new curate…

Evy heard from Arcilla now and then. Her Montague finishing school was nearby, so she sent Evy secret messages through one of the staff girls so they could meet at Regents Park. A message came on Friday afternoon, delivered by one of the maids who worked at the prestigious school: *Meet me at Regents Park at noon on Saturday. There is news to tell you.*

More than likely there was also someone Arcilla wished to meet.

Despite curtailed freedoms, the young woman had managed to rendez-vous with several men from the university, all while claiming that her heart belonged steadfastly to Charles Bancroft.

Evy went to the park and waited for Arcilla by the fountain. It was a sunny Saturday, and a good many Londoners were enjoying the day in spite of the chilly November weather. The lawn was well kept and filled with a scattering of colorful autumn leaves. An array of birds and pigeons were about the square and near the fountain. Evy wondered what kind of news Arcilla wished to tell her. Perhaps it was merely about her holiday plans. Arcilla usually anticipated gala affairs months in advance so she could have her father arrange for additions to her wardrobe. She told Evy that she did not wish to go home to Rookswood this year for Christmas, but preferred Heathfriar.

"Rookswood is too far," she had said. "Guests must stay the week-end or at least the night, and this limits many from attending. It's Rogan who prefers Rookswood; he likes the country setting."

"Well, with his dedication to riding, he would."

She remembered Arcilla's mock horror. "Riding! The very thought spoils everything."

Evy smiled at her extravagant friend. "You'd prefer dancing with a dozen attentive young men vying for your smile."

Arcilla laughed, then sighed in mock ruefulness. "Ah, how well you know me, Evy."

Evy was pulled from her musings by the sound of Arcilla's voice call-ing: "Evy, over here!"

She turned from the fountain and saw the parked carriage near the curbside. Arcilla was leaning out the cab window, beckoning her to come.

Now what? Arcilla usually walked down from Montague. Evy hur-ried across the grass toward the cab.

"Quickly, inside!" Arcilla scooted over, and Evy climbed in, the cabby closing the door.

"The gem show," Arcilla called to the cabby.

Evy looked at her as the carriage pulled away from the curb. "Gem show?"

"I'll explain in a few minutes. First, I've other news."

Arcilla was a beautiful sight in her stylish frock, hat, and fur-collared coat. She appeared quite the sophisticated young woman on the doorstep of marriage. And yet there was an unusual tension in her voice, and she was absent the hand gestures that she normally used for emphasis. She learned early on that she looked charming with a hand going to her heart as she expressed her sincerity, or up to a stylish hat when flirting, or reaching forth in a gesture of pathos when she wanted one's help.

The fact that she'd abandoned her favorite mannerisms told Evy that she was genuinely upset.

"*Everything* has gone wrong!"

"Surely not everything." Evy tried to smile at Arcilla's wail. "A few more months at Montague and you will graduate. That is something for you to be pleased about. No more schools, no more guardians—that should make you deliriously happy."

"I am serious, Evy. I've heard distressing news from Rogan. He came over to the school last night to see me. We talked in the parlor."

Evy's interest picked up.

"He showed me a letter he received from Parnell, who is in Capetown. Two pages, mind you. That should tell you how seriously Parnell takes his mission."

Evy raised her brows. "What mission?"

Arcilla's large eyes shone with misery. "Sir Julien is going to convince my father that I should marry Peter Bartley! So dear traitorous brother Parnell wrote Rogan telling him all the reasons why he must convince me, and why I should go through with it! Parnell has met with Mr. Bartley. In fact, Rogan has warned me that the man is here in London. Rogan said he arrived from the Cape a week ago. I'm expected to be introduced to him before we leave London for Christmas holidays."

Evy could see the worry in the other girl's eyes and dropped her teasing. "Parnell wants you to marry Peter Bartley? But why? I thought he and Rogan were both friends with Charles. They've certainly spent enough time together at Heathfriar these past few years."

"Well, Rogan is Charles's friend. It is Sir Julien who wants my father to arrange marriage with Mr. Bartley. Parnell wrote Rogan explaining what was being planned." Arcilla's mouth set in the stubborn line Evy knew all too well. "I won't do it, I tell you. I positively *don't* want to marry any man but Charles."

Evy was not surprised by Arcilla's unhappy news. She remembered hearing Sir Lyle discussing Peter Bartley and how Julien believed Bartley was the right man for her. But what did shock her was the role her brothers were playing. Parnell had to know his sister would resist.

"Why would Parnell want you to marry Mr. Bartley?"

"Oh, you know Parnell. He is for anything Uncle Julien is touting." She rested her chin in her hands, clearly despondent. "That's what he told Rogan in the letter too. It turns out that Mr. Bartley is related in some way to the Bleys, so I suppose he's in diamonds. Uncle Julien wrote Father that the marriage will bring a certain diamond mine under family control. So it is very important to him—and to the Chantrys. It is all quite involved, you see."

Evy could not help but notice that this fact—that it was considered important to the family diamond interests—seemed to appeal to Arcilla's pride. Evy knew she had always adored being the center of anything important. Well, if such a thing could sway her, then did she really love Charles?

"Does Rogan agree that it is wise for you to marry Peter?"

"Rogan told me he favors Charles. They're such good friends. Of course, Patricia is Charles's sister, and that has something to do with it, I suppose, since Rogan will marry Patricia. He has not proposed to her yet, but the family expects him to, perhaps before he leaves for Capetown next year. Parnell is also being groomed to marry into Uncle Julien's family. Even though the girl—I forget her name—is too young now. She is fourteen, I think."

She turned to Evy with wide, helpless eyes. "Oh, Evy, it is so dreadful. How lucky you are to be so inconsequential. No one wants to marry you—except Derwent."

"Thank you, Arcilla."

Arcilla batted at her arm. "Oh, you know what I mean. You are quite pretty, really. Except you are too prim. That frightens men away."

It did not seem to frighten her scoundrel brother, Evy wanted to tell her. She wondered what Arcilla would say if she knew of the advances Rogan had been making toward her. But Evy preferred that no one else know about it.

"Rogan is not convinced about Mr. Bartley," Arcilla was saying. "Parnell knows that Rogan favors Charles. That's why Parnell wrote him. You should see the letter. It was absurd. Rogan said it looked like a lawyer's treatise."

"I do not see how you can thwart your family's purposes, Arcilla."

"Not *everyone* in the family agrees, I tell you. Rogan is not convinced. He has yet to meet Mr. Bartley."

"What did Rogan advise you to do? He would side with your family's wishes, would he not?" After all, there would be family wishes and plans for *his* marriage as well.

"He will meet with Mr. Bartley and make his own judgment, then speak with Father about it over Christmas holidays when we all return to Rookswood."

"He would want a match that would be most sensible for you."

"I suppose Parnell does too, but he seems greatly swayed by Sir Julien since he went to Capetown. Thank goodness for Aunt Elosia. At least she thinks a match with the Bancroft family would be favorable."

"Then perhaps you have no cause to worry unduly."

"I wish it were that simple. Mr. Bartley will also be coming to Rookswood to meet with my father during the holidays. Now I'll have to go home for the season instead of being with Charles at Heathfriar, as we planned. But I *won't* marry Mr. Bartley."

Evy leaned back against the cushion. "You must not do anything rash."

"You are the only true friend I have. You must help me. If you don't, I won't have anyone to turn to."

"You have Rogan."

"Yes, but he would not stand for my running off with Charles."

Evy stiffened. Run off? Would Arcilla really do something so foolish? "I do not see what I can do to help you." What would Charles do if Arcilla suggested running away and getting married? Such a thing would bring sure scandal, and Charles would lose the favor of his family. Evy could not see Charles Bancroft giving up his right to inherit Heathfriar.

"There is something you can do for me." Arcilla was pleading now. "I'm to meet some friends at the museum at one o'clock for the diamond show. I want you to come with me."

"Me? But why?"

Arcilla looked away, and little alarms began to sound in Evy's mind. What was the girl up to now?

"Oh, just because I feel so unsocial. I need you there for support."

Evy laughed. "Since when do you need me to give you courage in a social gathering? Besides, I doubt my presence will be appreciated by your friends."

"Well, *I* shall appreciate it. Oh, Evy, do not protest. It will all be rather boring, actually. Diamonds from all over the world...but one can't *wear* them, can one? All one can do is *look*. And the event is really a show honoring diamond cutters. I need your company."

This was certainly not typical of Arcilla. Evy did not know what to think of her motive.

"Now, do not get that huffy look and say no before I explain. Because I need you to help me."

"To do what?"

"I'm meeting someone—alone." Arcilla waved off Evy's protest. "Oh, do not look at me that way. It is perfectly harmless."

Evy was not convinced. "If your brother does not wish you to go off alone, do not expect me to shield your recklessness. I've no desire to come up against his displeasure." Indeed, she'd faced enough of that in her race down the three flights of stairs at Rookswood.

"It is important, I tell you!" Arcilla's lip shot out in a pout. "Are you my friend or not?"

"It seems I am a friend when you need me to get you out of trouble."

Arcilla laughed. "Do not be silly, Evy. Of course we are friends. We have been together since childhood. Oh, very well. I will tell you. I'm meeting Charles. There...now you know. Is that so dreadful?"

"No, of course not. Then why must you slip away like this? Do you not see him most weekends at Heathfriar? And he *is* Rogan's friend."

"That's just the problem. They are close friends. Oh, do you not see my difficulty?"

"You are not being totally honest with me, Arcilla, and I shan't cooperate with your schemes unless you are truthful. I've my own reputation to safeguard, you know."

"But I *am* being truthful. Charles knows about Mr. Bartley, and we must meet alone and discuss the future."

"He learned so quickly?"

"Rogan met with him yesterday. Charles saw Parnell's letter. Rogan explained the difficulty facing my father should he oppose a marriage Sir Julien thinks is important to all of us. You look curious and confused, I know. I do not understand everything either. Rogan never explains all to me. He says I wouldn't understand. It does concern the Chantry interest in the diamond mines owned by Sir Julien. That should help you understand the horrid situation I've been forced into. I'm a pawn in the plans of relatives in Capetown as well as here in England. Rogan told Charles not to see me during Mr. Bartley's stay in London. Don't you see? It is so unfair to me and Charles."

"I'm sorry you're in this situation. But if you are not supposed to see Charles, then a secret meeting will only make matters worse."

"How will Rogan find out? You won't tell him, and neither will I."

"I'd rather not become involved in this."

"Of course not. But I must see Charles once more! Please, Evy!"

Evy was sympathetic, but she could just imagine her own difficulty if things went awry and Rogan discovered she had abetted his sister in something so reckless.

"Just this once." Arcilla placed a hand on Evy's arm. "I won't ask your help for a clandestine meeting with Charles again. I promise."

As if Arcilla could resist further opportunity to see the man she claimed to be in love with. And what of Charles? Did he not realize the situation he was placing Arcilla in by agreeing to meet with her in secret?

"If Charles is such a good friend of your brother, why is he willing to deceive him?"

"Oh, Evy, you are such a *novice* about love." She clasped her hands together, intertwining her fingers. "Charles and I are *deeply* in love. We should rather *die* than be forever torn apart."

"That sounds much like Romeo and Juliet. But I think you have felt the same way about several other men in your life."

Arcilla actually looked a bit wounded at that. "You laugh, but that is merely because you are so dour you do not know what love is."

Evy stiffened. "I know enough to realize that deceiving family and friends for a secret meeting is not likely to come to a good end."

"No lectures." Arcilla held up her hands. "I have endured enough of them!"

"Then I will go now and trouble you no longer."

"Oh, Evy, you are impossible. No, please, do not go. Say you will help me—just this once."

A heavy sigh escaped her. Did Arcilla have any idea how troublesome this could become? Did she even care? "How long will you be gone?"

"Not long. Thirty minutes, maybe less. All you need do is occupy Heyden van Buren with conversation until I return. Ask him all about the gem show. That will keep him talking. He is as boring as Rogan on the subject of diamond cutting. I will be as quick as I can. I promise."

Heyden. Evy fought the heat that threatened to surge into her cheeks. She hadn't seen the man since he'd witnessed that dreadful scene in the Rookswood library. "What is Mr. Heyden doing at the diamond show?"

Arcilla's pretty brow furrowed. "You look rather affected by him. Do you know him?"

"I met him in the library at Rookswood last August."

Arcilla gave her a quick scrutiny. "He will never marry you, so do not hope for such a thing."

Evy could not stop the bark of laughter that escaped her. "Whatever gave you such a silly notion?"

Arcilla arched her brows. "Oh, come. I know that wistful look."

"You know nothing of the sort."

"His family was one of the early *voortrekkers*."

"Boers, mostly farmers." Evy had studied up on the Hollanders, who had first gone to South Africa in the 1600s, while the Puritans had gone to America.

"Yes, well anyway…" Arcilla lifted her hand, showing she had little interest in history. She had hardly passed the subject when Aunt Grace taught it at Rookswood. "Rogan thinks that Heyden van Buren's family agree with the cantankerous Boers when it comes to who rules South Africa. Heyden's family is not well off, though he has a good education."

"I assure you, I have no romantic interest whatsoever in the man." Evy kept her tone calm and cool.

Arcilla's trilling laughter filled the cab. "That is why I like you, Evy. You are not afraid to say what you think. Too many others fear I will exclude them from my balls and dinner parties if they speak their true minds." She turned in the seat to face Evy, her hand extended like a waif pleading for crumbs. "Then you'll come with me to the museum?"

Evy nodded. She had her own reason for attending now. If Heyden van Buren would be there, then a few questions about the theft of the Black Diamond were appropriate. Rogan had said that Heyden had some suspicions of his own about who had taken it from Cape House.

"As long as you promise me you will not use this occasion to run away with Charles Bancroft, I'll go with you."

"You have my promise."

Evy gave Arcilla a quick look. The girl's meek response did not bode well…but never mind. Surely she would not be such a ninny as to run off with Charles. And even if she would, surely Charles had more sense.

At least, Evy fervently hoped so.

CHAPTER TWENTY-THREE

The carriage drew up alongside the museum, and they were assisted out. Evy saw Heyden van Buren standing on the wide steps. He came forward, smiling, and removed his hat, his eyes fixed on Arcilla. She exploited the moment, despite the negative things she had said about him in the cab.

"You are late, Miss Arcilla. I was beginning to worry. I should have met you at Montague and escorted you."

Her tinkling laughter showed delight, as though pleased he had worried.

"You are looking beautiful," he told her. "You shall put the diamonds to shame."

Again, she laughed and favored him with a sweet smile. "How kind you are with your compliments, Mr. van Buren. You make a humble young lady such as myself blush."

Evy was astounded she kept a straight face, and remained in the background unnoticed until his wintry blue eyes recognized her. There came a visible start of surprise as he must have recalled the scene in the library, then a small glimmer of approval as his eyes dropped over her. Evy resisted his flattery.

"Miss Varley, isn't it? This is a surprise. I think my friend Rogan Chantry failed to properly introduce us at our last encounter." He smiled and bent over her hand, his fair hair catching the sunlight. "Permit me to introduce myself. I am Heyden van Buren, and as you would know by now, my family is acquainted with Sir Julien Bley of South Africa."

"Yes. I have been informed. Will you be staying long in England?"

At the glint of curiosity in his eyes, Evy felt a twinge of apprehension. Was he putting events together? Was he linking her with her mother, and did he believe her mother had been at Cape House and run away with the Kimberly Black Diamond? The idea was so egregious that she felt her cheeks tint. If only she could disprove it and salvage her mother's reputation.

"A few more weeks," Heyden was saying. "Then it's home again to South Africa."

He was older than she had first thought, perhaps ten years Rogan's senior, which would make him around twenty-eight. He was browned from the South African summers, and the lines at the corners of his eyes were not the work of aging but of the sunshine. His accent was rather strange too, bringing to mind the man Evy had met in the woods so long ago. She preferred the richer tones of Rogan's precise British.

Inside the museum, guards were everywhere. One quiet, vaulted chamber of marble and glass was roped off, and diamonds of all shapes and sizes—some in the rough—were displayed on a background of black velvet under shimmering light. Special guests were invited to a catered luncheon to hear lectures by some of the most revered diamond cutters from around the world. In spite of her first inclination to refuse Arcilla's request to accompany her, she was now pleased she had come, not merely to ask questions of Heyden should the opportunity arise, but to see the glorious display of the world's diamonds.

Heyden seemed to appreciate her avid interest and informed her which diamonds had been sent from Capetown for the show. He pointed out a blue diamond, which was catalogued, "The Blue Rand, Kimberly, 1876."

"Sir Julien Bley's." There was tension in Heyden's pronouncement.

"I understand your Uncle Carl van Buren and Julien Bley were at one time partners in a diamond mine." She did her best to sound casual.

His brow twitched. "Yes, I was a small boy then. You probably know of the mining accident and how Sir Julien bought the van Burens out. We are not on the best of terms now… You have heard?"

"That you are an Afrikaner, yes."

"In British Capetown, Miss Varley, there is a great dislike for the Boers, to use a British term. Most of my people are loyal to Paul Kruger and the Transvaal Republic. That's where I grew up with my grand-mother. Though it's presently under Dutch rule, that may all change soon. Since gold has been found in the Transvaal, the British officials in Capetown, including Sir Julien, are trying to influence London to seize the area. They will not be satisfied until war is provoked with the hope that British sovereignty will be established throughout all South Africa."

Evy was aware of the recent newspaper accounts of disagreements between the British government and the Dutch farmers, but she had not formed an opinion on the matter. Perhaps that might change later, but with other, more personal concerns on her mind, trouble with the Boers seemed far away and of little consequence.

"Sir Julien Bley rightfully questions my allegiance to British rule in South Africa. I've never made any bones about my political convictions. But I do not fret… There are other ways to win my rightful seat at his banqueting table."

He studied her so thoughtfully that she grew uncomfortable. His look was much the same as Sir Julien's when he'd scanned her so intently in the parlor with Lady Camilla.

She gave a small shrug. "Sir Julien still has a great interest in what became of the Black Diamond."

"Then Rogan told you of the scandal surrounding your mother?" Evy started, and his mouth turned down. "That is most unfortunate. I feel she was unfairly blamed."

His words caught her off guard, and she gave him a smile of relief. "Somehow I thought you believed in her guilt and offered Rogan your convictions."

"I shall tell you a secret, Miss Varley. One of the reasons I came to England was to arrange a meeting with you about your mother. I have information that you will find very interesting. We cannot talk here,

however. I had hoped to speak with you at Rookswood, but Rogan"—
he smirked—"actually threatened me, the young cub. If I set foot again
on the estate, I'm quite sure he will have me thrown off."

She looked at him, trying to fathom this new development. Why
would Rogan not wish her to meet with Heyden about her mother?
"You feel my mother was innocent?"

"I do. If she took the diamond on the night of the storm when she
fled in the buggy, then what happened to it? I've questioned the old
Zulu woman."

"The one they say helped my mother escape in the buggy?"

"Yes, Jendaya. I've made a trip into Zululand since the war. I am the
only one who has managed to speak to her. She said there was no diamond because your mother was convinced that Henry Chantry betrayed her and ran off with it. Jendaya entrusted you to Henry who took
you to Natal. From there, arrangements were made to bring you to
Grimston Way."

Master Henry had betrayed her mother! Rogan had not mentioned
this...so he must not be aware of it. "Then it really *was* Master Henry
who stole the Black Diamond."

"I am convinced of it."

That could only mean Lady Brewster had been wrong when she
wrote him absolving him of guilt. But how to prove it? And how to convince Rogan?

Lady Brewster's letter would not help—in fact it would likely discourage Heyden. She did not think even he knew its contents. Rogan
had been quite closed about the matter.

"You do not know how your words lighten my burden, Mr. van
Buren."

"Heyden, please."

"I thought I was the only one who believed in my mother's innocence. I think the charge is incredible. She was a Christian missionary."

His golden brow went up. "A missionary?"

"Yes, of course, at Rorke's Drift. Why she would even be at Cape
House makes little sense to me. I told Rogan so, but he insisted my

mother was there that night. But I cannot imagine she would know Master Henry. So this supposed betrayal makes no sense. Unless— Yes, it is quite possible that my mother was at Cape House that night for some Christian purpose. A duty to perform, no doubt. I intend to find out someday."

She looked at Heyden and was startled at his intense regard. "I see… I believe you are in…some confusion about your mother, Miss Varley. We do need to talk. But now is not the right moment. When can we meet again? Alone?"

"I can meet you at Regents Park the first Saturday in December."

"Yes, very fine."

That Heyden understood her dilemma was tremendously reassuring. At last she had an ally.

"Tell me if I am out of line, Miss Varley, but witnessing that startling scene in the Rookswood library has troubled me on more than one occasion recently. May I ask what Rogan Chantry may have told you about the theft of Sir Julien's prized diamond?"

"Only what I just mentioned, that Sir Julien no longer believes it was his stepbrother Henry who arranged the theft, but my mother."

He was thoughtful again. "Do you mind telling me what was in the letter that made you want to throw it into the fireplace?"

She wondered how much to tell him, and yet why should she not trust him? He believed her mother innocent, when Rogan did not.

"Then Rogan did not explain?" She was opting for time to think.

"Rogan Chantry is a most secretive young man."

"It was an old letter from Lady Brewster apologizing to Henry Chantry for accusing him of stealing the diamond. She blamed my mother."

"Then…Rogan believes your mother was a missionary."

She blinked. What an odd thing to say. "Yes, of course he does."

In the thoughtful silence that followed, Evy came suddenly alert. *Arcilla…*

She turned from the showcase and glanced about the chamber, her heart plummeting. Arcilla was nowhere to be seen. Evy wasn't even sure which direction she had gone to meet Charles Bancroft.

Several couples entered the chamber, talking and laughing quietly. Evy's gaze rested on them, and suddenly she found herself confronting Rogan and Miss Patricia Bancroft.

Rogan was obviously surprised to see Evy—and when his fervent dark gaze found Heyden, Evy was sure he was displeased.

She assumed those with him were several of his university friends, along with the typically pretty aristocratic young ladies who would be dining with them after the diamond show. Why didn't Arcilla mention that Rogan would be here this afternoon with Patricia?

Evy hated to admit it, but Rogan and Miss Patricia made a handsome couple. Suddenly she felt herself a sparrow among peacocks—she hadn't dressed formally at all. She turned away as though to look down at the blue diamond Heyden had been pointing out to her just moments before.

Evy looked over to the clock. Arcilla said she would take less than thirty minutes. Her time was up. What on earth was delaying *dear* Arcilla? She endured a moment during which she wanted to turn and leave the museum at once and take a cab back to Parkridge Music School. She should have known better than to trust a Chantry! *She has left me here to make excuses during her absence, but this time it won't work.*

Heyden was watching her, and she tried to focus on what he was saying. "I understand you study piano at a notable music school. You must play quite well."

She managed a smile. "There are times when I wonder if I truly play at all. I shall have my concert solo in the first week of December. If I merit even a nod of approval from Madame Ardelle, I shall be delighted. It is very grueling."

"I can well imagine. I admire such determination. I have always wanted to play, but lacked the discipline to do it well. A public performance, is it? Then I should like very much to come and hear you."

Pleasure filled her at the thought. He was a most agreeable man.

The concert, she told him, would be held on a Saturday evening near the end of the term before the school breaks for Christmas and New Year's holidays.

"I shall make a note of the date and be in attendance."

"Am I missing out on something? Sounds like a party?"

Heyden turned to face Rogan. "Hello! Quite a display, is it not?"

He inclined his head, but his gaze was on Evy, not Heyden. "Quite. Only the Black Diamond is missing. I see Sir Julien's Blue is here. Stunning, isn't it?"

At the mention of the Black Diamond, Heyden fell silent. Evy tensed. Rogan must have known speaking of it would make the moment uncomfortable.

Rogan gave Evy a tenuous smile. "What a pleasant surprise. Where is Arcilla?" He glanced about.

"Arcilla?" Evy gripped her hands together. "She could, in fact, be anywhere by now."

Rogan was regarding her carefully. She could tell he suspected she was hiding something. Oh, a plague on Arcilla for putting her in such an awkward position!

If Heyden had not been there, Evy would have mentioned Arcilla's desire to see Charles. But family matters between brother and sister over a future marriage should be kept in a tight circle. Her inability to explain to Rogan left her no choice but to give an illusive answer. "She was right here with us when we came in." Evy cast what she hoped was a casual glance about the chamber. She saw Patricia talking with the friends they had arrived with earlier. She avoided Rogan's gaze and was relieved when Heyden, who saw nothing unusual about Arcilla's behavior, or perhaps did not care, went back to discussing diamonds.

"Sir Julien's Blue is attracting attention from the world markets," he told Rogan, "including the Vatican, but there's doubt Sir Julien will sell. Some suggest he's growing sentimental."

"About the Blue?" Rogan's smile was almost derisive. "It is not sentimentality that holds back the sale, but what Julien considers weak bidding. If the offer were high enough, he would sell in an instant. No, there is no sentiment lurking in my uncle's cool mind, unless it's over the loss of the Kimberly Black."

Evy frowned. Was Rogan baiting Heyden? She wanted to tell him that Heyden did not believe her mother was guilty, but decided against it. Besides, Rogan had not been looking at her when he mentioned the Black, but at Heyden.

Heyden turned a smile Evy's way and reached out to take her hand. "Miss Evy was telling me of her piano concert to be held in December."

Rogan lifted one rakish, dark brow. "How interesting. You invited Heyden to your performance?"

Oh, this was insufferable! "Well, yes…anyone is welcome. It is to be near the end of the term."

"But a solo concert nevertheless." He smiled. "I am sure I will find it of interest as well."

Heyden was looking across the chamber. "I see an old friend from the Angola diamond mines. He called and told me he'd be here. I worked for him some years ago. That was when I foolishly thought Angola diamonds were superior in color and clarity to South African." With that, Heyden walked across the museum chamber past several intimidating looking guards.

A man had entered the chamber and now stood by the door. Evy saw that he was very heavy, and in his fifties with a smallish, egg-shaped head. His warm-weather white Panama suit and wide-brimmed hat were most inappropriate for the setting.

Rogan, too, regarded him with mild interest. As the man and Heyden walked to one of the glassed-in security tables to look at the glittering array of stones, Rogan turned toward Evy.

"Who is he?" she asked. "The heavy man in the Panama suit?"

"One of the Boer officials from the Transvaal Republic. One of Paul Kruger's right-hand men. They came to see Her Majesty's Prime Minister to avert war. And now—where *is* that foolish sister of mine?" His gaze locked with hers. "With Charles?"

He knew. "You are wrong if you think I came here to help arrange her rendezvous."

"Then it is Charles?"

"Yes. I knew nothing of the museum showing until I was already in the cab with her. She asked that I meet her at Regents Park, and once I was in the cab she pleaded for me to come with her. She was upset over the family decision to have her marry Peter Bartley."

"Then she told you? I thought she might. Where does Heyden come into this?"

Evy cocked her head. "Why should you think he does?"

"Because he wanted to see you, and I warned him to stay away. He used Arcilla to bring you here so he could talk to you. What did he tell you?"

Her brows lifted. "*He* happens to believe my mother is innocent. He found out Master Henry betrayed my mother that night and ran off with the Black Diamond. Jendaya, the Zulu woman, told him so. He thinks Lady Brewster was quite wrong to have absolved Master Henry of guilt in the matter, all of which is very reassuring concerning my parents. Why then should I not want to talk with him?"

"Because he is more trouble than you are ready to handle." Rogan's gaze was as hard as his tone. "I'm asking you to stay away from him, Evy. At least until I have more time to look into the matters he's told me about."

"Then...he did tell you my mother was innocent?"

A look she had never seen before crossed his face. "Let us simply say he told me about your mother. The information he wishes to drop at your feet is not what you are expecting." Was he worried? He certainly sounded so. "I don't think you are ready to hear it yet. Stay away from him. The van Burens hate my family for a number of reasons I cannot get into now. Heyden will do anything to ruin us. He cannot be trusted."

She watched him, troubled, uncertain...yet unable to promise what he wished of her.

"Do you know why he is here in London?"

She looked to where Heyden stood talking with the heavyset man. "No, though he said wanted to talk with me."

"That's not all of it. As a Boer, he despises the British. He actually wants war. We consider him a serious troublemaker, trying to urge Paul Kruger to throw down an ultimatum to the British Government to get out of the Transvaal."

"I know little about the conflict," she admitted. Her interest in Heyden van Buren had to do with her parents, and Rogan knew it.

"This is the first time you've talked with him?"

"Yes. I have not seen him before except in the—" She caught herself before mentioning that debacle in the library, but it was too late.

He smiled, his eyes scanning her face briefly. "Ah yes…the library." The words came out in a deep, caressing rumble. "A fond memory indeed."

"I really must be going now." She turned to survey the room. "There is nothing I can do about finding Arcilla. I'm sorry it turned out this way. Sorrier still that she drew me here to enable her to escape more easily."

"Please accept my apology for her. We both know Arcilla well enough to understand her. But as long as she is with Charles, I won't worry unduly. I merely wish she had used her head and refrained while Bartley is visiting. He expected to meet her here tonight, and from the hound dog look on his face, his pride has been injured."

Evy could not help but smile.

"There is no telling when she will return," Rogan said. "I suppose she's gone off in Charles's carriage. Well then, you will need a ride back to Parkridge. I'll call you a cab."

"There is no need. I can arrange it myself, thank you."

His smile was broad. "I would not *think* of allowing you to go off alone. If I concern myself with Arcilla, I also feel some obligation toward you. After all," he said silkily, "you would not have gotten into this if it hadn't been for her conniving. I'll get you a cab."

"I am not helpless, Rogan. I have done my own arranging many times. I shall be quite safe."

He ignored her completely, falling into step with her as she headed for the door. The man was inexorable, and she could only wonder why.

Unless… She restrained a small smile. Perhaps his insistence had something to do with a vague notion that Heyden might feel obligated to bring her back to Parkridge.

True to his word, Rogan hailed a cab, rather imperiously, she thought, and handed her into the seat. "I shall let you know about Arcilla." He lifted her hand to his lips, and the contact sent shivers running through her. "Au revoir."

She sank back against the seat cushion, grateful to be free from the many layers of tension she'd just encountered. As she ran through the conversations in her mind, she felt her resolve grow.

She would talk with Heyden again and hear what he had to say. No matter what Rogan Chantry thought.

CHAPTER TWENTY-FOUR

Evy had trouble concentrating in class the next morning, so deep was her concern about Arcilla. What if she had actually convinced Charles to run off to France and get married?

After classes, Madame Ardelle entered the dormitory room that Evy shared with Frances and Victoria. Her round, olive-toned face was animated, and her brown eyes turned to Evy, who sat curled in chair with her music history book in hand.

"You have a caller, Miss Evy." The woman always used the formal *Miss* before the names of her students, even after three or four years under her tutorship. "Rogan Chantry waits for you with a coach. He is asking permission to escort you out to dinner, but I told him that was highly irregular for a Thursday night. I hope I have not disappointed you too severely. You may speak with him in the parlor if you like, but you must insist he leave for his university by eight o'clock."

Frances and Victoria slipped over to the window and peered down into the carriage yard.

"Oooh…look at that divine coach."

"Never mind the coach. Look at him!"

"Miss Frances, Miss Victoria?" Madame Ardelle looked at them, brows raised, then turned again toward Evy. "It is not befitting to keep a young man of such good breeding waiting."

What Madame Ardelle meant, of course, was that the Chantry name was associated with South African diamonds.

Evy hurried to freshen up and run a brush through her hair while

Frances and Victoria gave her advice on what would make her look her prettiest. She calmly changed into a pretty dress and added the saucy hat Rogan had bought her, setting it carefully on her thick, tawny hair. Again she noted how the ribbons and color emphasized the jade flecks in her eyes. Would he notice?

Evy smiled and left the room. Once away from the girls, she admitted to herself that she was not as indifferent toward her dashing caller as she pretended. She sped to the stairway and looked down into the quiet front hall. She hoped Madame Ardelle had not loitered, and she sighed when the woman was not in sight. Evy came down the stairs, looking toward the door that led into the parlor. It was ajar, and she knew Rogan had entered and was waiting.

She hoped the news on Arcilla would be good. Interesting…that Rogan had wanted to go to dinner.

She entered the parlor, where the gloomy late November weather was chased away by a glowing log burning in the grate. The large parlor was furnished in Madame Ardelle's old-world taste. Heavy wine-colored draperies, Louis XIV furniture, and a matching wine and cream Persian carpet. Through the floor-to-ceiling windows the bare branches of trees were starkly fingered against a pale five o'clock sky. She paused, lifting a hand to touch her smooth hair.

At the same moment, Rogan left the bookcase and came toward her, scanning her with obvious pleasure. He took in the hat. "Very charming. A perfect match of green." His genteel manner was in contrast with the lively gleam in his eyes. He took her hand, that enigmatic smile dancing across his features.

"How good of you to see me on a Thursday evening, Miss Varley. Madame has made it clear you need your sleep, and I am not to keep you up past eight."

From his exaggerated gravity, it was clear he was amused by Madame's strict code of rules for her music students. Yet his actions were smoothly calculated to represent the pinnacle of gentlemanly graces.

"Our first class starts at half past five," she said with a rueful smile.

"So, unlike spoiled fourth-year university students, we must adhere to a strict discipline."

He smiled. "So you still believe I am spoiled and arrogant. I'll have you know I am agonizing over final exams for graduation and going without sleep."

"Should I believe you? I wonder… You look well rested and alert."

"I cannot help what your stimulating presence does to me."

She laughed. He really was a rogue—and far too appealing when he was like this. She breezed past him toward the window, sitting primly on the cushioned window seat, her folded hands on her lap.

He watched her with a ghost of a smile, and she had the sense that he was still trying to understand her. She hid a smile of her own. Good. Let him wonder. He was altogether too accomplished in understanding young women as it was.

"I told you I'd come to let you know about Arcilla."

She inclined her head. "Thank you. I've been concerned for her. However, you could have sent a message and saved yourself a trip from the university."

"Would you have preferred that?"

She lowered her gaze, affecting a demure posture. "I was thinking of your busy schedule."

"I'm rarely too busy to see someone whose company I find so… intriguing. I was hoping you would come to dinner with me. I'd forgotten you were held under lock and key by the stalwart madame."

"I did not receive an invitation to attend dinner with you."

"Ah. A word to the wise, eh? I am expected to arrange things well in advance. You do not like surprises, then."

Did that displease him? She could well imagine that Patricia Bancroft rearranged her schedule to be with him whenever he wished.

"I assure you it is Madame who is inflexible." She quickly changed the subject. "I take it then that Arcilla is back at Montague, safe and sound?"

His wry smile was nonetheless indulgent. Clearly he cared about his sister. "Yes, alas, the emergency is over—for the present. My sister, as you know, is not above creating new storms to bring a bit of unwanted excitement into everyone's lives. Thanks to Charles, everything worked out reasonably well. He is from the old school of thought and prefers the status quo. Meaning he is not interested in galloping off to Paris in the dead of night to marry secretly. He knew what was expected of him and carried it through to the proper end. Instead of fleeing with her like two escaped lovebirds to France, he kept a stiff upper lip and brought her back to the school."

Charles Bancroft most likely had experience in avoiding awkward social positions, and Evy was fairly certain he must know Peter Bartley had arrived. Had Arcilla put up an emotional fuss and begged her beloved to flee with her to Paris? Poor Charles! The temptation to surrender to her pleadings must have been difficult to resist.

Rogan walked up to the window seat and looked down at her.

She refused to let his nearness unnerve her. "What do you think Mr. Bartley might have done if they had come back into the museum together?"

"I'd rather not imagine. But ol' Bartley does seem to be rather a sport. Like someone who would dutifully drink poison for the cause, rather than lose favor."

She laughed.

"In this case, it's Sir Julien whose favor Bartley fears losing. Not that matters are anywhere near being resolved where Arcilla and Charles are concerned. It's a gummy situation. Two men want to marry her, and the family must decide, but not according to which man will make her life most contented. That would be too simple. The choice must be based on social agendas."

And on what will bring more success to the diamond dynasty, she thought, remaining silent. She was a little surprised at Rogan's cynicism for his own social stratum.

He leaned against the wall near her. "I'm relieved the decision is in my father's hands. Naturally, I'll give him my opinion. I've promised Arcilla I would. I like Charles"—from the sincere tone of his voice,

Evy believed this—"though he's a bit of a lockjaw. He can be very pompous sometimes. But I do trust him. We've been friends since we were boys. But Bartley..." His gaze drifted to the far wall. "He is Sir Julien's golden boy. I don't see a bright outcome for Arcilla and Charles. Julien holds the purse strings to the family cache of diamonds—and mines."

"I'm surprised you can view the situation so clearly."

A brow lifted. "You think I am blind to the sins and foibles of the aristocracy? Only one who has never studied the French Revolution could be so. Sir Julien has feet of clay, as do we all, including the poor and downtrodden, by the way. I've never been one to believe in the righteous poor and the evil rich. What is that old saying? 'The Colonel's lady and Rosie o' Grady are sisters under the skin'?"

"I don't doubt that Rosie might pass herself off as the Colonel's lady if given half a chance," she said. "Anyway, I should hate to be forced to marry a man I did not love because his family had a stake in my marriage—and in the cache of diamonds."

"You are not suggesting that the aristocracy are the only ones who hold to the opinions of family and society, are you?"

She met his challenging gaze. "Yes, indeed. It does appear to be so. Arcilla has little to say about her marriage."

"You think she would make a wiser choice if it were left up to her?"

That stopped her. She had to be honest. "Well...in Arcilla's case—"

He smiled. "And in your case?"

"In my case"—she rose from the window seat and turned to look outdoors—"the same criteria do not apply. Your sister and I are worlds apart."

From the corner of her eye, she saw him contemplate the small explosion of wood and flames in the fireplace. "So your world is more generous with its young daughters, you think?"

She hesitated. She could see a trap coming, but she would not retreat. "Yes...I believe so."

His gaze came back to capture hers, and she thought she saw a fire reflected in the depths of his eyes. "Then why, unless something happens to force a change, is your future all but chiseled in stone? Why will you return to Grimston Way, become Mrs. Brown, and carry on in your aunt's footsteps?"

She started to respond, but he cut her off.

"And please do not tell me it is because that is what you wish, for I will not believe it."

Evy walked to the settee and sat down, refusing to let his taunts ruffle her. "I did not realize I was being forced to marry Derwent."

His cryptic smile set her nerves on edge. "Then am I wrong in thinking a match was made between your uncle and Vicar Brown when you and Derwent were still babes in arms?"

She had no answer for that—it was, of course, quite true—and so she simply remained silent. But when the stillness in the room grew oppressive, she gave a sigh. "Perhaps I wish to be a vicar's wife."

One brow arched. "Derwent and you, the perfect vicar's wife... I wonder. Ah, well. Life can be full of little surprises, can it not?" His unexpected smile was disarming. "Despite all the plans of mice and men, and, I might add, despite the promise of diamonds, people are known to do very strange things."

"I indeed hope so. I should be disappointed to think otherwise."

"Love wins out in the end, is that it?"

"I think so, yes."

"A man throws away everything for the woman he loves. Very romantic, but do you really believe that can happen?"

"Not often perhaps. I suppose, like Arcilla, more marriages are made to accommodate wealth and position than love and faith."

"Faith. I wondered if you would bring that into the equation. A vicar's daughter—in your case a niece—must marry her own kind, just as we must marry our own kind. Or as you would say it, someone *socially suitable*."

"One must marry of like faith, yes. Not because one is related to a vicar, but for obedience."

His head tipped at that. "Explain. I am interested."

"I am obliged as a Christian to marry a man of the same genuine commitment to the Christian faith as my own."

"'Be ye not unequally yoked together.' Is that what you mean?"

She stared at him. Was Rogan actually quoting the Bible? "Yes."

"So we are back to Derwent. You would marry him because he is…suitable. Very enlightening."

She did not argue, partly because he was right. But she also was reluctant to give away her doubts about marriage to Derwent. She was not in the least doubtful that it would be a comfortable marriage. But was that enough?

Rogan startled her by pushing away from the wall and going to snatch his coat and hat. Quick disappointment stabbed her that he was so ready to depart. Not, she assured herself, because she wanted his company, but because she had a question.

She leaned forward. "Why do I somehow think—dare I say it?— that you do not like Sir Julien?"

His cool gaze came back at her. "Whatever gave you that idea?"

She shrugged. "When you mention him I've noted…a bit of doubt in your voice."

"I did not realize my feelings showed so easily." He smiled. "I'd better watch myself around him, or he'll disinherit me."

She sat back, hands in her lap again. "Now you are being cynical again."

"Am I?"

"You did not answer my question. Maybe because you do not want to reveal how you think?"

He hesitated, then pursed his lips. "Maybe *dislike* is not the right word to describe how I feel about him. *Distrust* may be closer. I've never fully trusted him, not even when I was a boy. Remember when we were children and I brought you to Henry's rooms?"

"How could I forget? Sir Julien came in, and you told me to hide. It was frightening."

"I saw Julien search Henry's rooms the night before we went there. It was very late, so obviously he did not wish to be seen. I sometimes think he came to Rookswood to search."

To search…for what? She stood and walked toward him. "He was looking for the Black Diamond? Then he does not think Henry was innocent, as Lady Brewster maintained in her letter!"

His gaze held hers, but his thoughts seemed to be elsewhere. "I think it was the map he wanted. I wonder if it wasn't also the letter from Lady Brewster." He focused on her. "What did Heyden tell you about the diamond?"

She hesitated, then decided to tell Rogan exactly what Heyden had said. He needed to know there was at least one person in his family who did not hold her mother to blame.

Rogan listened, growing ever more thoughtful. "I suppose Heyden wanted to learn what it was you hoped to destroy in the fireplace that afternoon the three of us met."

"Why would he not be curious after such a dramatic, shocking scene?"

A small smile tipped his lips. "True, but he was far too curious long before that day. What did you tell him?"

"He already suspected that I wanted to destroy a letter. I told him it was from Lady Brewster."

"You told him what the letter was about?"

"Yes."

A frown drew his brow down. "That was a mistake."

"He believes in my mother's innocence. I saw no reason not to trust him."

"I *gave* you reasons. He wishes to use you for his own political purposes."

"But—"

"Never forget he's a ruddy Boer, disloyal to the British Crown. If a war breaks out in South Africa, which I fully expect, and perhaps sooner than anyone thinks, Heyden will support Dutch rule under Paul

Kruger. I've no intention of cooperating with him about the Black Diamond. Or"—his burning gaze swept her face—"about you."

After a moment of charged silence, he smiled. "Well, I'd best be on my way."

Evy followed him into the hall to lock up for the night.

"I regret you are not having dinner with me."

Swift pleasure warmed her, but she schooled her features, careful not to give him the notion that she, too, was disappointed. "It would have been pleasant."

"Another time perhaps, when you are not so limited by Madame." He took her hand and lifted it to his lips, but rather than kiss the back as she expected, he turned it over and pressed a kiss to her palm. At the warm pressure on her skin, she caught her breath, suppressing a shiver. His smiling eyes told her he was well aware of her reaction. And pleased by it.

"Au revoir," he murmured and went out the door.

Evy watched as he entered the coach and shut the door. A moment later she heard the clop of hooves as the coach pulled away. Her gaze followed the coach down the cobbled drive until it disappeared into the London fog.

She bolted the front door and turned to the staircase. How Rogan disturbed her. She could still feel the touch of his lips on her hand. There was more to Rogan Chantry than the surface revealed. He disapproved of Heyden, but there was much he was not telling her. Somehow she was sure it involved her—and her parents.

But Heyden had a side to him that she found rather comforting; he had been sympathetic about her mother, and he lacked the social status—and the accompanying arrogance—so nettling in Rogan.

Evy went back upstairs to her dormitory room and tried to concentrate on her language studies, but Rogan's words echoed in her mind: *I've no intention of cooperating with him about the Black Diamond. Or about you.* What had he meant? Could he have found out about her upcoming meeting with Heyden?

On Friday a letter arrived from Aunt Grace.

Vicar Brown died peacefully in his sleep of heart failure on November 3, and the new vicar has arrived. It is all quite sad for our sakes because we will miss him, but not sad for Vicar Brown, who has joined your uncle in the presence of Christ.

At the end of the letter, she wrote part of the verse from the first chapter of the epistle to the Philippians: "…to depart, and to be with Christ; which is far better."

Evy wrote her condolences to Derwent. It was far too soon after the loss of his father to inquire about his plans for the future. Though she fully expected that in time he would become the new curate, he would first need to return to divinity school for his final year.

Life was definitely changing by large steps and small. Sometimes it seemed the most significant changes came by way of the most unlikely events. Yet over all things, great and small, the Lord God reigned supreme. Only in moments of human weakness did doubt and fear steal away her confidence and set her heart beating uncertainly.

If only those moments did not center so very often on Rogan Chantry.

CHAPTER TWENTY-FIVE

The end of the school term and the Christmas holidays drew near…as did the night of Evy's concert. The other girls were as excited as though they had been chosen to do the solo performance for an audience of London's avid music lovers.

"I know you'll do well," Frances told her. "I have listened to your practice, and it's flawless."

Evy laughed. "I think you're too generous. I'm far from becoming a concert pianist, and this whole thing has put butterflies in my stomach."

"You will do well," Frances said again, and left Evy to her practice.

She was having a new dress made in a London shop for the occasion. Aunt Grace had known of the honor since October and had written Evy insisting a gown be made for the evening of Evy's performance:

Do not concern yourself for the expense, dear. To have been selected from among the students to be the featured pianist is obviously a thrilling event, and I want you to have the best. You have worked hard indeed and deserve a special gown. I only wish my strength were such that I could be there to hear you play. My prayers will be with you, and I'll be waiting anxiously for you to come home for the holidays to tell me all about it.

Evy was thrilled. She had worried about what dress to wear, for she had nothing elegant enough for the occasion. She wasted no time in trying to find the right shop and seamstress. Madame Ardelle recommended a French shop, for she was acquainted with its widowed owner.

"You are making a mistake," Frances said. "Do what Madame says, and you'll be wearing stiff black taffeta on stage. I can hear it now as you bow before the audience and sit down at the piano. Then you'll begin to play the funeral dirge." Frances began humming a doleful march.

"Oh Frances, you are being silly," Evy said, laughing. "Just because Madame wears black doesn't mean her friend cannot work with colors. What color do you think I should choose?"

"Burgundy," Victoria sighed.

"Emerald velvet," Frances countered. "It suits your eyes."

Evy pursed her lips. "Emerald green. Velvet, yes. Luxurious velvet."

And so it was. Accompanied by her roommates, Evy went to the shop in downtown London and chose from the available patterns and materials. When she returned two weeks later to collect the gown, Evy tried it on before the mirror to make certain everything fit. It was all Evy could do not to echo the *oohs* and *ahs* of her two friends. She turned before the mirrors as the seamstress looked on proudly at her handiwork. The skirt was long and flowing; the tightly fitting bodice, according to the latest style, had a lower neckline for evening wear, and the popular sleeveheads were large and puffed. "Do you think it's a bit too daring?" she whispered to Frances and Victoria.

"It fits you so well, Evy. Anything else would make you look stuffy and disapproving. Besides, it is just a *wee* bit off the shoulder."

"And you *did* choose that pattern." Frances eyed her. "So you must have wanted that style."

"Yes, it is so lovely… I saw Patricia Bancroft wearing a style like this at the diamond show at the museum some weeks ago."

"There! You see?" Frances clapped her hands. "You are all set for the musical. Hurry now, let's go back to the school to show the other girls. I cannot wait to see their faces. And wait until we do your hair the night of the concert." She sighed. "'Tis a pity Rogan Chantry won't be there." She cast Evy a sly glance, but Evy avoided her eyes in the mirror.

Now the night of the concert had arrived. Evy had had one disappointment that morning—a letter from Heyden. It had read quite simply:

Dear Miss Varley,

I regret that I cannot keep our appointment at Regents Park for this Saturday. Urgent political concerns demand that I accompany Paul Kruger

to the country home of the Officer of Colonial Affairs. I look forward to con-
tacting you as soon as possible.

    H. van Buren

    But she scarcely gave him a thought now. Dressed in her gown, her hair meticulously upswept in curls and waves, Evy had to admit she felt like Cinderella going to the ball. Victoria had lent Evy her mother's pearls and matching fan comb. And Claudine, who hailed from a wealthy London family, lent her a darling pair of velvet slippers and a feather fan. Victoria, who had as little as Evy, kissed a lace handkerchief and turned it over, a twinkle in her eye. "From great-great grandmother Fanny Wilshire, for blessing."

    Fifteen minutes before Evy went on stage, she waited near the entrance to the raised dais in the great hall. She was shocked to see Arcilla, adorned in a lovely outfit of blue satin, come floating into the room.

    "Arcilla!" Surprised delight filled Evy at the sight of her friend. "What are you doing here?"

    Arcilla's tinkling laughter was warm as she came up to take Evy's arm and turn her about. "*C'est magnifique.* Evy, I hardly recognize you. What do you mean, what am I doing here? Would I miss your crowning moment?" She grimaced. "Mr. Bartley is here with me. He's my escort tonight. We were to attend a dinner party, but once I knew this was your night to shine, I insisted he bring me to hear you play. Afterward we are all going to our family townhouse on the Strand for a little dinner—and you are coming with us. We must toast you and make a fuss over your success, you know."

    We? Evy's heart thumped irregularly. Was Rogan actually there?

    The butterflies in her stomach were getting worse. Even her hands felt cold and clammy. Suppose her fingers fumbled over the keys? *Dear Father, please help me to play for Your honor tonight.*

    She tried to focus on Arcilla. "Me? Go to the Chantry Townhouse?"

    "But of course. We think highly of you, you know." She laughed. "We have a surprise for you there as well, but you won't learn what it is until you get there. We'll take you in the carriage. That way you can meet my Prince Charming, Mr. Bartley." She looked toward the ceiling, as though he were anything *but* Prince Charming.

But Evy's mind was too full to think about Arcilla's problems right now. *"We* have a surprise? Who is *we?"*

"Rogan, of course," she said airily. "Most of this was his idea. He was the one who told me you were playing solo tonight, chosen from among all the students at the school. And this"—she produced an orchid—"is from both of us. Here, let's pin it to your gown, it goes so well."

Rogan *was* here! Evy's agonies increased at the thought. What if she gave less than her best performance?

Madame Ardelle appeared and drew Evy from among her well-wishers. It was time. A few minutes later, Evy stood beside Madame in the dimly lit utilitarian backstage area behind enormous curtains. She must be calm, Madame told her quietly. Yes, she would be confident, and play from her soul. Madame would not have chosen her if she thought otherwise.

With these words in her mind and a prayer on her tongue, Evy waited for the end of her introduction. She found herself leaving parted curtains and walking onto the stage, something she had practiced scores of times. She walked to the grand piano, turned to face the large audience, whose faces she could not see, offered the practiced little curtsy, then sat down on the bench. The keys stared up at her, waiting, as though holding their breath. *Play us well,* they seemed to implore, *with all your heart.*

Evy's fingers took command of the keys, and glorious notes resonated throughout the hall. It was no accident that she had chosen Beethoven's Piano Concerto no. 4. She smiled as she imagined Rogan's reaction. He would have no doubt that she had fulfilled her part of their music bargain made on the windy hill overlooking Rookswood, when he had challenged her to play this very concerto for him.

But she dared not imagine him sitting out there, watching her and listening. Not unless she wanted her nerves to go out of control. Instead, she gave herself up to the piece, and soon she forgot everything but the glorious images in her soul that the music stirred to life.

She went on to play a number of pieces for her finale, including some Chopin nocturnes. When her fingers stilled and the last notes drifted on the still air of the room, there was a moment of hushed silence. She held her breath—and then it came: applause, breaking out in waves of wholehearted approval, but she understood it was for more than her ability. The enthusiasm was for the matchless music itself filling the listeners' souls with wondrous joy, even as it had her own. And if she had been able to elicit this emotion in the audience, she had accomplished her goal.

Evy stood, blinking back tears, thankful to her Creator for endowing her with the abilities she had been able to cultivate and use tonight. This achievement had been years in the making, and many were her enablers, not least Aunt Grace at home in Grimston Way, praying for her as Evy knew she would be. Aunt Grace, ill, yet wholeheartedly involved.

Thank you, Father God.

Evy bowed to the audience.

When she left the dais, Madame was there in the waiting room, her hands clasped and her eyes shining. "Magnificent."

At the woman's simple praise, Evy smiled her delighted gratitude.

"Now you must meet some guests. They are waiting to congratulate you."

It was some time before she met Arcilla and Mr. Bartley. She looked behind them and felt a small stab of disappointment. No Rogan.

"Evy, you were grand!" Arcilla turned to Mr. Bartley. "Was she not, Peter?"

"Indeed, most excellent, Miss Varley. I look forward to hearing you again."

"Thank you," Evy repeated over and over to her well-wishers. But her focus was elsewhere. Where was Rogan?

She turned and almost bumped into him. He was unaccompanied. Evy's heart tripped. Where was the ever-present Patricia? Had she not wished to accompany him? Or had he decided against her company tonight? She felt a little thrill at the possibility.

Rogan's eyes shone, and the unrestrained admiration in his dark gaze brought a warmth to her cheeks. Unlike the others he took her hand and bent over it, kissing it. Once again her heart leapt at his touch.

"You were wonderful."

His low murmur moved over her like a sweet summer rain. "Thank you," she managed, withdrawing her hand, but still feeling his touch. "Did you approve of my first choice?" She barely restrained a grin.

A faint, knowing smile touched the corners of his mouth. "It was superbly done."

Evy had never known such joy as filled her in that moment.

It was some time before she could break away, and when Madame Ardelle gave permission for her dinner out with the Chantrys, she escaped with them to the coach. Arcilla and Mr. Bartley got in first. Arcilla was busy chattering as Rogan handed Evy inside. He then got in beside her, shutting the door. The horses' hooves clattered across the damp cobbles on the way toward the Chantry Townhouse located on the Strand.

Arcilla was still laughing and chattering with Mr. Bartley, looking very unlike the forlorn young lady she had portrayed only a few weeks ago. So much for the deep, undying love she had vowed! Or was this apparent happiness only affectation? It was difficult to tell. Evy would rather believe Arcilla had decided Peter Bartley was not such a dreadful choice after all.

She glanced at Rogan, meaning to look away again, but his gaze would not relinquish hers.

"Unlike some others, I am not surprised at how lovely you look tonight. I have always credited myself for seeing beyond the unadorned rectory girl to the real woman who is Eve Varley."

That gave her pause. "I am and always shall be the rectory girl, Rogan."

His smile wrought havoc on her already heightened nerves. "I hope so. It's the rectory girl I find most appealing. She remains the same, even when adorned in pearls and velvet. Someday it must be diamonds."

She flushed, nearly overcome with a pleasure she did not want. She must not feel this way... It made her foolishly vulnerable. It had been a mistake to come with him tonight, to act as though she belonged to this social echelon. And yet, there was not another place she would rather be than sitting beside him, warmed by his attentive interest and what appeared to be genuine compliments.

And so for a moment, she allowed herself to deny that she was climbing a precipitous cliff. Or that the fall, should it occur, would be a dreadful one.

Aware of a sudden silence in the coach, Evy looked quickly across at Arcilla. It would be dreadful if she could read Evy's thoughts! Arcilla had already seen fit to warn her not to fall for Heyden van Buren. What would she think if she knew her true feelings toward her brother, upon whom Arcilla thought the sun rose and set?

The Chantry Townhouse was exactly what Evy would have expected: It stood in a class all its own surrounded by other two-story houses in the socially elite area of the Strand, known for royalty and titled families.

"Mum used to like coming here," Arcilla reminisced, after exiting the coach. "Do you remember, Rogan?"

Of course he would, and made no unnecessary comments as Arcilla continued in her nostalgia. "There was something about the rose garden that was special. Mum would say, 'You can smell them tonight. The little fairies are out playing on the velvet petals.' No sooner would we all arrive than Mum would take my hand and we'd go off to check on her special scarlet roses. If she thought anything was not just right, she'd call Simms—our old butler, the dear—and she would chide him about the health of her *babies*. Simms used to be so gentle with Mum, as though she were a child herself."

Rogan interrupted, but there was gentleness in his voice, as though he felt sorry for his sister. "Come along, Arcilla. We'd best go inside. Simms won't like it if the supper gets cold. Besides, I suspect after giving so much of herself tonight that Evy must be hungry."

Actually, she hardly had an appetite. She was too excited. As they went up the walk she knew she would always remember this special

night when she had played to an approving audience and dined in
December moonlight with Rogan Chantry.

The townhouse must indeed have been one of Lady Honoria's
favorite places away from Rookswood. Evy could see it in the choice of
furniture and paintings. The rooms were narrower, the house taller, and
the intricately carved steep wooden staircase had been refinished so that
it looked like a polished wooden gem. Three narrow flights of steps
wound upward in a half spiral. The gallery railing on the middle floor
was also highly polished, and ornate and lovely crystalline chandeliers
shone and glittered like carved chunks of ice.

"It is beautiful," she murmured as Rogan took her wrap and handed
it to Simms.

Simms and his niece, a young woman with berry cheeks and thick
brows, had prepared a cozy room facing the garden for the supper.
There was a long table covered with festive linens and full of platters of
all sorts of foods and delicacies. Candles gleamed on either end and
above another smaller chandelier.

Comfortable chairs were arranged in a semicircle about a round
table with a mammoth bowl of Christmas flowers and greens. Evy kept
the surprise she felt to herself. She had expected other guests to be here,
but the comfortable arrangement was set for a foursome.

She gazed about, aware of the thought that had gone into this.
Warmth filled her at the realization of the care and honor that had been
afforded her. Was it Rogan or Arcilla who had been the driving force
behind it all?

They each were to choose whatever delectables they preferred.
Evy felt as though her head were spinning. *Here I am, dining cozily
with social aristocrats in a townhouse that once, long ago, entertained
King Charles!* Surely this opportunity would not have been possible
without Rogan. He must have been the instigator. The thought was
exciting and dangerous—but she didn't care. She was here, in her
new gown and hairdo, after a successful performance, enjoying the
attention of quite possibly the most sought-after young bachelor in
London.

Miss Patricia Bancroft was not here, but Evy Varley was.

The dining was quite pleasant and the company exhilarating. Even Arcilla, with whom Evy was so accustomed to chatting, entered whole-heartedly into the relaxed conversation. Mr. Bartley, or Peter, as both Arcilla and Rogan called him, talked extensively about South Africa and Capetown. Evy found it all quite intriguing. Peter told them he had been born in England and taken to Capetown when he was three years old, when his father was appointed a governing official.

"Peter may be appointed to aid the governor-general in dealing with the troublesome Dutch," Arcilla told Evy.

"Boers," Peter corrected her, though Evy noted his tone was most patient. "A proud and uncivilized band of farmers. Do you know much about them, Miss Varley?"

"No, I cannot say I do. I understand they settled there before the English arrived."

"That is true. They call themselves voortrekkers. Their commander is Paul Kruger. A thornier, tougher-minded old Dutchman you'll not likely meet."

Evy thought of Heyden at that, and her eyes met Rogan's. He looked a bit provoked.

"War is inevitable, don't you think, Peter?"

He studied Rogan at that. "If we do not force the Boers to accept British rule, then the Union Jack isn't likely to be flying over any new Rand that may be discovered. Therefore war, in my mind, is a necessity."

"The Rand?" Evy asked.

Rogan turned his head toward her. "Witwatersrand. Where the first big gold rush took place. The name was shortened to The Rand."

Had Rogan mentioned his idea of a second great gold find to his future brother-in-law? She guessed that he had not. Rogan listened more than he spoke, as though willing to learn everything he could from those who had been born and raised in South Africa. It was this tendency that made her think he would become an expert in whatever he set out to do. More and more she realized that he was not arrogant, as she had once thought, but confident. His interest in the Cape, in gold especially, had not waned since childhood. Nor had his belief that he would be successful.

"Why do you think there will be a war?" Evy directed her question to both Peter and Rogan.

Arcilla yawned and nibbled at her dessert, a small custard tart with raspberry sauce.

"I can sum it up for you in one meaningful word, Miss Varley," Peter said with a twisted smile. "Kruger. The soldier, the warrior, the stubborn Dutchman who refuses to see the sunrise of the British Empire spreading across Africa."

She shifted in her chair at this passionate outburst.

Rogan had long since finished his supper and was stretched in his chair opposite her, hands behind his dark head. He had removed his dinner jacket and loosened his white frilled shirt around his throat.

"Gold and diamonds," Rogan told her lazily. "You've heard of Cecil Rhodes, have you not?"

She looked at him. *I would have studied up on this before I came if I'd known I'd be drilled on South Africa.* She feared she might look as blank and bored as Arcilla. "I believe your father mentioned a colony…somewhere in Mashonaland."

Rogan nodded. "Rhodes wants to push farther into the region and form a new outpost that he dreams will one day be a small country all its own—Rhodesia. Named for himself, of course. There are likely to be diamonds, gold, and perhaps emeralds in that region. He has gained a charter from the queen allowing him to form a company of settlers to make the trek inland. Peter is likely to be sent to Rhodesia as an official representative of the governor-general in Capetown."

Evy looked at Arcilla to see her reaction. She had come alert and looked with shock, first at Rogan, then at Peter. "Rhodesia? You're being sent there by the governor-general?"

Peter looked a trifle uncomfortable and glanced at Rogan as if to ask why he'd told her so soon. But Rogan sipped from his glass, his expression bland and unreadable.

Had he done this deliberately? She recalled how he had said that he preferred Arcilla to marry Charles. Perhaps she had settled in too comfortably with Peter, and Rogan was trying to alarm her, to make her put up more of a fight for the man she wanted. Did Arcilla wish to travel deeper into Africa as the wife of a commissioner?

But while the news had startled Evy, too, she found the idea of such a journey as exciting as it was dangerous.

"The governor-general of Capetown and your uncle, Sir Julien, will be sending me," Peter said.

"Leave it to Uncle Julien," Rogan commented. "He has his fingers in everything."

"What of the tribes in the area?" Evy looked to Peter. "Do they agree on allowing more white settlers?"

Rogan cocked a brow and looked at Peter. "What say you, Peter?" Amusement tinged his casual words. "Will they welcome Rhodes with open arms, do you think?"

Peter emptied his glass in one gulp and set it down with a click of determination. "They will. All we need is more time to convince them it's in their best interest."

Rogan looked over at Evy, a faint smile playing at his lips.

Arcilla was frowning, most likely imagining herself in a company of new settlers moving off into the unknown wilds of Africa. Evy saw her shudder a little, and at that moment her heart went out to Arcilla. Did Sir Lyle understand what he was doing by allowing Sir Julien to dictate his daughter's marriage?

Rogan stood, startling Evy, and looked at his timepiece. "I think we need a change in mood. One moment." With that, he left the room.

Arcilla lapsed into thoughtful silence, and Evy did her best to carry on the conversation with Mr. Bartley, steering clear of his future in Rhodesia. Was he finding everything in London as he had expected? Was the cold weather difficult on him? How were the seasons in the Cape? Then she heard it.

The vibrant notes of a violin.

Emotions washing over her in waves, Evy sat straighter and turned her head. Rogan had reentered the room. He had his dinner jacket back on, his shirt collar buttoned precisely, and held a magnificent violin. He bowed to Evy.

"I keep my promises, Miss Varley. After your superb performance at Parkridge, tonight seemed the perfect time."

Arcilla's face was wreathed in smiles. She clapped her hands, looking at Evy with a childlike delight. "I *told* you we had a surprise for you."

She stood and offered a sweeping curtsy. "Ladies and gentlemen, may I bring to your august attention the musical expertise of Master Rogan Chantry playing...?" Apparently she had forgotten the official name, for she covered her mouth with a laugh and looked over at her brother for help.

Rogan bowed deeply to Evy. "Paganini's Violin Concerto no. 2 in B Minor."

As he set bow to strings, Evy leaned back in her chair, her eyes drifting closed. The music rose and swelled, filling the room as completely as it filled her heart. Rogan's suave yet dynamic performance of Paganini's concerto left a tingle running down her spine. She opened her eyes and saw his gaze fixed on her, and knew he was playing for her. Her breath caught in her throat at that, and she gave him a smile from the depths of her heart.

After Paganini, he broke into "La Campanella." She would never have guessed Rogan had such drama and beauty of interpretation in him. The rendition called for a quivering command of the strings. She envisioned a lone violin player late at night on the streets of Paris telling a story of love, danger, and loss with just a touch of wry humor. How well that piece fit Rogan's personality.

When he finally lowered his bow, Evy stood with the others, applauding madly.

Rogan's questioning gaze held hers, and she knew what he wanted. She did not hesitate to give it to him. "It was marvelous."

"Encore!" Arcilla's eyes shone as she looked at Evy. *This is my brother,* they seemed to say to her. *He is a Chantry. He is exceptional.* "Encore."

He gave his sister a small bow and played Bach's Violin Concerto no. 1. And as Evy sank back into her chair, she thought she would never know another night such as this.

The evening ended as it had begun, at Parkridge Music Academy. Rogan escorted her to the door and inside to the front hall, while Arcilla waited with Peter in the coach.

She gave him a warm smile. "Good night, Rogan. Thank you for the lovely evening. I enjoyed it very much—especially your violin."

"It is you who are the musical talent. You won accolades tonight, you know. I suppose you'll go on for your final year. What then? Have you any special plans?"

"Everything depends on my aunt's health." And their finances, but naturally she did not tell him that. Aunt Grace wanted to keep her in Parkridge, but the final year would be almost twice as expensive, since Madame Ardelle's graduates would attend classes at Eldridge Music School under the direction of Master Eldridge himself, a very demanding instructor.

Rogan nodded, and Evy thought there was sympathy in his eyes for Aunt Grace's health. But there seemed to be a question as well. "I suppose Derwent has written you of his plans now that the vicar has died."

Derwent! She hadn't thought of him once that night. She looked away, wondering what that meant. "I think it far too soon for him to make any decisions."

"He only has two choices, as I see it. Return to divinity school and hope for a vicarage, or find other employment."

"He might get the curate's job in Grimston Way."

"At St. Graves Parish, you mean?"

"He mentioned it in his last letter."

"I suppose that would please you. You could remain in Grimston Way. That is, unless you're the adventurous sort who wishes to travel and see something of the world."

Was there a question behind this casual statement?

Evy didn't hesitate. "Unlike Arcilla, I think I would very much like to go to South Africa. But...I suppose I shall settle in Grimston Way and carry on as I always have."

"Ah, well, there is still this year of studies to complete, isn't there—for both of us. That reminds me, I have horrendous exams in the morning. I had better get back to the university. If not, I may be out on the streets playing my violin for a tuppence."

She laughed at that. "I hardly think you'll need to worry about such a thing."

He opened the door, his thoughtful gaze lingering on her face. "One never knows. Especially if I end up balking against Julien's will and plans." He smiled. "Good night." The door closed behind him.

Evy stood there, wondering. What did Rogan mean? Contesting Sir Julien Bley's will and plans? Did Rogan have Arcilla's marriage to Peter Bartley in mind, or something else? His own marriage, perhaps? Could there be someone special that Sir Julien wanted Rogan to marry? Maybe a girl in Capetown?

Evy realized she'd been biting her thumbnail and lowered her hand.

Or maybe the confrontation would come over Henry's Mashonaland map? It was no coincidence, was it, that Cecil Rhodes's ambition for a new colony was directed toward Mashonaland?

She pushed all this from her mind, determined instead to remember and relish every moment of the exceptional evening. She wrapped her arms around herself and stood there, basking in the warm afterglow. She could still feel the pressure of Rogan's hand holding hers as he had helped her from the coach.

But it was another moment they'd shared—one long ago in a darkened library before a blazing fire—that was indelibly burned upon her lips. And her heart.

CHAPTER TWENTY-SIX

Evy returned home to Grimston Way for the Christmas holidays. She had expected Derwent to meet her at the train depot but he did not appear. It was Mrs. Croft who was all smiles, driving the jingle. Strange...that Derwent did not come.

"That Derwent be a foolish young man," she snorted, but would say no more when Evy questioned her. She spoke instead of Aunt Grace's deteriorating health. "Though she won't be admitting she's failing to anyone, leastwise to you, Miss Evy."

Evy suspected her aunt wished to keep Christmas a joyful and hopeful season for them both. When she arrived at the cottage, Aunt Grace met her on the porch with a smile.

"Welcome home, Evy dear."

"Aunt Grace." Evy took hold of her shoulders and looked at her thin, pale figure. "You haven't worn yourself out getting everything ready for Christmas, have you? You know I would have enjoyed doing the decorations and baking with you. You must not tire yourself."

"No, no, I am fine now." She laughed. "I've been so looking forward to your coming home since last month. Just a mild winter cold again."

Evy looked about the cottage with warm pleasure, well aware that their home came from the generosity of the Chantrys. "Everything is just as I remembered it. Oh Aunt, it's so good to be home again." She threw her arms around her. "I only wish you could have been there the night of my recital. It was thrilling, stunning, and even Arcilla came— and Rogan."

Aunt Grace's brows shot up. "Indeed? Rogan? My! Well—I shall need to hear every exciting detail. I've got a nice pot of tea on, and Mrs. Croft brought over some peppermint cookies."

Evy smiled her pleasure. They stayed up late talking about everything while slowly decorating the cottage with baskets of fresh pine and berries.

"Where did you get the pine?" Evy did not think her aunt could go foraging in the woods as she used to when stronger.

"Alice brought them over. Very kind of her, I thought."

Evy paused, turned, and looked at her. "Alice? Yes, I'm surprised, too. How is she?" Evy had never quite understood why it was that Dr. and Mrs. Tisdale, who were comfortably affluent, had held back from sending Alice to pursue her music. They could afford to send Alice to France, considered to have the crowning glory of music schools.

"Oh, Alice is well enough."

Evy waited, expecting more explanation, but it did not come. "She is not ill, is she?"

"Oh, my no. She is—just the same girl she always was. More grown-up, of course. She is quite a young woman now, a year older than you."

"Yes, she's Arcilla's age. I suppose I'll see her during the season."

"I'm sure you will." Aunt Grace added a red bow to the pine garland she had strewn atop the fireplace and stood back to judge its effect. "The new vicar and his wife are giving the traditional afternoon Christmas tea on Saturday. You'll like Vicar Osgood and his good wife, Martha. She is just as busy and hard-working as Martha of Bethany. Vicar Osgood served a parish in Runnymeade before being sent here to us after Vicar Brown's departure. You'll like them, dear."

"I'm sure I shall." Evy was still wondering about Alice. What could have happened to her? Aunt Grace did not seem to want to discuss it, and Evy thought it wise to drop the subject for now. She was sure she would learn more in the days to come.

They baked ginger cookies and mince pies and placed them in the little pantry to cool. They would wrap them up and tie them with ribbons and then go calling on the villagers to wish them Merry Christmas on Sunday. She had joined Aunt Grace on this traditional outing since she was a little girl riding along in the jingle, the big basket of goodies on her lap. Oh, the happy days of childhood. And yet how the holidays, so precious in their Christian foundation, could also bring painful memories of lost loved ones and a world no longer sunny with childhood expectations!

Dear Uncle Edmund. Evy could see him busy at his rectory desk preparing his sermons, smiling at her with such patience if she loitered in the doorway of his office hoping for attention. Evy sighed. She missed him terribly at times like this. And it brought a qualm to her heart as she looked at her aunt and saw the visible decline in her health, clear warning that their time together was drawing to a close.

Don't think about it, she told herself. *Enjoy the time God has graciously given you. Who knows what a day may bring forth? But my heavenly Father does, and that's my consolation.*

This year would be a special holiday, one that she would always look back upon with fondness. She would make sure of it and enjoy it to its fullest.

The next day she did not see any of the Chantrys, though Arcilla and Rogan had both returned to Rookswood within a day of Evy's arrival from London. Peter Bartley was to have come back with them to meet Sir Lyle and Lady Elosia. Evy wondered about Heyden van Buren. She was disappointed that he had not gotten back in touch with her yet, but she fully expected him to do so.

The next day the Chantry coachman, Mr. Bixby, delivered the yearly goose for Christmas dinner. And for Aunt Grace there was a sealed envelope containing a generous gift of money from Lady Elosia.

"Bless her! Now we can buy presents." Aunt Grace's features lit up. "It's a sunny day too. Perfect for a bit of shopping in the village. We will have a few days for wrapping as well."

"It should be enjoyable, but are you sure you're feeling strong enough?"

"I'm feeling fine," Aunt Grace said with determination.

"I'll drive the jingle. And maybe we can stop afterward at Miss

Henny's shop for tea and some of those honey cakes I remember from childhood. It seemed back then the cakes were the most wonderful in all England."

Aunt Grace laughed. "I suspect you will still enjoy them, even though they may be a bit lumpy at her age."

The shopping trip was as fun as expected, and they laughed riotously as they tried to buy a gift for one another while the other turned her back and pretended ignorance. Afterward they stopped at Miss Henny's tea shop and enjoyed a pot of the best tea in Grimston Way along with the slightly overdone honey cakes baked by the eighty-year-old proprietress, who was delighted to see them.

"Bless my soul, but you're getting prettier with every year, Evy. And so talented with that music learnin' of yours that Grace tells me you're studying." She shook her gray head. "I just can't understand the likes of the vicar's son."

Before Evy could ask what she meant, the door opened, and Mr. Croft came shuffling in. He looked unchanged since the days of Evy's childhood, when she watched him digging graves. He saw her but did not appear to recognize her. He grinned at Aunt Grace, however, and removed his sock cap. "Afternoon, Mrs. Vicar. A pleasure to see ye out and about on such a sunny day...ah, that be *you*, Miss Evy? Praise the Lord, it is!"

"Hello Mr. Croft," she said with a warm smile. "How are you?"

"Oh, I be fine, yessir, just fine. Ye be coming to the new vicar's Christmas tea, miss?"

"I'm looking forward to it."

"Mrs. Croft be helping out the new vicar's wife that day. She be glad to hear you'll be there, miss."

He went to order his lunch of milky tea and sweet biscuits, and Miss Henny went to wait on him.

Evy studied Aunt Grace as they drank their tea. "Why did Miss Henny say that about Derwent?"

Her aunt contemplated her tea as though it were quite profound. She gave a heavy sigh. "Because Derwent has been seeing a great deal of

Alice. Let's not worry about that now. Derwent will come to his senses. His mind is filled with South Africa, and I feel certain Alice is encouraging him in this."

Evy set her teacup in its saucer, giving a slow nod. "I thought it might come to this. He has always wanted to go there, since we were children."

"Nothing is certain yet."

She thought she should feel something, some disappointment perhaps. But she didn't. It was strange... She felt so little concern about Derwent and Alice, so little disappointment that her old friend hadn't come to see her. But let her wayward mind conjure one image of Rogan Chantry paying close attention to Patricia Bancroft—perhaps kissing her palm as he had Evy's, or—*forbid it!*—kissing her the way he had kissed Evy in the library that day...

She closed her eyes. *I not only feel like I've swallowed a rock but as though I could cry my heart out! Drat Rogan Chantry!*

When they finished their last cup and the teapot was empty, they said good-bye to Miss Henny and went out to where the jingle was parked and waiting with their packages.

As Evy walked to the jingle, she saw Mrs. Tisdale and Alice just getting out of the family carriage. Mrs. Tisdale looked over to see Evy and Aunt Grace, and she smiled and waved. "Oh, hello!"

Evy held the reins while mother and daughter walked up.

"Well, Grace, you are looking much better today. Must be Evy's homecoming. Hello, Evy, how are you?" Mrs. Tisdale went on talking to Aunt Grace, so Evy turned to Alice.

"Alice, hello!"

Evy had not seen Alice for nearly a year. Aunt Grace was right— Alice indeed had changed, at least on the outside. She was nineteen now. Her strawberry blond hair was elaborately styled under a blue hat with a matching satin rose. The colors made her already pale face look waxen. The narrow chin, the tight little mouth, the rather wide forehead with a coquettish curly lock deliberately arranged there seemed testimony to Alice's usual self-satisfaction. Her light eyes reflected whatever color she wore, so that they now appeared gray-blue, fringed with reddish lashes.

"Hello, Evy." She played with her gloves, looking at Evy's bare hands holding the horse's reins. "Congratulations on being chosen to play the solo at the school concert. Mrs. Havering told us about it."

"Thank you. I'll always remember that night."

Alice smiled. "I don't suppose the competition among Madame Ardelle's students was very rigorous this year. So many of *us* that would have competed weren't there."

Evy ignored the clearly self-serving remark. It was, after all, Christmas, and the season of goodwill. "Are you still playing, Alice?"

"Not as seriously as before. I enjoy playing the piano at the rectory each Sunday." She paused, and Evy thought her look held some special meaning. "Unless you wish the position now that you're home again? You always used to do it."

"I'm sure you do wonderfully." Evy hoped she showed no curiosity over Alice being involved at the rectory. She had never appeared to like such involvement before. She had changed all right…because of Derwent? But was her faith genuine? Derwent had best find out.

"Then I shall keep the plans as they are," Alice said. "I'll be playing the carols in the chapel on Christmas Eve as well."

"Perhaps you should ask Rogan to join you on the violin." Alice looked startled, and Evy smiled. "He plays beautifully. So serious, yet he has a certain flair for lightness."

Alice's brows went up. "Rogan?"

Evy felt a small prick of pleasure at Alice's discomfiture. Now Alice was aware how little she knew about Rogan.

Mrs. Tisdale had concluded her chat with Aunt Grace and was bustling herself and Alice off toward the local seamstress shop. "Miss Hildegard has opened her own shop, Evy, did Grace tell you?"

Miss Hildegard had been sent for by Lady Honoria some years ago to make dresses for herself and Arcilla. At that time Miss Hildegard had lived at Rookswood. Since Arcilla had long ago departed for London and had all her clothes made there, the seamstress had opened up a small shop in Grimston Way. Evy wondered if she received much business other than that of Mrs. Tisdale and Alice—and perhaps Lady Elosia.

"We visit her shop often." Mrs. Tisdale's rather proud tone grated on Evy's nerves. "Naturally Alice likes to look well. Especially now." She smiled, and Evy thought, as Mrs. Tisdale glanced sideways at Alice, that the two acted as though they shared some special secret. Alice offered a little smile and touched the rose on her hat. Changed or not, she still had that sidling way about her.

Evy's suspicions grew.

"Well, we're off, girls. We must run. Toodle-oo. Come along, Alice. I'm anxious to see the lace from Brussels."

Evy picked up the reins to drive back to the cottage, smiling at her aunt to show the Tisdale women did not worry her. Aunt Grace, however, was not smiling. She looked ahead, down the narrow village street.

"Mrs. Tisdale still seems the same," Evy commented, but not without affection.

"Yes, indeed. Beatrice has always forged ahead with her plans and needles Dr. Tisdale into using every ounce of his influence in the village to get things done the way she wants them."

Evy glanced at her aunt. It seemed Aunt Grace was more disturbed by the Tisdales than she had been in the past. She must not be feeling well.

"Beatrice has managed to become friendly with Lady Elosia."

She pondered this. "That should please both Mrs. Tisdale and Alice. They were always quite concerned about getting on socially with Rookswood."

"Oh, it isn't social, exactly. That is, Beatrice gets on with Lady Elosia on some matters that concern the village and rectory, but the relationship ends there. Neither Arcilla nor Rogan is likely to include Alice in their inner circle. But Beatrice does influence Lady Elosia on some important decisions connected with the rectory."

Evy waited, but her aunt must have decided she had fallen into gossip, because she stopped and said nothing more for the ride back to the cottage. Evy couldn't help wondering if some of those decisions included Derwent. The gay holiday mood had evaporated. Perhaps her aunt had overdone herself. Evy would insist she rest for the afternoon until she made their supper. *Tonight I shall make sausage and eggs, and use some of the sweet white bread we bought at the bakery.* Derwent would be coming over as he usually did on Friday evenings. This would be her first time to see him since her return from school. She was anxious to discuss matters with him about divinity school—and his deeper friendship with Alice.

That evening after Evy wrapped her Christmas presents and put them in the cupboard out of sight, she set about to fix their supper. It was six o'clock when Aunt Grace came out to join her. She looked much more peaceful.

"Why the third place setting, Evy?"

"Derwent always comes on Friday nights."

"Yes, of course, I should have told you. He's in London."

"London?" Evy turned to her aunt.

"Yes, he said he had some business there."

"When did he go there?"

"Oh…a day or so before your return." She shuffled her dinnerware around.

Evy watched her. "What sort of business could he have?"

Aunt Grace either did not know or did not wish to discuss it. She simply said, "He will be back before Christmas."

Evy dropped the matter and forced a smile, trying to seem cheerful so as not to worry her aunt. "I do not mind the extra sausage and eggs. I can warm them over for breakfast. "

Christmas drew closer, and Evy could see the various coaches arriving for the drive up the winding road to Rookswood to attend the dinner balls. She did not see Arcilla or Rogan, but she heard from Mrs. Croft that Lizzie had told her that Miss Patricia Bancroft had arrived for the weekend. Her brother Charles was noticeably absent.

"I hear Miss Arcilla has herself a new beau," Mrs. Croft said with a curious glint in her eyes. "There was quite a going-on up there, before them guests arrived, there was, says Lizzie. Miss Arcilla is in a weepy state one day, then all stoic, and cheerful as a wee elf the next, but keeping firm company with that Peter Bartley from Capetown."

Evy did not tell Mrs. Croft that she already knew what was happening in Arcilla's life. Sir Lyle must have decided that his daughter would indeed marry Peter. Evidently Mr. Bartley's pending political position in South Africa was deemed more important than any danger of war upon Sir Lyle's only daughter.

Evy shook her head at the idea of spoiled, flighty Arcilla in South Africa! How would she ever endure?

On a crisp, sunny morning near Christmas, Evy walked the trail up to the hillock, where she could enjoy the wide, sweeping view of Rookswood and the surrounding estate grounds. She'd come here nearly every day since her return…though she finally admitted it wasn't for the view.

Sadly, Rogan did not once ride up to the hill as he had that day in what now seemed the distant past. It was foolish to expect him to come, of course, with Patricia staying in the great house.

Evy pressed her lips together. How had she ever permitted her emotions to get out of hand? It was unwise to wish to see him again, to walk here thinking he might show up, but neither could she stay away.

It was his presence in London at the concert that made her think so unwisely about him, and his playing the violin. She had mistaken his interest in her plans for an interest in her. *Foolish, foolish girl,* she chastised herself. *That will never be.* It was clear that when Patricia Bancroft occupied his time, Evy Varley did not enter the picture. She was, and always had been, little more than Arcilla's childhood companion—the rectory girl.

Clearly attending her concert and inviting her to the Chantry Townhouse for supper had been suggested as much for Arcilla's sake as for Rogan's.

Nevertheless she remained on the hill, determined to enjoy the view, looking toward Rookswood. She drank in the sight of the sun shining on its windows, fondly recalling events, then turned away and walked back down the trail.

She came to the bottom of the hill. Before she turned on the path leading toward the cottage, she heard male voices and the *clop* of horses' hooves. Reluctant to meet anyone with her emotions still so raw, she stepped aside where trees grew close together. A few moments later she was surprised to see Rogan and Derwent riding by, side by side.

They rode past her, going away from the cottage, and Derwent was laughing.

Evy waited until they rounded the fork in the road and then resumed her walk home.

The rooks gabbled in the tops of the trees, and a chill wind blew against her. Strange that Derwent had not been by the cottage to see her since he had returned from London yesterday... Or was it? Perhaps stranger still, that he was to be found in Rogan's company.

What, if anything, did it mean? The happy ring of his laughter had conveyed a carefree message she believed was clear.

CHAPTER TWENTY-SEVEN

Christmas tea took place as it always had at the vicarage, with one distinct difference. Derwent did not attend.

"Derwent is working today," Vicar Osgood told Evy when she inquired.

"Working?" Evy was unable to conceal her surprise.

"For Rogan Chantry. He's been spending quite a lot of time at Rookswood with the Chantry horses. We are hoping the position of curate opens soon… I'm certain it will."

His sympathetic look told Evy he understood that marriage could only take place once Derwent received the position. Evy's annoyance with Derwent was growing. How much had he told the new vicar?

It appears as though he is doing a good deal of explaining about his situation to everyone except me.

So Derwent was working at Rookswood estate for Rogan! Then that explained why she saw them riding together yesterday.

Derwent was not the only absentee. Lady Elosia, who made it a point to maintain her influence in the village, did not attend either. Someone mentioned she was "a bit under the weather." In fact, none of the Chantrys were present, nor were the Tisdales. Evy's girlhood friends Meg and Emily, now married, were there. Meg had married Emily's brother, Tom; Emily was married to Meg's brother, Milt. Both women were expecting babies. They were quick to embrace Evy and welcome her home, smiling and congratulating her on success at music school. Evy had always liked the two. They were plain, humble, and genuine. But even they watched her as though they were on the verge of asking her a question about some matter that troubled them. An exchange of glances between the two appeared to discourage either one from doing so.

When the first group left early to take their children home, Evy used their departure as an opportunity to get away. She left Aunt Grace chatting with the new vicar's wife and wandered out the rectory gate, onto the road. It was odd how everyone watched her. Could her worst fears be true? Could gossip have escaped Pandora's box somehow about her mother stealing the Kimberly Diamond? No, that could not have happened. Not many knew about it, not even Lizzie or Mrs. Croft. Rogan, while a scamp in some ways, would not embarrass or hurt her reputation in the village.

But might Heyden have been here asking questions?

Evy walked along the road toward Rookswood. Aunt Grace would come home in the jingle, so there was no need to worry about her. Evy wanted to be alone.

Though it was far from an unpleasant day, she could think of little to cheer her mood. The holiday festivities no longer seemed as bright as when she had arrived three days ago. The excitement of returning to Grimston Way had fizzled. Except for seeing Aunt Grace, little remained of the old life she remembered when Uncle Edmund was the beloved vicar. Even Derwent and her village friends had changed. It was as though she were no longer one of them. Even Aunt Grace seemed different…a little sad, perhaps? Or perturbed? Yes, that was it. Perturbed. It must be on account of her poor health. *Undoubtedly she misses her life as it was in the rectory, too.* What else could it be except disappointment with Derwent?

Evy thought of the Kimberly Diamond again. So far, she had avoided upsetting Aunt Grace by discussing it with her. But if Heyden had been asking around the village and word had gotten back to her aunt as well, perhaps it was time to speak to her about it.

Rogan believed her aunt knew something, though even he had not forced the issue with her. He would graduate soon and be off to South

Africa, so surely he would want to learn everything he could before leaving Grimston Way.

Evy cast a glance at the sky now turning as dark as her mood. Yes, perhaps it was time.

The next day, however, Aunt Grace took to bed with a mild fever.

"You must not worry so, Evy. I overdid it a little at the tea, is all. A rest in bed today and I shall be feeling much better tomorrow. But perhaps you should go ahead with our plans to deliver presents today. That is if you do not mind going without me?"

"No, I wouldn't think of your going. The weather has taken a turn for the worse. It looks like a foggy evening."

"Then do not be late. Mrs. Croft is coming over to make us a good chicken soup."

Evy's mood was far from festive as she loaded the basket with the cakes and candies they had made on her arrival and carried it to the jingle.

She rode into the village alone, forcing a cheery spirit and trying to leave a blessing in the homes where she called. She delivered the preserves and cakes to Old Lady Armitage, who was still spry and alert in her advanced years. The old woman came out her door to the wicket gate and up to the side of the jingle. The wind blew her thin white hair, and she drew her fringed shawl around her bony shoulders. A gleam flickered in the still-shrewd eyes.

"So it's you, is it, Miss Evy? I daresay you've changed a bit since tripping off to London to play that piano. You look a mite too pretty for the young scoundrels of Grimston Way." She studied Evy up and down. "Unless it's that chief scoundrel, Rogan Chantry, you've an eye on."

"Merry Christmas, Miss Armitage." Evy forced a smile and ignored her comments. "Aunt wanted me to bring you some of her summer preserves."

"Bless her soul. True blue, she is. Always was. Can't say the same for the rest of 'em… And now Vicar Brown is gone to his reward too. The new vicar laughs too much. I don't care for it. That silly boy of Vicar Brown's hasn't half the wit of his father, either. Derwent lets himself be pushed around like a wet mop. You'd think he'd stand up on his hind feet and demand to chart his own life, wouldn't you? But oh no, not him. Knuckles under to Lady Elosia like a puppy grabbed by the scruff of its neck. A shame, really… Ah, thank you, dearie." She took the box of preserves and cakes. Evy had put extra inside, along with a new shawl and bonnet she had bought for the woman in the village.

"You're not missing much when it comes to Derwent Brown." Miss Armitage gave a sage nod of her head and a wink. "Let him have that silly Alice if that's the way of it. Well, Merry Christmas, Miss Evy. You keep playing your piano."

It was a few moments before Evy could reply, but she finally gathered her scattered wits. "Yes, Merry Christmas, Miss Armitage."

So that was it! Derwent and Alice! *My suspicions were right.*

Evy drove on, and by the time the jingle was empty, she was in a better mood. In fact, she almost overflowed with relief! She did not love Derwent the way a girl should love a man. She'd known it for some time but never really admitted it, mostly because Aunt Grace had always expected the union. *I was told from a child I should marry Derwent.*

The relief she felt over admitting this, combined with giving and sharing Christian love with others, cheered her heart and utterly lifted her burden. She was humming "silent night, holy night" when she left the village proper and was on the road back to Rookswood estate. She had not gone far when she met Arcilla riding one of the mellow mares from the Chantry stables. She called to Evy and waved for her to pull over. She came riding up, her cheeks tinted pink with cold and her blue eyes bright. The wind tossed her hair beneath the pert riding hat.

"Hello and cheers! I've been looking for you, Evy. Your aunt said you had come into the village."

"What brings you out riding alone?"

"I'm a big girl now," Arcilla jested.

"Yes, but surely any mission important enough to get you on horseback must be worth some kind of escort," Evy said with a laugh.

Arcilla played with her whip. "Exceedingly important, if you want to know."

"A dinner ball?"

Arcilla stared at her, clearly amazed. "How did you know?"

Evy laughed. "I know you. When is this one?"

"Tonight. And you *must* be there."

"Me, tonight? Oh come, Arcilla, you are teasing."

"No, indeed. There is an emergency, and I need you."

"Well, it is so grand to be wanted, even if only when an emergency demands it."

"Oh, you know what I really mean."

"Yes."

Arcilla laughed. "Now don't be so moldy. You need some fun as well, so let us conclude we are helping each other. Do say you'll come. Aunt Elosia approves of you, and so does my father. They wouldn't have had your aunt as my governess years ago if they hadn't."

Evy toyed with the reins. Would Rogan be there? Of course… Patricia Bancroft would no doubt be at his side.

"Aunt Grace is not well and needs me to be home tonight."

"I already spoke to her. She tells me she will have the company of Mrs. Croft. A party will do you good, she says. So there! No more excuses."

Arcilla was never one to mince words when it came to protecting someone else's pride or feelings, and she did not do so now. "It's Rogan's friend, Abbot. He's here at Rookswood. I had planned for Cicely to be Abbot's partner tonight, but she became ill this morning. And you have the perfect gown to wear, too. The one you wore to your concert in London. It looked very pretty on you, I must say."

Evy knew Arcilla would give her no peace if she did not capitulate. "Very well, I will come."

"I *knew* I could depend on you." Arcilla's smile beamed on Evy. "I will send Bixby to bring you up to the house around seven."

❧   ❧   ❧

It was raining when Bixby helped her into the coach and closed the door.

Evy arrived at the front carriageway, and the footman came to open the door. He carried an umbrella for Evy and escorted her up to the open doorway of Rookswood.

The glittering chandeliers, the decorations of pine and berries, red and gold ribbon, all glowed with festive color. Lilting voices reached her ears, and she realized they came from the expanded ballroom off to her left. Evy held her breath as she waited near the wide double doorway that led into the aristocratic foxes' lair.

Arcilla saw her first and rushed toward her, bringing a handsome young man in evening dress with her.

"This is Abbot Miles. Abbot, my very best friend, Evy Varley."

He bowed over her hand and smiled. "Fortune has smiled upon me."

He took her arm, and they stopped at the doorway of the ballroom as their names were announced to the small group, all of whom had turned in their direction. Then Lady Elosia came toward them, a smile on her face, her elegant hand outstretched, the gems glittering on her fingers and wrist.

"Ah, dear Evy, how charming of you to come. And how positively enchanting you have become."

"Thank you indeed, Lady Elosia."

"Come, let me introduce you to the others."

In the next few minutes Evy found herself murmuring all the right responses to all the right greetings from all the right holiday guests— mostly lords and ladies, of course—from London's elite. She felt a little breathless when introduced to an earl and his countess. Then, of course, there was Peter Bartley, looking quite distinguished. Even Arcilla seemed more mature than when Evy had seen her that afternoon. She actually seemed to change in Peter's company, to stand straighter and carry a more somber demeanor. Evy could not help note, however, that the girlish glow that had shone in her eyes when with Charles Bancroft had dulled to a look of resignation.

A stir passed through the gathering as everyone turned to look toward the doorway. The handsome younger son of the squire himself had arrived, Patricia Bancroft on his arm. Rogan's dark gaze slipped over the faces of those present and then focused on Evy. He looked genuinely shocked for a moment before he recovered. His jaw hardened, and Evy frowned. He did not look pleased.

He did not know I would be here.

"Rogan Chantry and Miss Patricia Bancroft," the male reader intoned, and the couple advanced into the ballroom, Patricia's hand resting lightly on Rogan's arm. They made the rounds of the guests, exchanging greetings, until they came to Abbot and Evy. Evy felt her heart skip a beat as her gaze met Rogan's.

Yes, he was displeased. She could see an angry spark in the depths of his eyes, and it brought a heat to her cheeks.

"Why didn't you tell me you had such a beautiful neighbor, Rogan?" Abbot grinned. "Or maybe I should say now I *know* why you didn't tell us all these years."

"Where is Cicely?" Patricia asked the question of Abbot, though her narrowed gaze was fixed on Evy.

"Ill, in her room."

Patricia's cool gaze slipped from Evy, and she looked at Rogan. "There is Peter... Come, Rogan, I think dinner will soon be served."

Evy refused to be intimidated by the cool reception. Had she not told Arcilla it would be this way? But she had not expected Rogan to be in opposition to her presence. Was it because he was with Patricia? Rogan had not actually spoken to her yet and now walked Patricia away toward his sister and Peter Bartley.

They all made their way to the table, and Evy lifted her chin. She would not dart away like a timid mouse. She determined to enjoy the evening no matter how coolly Patricia treated her.

Never had Evy seen such elegance. It almost made her head spin with the wonder of it all. The long dining table was adorned with silver and crystal, all aglitter under the great chandelier. The dining hall must have witnessed many splendid occasions through its years, but never more so than tonight, she thought. Flowers had been brought in from Rookswood greenhouses and were in great ceramic pots on urns and side tables. Candlelight did wonders for the gowns and jewels that adorned the women, as well as the gentlemen adorned in dinner black with startling white frilled shirts. Evy sat toward the end of the long table to the left of Abbot, and though she was aware of the interested glances cast her way from the young men in attendance, she pretended not to notice.

If only she could also have ignored the fact that Rogan was fully attentive to Patricia.

The meal was sumptuous. Evy had never seen such food, including three kinds of roasted meat and a number of side dishes and breads. The conversation as well was stimulating. On her right was an older gentleman, a friend of Sir Lyle's. Evy carried on a fascinating discussion with him through the meal about the prospects of war between England and the Boers of South Africa. He was in favor of ousting the "Boers under that uncivilized Paul Kruger" and planting the Union Jack squarely in the Transvaal, the area controlled by the Dutch.

After an assortment of English and French desserts, teas, and coffees, liquor was served in the next room. Evy declined and accepted lemon water with a sprig of mint.

Later in the evening the dancing began in the ballroom. Sir Lyle and Lady Elosia led the first waltz, followed by Rogan and Patricia, then Arcilla and Mr. Bartley. Afterward, Sir Lyle and Rogan performed their social duty by choosing other partners from among their guests.

Evy's heart fluttered when Rogan stopped in front of her, bowed lightly, and escorted her onto the glossy floor. As she moved into the circle of Rogan's arms, she could sense Patricia's cool indignation. Sir Lyle chose Lady Elizabeth, and the four of them waltzed about the huge ballroom floor. Despite her pleasure at being chosen for such an honor, she couldn't help a touch of nerves.

If I miss a step, I shall wish to sink through the floor. Happily, she did not, and soon she relaxed and let the music overtake her.

It was an astounding moment to be in Rogan's arms, with the grand notes of Johann Strauss's music echoing about them. She was waltzing where great ladies of the blood had done for nearly two hundred years, and the man she was with was heir to its history and future. For a moment she felt like Lady Eve Varley, her beautiful skirts swirling in a show of color and promise. She was aware of Rogan's nearness, of the way he held her, his arm around her waist, the other hand enclosing hers...

For just a moment, her rebellious memory flashed to the moment in the library all those months ago, when his kiss had sent her head spinning and her heart dancing. For a moment, all was magical and all her girlish daydreams were coming true. For a moment...

Her gaze met Rogan's. He stared back evenly.

"You have made me the center of attention," she said breathlessly.

"You already were. The rectory girl is not supposed to be so beautiful, or so poised and polished."

Her heart beat faster at that. *He thinks I'm beautiful!* "Everyone will talk, now that you asked me to share the first waltz. You dance well."

"It is not hard when holding you." Something burned deep in his gaze. Something heated and disturbing. "Yes...I would like the waltz to continue indefinitely."

She let her gaze drop. "You must not say such things."

"I could say a great deal more."

"But it would not be fitting for you to do so...*Master* Rogan."

At her use of his title, they lapsed into silence. Evy focused on enjoying the music. Waltzing beneath the glowing chandelier was like a fantasy. And like any fantasy, it would certainly come to an end.

She might be as beautiful as any woman there, but she was, and always would be, the rectory girl.

She pulled her dismal thoughts another direction. "Arcilla does not look happy tonight, but subdued."

"I'm hoping she will get over losing Charles. She's young."

He spoke as though he himself were old and seasoned in such matters.

"Then you've changed your mind? You think Mr. Bartley will be a proper husband?"

His shoulders lifted. "I doubt either man would be a proper husband, as you mean it. They love their pleasure too much for both marriage and their ambitions. It's not that I have changed my mind about Arcilla's marriage. South Africa does not suit her nature—she is too flighty—but my father has decided the matter, as is his right. She will marry Peter and go to South Africa."

"Soon?"

"Quite soon."

Evy lapsed into silence for a moment, then, "She will be forced into a marriage she does not want, to a man she does not love. How could it be worse?"

"It could be worse, because as we discussed that night in the townhouse, Peter is likely to be sent inland to the Rhodesia colony. Can you see my sister as the governor's wife?"

No, she could not. Arcilla would be most unhappy. She belonged in London among her elite friends. "Then—it could come to that, do you think?"

"I hope not. I've discussed the matter with my father. He has yet to convince Sir Julien, though. Perhaps when Julien meets her at the Cape, he will understand and change his mind about the governor's post, at least. Sending Arcilla with Peter into Mashonaland is like sending a lamb into the wolf pack. She would become ill and depressed."

"You *must* convince them."

One brow arched, and he met her earnest gaze. "I have tried, and will continue. It is kind of you to concern yourself. You have been a good influence on her from the beginning."

She was pleased that he would think so.

"But you mustn't worry too much about Arcilla. You have your own concerns, it appears. I hear you have lost the humble, kindhearted boy your aunt expected you to marry these years."

Derwent.

Rogan's lively dark eyes studied her a moment too long, and then a hint of something like satisfaction showed itself. Whenever Rogan wore that satisfied smile, she worried.

He cocked his head. "Then you have not heard the romantic news?"

"I have my suspicions and"—she inclined her head—"a bit of gossip from Miss Armitage, but I have heard nothing from Derwent, and until I do…" She let her words fade.

His smile loitered. "Why, I am indeed scandalized that Derwent—fine upstanding saint that you say he is—has not come to you to explain the change in his future plans. What could he be afraid of, I wonder?" He scanned her lightly. "Do you have a temper, Miss Varley? They say hell has no fury like a woman scorned."

That got her. "Afraid! Of me! Because of an interest in Alice?"

"Rather shoddy of him not to tell you sooner. Even if his courage is lacking, he might at least have written you while you were in London to prepare you for the surprise. You are surprised by this turn of events, are you not? Come, admit it. Surely your reticence does not come from your feminine pride being stepped on?"

She was tempted instead to stomp on one of his finely clad feet. "If you have news worthy of being believed, and not mere gossip, then please do get on with it."

"My, my, such lofty indignation. The news that has the village buzzing of course is marriage, what else? Between Derwent and Alice Tisdale."

Then Old Lady Armitage had known what she was talking about after all. Evy might have expected this outcome about Derwent, but hearing it now so bluntly put was startling. For a moment she was tongue-tied under Rogan's alert gaze.

"Did Derwent tell you he wanted to marry Alice?"

"Yes, when we were out exercising the horses recently."

He watched her, but she scarcely noticed. She was turning the news over in her mind. If Derwent had confided in Rogan, it must be true.

His arm tightened around her. "I am waiting for you to faint in utter despondency over your loss. Do I take it then that you are not disappointed?"

She pulled away a little, finally finding her voice. "Disappointed? Perhaps I was expecting it. But until Derwent himself tells me, I think it best not to rush to conclusions."

"Mrs. Tisdale has been calling on Aunt Elosia for the last few weeks. There was a lengthy discussion between them just a few days ago. It appears there will be an arrangement made between Dr. Tisdale and Lady Elosia to have Derwent and Alice marry in the new year."

Apparently Mrs. Tisdale had decided Derwent would be a good catch for Alice. But why? What had changed Mrs. Tisdale's mind so that she would seek out Derwent?

She realized Rogan still watched her with keen eyes and forced a smile to her lips. "If what you say is true, then I hope they shall be very happy."

She thought that beneath his grave mood there was satisfaction.

"They are well suited then, you think?"

"I would not know." Her words sounded stiff even to her own ears, and she tried to ease the tension in her voice. "That is for Derwent to decide…and Alice." No wonder Alice had looked smug and secretive when she had seen Evy the other day in the village.

"It is just as well then, that you are not too disappointed. Derwent will soon be going to South Africa with his new bride. Thanks to my father, Derwent has a job that pleases him—and the Tisdales. Derwent will be working for the family. He will also get some training in geology. I understand his pay will be generous. And that, along with his prospect of owning shares in any new gold discovery, has made everyone happy."

She stopped dancing. "So *that's* it!" She struggled to keep her tone hushed. "You were partly behind all this. What did you do, bribe him to abandon divinity school, marry Alice, and go to South Africa?"

He gave her a look of utter innocence. "What suspicions you nurture. I am shocked you would think this of me. My thoughts toward Derwent are supportive and kind…" His gaze captured hers. "As they are toward you. Besides, we know, do we not, that he's long spun dreams from cobwebs about South Africa."

In fairness to Rogan, yes, she did know this about Derwent. Nevertheless—

"Come, Evy, you are not in love with Derwent."

The music ceased, and she stood on the ballroom floor, still held captive in his arms, staring at him. She had no trouble reading the challenge in his eyes, yet she refused to give in. How could she, when doing so could only mean disaster for her?

"How would you know *what* I feel?" No sooner had she said this, than she wished ardently she hadn't.

His arm around her waist tightened a little. "Because you are not as indifferent toward me as you pretend."

"Indeed?"

"Nor am I indifferent toward you." There was a husky quality to his voice that sent shivers tingling across her nerves. "You must know that."

Of course she knew it. She'd known it for years. But she also knew any relationship between them had only one end. And it was not a good one.

"Don't you see, Evy? I am not willing to lose you so quickly. You are too young to be snatched away from me."

She swallowed as a trembling seemed to take hold of her. He sounded so determined. *Lord, how am I to resist him when all I want to do is give in?*

"I do not want to come back from South Africa in a few years and find you the wife of Derwent Brown. Or of anyone else, for that matter."

She closed her eyes. And when he did come back, what then? His family had their expectations, and they would hardly be willing to permit the marriage of Master Rogan to Evy Varley—not, she reminded herself, that Rogan had ever mentioned marriage.

"You should be pleased you are not like Arcilla," he said, "being forced to marry without love. Derwent is a fine fellow, but losing him to Alice is not the end of the world."

She raised her chin. "How do *you* know what is best for me?"

"You forget, my dear Miss Varley, that I, too, have known you since childhood. If Derwent wishes to go, you should reconsider your feelings toward him."

"What do you mean by that?" And yet, she knew quite well what he meant.

"Is it not obvious? He either allowed others to make up his mind for him, which does not bode well for his courage, or he freely made up his own mind. Which is it?"

"The latter, I suspect, with a bit of bait dangled before his eyes."

He shrugged and a brow lifted. "The glare of gold blinded his vision, you mean? I won't deny life is full of testings and temptations. One must still show what one is made of by one's decisions. I say Derwent wants to marry Alice and go to South Africa. In which case, free him to go."

That was too much. She stared at him, letting her irritation show. "I have no intention of holding him here!"

He flashed a smile. "Good. His only mistake, as I see it, is his timidity in coming to you and admitting it face to face. I shall have a little talk with him."

She stiffened. "Please do not."

"If he feels he cannot face you, then he can write you a letter."

She narrowed her eyes, but Rogan seemed to ignore her. After a moment, she tilted her head. "Very well, you may be right about all this. Even so, there must be some other reason for his not telling me of his change of plans sooner. We've been friends since childhood."

He gave a nod. "Though I don't know this for a fact, I suspect his reluctance stemmed from his concern over the convictions he believed he must live up to in becoming a vicar. That they worried him, I think, is not a surprise to you."

She did not reply, but he must have seen from her expression that he was right. He gave another nod. "Perhaps Derwent simply cannot face disappointing you, and others."

He was probably right, but she did not want to hear it now. She turned. "I am going back to the cottage."

He refused to release her hand. "Wait. Leave now, like this, and we will both be the talk of the village gossip tomorrow. We are being observed by everyone in the ballroom. Besides, the coach is not ready, and it's pouring rain."

She glanced about the room—he was right. They were indeed being observed.

"Shall we dance this waltz also?" Not waiting for a reply, he led her in step with the music.

She eased back into his arms, letting him direct her, letting his arms support her. *Only for a moment,* she told herself.

His low voice whispered in her ear. "Forget Derwent. He was never truly right for you."

"You are so certain…"

His embrace tightened again, and he leaned close so that his warm breath caressed her face. "Oh yes. Quite certain."

CHAPTER TWENTY-EIGHT

It was only two days before Christmas, but Evy could not bring herself to ask the sexton, Hiram Croft, to come and kill the white Christmas goose already delivered from Rookswood.

"You've a tender heart, that's what," Mrs. Croft said.

"She is so white-breasted, so sleek of neck," Evy said. "It seems a pity to destroy her—especially when neither Aunt Grace nor I have caught the festive mood for a big Christmas feast."

"She is right."

They turned to find Aunt Grace joining them to look over the wire fence at the goose walking under the willow tree.

Mrs. Croft rubbed her chin. "I saw a hen already prepared at Tom's butcher shop."

Evy looked at her aunt, who smiled. "Very well. A hen it is. We ought to have a small celebration at least, in honor of the Savior's birth."

Evy agreed, though she could find little to be joyful about this year. She had not yet mentioned the news about Derwent and Alice to her aunt. It was true that she was not in love with Derwent; but she was fond of him...had been connected to him since childhood.

"You best get indoors where it's warm, Miss Grace; this be bad weather for chest colds."

When Aunt Grace went to take her afternoon nap, Evy was alone with Mrs. Croft in the kitchen, and the silence between them lengthened. Mrs. Croft was helping Evy bake the week's bread supply, a task she had done on her own when Evy was in London.

"I do not know what Aunt Grace and I would do without you, Mrs. Croft. You and Mr. Croft, both. He chopped wood for us on Saturday. And you've been such a help and consolation to us."

Mrs. Croft smiled, and pleasure shone in her eyes. "You're both as much family to me as my own kin, Miss Evy."

At Mrs. Croft's subtle glance, Evy wondered if she knew about the upcoming marriage. There was little she did not know of the goings-on in the village. How could anything of this magnitude escape her?

"You are very glum," Mrs. Croft acknowledged. "Ever since you went to that ball up at the big house. Did it not go well for you, child? You looked so pretty that night. I'd have thought you would be asked to waltz most of them dances."

"Oh, it was a lovely ball. That's not what is troubling me."

"That Master Rogan again, I suppose." Her lips were pinched. "A sly one, he. Has his eye on you plenty, I'm thinking, and with no good purpose in mind. He can do little else 'cept marry that Miss Patricia even if he wanted someone else."

Evy realized with a sinking heart that if she did not explain soon, Rogan would be blamed for trifling with her. Well, no time like the present. "I think you already know about Derwent and Alice Tisdale, Mrs. Croft."

Mrs. Croft frowned. "Aye, I do. The story's been buzzing about since you went off to school in London. It's why Mrs. Tisdale kept Alice home, I'm thinking. To make their sneaky plan for catching poor Derwent. I'll tell you something else too. Miss Grace knows all about it."

"I thought she might."

"She was hoping—probably still is—that Derwent would come to his senses. He'd never be allowed to get by with this foolishness if Vicar Brown was alive. You were away at school when Mrs. Tisdale came to see your aunt. She came all huffy like. Insisted Derwent had fallen in love with Alice and was reluctant to break the news to you. In love, my *foot*." She sniffed her disapproval and held up her floured hands. "It's the job working for the diamond family that Derwent wants. I say the

Tisdales helped arrange it with the squire, knowing it would lure Derwent away from his schoolin' and marriage to you. Squire gave Derwent the job offer because Lady Elosia agreed he ought to marry Alice. Promised him shares in a mine. And that offer went hand in hand with marrying Alice. Well, it figures, I daresay. Derwent never was much bent on following the vicar's footsteps."

She slapped and kneaded the lump of bread dough with robust force. "Miss Grace went on hoping and praying Derwent would see the light. But the glitter of gold and diamonds has him packing his bag. That's what Mrs. Tisdale is excited about too."

"About the diamond mines?"

"I daresay. After all, her Alice will be married to Derwent when Rogan Chantry strikes gold—if he can make good on his Uncle Henry's map. That's how they're thinking, anyway. Her and the good doctor both. And Alice thinks Derwent could end up with a great reward from Rogan if he shares the burden of the work."

Evy could see the way Alice was thinking, that Derwent might even end up partners with a Chantry. That would never happen, of course. Neither Rogan nor the family, including Sir Julien Bley, would allow anyone to become a partner.

"Diamonds, and now gold." Mrs. Croft said it as if discussing measles and the plague. "That's what's been rattling 'round in Derwent's head. Believes all of Master Rogan's talk. There isn't anything he wouldn't do for Rogan Chantry."

As Evy had known since childhood. Just as she'd always known she saw Derwent more as a brother than a beau. It had just seemed the easiest path to agree to what everyone expected: that they would one day marry. She'd spent so many years walking that path without ever really wanting to do so. Not to say that her pride was not stung by his turning her down for Alice and employment with Rogan at Kimberly. Without the prospect of marriage to Derwent, her future was decidedly unsettled. But perhaps it had always been so.

"Maybe you ought to be counting your blessings. You found out early enough what Derwent was like," Mrs. Croft said.

"What do you mean, what he is like? It's true I have always known about Derwent's dreams of going to South Africa."

"Well, that's so, it's plain as the nose on your face if you ask me. But what I mean is, he could be bought, couldn't he? And he was quick to betray you to get what he wanted."

At this echo of Rogan's words at the ball, Evy frowned. "I do not know if I see it as betrayal."

"What else? Nice young man, indeed! He's not strong enough for you, that's what I say. And you're worth two of Alice."

Evy smiled. "You are loyal to me, that's all. Alice is all right."

"I don't understand you, Miss Evy. I'd be hopping mad if she stole my beau from beneath my nose like that."

"Maybe I'm not really in love with Derwent, Mrs. Croft."

She looked at Evy, brows raised. "You was planning to marry him for years."

Evy had no response for that. But she knew, deep inside, that while she'd been planning it, she hadn't been looking forward to it.

Aunt Grace said very little about Derwent after Evy told her she knew of his decision. "You'll graduate from Parkridge next year," she assured her. "You will be able to get a decent position teaching music."

Evy understood, and even agreed. If there was no one else to marry, she would at least be able to support herself doing something she loved.

Christmas dawned damp and foggy. Evy dressed in a frilled white blouse and ankle-length skirt of blue, then brought the present she would give Aunt Grace from its hiding place in the cupboard by the window. It was a cluster of red, blue, and green glass hummingbirds formed into a wind chime. Aunt Grace loved wind chimes, and Evy had found this one in a shop in London. It had taken most of her meager savings, which she had earned while sometimes helping out in the kitchen at school, but every coin she had spent would be worth the sparkle in her aunt's eyes when she hung it from the window and the first spring breeze sent it tinkling.

Aunt Grace must have heard her getting dressed, for when Evy came into the kitchen she was waiting. Evy took a deep breath of the aroma of fresh-brewed tea. Aunt Grace was sitting at the table with her worn Bible open.

"Merry Christmas," Evy called with deliberate cheerfulness. She bent and kissed her aunt's cheek.

"Merry Christmas, dear. Shall we have breakfast first, or open our presents?"

"Oh, you should not have troubled yourself," Evy said, but was pleased to see the scrambled eggs and ham slices on cornbread staying warm on the back of the stove. Aunt Grace must be feeling stronger.

"Believe me, it's like old times," Aunt Grace said. "I enjoyed being able to cook for a change. Mrs. Croft has already been here—look."

Evy followed her smiling gaze to the decorated pine bush, where two small packages sat next to their own presents. Evy saw that her present to the Crofts, along with Aunt Grace's for them, was gone. She hoped Mrs. Croft liked the new shawl she had bought for her. She knew Aunt Grace had made Mrs. Croft a new woolen nightgown and cap.

"Since breakfast is staying warm, let's be like children and open our gifts first!"

Aunt Grace laughed. They handed each other a gift, then tore them open with exclamations of joy. Aunt Grace had bought her a new blue-gray hooded woolen cloak, and Evy was delighted. She realized what it must have cost and how little money they had between them, yet somehow, strangely enough, Aunt Grace always seemed to have whatever money was needed—both for schooling and for school clothes. Whenever she asked about it Aunt Grace would always say cheerfully, "Oh I have my little secrets, dear."

"Aunt Grace, you shouldn't have—"

"You'll need it. You still have a year and half of schooling, do not forget. The other was getting frayed."

"It is the perfect color. I adore it, thank you."

Aunt Grace made much of the glass birds, and Evy could see by her happy expression that she truly liked the gift. "Ah, a sweet sign of spring and better days ahead," Aunt Grace predicted.

They made the most of their Christmas and then prepared their dinner, ready to receive several village friends who were coming to offer well wishes. Emily came by with her husband, Milt, followed an hour later by Meg and Tom. Once again Mr. Bixby showed up from Rooks-wood with several gaily beribboned gifts. Arcilla had sent Evy new gloves and a small beaded handbag. A second gift was wrapped in shiny red paper with a golden ribbon. Evy stared, speechless, when she removed a pair of golden earrings with emeralds. They could not be real...could they?

But they were. The gift card was signed simply: *Merry Christmas, Rogan.*

She gazed at the gift, knowing she could not possibly keep them, yet also knowing she would never be able to afford anything like them on her own. She took them out and ran to the small mirror by the hat tree and tried them on, pushing her tawny hair aside and turning her head in both directions so the flash of gold and green would dazzle her.

"Oh...they're stunning." She sighed.

Aunt Grace watched her, a slight frown on her brow. "From Master Rogan?"

"Yes."

"I thought they might be."

She did not say why she had thought so, and Evy avoided her gaze in the mirror. She waited, expecting her aunt to tell her she could not keep them, but Aunt Grace was silent and went to the stove to bring their breakfast to the table.

"They are expensive and beautiful."

Evy studied them again in the mirror. "Yes, I cannot think why he would give me such a gift."

Aunt Grace looked over at her. "Perhaps he is trying to cheer you after the disappointment with Derwent."

Evy looked at her reflection. The emeralds brought out the flecks of green in her amber eyes. "I hardly think so, Aunt. When he told me about the upcoming marriage, he seemed rather glib about it, as though he liked the idea of Derwent going to South Africa."

"That is what I mean."

Evy turned and looked at her aunt. "I beg your pardon?"

"It has not escaped me that Master Rogan has noticed you on more than one occasion. I've known from way back, even when I was governess at Rookswood, that he always took a special interest in you."

"Oh, I hardly think so—"

"Yes, he has. No use denying it, dear. Mrs. Croft has noticed it too. The question is, what does he have in mind?"

Evy flushed and reached up to pull off the earrings. "Nothing. He has nothing in mind. He will marry Miss Bancroft and go away to Capetown."

"Naturally the squire and Lady Elosia expect him to do so. You saw what they expected of Arcilla. I suspect she will be married off to Mr. Bartley very soon now. The family has their expectations and they will not be easily thwarted. Especially Rogan's uncle, Sir Julien Bley."

Evy placed the earrings back into the small red velvet box and closed the lid. "Yes, I know. If you are trying to warn me not to fall for Rogan Chantry, you need not worry. I am well aware of his reputation…and that no Chantry will ever marry beneath his social level."

"I do not worry, dear. I know you have twice as much sense as the silly young ladies who make fools of themselves chasing after him. You have too much dignity for that. I suspect that is one of the things about you that captures his attention so."

"Why have you not told me to send the earrings back?"

"Because you do not need me to lecture you. You will do what is best."

"Suppose I wish to keep them?"

Aunt Grace poured tea. "Then you will do so. You are nearly grown up now."

"They are worth a lot of money. If worse came to worst I could sell them. A little nest egg, so to speak."

"Yes." She looked up from the teacups. "Do you want honey in your tea?"

She trusts my judgment. Evy smiled, knowing she would not disappoint her aunt. She would make the appropriate decision.

But oh! How she wanted to keep the earrings!

With the New Year upon them, it was soon time to return to London. A day before Evy was to board the train she received a letter from Derwent. Mrs. Croft delivered it.

"Aye, Derwent is knowing what I think of him," Mrs. Croft said shortly. "I told him before he left Grimston Way."

Evy took the envelope and held it for a moment. Then she looked at Mrs. Croft. "You must not be too hard on him, Mrs. Croft. I told you, I'm not in love with Derwent. I suspect he did not want to hurt me and couldn't endure a face-to-face meeting. Down deep in his heart he probably believes he did betray me. His father, too, and Aunt Grace. Expectations were so high it never gave either of us much choice. I'll need to let him know I hold nothing against him. I only wish Alice and him well. Has he left the village?"

"He has, indeed. Squire sent him off to do some work in London at the family company there. Seems Master Rogan will be giving him some training now that Rogan's graduated from that university. In about a year's time they'll both be going to the Cape…after Alice ups and marries him, that is."

Evy opened the envelope.

"Well, you've guessed how it is. He writes 'cause he can't look himself in the mirror. He don't have the courage to look you eye to eye either and admit he betrayed you," Mrs. Croft stated.

Evy shook her head. "I do not think he betrayed me, Mrs. Croft.

This may sound strange, but Derwent and I never talked of marriage outright, or even said we loved each other."

"Well, it were certainly planned by the good vicar your Uncle Edmund before he were killed the way he was that stormy night. I daresay he would be upset with Derwent for turning his back on you and running away to the diamond mines. Adventure, that's what he wants, and that silly little Alice. Mark my words, she'll regret it once she gets over to that land of savage Hottentots. An' I'll wager Derwent will want to kick himself once he's been married to her a time. He'll be thinking back to the vicarage and the old ways and what he gave up for big dreams." She gave a sharp, quick nod. "He'll be regretting his quick decisions, all right. I've been around too long not to know that's how life goes. You reap what you sow, that's how it is…"

Evy was barely listening. She read to herself as she sat on the kitchen stool.

I have Squire to thank for this grand opportunity. We talked at some length in the library at Rookswood. It is no secret to you how I have wanted to go to the Cape to make my life and fortune. I never was cut from the cleric's cloth the way my good father was, or your Uncle Edmund. When my father was so ill and I filled in for him behind the pulpit, even writing most of his sermons, it gave me the opportunity to learn that I was not called to the vicarage, and do not at this time have a strong desire to return to divinity school. You are such a fine, upstanding girl that I guessed long ago I was never good enough for you, Miss Evy. Even Lady Elosia said you would never be pleased with me because I was not like your uncle. Alice thought so, too. Lady Elosia thought marrying Alice and beginning a different life in the Cape would be the wisest thing I could do for you, and for me…

I hope you will forgive me if I led you to believe falsely of my intentions toward you. It was always more what your aunt and uncle, and my father, wanted than what either of us wanted. I love you as a sister and think highly of you and always will.

As ever, faithfully your friend,
Derwent T. Brown

Evy blinked back tears. She folded the letter and replaced it inside its envelope.

"That rascally scoundrel, Derwent!" Mrs. Croft scowled, evidently taking Evy's tears to mean heartbreak.

"My tears are for fond childhood memories, Mrs. Croft, not over losing Derwent. You see, he is right," she said firmly. "And I think we all did him an injustice in not listening to him these years. He was not *called* to be a vicar. I'm seeing now that his gifts and abilities lie elsewhere than behind a pulpit."

"Humph. I'm not convinced any." She shook a finger. "Bad company corrupts good behavior, is what I say. It's that Master Rogan who planted all those restless seeds in Derwent's mind from the times they was boys."

Lady Elosia said you would never be pleased with me because I was not like your uncle... Marrying Alice and beginning a different life in the Cape would be the wisest thing I could do for you, and for me...

Evy stared at the letter. Strange...about Lady Elosia.

The January morning was cold and frosty as Evy boarded the train for London. The evening before, when Evy questioned whether or not they could afford her return to music school, Aunt Grace assured her all was well.

"We will manage the expenses somehow. It's even more important now that you continue your music studies."

Once back at Parkridge, school life and her love of music overshadowed past disappointments. She wrote a brief letter to Derwent in care of the Chantry Diamond Company assuring him that his decision to marry Alice Tisdale and go to South Africa in no way caused her either unhappiness or disappointment toward him. She wished him and Alice much joy and prayed God's blessings on their union. She also wrote Rogan:

Dear Rogan,

I thank you for the exquisite pair of earrings, but I cannot accept a gift so expensive. It would not be suitable. They are now safely stored at the cottage with my aunt, Mrs. Havering. If you would have Arcilla stop by and claim them, or do so yourself on one of your visits home (perhaps for Arcilla's wedding?), I would be appreciative.

 Miss Evy Varley, Parkridge Music School, London

In the months that concluded Evy's third year of studies, she did not hear back from Rogan, nor did she hear again from Derwent. As for Rogan, it was unclear when he would sail to the Cape. The last she had heard, he remained in London becoming familiar with the inner workings of the family company under the headship of Sir Julien.

Since Arcilla had already graduated from Montague, she remained at Rookswood, as did Peter Bartley. Aunt Grace wrote her that the engagement had been announced and that the marriage would take place in April. Within a week they would then sail for the Cape.

During this period Evy heard from Arcilla twice. She had sent a letter bemoaning the fact that she must go to South Africa, and deplored the notion that Peter might get a government post inland at the colony to be called Rhodesia.

I feel as though I am being sentenced to prison.

Evy felt compassion for her plight, but what was there to do? At least Peter Bartley had seemed a patient man who would deal kindly with Arcilla's whims.

Another letter came at the end of March.

I am getting married at the rectory on the 15th. Everyone will gather at Rookswood afterward, including Rogan. He has finally accepted Peter as a future brother-in-law. They are getting on quite well now. I would invite you to the ceremony, but you would need to miss some of your exams, and that doesn't seem wise considering you lost Derwent to Alice. You may need to work as a music teacher in the future, so you had better study hard.

That reminds me—Alice is such a copycat! A week after my marriage, she will marry Derwent in the rectory. Amusing, don't you think?

We sail for Capetown immediately after our marriage, and Derwent and Alice will sail in May. I don't know if I shall see you again before I sail to my doom… If not, I wish you well on your music and future teaching. I will write you from Capetown.

Arcilla

In April, Evy read of Arcilla's marriage in the society page of the London paper. "Diamond Heiress Marries South African Government Official," the caption read.

There was a stunning photograph of the wedding. Arcilla looked like a princess in white, and Peter Bartley was quite distinguished. But it was Rogan who stood out, and in the background stood Miss Patricia Bancroft as bridesmaid. She held the bride's bouquet. Would she be next to marry?

Aunt Grace did not write about Derwent's marriage, which followed a week later, but she mentioned that Arcilla and her husband had indeed set sail for the Cape, and that Derwent and Alice, now Mrs. Brown, would sail on the first of May.

Evy turned her full attention to her graduation next year from Parkridge. She wondered and prayed about her own future, what she would do, and what God might have in store for her.

And yet, despite her best efforts, she could not shake the awareness that Rogan Chantry had not yet become engaged to Patricia Bancroft.

Chapter Twenty-Nine

Near the end of the school year came the emergency that Evy had been expecting. The letter was from Vicar Osgood: *Your beloved aunt is quite ill. Dr. Tisdale has concurred with me that it would be wise if you came home as soon as possible.*

Evy wasted no time packing her portmanteau and boarding the train for Grimston Way. She had sent a wire to Dr. Tisdale asking that he inform Mrs. Croft of her arrival.

Mrs. Croft was waiting in the jingle when she arrived. She appeared haggard and discouraged.

"It's that nasty business with the lungs, dearie. Doctor says she has pneumonia."

Evy's heart grew even heavier when she saw Aunt Grace, who was feverish and delirious.

"She has congestion and inflammation of the lungs." Dr. Tisdale's grave tone and countenance told Evy more than she wanted to know. "This is serious business, my dear. I would not have asked you to come home if it were just another of her colds."

Evy nodded and knelt beside the bed, taking Aunt Grace's hand in both her own. She searched her feverish face anxiously. "I'm here, Aunt Grace."

Aunt Grace's eyes fluttered open, and she tried to focus on Evy's face. She managed a faint smile, to reassure her, Evy was certain, that she would be all right. How like her aunt. Unselfish to the end. A woman who had stood by her sister—and her sister's child—through thick and thin. A woman who had wanted children of her own, had been denied them by God's providence, and had opened her arms to embrace Evy as her very own. She had worked to help support Evy, had been a faithful vicar's wife, had been stout-hearted to the end.

"Many daughters have done virtuously, but thou excellest them all," Evy whispered in her aunt's ear, quoting from the last chapter of Proverbs. Although Aunt Grace was too ill to answer, Evy sensed that she had heard.

The next days were some of Evy's unhappiest. To see Aunt Grace lying there, propped up with pillows, her skin hot and dry, her eyes glazed... It was almost more than Evy could bear. It came to her then...the sad truth that her aunt's chances of recovery were as feeble as her body. Evy prayed, as did all their friends in the rectory. Mrs. Croft stayed with her, helping to care for her aunt's needs and lending loving strength to Evy as well, making sure she had her soup and enough rest.

"It was bound to come to it, child," she said more than once. "Miss Grace's been on borrowed time from the Lord some years now. She knew it too, but she tried to keep joyful for your sake. If it weren't now that the Lord was going to bring her home, it would be next winter, or the winter after that. She's been sick like this before, but never this bad."

Aunt Grace's eyes opened. "Is...that you, Evy?"

She came quickly to the side of the bed. "Yes, Aunt, I'm here."

Mrs. Croft murmured she would put tea on and left them alone, closing the door behind her.

"Evy, I am going home to be with our heavenly Father...and dear Edmund..."

Sorrow choked Evy's throat. "Oh, Aunt, try to get well. You must! What will I do without you? I have no one else...no one." Tears trickled down her face as she clutched Aunt Grace's hand. She suddenly felt alone, abandoned, an orphan once more. She was losing everything she cared about. First her Uncle Edmund, then loyal Derwent, and even Arcilla was gone...silly, spoiled Arcilla, yet her dearest friend. And now Aunt Grace. What would she do alone?

"You must be strong..." Her aunt's voice was firm for all that it was weak and thready. "God is a very present help in trouble. You can trust Him to provide, dearest… His plans are well laid…all for your good."

"Don't talk, Aunt, you must save your breath and rest. You'll get better. This will pass."

She shook her head, and Evy could see what the action cost her. "Not this time…I know. There is something I must tell you…about your mother."

Evy stiffened and met her aunt's fevered gaze. Aunt Grace reached a hand toward her as if to touch the side of her face. "Rogan came to me…months ago… He asked, and I told him the truth. I could do naught else. I sinned in not telling you, but I did not want you unhappy… You were so proud to be the daughter of missionaries—martyrs—that I kept it from you…"

Evy swallowed, her throat suddenly dry and raw. She leaned closer, catching every syllable. "What…truth?"

"Clyde and Junia… They were going to adopt you…"

Evy clutched her aunt's hand. "Adopt?"

"Your mother was a van Buren…Katie…Sir Julien's ward…"

Evy felt unable to catch a breath. Her heart pounded in her chest as she struggled to absorb those words. Her mother…not the wonderful missionary she'd always believed? But a van Buren? How could this be?

"My mother is…Katie van Buren?" Saying it out loud didn't help. She couldn't believe it.

But Aunt Grace's weak nod told her it was so. "She ran away. From Sir Julien…because he took you from her. She tried to find you…to get you back. But she was killed. At the mission station. With Junia."

Evy swallowed again as understanding began to dawn. "Then it was Katie—my mother who took the prized Black Diamond? When she ran away?"

Aunt Grace closed her eyes, as though the effort to speak had drained all her energy. She moistened her cracked feverish lips. "That, I do not know…only that Katie was your mother… I know not who your father was."

Evy laid the side of her face against her aunt's hand and let the sobs come. "It matters not," she said over and over again. "*You* are my mother, dear heart. The only mother I've ever known. Do not fret."

Aunt Grace looked at her with pleading eyes and managed another weak smile. "You mean that?"

Evy buried her face against her aunt's thin chest. "Oh yes! I love you, Mum."

Aunt Grace smiled and reached a trembling hand to Evy's tumbling hair. She caressed it gently, and Evy recognized the action for what it was. A farewell.

Aunt Grace died in the night during the prayer vigil led in her room by Vicar Osgood. Prayers and scriptures were read, while candles flickered and cast trembling shadows on the cream walls beside the bed. Evy was silent, remembering all that they had been through together, well aware that she now trudged the future's path alone.

Grace Havering was buried in the churchyard at the rectory on a summer day in late June, next to the grave site of Vicar Edmund Havering. No gray day, this. The sky was a cloudless blue, and the birds sang merrily.

Only Evy's heart still felt the grief of winter. What would she do now? This was why she had gone to music school, of course...to work as a music teacher and support herself through the years. Her aunt had sacrificed financially to make sure of her education. But would she be able to finish her final year?

To represent Rookswood, and in fond memory of Vicar Edmund's wife, Lady Elosia came to the funeral. To Evy's surprise, Rogan stood with her in solemn black. Mrs. Croft and the sexton were there too, and Meg and Emily and their families. Even Dr. and Mrs. Tisdale came.

But Evy was aware of little else except her sense of sadness tempered by the Christian hope of being united once more with loved ones who had gone before. The words of Christ echoed in her mind, bringing consolation: "I am the resurrection, and the life: he that believeth in me, though he were dead, yet shall he live."

Mrs. Croft returned with Evy to the cottage to spend the night. "You ought not to be alone," she said.

Evy was grateful for her company. The cottage was empty and too quiet. She went to her bed and tried to rest, for she was exhausted. At last she slept and awoke to drink the strange tasting tea that Mrs. Croft gave her.

"A sedative from Dr. Tisdale," she explained.

Evy did not awaken until midmorning the next day. The song of birds filled the room with hope. Life went on. Summer went on. Her heavenly Father was sovereign and reigning on His throne, her future in His hand.

The future, however, did not share its secrets with her. It only stared at her blankly. *I am the daughter of Katie van Buren.* The thought rattled around in her mind until it was joined by another. *Then…I must be related in some way to Heyden van Buren!* She shook her head. *And my father? Will I ever know who he is?*

Then, as though stepping from the mist of her memory, she saw again the stranger in Grimston Woods…remembered the look of sadness in his eyes as he had scrutinized her. What had he seen that made him so sad? Could he actually have been some distant cousin of Lady Camilla's, as Evy had been told? John…that was his name, wasn't it? Had he really gone to Australia?

And on the heels of that thought came another. Lady Camilla had been sure that her husband, Anthony Brewster, had fathered a child in secret. Evy's heart pounded at the question that nagged at her: Was it possible there was truth to this, after all…and that Evy was that child?

Her blood thundered in her ears. She sat up in bed and stared at the fluttering curtain. She pressed her trembling hand against her forehead, and her eyes closed as she tried to make sense of all the ideas tumbling about in her mind. Of course it could be true! Anything could be true now that she knew her mother was Katie van Buren, Sir Julien's ward. Sir Julien Bley! No wonder he had searched her face the way he did that day in the tearoom with Lady Camilla. Was it he, then, who had covered all this up? And Heyden van Buren—he had wanted to tell her something about her mother, but had suddenly vanished from her life. Why? Sir Julien again?

Evy tried to quiet her emotions. She must be calm and not jump to conclusions, though the truth appeared to be staring her in the face. She must give her heart time to adjust.

She forced her thoughts away from her parents. It was still too new and painful to ponder for long. The truth would be there tomorrow. There was time to let things settle, to let the shock ease a bit. Instead, she looked to the future. She supposed she would return to school in September, but that would depend on finances. She had known little about them; Aunt Grace had managed the purse strings. Evy knew she would have to look into what she had to depend on. Her aunt always kept their money in a small metal box hidden away in a trunk that held her and Uncle Edmund's mementos. Evy slipped from bed, dressed, and went to find the trunk. She removed the metal box and opened it to count the contents.

There was ten pounds in it. She was shocked. She would have expected at least a hundred. And making matters worse, now that Aunt Grace was gone, her retirement wage for faithful service to the vicarage would not continue. Even the cottage had been theirs to use only because Lady Elosia had awarded it to Aunt Grace because of Uncle Edmund. Evy had benefited, but now that would all change. She did not think those at Rookswood would immediately ask her to go, but she would need to leave sometime, and probably soon.

Ten pounds. Evy sat down hard on the ottoman. How had her aunt possibly believed she could attend her final year at Parkridge if that was all she had?

I will not be able to go back. That's clear. I must make careful use of this money. It will be some time before I can make any on my own.

Yes, she would need to find work by September, either here in Grimston Way or in London. This revelation coming on top of her sorrow made the burden far heavier to bear. For a moment she was tempted to give way to self-pitying tears. *No.* She clamped her jaw. There was no other recourse than to find work. She would be unwise to spend what she had knowing there would be no more until she earned it.

Still, she consoled herself, she had nearly three years of training, enough to possibly get a position as music teacher—if not at a prestigious girl's school, then certainly she could find young private students in London.

Evy took her Bible and found solace in reading the Psalms and Isaiah. She prayed for guidance and strength, to be wise and trusting. Over and over, verses that told her to fear not seemed to jump out at her. "Fear thou not; for I am with thee: be not dismayed; for I am thy God.... Fear not: for I have redeemed thee, I have called thee by thy name."

Later that afternoon Mrs. Croft came to Evy, clearly reluctant to impart her message. Lips pinched, she finally said, "Master Rogan wants to see you. Shall I tell him you aren't up to seeing visitors just now?"

Evy's heart skipped a beat. Did she dare see Rogan now, with her emotions in such a riot? But she could not bear to have him come and be turned away.

"No, I want to see him. I'll be there in a few minutes."

Mrs. Croft looked none too pleased. Evy knew she blamed Rogan for taking Derwent away from her, but at least the woman didn't say anything. She just nodded and left the room.

Evy brushed out her hair and smoothed the skirts of her black taffeta funeral dress. She glanced at herself in the mirror, frowning at the wan and distressed image that met her. She pinched her cheeks, trying to bring some color into them, and smoothed her thick, unruly hair. She scowled at her image. She looked young and frightened.

Determined not to appear so to Rogan, she bound her long hair up into a semblance of dignified order and, drawing a deep breath, went out to meet her caller.

Rogan paced about the small room and turned when he heard her enter. He came toward her, took a careful look, and a frown formed. He took both her hands into his and looked into her eyes. "No need to tell you how sorry I am at your loss."

She knew she should withdraw her hands, but she did not. "Thank you. I saw you and Lady Elosia at the funeral. Thank you for coming."

"But of course I would come. I would have called on you sooner, but I knew you needed time to be alone. Are you up to talking for a few minutes? I would not disturb you now, except I have little choice. My plans to leave for Capetown were already made before this happened, and my ship leaves next week."

"Oh"—her dismay was swift and fierce—"then you are leaving so soon?"

His jaw tightened. "Yes, I must. Why not come to Rookswood to dinner? It will do you good to leave the cottage for awhile."

"I couldn't…"

He inclined his head. "I understand. Then we will talk here or go for a walk. It is a pleasant enough afternoon. You could use some fresh air, I think."

He probably wanted to talk with her alone, without Mrs. Croft loitering in the kitchen with one ear peeled in their direction.

"I really do need to talk to you, Evy."

Evy. The warm way he said her name sent her heart scurrying. She knew she should not… Walking unescorted with a man when one was single and alone in the world was more than enough cause for gossip.

But he was leaving next week. "All right, a walk. Excuse me a moment first. I want to get something from my room."

"I'll wait for you outside."

Evy went to retrieve the earrings Rogan had given her for Christmas. He had never come to claim them. She slipped them inside her handbag, then took a black scarf that had belonged to Aunt Grace and put it around her hair.

Rogan waited near the gate, opening it for her as she joined him. She allowed him to lead the way. He was right: Being outdoors, feeling the afternoon sun on her skin, breathing fresh air, and hearing birds and humming bees filled her heart like a refreshing breeze. All was not lost. Her wonderful heavenly Father still ruled.

They walked for a while in silence.

"That black scarf is rather disconcerting."

Slowly, she removed it and let the breeze play in her hair. "It is not proper to go out so soon after a funeral without black."

"The villagers all know you. There isn't one of them in their right mind who would think ill of you if they saw you, which they will not. We are alone. As I already suggested, I would have waited to see you except there is so little time. I leave for London in the morning, and I do not know when I will be back to England. A year, maybe two."

Evy remained silent, but her heart cried out against this news. Two years! He was leaving for two years. She would not have him...or Arcilla...or Derwent...

He turned toward the grassy area facing the pond. There were benches here, and the ducks, geese, and peacocks were enjoying the grass and the water. Evy sighed. "Aunt Grace told me about my mother before she died."

His head turned sharply toward her. "Did she tell you I had spoken with her a few months ago?"

She nodded.

"What did she tell you about...your mother?"

"The truth. That her name was Katie van Buren, and she was your Uncle Julien's ward. That Dr. Clyde and Junia Varley adopted me...or had planned to do so. And"—her throat constricted, but she forced the words out—"that Katie very likely stole the Black Diamond."

She blinked away the tears that burned at her eyes. "Lady Brewster's letter was accurate after all. But when she spoke of my mother, she meant Katie van Buren, whereas I was thinking of Junia Varley. That's why her being a"—she could not say it, could not call her mother a thief—"made so little sense to me."

Rogan was silent for a moment. Then he nodded. "I was under the impression Lady Brewster was speaking of Junia, as well." He regarded her. "But there may be more to all this than what we now know, Evy. While I'm in Capetown I shall find out the entire story from Sir Julien."

She turned to face him. He would do that…for her?

"I was not going to say anything yet. I still need to do some research." His gaze grew warm, and she wondered whether it was sympathy that she saw there…or something more. "But you have had enough depressing news, and I'd like to leave you with something on a more hopeful note." He took her elbow and walked her across the grass toward the pond.

"There is something about this tale of your mother betraying my Uncle Henry that has troubled me since Grace told me who your real mother was. And that is the death of Henry."

"Yes, Henry… What about his death?"

"*Think*, Evy. If neither Katie nor Henry had the diamond, then why would someone follow him here to England—someone who murdered him? It suggests to me that someone followed him here for another reason. The map, most likely. I always thought that. And if he *was* murdered, that implies that he knew something that placed him in danger."

She began to understand, and her heart quickened. "He may have found out who had the Black Diamond?"

"Quite possibly."

"Perhaps the man who murdered him?"

His nod was quick. "Yes. Henry may have confronted whoever it was and threatened to unmask him."

"But that would imply the person was living in Rookswood!"

"Not necessarily. Someone may have followed him to Rookswood. I think," he said firmly, "that Heyden knows more than he is telling me."

"I am quite likely a relative of his, you know." Evy still could not believe that. "He had planned to meet me in London long ago and tell me more about my mother."

"Yes, I know. He came to me and told me. I asked him not to say anything to you about Katie. I wanted more information first, and I did not want you hurt. I had no idea your aunt would confess before her death. But now that she has told you—yes, Heyden is your cousin. He has returned to South Africa—with a few thousand pounds in his bank account."

"Oh, Rogan! You gave him money to go away?" She stared at him, not sure if she should be angry or pleased.

"It is over and done. What pleases me is that you are not too unhappy to know you are the daughter of Katie van Buren."

She gazed out across the pond. "I don't know how I feel about all this yet. I am still dazed. But Rogan, how would someone from Capetown get inside Rookswood to confront Master Henry without some of you remembering him?"

"There is no secret there. Members of all sides of the family were nearby in London when Henry died. My mother's family, the Brewsters, were here also. For that matter, so were Anthony and Sir Julien. Even Camilla."

"Oh, surely you do not think—?"

He frowned. "I don't know yet what I really think about all this."

"Then...what you're saying is that it could have been any of them?"

"They all had opportunity to silence Henry."

She walked over to the bench and sat down. "Thank you for telling me this. It helps more than you know. Is this the matter you wished to see me about?"

"No." He walked over to the bench and stood looking down at her. "I will come straight to the point. It is not lost on me that you are alone now. I should like to go away to South Africa knowing you are well taken care of."

Her brows lifted, and she could not hold back the rueful words. "Do you wish to arrange a marriage for me with the village shoemaker, Rogan? Perhaps you regret the haste with which Derwent was taken from me after all?"

A glint of derisive challenge burned his dark gaze. "You misunderstand me. I think you already know what I meant."

She met his gaze, barely daring to breathe. *Did he mean...?*

"I do not."

"I certainly am not advocating marriage—to anyone, least of all the shoemaker. And you misjudge me about Derwent."

"I am not altogether convinced of that. I believe you were involved. Derwent said so in his letter back in January when I returned to Parkridge. The only thing that is unclear to me is why you would meddle."

"Meddle." A small smile played at his lips. "Such a potent little word, implying malice. I would think my interest in the matter should be simple to understand. I did not fancy the notion of your marrying him while I was away. I already told you that at the ball, back in December."

His bluntness embarrassed yet elated her. "Why should it matter to you?"

His smile was full now, and she saw the imp dancing in his dark eyes. "What a leading question, Miss Varley! Naturally, as I've told you before, I am…fond of you."

"Fond of me?"

He placed hands on his hips. "I have known you most of my life. I find myself concerned for your future. I did not twist Derwent's arm to get him to marry Alice. He did so of his choice and at the prompting of Mrs. Tisdale and Aunt Elosia. It was my father who offered him a good position in Capetown." He gave her a slanted look. "Of course, offering him some shares in the gold I expect to discover did not hurt the prospects either."

She folded her arms and tapped her foot. "Well, you proved yourself quite successful."

"Just between you and me, I am not the least sorry Derwent is gullible and, where you are concerned, foolish."

The way he looked at her, as though she *belonged* to him, did odd things to her heart. She folded her hands in her lap, forcing herself to breathe slowly. *Do not be foolish,* she scolded. *His interest in you is as a friend, as one who wants the best for you. That is all.*

He crossed his arms, watching her closely, as though trying to read her reaction to his words. "I have the feeling Derwent and I will be friends for years to come. He trusts me. I will be forced to honor that trust."

She smiled at that. "Sometimes I think you actually are fond of Derwent."

"If I confessed, that would spoil your convictions that I am arrogant and a scoundrel."

"Oh? Is that how you want me to think of you?"

"I think I told you before that I would prefer your good opinion of me."

The breeze blew against her, and she watched it ruffle his shirt. "Your opinion that casts my mother in a new light is definitely in line with your wish."

He bowed lightly. "Thank you. And now I shall get straight to why I wanted you see you. I am aware that your expenses must weigh heavily on your shoulders, particularly at this time."

She thought of the ten pounds in the treasure box. She did not like to discuss such a personal matter with him, but he seemed quite relaxed about it, showing no embarrassment at all.

"That is why," he continued, "since I must go away for some time, I would secure a measure of peace knowing you had sufficient funds to care for yourself. Lest you think the removal of Derwent is to blame for this, I hasten to contradict the idea. I knew for some time about your aunt's dwindling finances. She confided in Mrs. Croft—and we know, do we not, that Mrs. Croft loves to chatter. So it is no wonder it all got back to me. You have ten pounds. Am I right?"

Quick heat filled her cheeks. *Oh, Mrs. Croft!* Though pleased by his concern, she wondered why he felt it. She searched his features, seeking some clue to his motivation...but he was veiled.

"Naturally I would be sorry to see your final year at the music academy foiled. I would be quite amenable to seeing the tuition paid—as I've paid the first three years."

She sucked in her breath, then surged to her feet. *"You?"*

"Why not? It was our little secret, your aunt's and mine. She wanted you to attend so badly that she accepted the gift as a loan. If it makes you feel better, we can consider the final year a loan as well, with the idea you would pay it back at some time in the future."

Evy silenced an intake of breath. Could she possibly be hearing right? "Are you saying you wish to give—lend me more money?"

He inclined his head, looking as though he was fighting a smile. "Yes. Enough to pay for your final tuition, and then to set you up in your own music school. Preferably here in Grimston Way. London is full of scamps. Here Mrs. Croft could keep an eye on you, as would the new vicar and his wife."

She could not take it in. "But—*why?* Why would you wish to do such a thing?"

"I told you I am fond of you…actually, quite fond." He walked toward her. "It was always your aunt's wish that you should support yourself. If you are financially independent, then there will be less reason for the well-meaning but errant ladies of the village to try to marry you off to the farmer's son"—he allowed the smile now—"or the shoemaker. And you will be under far less pressure to agree. You will have time to…make decisions."

"That is exceedingly thoughtful and generous of you."

"I have my own reasons as well. We both enjoy a genuine interest in music. I would like to see you pursue it."

Evy did not know what to say.

"If, in your proper way of thinking, you believe taking money from me is unsuitable, then we could work through a third party. Vicar Osgood, for instance, would do nicely."

"You are serious, then."

"Of course. I hoped I made that clear. Well?" He smiled again. "Is it a bargain?"

"But I… Well, it is very considerate on your part. I must say I am astonished. What can I say? You have already paid my schooling for three years."

"I enjoyed the little secret."

She could well imagine he did. "However, it is quite out of bounds to even consider taking money. And I must pay you back what you've already paid." She closed her eyes. How on earth would she do that? It had to be thousands of pounds... *Oh! What would people think if they knew?*

"Nonsense."

Her eyes opened at his firm assertion. His expression was as unyielding as his tone. "Everyone in the village knows you are virtuous."

How did he do it? How was it he could read her thoughts so easily? Did he know her feelings toward him as well? *Oh, please...no.*

His gaze softened. "A loan is not as improper as you imply. After all, I am the squire's son. One day I will inherit Rookswood and my father's title, and I shall be squire. All that has been settled years ago."

Her eyes widened at this. So Rogan would not inherit the Chantry shares in De Beer Consolidated. "Is that why you have your own interest in locating gold?"

"Partly. I always wanted Rookswood; Parnell always wanted the diamonds. So for once you hear of two brothers who have completely agreed on the inheritance that will be left them. Arcilla, of course, will share in the diamonds, but most of the shares go to Parnell. That is one of the reasons my father and Sir Julien thought it so important for Arcilla to marry into position and wealth through Peter."

"I see..."

"Look, never mind about me. As I said, I am interested in *your* future, Evy. I want to make sure you will be financially secure. Please, will you allow me to help you?"

She looked away from the kindled warmth in the dark eyes, afraid of what was there, knowing that it could never come to fruition. "I— I will need to think about it. Thank you for your offer."

He looked amused at her grave hesitancy. "All right, think about it, pray about it. But you will need to make your decision soon. I leave for London tomorrow early, and for the Cape next Thursday morning." He handed her a calling card. "Here is my town address in London. Contact me before Thursday. In the meantime, I will go ahead and draw up the necessary papers. How do you wish it to be written? Through Vicar Osgood and the rectory, or directly to you?"

He smiled faintly. "That is, of course, should you decide to go along with this."

She plucked at the black scarf in her hands, aware of the wind, aware of him, of his gaze and how near they stood. She looked away toward the pond. "If I decide to accept your kind offer, I should prefer to deal through the vicar."

He smiled. "Very proper. Then the vicar it is. As a matter of fact, I have already talked to him about this. He is in full agreement."

She looked at him and saw his smile. Suddenly she smiled too. "You were quite certain I would accept."

"I was hoping."

"My own music school." The mere thought of it filled her with inexpressible joy. "Oh, Rogan, how could I resist? It is something I've always dreamed of, but never thought possible. I thought marriage to—" Rogan's mouth turned slightly, and she hastened on, "I expected my life to be different."

"I think you will agree that life's plans are not always tied up in neat little packages. Occasionally we find ourselves at unexpected crossroads with more than one opportunity from which to choose. Time itself is often the best indicator of which decision to make, for it can tell so many things that are now hazy. Do you not think so?"

His soft words, his warm gaze wrapped around her, enfolding her. Once again, her heart beat faster. "Yes…only time will tell."

The awareness between them all but crackled in the warm air, and she forced her gaze away from his, reaching into her handbag and drawing out the small red velvet box. She hesitated, then handed it to him. "I see that neither you nor Arcilla came by for this, so I wanted to return it now. Again, it was kind of you to think of me at Christmas, but…"

"I think of you a great deal, Evy. There is a special relationship between us."

She was not so certain about this special relationship and believed he was not either. "But a Chantry heirloom…"

"It is not from the Chantry family jewels. I chose this myself in

London while looking over some of the diamond and emerald collections at the Company. The green and yellow diamonds reminded me of your eyes. Please accept it from me, Evy. It is simply a Christmas present."

She was overcome. "But, Rogan—"

His eyes glittered. "If you will not accept it, I will toss it into the pond."

She gasped. "You would not!"

"I will. I can be rash sometimes."

There was a half smile that denied this challenge, and laughter bubbled up from deep within her. She snatched the red velvet box back from his hand.

"Such a display of emotion on your part, Master Rogan, would not be fitting. But…since I never know how far you will go to surprise me, I will humbly accept this gift and will treasure it always." All jesting gone now, she let her sincerity show in her eyes. "Thank you. I am afraid I did not have a proper gift to give you at Christmas, however—"

"However?" His gaze dropped pointedly to her lips.

Her breath caught in her throat. "*However,* I am sure you understand."

His smile was rueful. "Hmmm. Indeed. Well, with that settled, I am sorry to say I must be on my way. I will walk you back to the gate. Unless you wish to sit a while by the pond and enjoy the sunshine?"

He was leaving… And though he was making a generous financial provision for her security and safety, who knew when she would actually see him again? Or whether she ever would? Anything could happen in two years. Anything. He might find someone he cared for in Capetown. He might forget all about her. She had heard that there were quite a few English girls there with well-to-do families serving Her Majesty's government.

Or Miss Patricia might join him in Capetown, and they might marry…

No, nothing was certain, least of all this shaky relationship that she and Rogan seemed to share. Yes, he said he was *fond* of her—a fact this present generosity seemed to support—but fondness was not undying love.

His brow lifted as he watched her, but his tone was gentle when he spoke. "You are frowning."

She looked away. "Was I?"

"Still disappointed about losing Derwent?"

Oh, Rogan! She looked at the box in her hand and shook her head. Moisture filled her eyes and before she could stop the flow a splotch dropped on the velvet, darkening it.

"Evy." Sympathy deepened his voice.

No… That was the last thing she wanted from him…

She looked up at him, and her heart contracted. Their gazes held, and he reached with gentle hands to take her arms. As the June breeze blew her hair and rustled the skirt of her mourning dress, Rogan's arms encircled her, drew her close. A small sigh escaped her as his lips lowered to hers.

A searing flame scattered the dismal shadows and the blackness of gloom. The moment was wonderful, even if it was only a moment. This was *now.* This she would always remember. The memory of his lips on hers would warm her in the long, lonely nights ahead. Her arms went around him, and he held her tightly, his kiss deepening, lingering.

After what seemed an eternity of wonder, Rogan withdrew. His hands moved to her shoulders.

"I will come back, Evy, and when I do, I expect to find you here waiting for me. Until then, it is never good-bye." He studied her face, as though memorizing it. "It is merely au revoir."

She was unable to speak, though her heart cried out when he released her and turned to walk away toward Rookswood…and Capetown. Her gaze followed Rogan until he was out of view, then she turned, blinking back scalding tears, and looked toward the silvery-blue pond rippling in the warm breeze. A graceful white swan glided peacefully toward the shade of a willow whose long branches swayed over the water. A meadowlark sang in the lilac tree nearby, while out of view in the distance its mate answered sweetly, confidently.

Evy turned and looked back toward Rookswood, where Rogan had disappeared. Out of sight, she thought with a sudden glimmer of hope and confidence, but not forever gone.

"Au revoir, Rogan," she whispered. "I promise I will be waiting for you when you return."

About the Author

Linda Lee Chaikin has written eighteen books for the Christian market. *For Whom the Stars Shine* was a finalist for the prestigious Christy Award, and several of her novels have been awarded the Silver Angel for excellence. Many of Linda's books have been included on the best-seller list.

Behind the Stories, a book about writers of inspirational novels, offers Linda's personal biography. She is a graduate of Multnomah Bible Seminary and taught neighborhood Bible classes for a number of years before turning to writing. She and her husband presently make their home in California.

Dear Reader,

I hope you will look for the second book of the East of the Sun trilogy, when the story of Evy Varley and Rogan Chantry continues to unwind toward their destiny in Capetown, South Africa.

I would be pleased to hear from you. You can write to me through my publisher:

Linda Lee Chaikin
c/o WaterBrook Press
12265 Oracle Boulevard, Suite 200
Colorado Springs, CO 80921

Sincerely,

Linda Lee Chaikin